ASPEN IN
MOONLIGHT

By the Author

Holding Their Place

Aspen in Moonlight

ASPEN IN
MOONLIGHT

by

Kelly Wacker

2019

ASPEN IN MOONLIGHT

ISBN 13: 978-1-63555-470-0

This Trade Paperback Original Is Published By
Bold Strokes Books, Inc.
P.O. Box 249
Valley Falls, NY 12185

First Edition: November 2019

CREDITS
Editor: Shelley Thrasher
Production Design: Stacia Seaman
Cover Design by Melody Pond

Acknowledgments

I would like to express my gratitude to the many people who have helped make this book a reality.

A deep thank you to the team at Bold Strokes Books, especially Shelley Thrasher, my keen-eyed editor. She helped to refine and polish the first draft into the book you are now reading. Working with her has been enlightening and a pleasure. Amy Feger, my wife, has supported my creativity and craft with unflagging enthusiasm and without complaint when I needed to sequester myself to write. I am thankful for my beta readers who graciously provided their fresh and varied perspectives. Michelle Lisper asked good questions. Gaby Wolordarski's mirthful engagement with the story kept me smiling. Officer Angela Velarde kindly answered my questions about police procedures. Conversations with Paul Corrigan improved my writing about fly-fishing for trout. Tawny and Spottie, the finest and most loving feral cats I've had the pleasure of knowing, provided feline inspiration. Finally, I am deeply indebted to my dear friend and fellow author Karen F. Williams for countless hours of conversation that improved the story greatly and for continually reminding me of the extraordinary power of wonder.

I would be remiss in not acknowledging the deep influence of my time spent in the Rockies of Colorado, visits to the site of my great-grandparents' mountain homestead, and landscape paintings by the nearly unknown painter Newt Thomas, including one my grandmother received from him in the early 1920s that now hangs in my home.

This is for you.

Prologue

The bear ascended through a forest of aspens and conifers, climbing up and over a steep ridge in an easy gait made possible by her long, powerful legs. She ambled over to a wide rock ledge and sat down. The trunks of the pines that survived in this place were bent outward, bowed where the winter's snow pushed against them. But their roots were strong, and they wrapped around the rocks, clinging to them. Spring snowstorms had continued into summer, and patches of snow still sparkled on the ground here and there.

The ledge was a good place to watch. The headwaters of the river that ran through the valley below were here, a basin where the snowpack melted slowly, forming streams that meandered through the upper valley and coalesced into a river at the lower end. The water followed the lay of the land, flowing into a canyon where it lost its clarity as it picked up speed, becoming turbid and milky white as it rushed over rocks and boulders, curving and twisting its way downslope to the dry plains beyond the foothills.

Above, a red-tailed hawk circled, riding a warm rising current, and let out a sharp cry to claim this territory as his. In reality, the place belonged to many creatures. It belonged to the other creatures of the air—to the small songbirds that visited in the warmer months and made long journeys south to escape the harsh winters, to the observant eyes and loud voices of the jays and crows, and to the night owls who trilled and hooted, but flew silently through the trees and across the meadow. It belonged to the mule deer and to the elk that grazed on the grass in the meadow of the valley floor at night and then worked their way into the safer cover of the forest during the day. It belonged to the cicadas that clung to the coarse bark of the pines and sang, filling the resin-scented air with a raspy chorus. It belonged to the raccoons that slept contentedly in their dens and waited for night to fall before emerging to hunt. It belonged to the beavers who feasted on the soft inner wood of the trees they felled, and who engineered lodges for their families in the lake and the creek, altering and slowing the flow of the water through the valley. It belonged to the pine squirrels and the striped chipmunks that rushed from rock to tree, and from tree to rock, looking for good things to eat, all the while watching for predators from both the air and the ground. It belonged to the coyotes who hunted the ground squirrels and the chipmunks, but who also loved to eat sun-ripened blackberries.

It also belonged to the mountain lion whose presence the bruin detected. The big cat had passed by here within the past few days. The sharp acrid smell of his marking scent still permeated the air. The lion was much like herself, a watcher who preferred not to reveal himself, especially to humans. Humans were complicated, their actions difficult to comprehend. She wasn't fully convinced that this place belonged to humans, though they thought it did. Most of them failed to see that they were not the only ones to whom the land belonged.

The bear lowered her head and sniffed the ground where the lion's scent was strong. She scratched the ground lightly with her long, dark claws, stirring up the scent and, in the process, dislodging a few rocks that tumbled and rolled off the ledge.

As the rocks fell, she scanned the valley again. Directly below stretched one of her favorite places, a deep pool that appeared to be watched over by two large owl-shaped boulders sitting shoulder to shoulder above the river. She imagined wading into the cold, deep water, grabbing a wriggling, fat trout with her strong jaws, and tearing into it with her teeth. She found the pleasure difficult to resist. She sniffed the air again, this time seeking to detect the scent of a human, the only animal she truly feared. The air was clear. The bear stood and grunted softly as she shook the dust from her thick, shaggy coat. Then she began to carefully descend the side of the mountain to the river below.

CHAPTER ONE

Lugging a canvas tote bag, Melissa walked across the tree-shaded main quad on her way to her office in Fuller Hall. One of the oldest brick-and-stone buildings on the university campus, its exterior had a stately feel, with limestone columns and a triangular pediment marking the main entrance. It was the last week of the first summer term, and the campus was quiet compared to the regular academic semesters.

As she approached, she slowed her pace under the canopy of a big burr oak, her favorite tree on campus. The trunk was wide, maybe four feet in diameter, covered with rough, dark bark. Its lateral branches seemed like twisting arms, some of them stretching out twenty or thirty feet. The leaves, bigger than her hand with fingers outstretched, were a deep, verdant green. Everything about this tree seemed animated and very much alive.

"Hey, Professor Warren!"

Melissa startled at the sound of her name coming from above her head. Squinting up at the branches, she tucked a loose strand of her blond hair behind her ear and looked for the source of the voice. One of her students sat on a branch about fifteen feet from the ground, leaning back against the trunk with his legs dangling over either side of the wide resting place. His backpack was balanced between his legs, with an open textbook on top. Melissa raised her hand to shield her eyes from the sun breaking through the branches.

"Hey, Theo. What are you doing up there?"

"Studying for my last physics exam." He pointed to the textbook. "Everyone said it's supposed to be easier in the summer, but I'm not so sure. I've got to pass it if I'm going to graduate in the fall."

"It seems like you were just in my freshman class. You're finishing up already?"

"Yes, ma'am." Theo spoke politely, revealing his Southern good manners. "But I'm glad I'll get to have one more class with you before I graduate."

"Yeah? Are you registered for my ancient art history class in the fall?" He wasn't one of her strongest students, but she liked having him in class. Full of curiosity and enthusiasm, he could get classroom discussions going.

"Yes, ma'am."

"Well, I look forward to seeing you then. Good luck with your summer classes."

"Thanks. I need it!" He beamed at her from his arboreal perch.

Melissa wagged her finger at him. "And don't fall out of that tree."

"No, ma'am. I'm not planning on it," he said with a laugh.

She waved good-bye and continued walking. A student coming toward her looked at her strangely, and she realized it probably seemed as if she'd been talking to the tree. She smiled at him as she passed and continued to Fulton Hall.

As she walked through the portico and entered the building, she felt relieved to enter air-conditioned space, as the temperatures had been rising steadily. Melissa wiped perspiration from her forehead and tucked an errant strand of hair back behind her ear. She'd gotten a haircut a few days ago, and her hair was a little shorter than she was used to. Cool gray terrazzo floors, plastered walls painted a warm cream, and doors and windows cased in a dark wood trim that gleamed from decades of polishing greeted her. Offices even had transom windows above the doors that, for some reason, Melissa always associated with detectives' offices in old film noir movies. They were practical in a building constructed before air-conditioning and that had been heated with cast-iron radiators, the high tech of an earlier era that still worked well.

She walked down the deserted hallway. Students who would normally be seen milling around or sitting on the floor waiting for class, studying, or staring intensely at the screens of their mobile phones in between classes were absent. During the summer the on-campus student body was only a fraction of its regular size. Melissa usually taught an art appreciation course during this term, but this summer she was forgoing the extra class to use the time to prepare her tenure application. Although it wasn't due until the fall, by completing it now she could finally take a break and work on a personal project that she'd kept on hold.

Melissa entered her office and hoisted her tote bag to her desk.

After she removed the four large white binders containing nearly a thousand pages that documented her academic teaching and research career for the past six years, she lined them up on her desk for inspection. Seated at her desk she went through each binder, comparing its contents to the checklist. It was tedious but necessary. Everything seemed in order, all as complete as they could be. She just had to turn it in to her department chair in the fall. Her stomach growled, and she realized she was hungry. She looked out the window—the sun was low in the sky and dropping below the tallest trees in the quad. As she glanced at the antique regulator clock on the wall across from her desk, she was surprised to see that it was nearly six.

Melissa had inherited the round-faced clock encased in a dark oak case from her grandmother. Invented in the late eighteenth-century, when the first factories were being built and people needed to pay more attention to the time, regulator clocks were simple. They lacked amenities such as phases of the moon or days of the month but were very precise, so they were often used in schools and train depots.

It complemented the architecture so well, Melissa had wanted to hang it in her office. It wouldn't even keep time when she received it, so she'd sent it to an antique-clock restorer in Alabama, someone that Beth, her colleague in the department and friend, had recommended. She had warned Melissa that he was rather eccentric, and if she talked to him on the phone she should be prepared for a long, interesting conversation. Melissa had come to learn that, in this part of the country, someone described as "a little" eccentric was actually a *lot* eccentric. The people of the Deep South had a well-deserved reputation for intolerance and resistance to progressive change, but when you dealt with them at the micro-level, in small towns and rural communities, they were surprisingly tolerant as long as you observed the basic rules of politeness. She had never talked to the horologist on the phone, and eccentric or not, he had returned the clock polished, gleaming, and once again keeping time accurately.

"Ticktock, it's time to stop," Melissa said to herself. She placed her hand on top of the first binder, a gesture that felt like a benediction. With tenure, she would have job security. Without it, she'd have to start all over again somewhere else. She didn't want to think about that possibility, as the academic job market was grim and only getting bleaker.

Before leaving the office, she checked her email one last time. She had several new messages, most of which she would ignore until later.

But one caught her eye—a reservation reminder from the Buckhorn Creek Ranch, the guest ranch in Colorado where she would be staying soon. She opened it and smiled at the photo at the top of the message, a panorama of a blooming meadow, pine trees, and snow-covered mountains in the distance.

She'd found herself daydreaming more and more about exploring Buckhorn and sitting on the porch of a cozy rustic cabin in the cool mountain air while drinking coffee, thinking, reading, and maybe even writing. Smiling, she logged out of email, put the computer to sleep, and left the office.

When she reached her silver Subaru Forester, she tossed her bag and the empty tote onto the passenger seat. Her stomach grumbled again as she started the car. Feeling in a celebratory mood, she decided to pick up something on the way home.

The Depot, a popular restaurant and bakery housed in the old train depot, was one of her favorite places in town. Its main building held the kitchen, a bar, and dining room, while the covered waiting platform provided space for dining al fresco. The train had long ceased to run through town, replaced by a walking trail where the tracks used to be— part of a regional rails-to-trails project.

It was still early for the dinner crowd, so the restaurant wasn't busy. The hostess greeted her, and Melissa gestured to the bar, saying she planned to order something to go. Quite a few people were gathered there, taking advantage of happy hour. She glanced around but didn't see anyone she knew. She took a seat at the bar and waited for the bartender, a young woman with short, spiky, blond hair, who stood at the other end filling pint glasses with ale. She nodded at Melissa and smiled.

"Be with you in just a minute."

"No hurry."

Melissa grabbed one of the menus. She thought she knew what she wanted, and a quick scan of the menu confirmed her choice.

"How are you today?" The bartender, speaking in a cheerful tone, set a coaster down in front of Melissa.

"Great, actually."

"I'm glad to hear that," she said. Melissa found her rather attractive, especially when she smiled and two dimples suddenly appeared on either side of the corners of her mouth.

"What can I get you?"

"I'd like a cheeseburger with sweet-potato fries to go." Melissa glanced back at the menu. "And an Italian soda while I wait."

"You got it."

The bartender entered the order into the register and then grabbed a tall glass, put a scoop of ice in it, and glanced at Melissa.

"What flavor?"

"Almond, please."

"Cream?"

"Of course."

The woman nodded and smiled as she stirred the syrup into the seltzer and then floated a little cream on top. She set the glass on the coaster and winked at Melissa.

"Your order will be out in about ten minutes."

Melissa thanked her and observed while she talked with a group of people clustered at the far end of the bar. She checked her thoughts. *Too young.* Melissa took a sip of her soda and spun the other way on her barstool, beginning to daydream again about her upcoming journey to Colorado. It would take her two long days of driving to get to her parents' house and then a few hours more to the mountain town of Buckhorn. She really liked her job and had become accustomed to where she lived, but she still longed for the big sky and the clear dry air of her western home state.

"Here's your order."

The bartender placed a paper sack on the bar, and Melissa handed her a debit card. When she returned with the receipt, Melissa signed it, put a cash tip on top, and pushed it back toward the edge of the bar.

"Have a good night."

"Thanks. You, too."

The bartender raised her eyebrows and smiled at Melissa, her gaze lingering a little longer than it needed to.

Melissa smiled to herself as she left the restaurant and walked back to her car. The bartender might be too young for her, but at age forty, she didn't mind feeling like she could still turn a head. Her house was only a few minutes away from the restaurant, but the aroma rising from the paper sack was irresistible. While driving, she snuck a few hot fries out of the bag and ate them carefully, trying not to burn her tongue.

By the time she pulled into her driveway and then under the carport in the back of her yard, the sun was beginning to set. As she got out of the car, she looked up to see crepuscular rays shooting from behind a large cumulous cloud. The edges of the cloud were golden, and the sky above was turquoise, complementary warm and cool colors. It looked like something in a Baroque ceiling fresco.

"Hey, Melissa!"

Her neighbor, sitting in a lawn chair in his backyard smoking a short cigar with a beer in his hand, shook her from her reverie. It was his nightly ritual, and she suspected that his wife demanded that he complete it outside. She suddenly felt self-conscious.

"Oh, hello, Stan. The sky is really beautiful, isn't it?"

Stan, a Georgia State football T-shirt stretched tight across his pot belly, didn't seem to give much thought to nature. He looked up at the sky a little skeptically.

"Yeah, sure is."

Melissa grabbed the paper sack and her bag, nodded to Stan, and headed for the house.

"Have a nice night."

"Yeah. You, too."

Stan took a swig of beer from the bottle and looked back up at the sky, as if wondering what exactly she was looking at.

Inside, Melissa dropped her things onto the counter and quickly poured some food into Alex's bowl. The big gray tabby had been talking to her, complaining, as soon as she put the key in the lock. While he crunched away on the kibble, she grabbed a beer from the refrigerator and took the sack to her back deck. It was screened, and because of the curtains she'd hung for privacy, she didn't have to see or be seen by Stan or any of her other neighbors if she didn't want to. She practically lived on the deck for many months out of the year until it was either too cold, or too hot and humid, to enjoy being outside.

She lit a small oil lamp on a table and sat in a wicker chair, slowly eating her burger and fries while sipping her beer. In the growing twilight she could still see the outline of her garden. Knowing that she would be gone from mid to late summer, she hadn't put in a vegetable garden, as she usually did over spring break. Instead she'd planted rows of crimson clover and sunflowers, plants that were good for the soil and wildlife and would help keep the weeds at bay while she was gone.

As the sky darkened, fireflies began to rise out of the clover. Blinking slowly and emitting a greenish-yellow light, they flew erratically into the branches of the tall pecan and elm trees, looking like tiny stars in the night sky.

Not having a vegetable garden this summer reminded her of

her ex, Teresa, who had no interest whatsoever in gardening. Melissa should have taken that as a warning sign that the relationship wouldn't work out.

"What's the point of doing all that work when you can just go to the store or a farmers' market and get the same thing?" Teresa had argued. As Melissa discovered, Teresa didn't like getting her hands dirty, and she didn't like being sweaty, unless it involved sex. Melissa realized, for the first time, that the only thing she really missed about Teresa now was the sex.

A scampering sound caught Melissa's attention. Alex came running through the open kitchen doorway, probably chasing something, a fly perhaps. Wild-eyed, he launched himself on to the screen and started to climb it.

"Oh, no you don't, mister!"

Melissa jumped up, grabbing him before he could tear a hole in the screen, and let him drop onto the decking floor. Seeming unperturbed, he ran back into the house, presumably after the fly. She picked up her bottle and carried it into the garden. A glowing firefly hovered in front of her, and she watched it ascend slowly, her gaze going beyond it to the stars visible in a narrow window between the edges of tree branches. She spotted the tip of the tail of Ursa Major, the Big Bear or, as her grandmother had taught her to call it, the Sky Bear. She could hardly wait until she was back in the western landscape with unfettered views of the vast night sky that would allow her to see the bear in its entirety.

CHAPTER TWO

"Hey, Beth. Come on in!" Melissa had just taken a shower and was dressed in jeans and a T-shirt, and had a towel wrapped around her head.

"Oh, are we too early?" Beth stepped in, followed by her eight-year-old daughter, Emma.

"It's not a problem. Just give me just a minute to deal with my hair. There's coffee in the kitchen if you want some. Emma, would you like some chocolate soy milk? That is, if it's okay with your mom."

Emma flashed a toothy grin at her mother.

"A small glass," Beth said.

"You know where everything is. Help yourself." Melissa nodded toward the kitchen and went back to her bathroom and finished drying her hair and put on a little makeup. As she walked back to the living room, she heard Emma talking to Alex. When she turned the corner, she found Emma seated on the couch. The tabby was curled in her lap. Beth sat in an armchair sipping coffee and watching them.

"Good Lord, that cat loves you, Emma. I've never seen anything like it."

"He's so sweet," Emma cooed at him, drawing out the words. She petted him in long strokes from the top of his head to his tail. Every time her hand hovered over his head, he bumped it with his nose and ran his cheek across her palm.

"I appreciate you being willing to take him home with you while I'm gone. Six weeks is a long time to leave him alone. You really don't mind?"

"Look at that love fest." Beth tilted her head toward Emma. "We've already gone on our summer vacation, and I told Emma that if she takes really good care of Alex like she says she will, we'll look for a kitten after you get back."

Emma's face lit up. "I'm going to take great care of him!"

"I bet you will. Hey, why don't you stay here with Alex while I show your mom how the garden gets watered?" Melissa said.

"Okay." Emma turned her attention back to the purring tabby.

Walking around the yard, Melissa pointed out the new soaker hoses running through all the flowerbeds and explained that they were attached to programmable timers at the front and back spigots. She showed Beth how they worked and told her that, unless it rained too much or too little, she probably wouldn't need to adjust them. "But you should check on them to make sure they're working right."

Beth nodded and pushed her sunglasses down her nose, squinting at Melissa in concentration. "Something's different about you. Did you get highlights in your hair?"

"No. It's still the same mix of my father's blond and my mother's chestnut." Melissa ran her fingers through her shoulder-length hair. "I got a haircut last week."

"It suits you." Beth smiled, pushing her dark glasses back up. "Still, something's different about you. You seem happier than I've seen you in months."

"I finished putting my tenure application together yesterday."

"Good for you, getting it done early. I'm impressed. But it still seems like something more than that."

"Well…" Melissa stared at a fuzzy mason bee searching a nearby coneflower for nectar. "I'll be in Colorado for six weeks. I'm pretty excited about that."

"Maybe that's what it is…" Beth searched Melissa's face. "I was wondering if you'd met someone."

"You mean you were hoping I had. But no," Melissa said with a dry laugh. "In this town? The pond is small, and the lesbian fish are few."

"There is such a thing as online dating, honey. And Atlanta's not that far away." Beth arched an eyebrow.

Beth had a point. Buck Springs, Georgia, home of Dreighton College, had less than twenty thousand people living in it. In contrast, several million people lived in the Atlanta Metro area, which was over an hour away. Some faculty actually lived in the suburbs and made long commutes, about which they usually complained. Melissa had considered doing that when she first took the job but decided she didn't want to spend hours of her life every day driving.

"Or are you just not over Teresa?"

"Ouch, Beth."

"It's true, isn't it? Some little part of you thinks she's going to come back."

"No. I know she isn't. She went to Asheville to escape from here, and from me. I know that."

"I think it was less about you and more about here," Beth said. "Don't get me wrong. I think y'all were a great couple, but she didn't seem ready for a long-term relationship, *and* she wanted a new view."

"Clearly." Melissa touched the stems of a lavender plant to release its fragrance. She loved its scent.

"Still bitter, I see." Beth looked at her sideways.

"What's not to be bitter about?" Melissa tried not to let a sharp edge creep into her voice. "I really loved her, and I thought we were a good thing."

"You *were* a good thing," Beth said gently. "But sometimes situations change, and you forget that she grew up around here. The appeal of experiencing another place was, well, appealing."

"You're defending her."

"No. I just understand her. You know I was raised in Marengo County, Alabama, knee deep in kudzu and miles from a town that had only one stoplight. I couldn't wait to get out into the world. I *know* that itch." Beth paused and looked at Melissa with a gentle expression. "But that doesn't mean I approve of her breaking your heart, you stuffy old art historian."

"Me? Old? Stuffy? Oh, no, has it happened already? I haven't even gotten tenure yet." Melissa appreciated Beth's attempt to make her laugh and responded to their old joke by patting herself all over dramatically. "I'll never get a date now!"

Melissa had first met Beth when she was carrying a box of books into Fulton Hall. Fresh out of grad school, she was moving into her new office when she bumped into Beth, a recently tenured professor of graphic design. Beth introduced herself and had joked that she was glad to have gotten rid of the stuffy old art historian in exchange for a fresh one. Melissa warned her that she might become the next stuffy old art historian if things worked out and she was awarded tenure. Beth replied that she hoped to be retired before that happened and then clarified that she meant the stuffy part, not the tenured part. They'd both laughed. Over time Melissa had come to rely on her for both professional and personal advice, and more recently, when she needed a shoulder to cry on.

Beth put her hand on Melissa's shoulder. "Give it time, honey. The right one will come along."

"So you say." Melissa sighed and shrugged. "Let's go back inside before it gets any hotter."

As they walked up the deck stairs, Beth gestured toward a flowerbed brimming with salvia, echinacea, butterfly weed, and day lilies—all in full bloom. "Your yard is always so pretty. Won't you miss it?"

Melissa paused on the steps and thought about the possibility for a moment. "Yes. But I'll get to exchange this for cool mountain meadows of foxglove, lupine, and columbines."

"Hm. Good point."

Melissa led Beth back inside and removed a printed note tacked to the refrigerator with a magnet. It listed her parents' contact information in case she had a problem and couldn't reach Melissa. There was also information about feeding Alex.

"Please follow the instructions. The last time I was out of town for two weeks, my house sitter overfed him. Don't let Emma overdo the treats."

"I promise not to feed him too much," Emma said, walking into the kitchen. She cradled Alex in her arms like a baby.

"Thank you, Emma. It's for Alex's own good. He'll live a longer, healthier life," Melissa said and rubbed the cat between his ears.

Emma nodded and stared at the kitchen table.

Beth turned to see what had gotten her daughter's attention. "Are those maps?"

"Yeah."

"Why don't you just use your phone like the rest of the modern world?"

"I could and I do, but I like to plan my road trip with an atlas."

You're so old fashioned..." Beth playfully nudged Melissa with her elbow. "Stuffy old art historian."

"Ha. What can I say? I like to see the big picture. Out West, sometimes you don't have cell service." Melissa noticed that Emma was regarding them with curiosity. It was like she'd never seen a paper map before. Considering Beth's response, maybe she hadn't. Melissa flipped the atlas open to the two-page complete map of the interstate system and put her finger down north of Atlanta and then again north of Denver. "I'll start here and end up there. I've made this trip several times, so the map is really more of a reminder."

Emma put Alex down and looked more closely. "You're going to drive all by yourself?"

"Yes. I'm looking forward to it. I can't wait to hit the open road."

"That sounds rather romantic," Beth said.

"It is." Melissa grinned at Beth. "*And* old fashioned. But definitely not stuffy. There's something about leaving town, getting away from it all—something about having my hands on the wheel and the wind in my hair, though I don't have a convertible. I'll be keeping the windows up and the air-conditioning on."

"We would die without air-conditioning," Emma said.

Beth rolled her eyes at her eight-year-old's dramatic proclamation, and Melissa laughed but couldn't help but agree with her. Southern summer heat and humidity were brutal.

"You're leaving Friday, right?" Beth asked.

"Yes. I'll head out early. I'll feed Alex before I go, so you don't need to come over to get him until later in the day." As if on cue, Alex hopped up onto the table, strutted across it with his tail straight up, and then sat down in the middle of the open atlas.

"I read somewhere that when a cat sits on whatever you're reading or writing, they're blessing it." Beth reached out to pet Alex.

He began to bathe himself and pointed a back leg, yoga-like, up toward the ceiling. Melissa gestured to him with a nod. "Well then, I'll take *that* as a good omen."

When Melissa gave Beth the house key, her friend seemed to intuitively understand that she still had many things to do before leaving town. She gave Melissa a hug and wished her a safe trip. While crossing the porch, Emma again promised to take good care of Alex. Melissa sensed she was going to work hard for the promised kitten.

Closing the door behind them, Melissa walked across the living room, stopping in front of the paintings hanging there. These Rocky Mountain landscapes were the subject of her new research project, the one she'd put on hold while she worked on publications derived from her dissertation that were necessary to be awarded tenure. It was a uniquely personal project. She'd received them as part of her inheritance from her grandmother. They were painted by the same artist who had neatly signed her name, Ursula Bergen, on the back of each canvas. Aside from a name that Melissa was able to connect to the town of Buckhorn, she was an unknown artist. Melissa longed to find out who she was and to give her paintings a place, even if a small one, in the history of art.

The two larger canvases, each roughly sixteen by twenty inches, hung together on a wall above a long, low bookcase. She'd considered putting them in different rooms, the way her grandmother had, but it seemed like they should be companions. They didn't depict the same place, but they balanced each other compositionally. The same color palette had been used in both, and the pattern of the brushwork was consistent. Likely they had been painted around the same time—either that or Ursula was a very consistent painter.

Melissa had spent a lot of time scrutinizing the paintings, engaged in what art historians called "slow looking." Ursula had mixed her colors from a restrained palette of Naples yellow, cadmium yellow, ultramarine, and cerulean warmed and darkened with ochre, or tinted and highlighted with titanium white. Melissa also detected traces of cadmium red, a pigment invented in the nineteenth century and beloved of modern and contemporary artists for its intensity.

In most areas, Ursula used a type of brush called a bright, its bristles short and square and capable of being loaded heavily with thick paint. Melissa could see how Ursula had manipulated the brush, pulling the paint in long, straight strokes, zigzags, or short strokes made in quick succession. Highlights and details revealed where she had used a brush with a pointed tip, known as a round. Sometimes the paint was laid in with pressure, forcing paint out along the sides of the brush, creating little ridges of impasto. These ridges, in addition to the lively brushwork, added a sense of vivacity to the paintings, bringing them to life.

The painting on the left showed a meadow with rounded, cool-hued boulders in the foreground. One boulder was cracked, a rangy pine tree growing from the cleft in it. Its branches curved, drawing the viewer's eye from the left edge of the painting to the golden meadow in the center. A large log building with a steeply pitched roof sat between several boulders. Was it a house? Or perhaps it was a lodge for a camp of some kind. Melissa wasn't sure, but it didn't look like a modest homesteader's cabin. The bluish mountain peaks in the distance still had a little snow on them—as expected in the high country in mid to late summer. The sky was clear blue and dotted with a few small cumulus clouds.

While the image of the meadow was bucolic, the painting on

the right captured a very different scene—a mountain river, white and raging from a passing storm, cascading from the upper right to the lower left corner of the painting. Turbid water rushed over rocks and over the trunk of a splintered fallen tree, the torn bark revealing bright heartwood underneath, a fresh wound. Although threatening dark clouds hovered in the distance, everything was bathed in a warm light, and the sunlight that broke through the clouds highlighted two owl-shaped rocks, seemingly sitting side by side, in the distance.

When she stood back and looked at both paintings together, the curving arc of the pine and the flowing river almost seemed intentional. She enjoyed the tension between them. While one was calm, pleasing, and inviting, the other was sublime in its truest sense, awe-inspiring, even a little frightening.

Melissa especially recalled this painting hanging in her grandmother's dining room. As a child, she had been scared of white water. Her family had almost always camped or picnicked in the mountains and near a river. Invariably, her parents had warned her not to go into the cold and powerful river lest she be swept away. Even so, she would get as close to it as she could without being scolded and would sit quietly and watch. Sometimes she saw the dark shapes of trout hiding in the shadows of rocks in the clear water. Jays often paused in the branches of nearby trees to check her out, looking to see if she had some crumbs of bread or, better yet, peanuts. She usually did, and some jays were bold enough to swoop down and take them from her small, outstretched hand. Little striped chipmunks, also looking for an easy meal, scurried from rock to rock with their short tails straight up in the air and their legs a blur of movement. Peering at her over the edges of the rocks, they would also be rewarded for their bravery. In her grandmother's dining room, she was equally mesmerized by the painted river and would sit on one of the creaky chairs and just stare, imagining she was there at the river's edge, surrounded by life.

Melissa turned her attention to the third, smaller painting hanging on the wall opposite, between two tall bookcases. Different from the other two paintings, it contained figures. The painting depicted a glade, a brightly lit area ringed by dark ponderosa pines. A woman stood in the center with one arm bent, the fingertips of her right hand lightly touching the center of her chest just above the swell of her breasts, her left arm outstretched with the palm up—a gesture of beckoning. The pose reminded Melissa of figures in early Italian Renaissance paintings, especially those of Sandro Botticelli and Giovanni Bellini.

At first, Melissa thought the setting might be an alpine Garden of Eden, but no Adam was present, no snake, not any of the other animals common in such a scene. The woman in this painting peered into the forest, at a solitary dark figure with a shaggy coat and rounded ears. The figure gazed back with intensity, its eyes highlighted with tiny dots of titanium white—unmistakably a bear.

This painting had also captured her imagination as a child, and she had invented many stories about the woman and the bear. Most clear in her memory was a story in which the bear was lonely and the beautiful woman coaxed it out from its forest of solitude. Melissa imagined herself there in that glade, with both the kind woman and the fearful bruin, the three of them playing together. The reminiscence brought a smile to her face.

As an educated adult, Melissa had come to realize how very different this painting was from the others. It had a fairy-tale-like quality, and Melissa wondered if perhaps Ursula had received a commission to illustrate a story. Maybe yes, maybe no, and perhaps she'd never know.

Yet, Melissa thought, people made strong connections with the people they knew and loved, the places they lived, and the things they owned. Traces of those connections often remained, even across a long expanse of time. But a researcher had to look for them, sometimes very carefully. This was why she'd be traveling to Buckhorn, the mountain community where Ursula Bergen had lived, hoping to find any trace the artist might have left behind. Even incomplete fragments of an artist's life could help reveal why the artist painted in a particular way or why she chose particular themes and subject matter. It was a bit like forensic science: the more pieces of evidence the investigator uncovered, the clearer the picture.

CHAPTER THREE

Sula Johansen slid carefully into the booth in the Blue Mountain Diner. Thanks to her Scandinavian heritage, she was a little over six feet tall and had learned to be mindful not to bump her knees into the metal supports under the vintage red Formica-and-chrome tables.

"Good morning, Sula," said the waitress, Danni. Sula was a regular customer, and Danni was always especially nice to her. When she'd first started working at the restaurant she often commented about Sula's naturally wavy hair or her unusual amber eyes. Danni would have grabbed the opportunity for a date, should Sula suggest it, but she never did. Eventually Danni seemed to realize that Sula just wanted to be a friendly customer.

"Ah, my morning just improved greatly," Sula said as Danni brought her a cup of coffee without asking.

"Because of me or the coffee?" Danni joked, placing the cup in front of Sula. "Wait. Don't answer that! You want to see a menu?"

"No. I'll just have my usual."

"You got it, hon. I'll go put your order in right now."

"Thank you." Sula poured some cream from the little stainless-steel pitcher on the table into her cup.

After the bell on the front door tinkled, a familiar voice resounded.

"Hey, Smokey!"

"Hey, Officer Martinez," Sula said without looking up. "You looking for doughnuts?"

"Ha-ha." The police lieutenant spoke flatly but with a smile. "Nope. I'm looking for you."

Sula had known Lee Martinez for years, and there was no animosity between them. Quite the opposite, actually. As a bear biologist and the executive director of the Colorado Bear Conservancy, Sula worked hard to develop good working relationships with local law-enforcement officials to try to reduce the frequency of bears killed by car accidents or on purpose because they had been labeled as nuisance animals. The conservancy's "keep bears wild" program had been successful. Fewer bears were being killed, and she was known in the community for being a strong bear advocate.

A number of people, especially hyper-masculine wildlife officers and law-enforcement types like Lee, sometimes called her Smokey, as in Smokey Bear, no doubt due to her affinity for the bruins but also because of her size. She always figured that she made them a little nervous and that the teasing was a way of compensating. But Sula also knew that Lee teased only people he liked, so she suspected him of starting the nickname. While she didn't hate it, she didn't love it either.

Sula reached for the bear-shaped plastic bottle next to the sugar dispenser and squeezed honey into the cup. While she stirred her coffee, she looked up to see Lee striding toward her across the diner in his dark-blue City of Buckhorn police officer's uniform. He stopped and stood by the table, resting his hands on his thick leather belt with the tools of his trade attached—handcuffs, mace, flashlight, gloves, radio, and a 9mm Glock.

"How do you put that in your coffee?" Lee grimaced.

"It tastes good, and it's better for you than refined white sugar." Sula lifted her chin, gesturing to the empty seat across from her. "Care to join me?"

Lee sat and declined a menu from Danni but asked instead for a cup of coffee, black.

"So…what's up?"

Before Lee could answer, Danni returned with his coffee and, resting her fingertips lightly on Sula's shoulder, she topped off Sula's cup.

"Thanks."

"You're welcome," Danni replied sweetly.

Lee sipped his hot coffee, watching the waitress make eyes at Sula. After she left the table, he stroked his mustache and said quietly, "A bear mauled a camper, a sixteen-year-old Scout, last night."

"I'm guessing you didn't find it, or you wouldn't be talking to me about it right now."

Lee shook his head. "No bear."

"Is the kid okay?"

"Yeah. He's banged up and has about twenty stitches in his leg. He'll have a good story to tell."

Danni returned carrying an oval platter heaped with food. She leaned across Sula, allowing her a clear view of her ample cleavage and the lacy edge of her purple bra while she placed the plate in front of her. She touched Sula's shoulder again.

"You need anything else?"

"No. This is all I need." Sula smiled and spoke in a smooth voice. "Thanks."

Lee shook his head at the one-sided flirtation clearly happening in front of him. Sula knew he didn't understand the attraction. He once said that he preferred to date women who didn't look like they could beat him in an arm-wrestling contest. It was his way of telling her she wasn't his type. Sula was tall and anything but delicate. Most days she wore what she referred to as her conservancy uniform: hiking boots and outdoor clothing monogrammed with the conservancy logo. It was practical, given that her job could take her anywhere in a day, from meeting with wealthy donors to going out in the field with biologists. Once, Sula couldn't resist teasing him and told him he might reconsider if he saw her dressed for a date. His wide-eyed expression nearly brought her to tears while laughing. When she explained that she was a lesbian and he had nothing to worry about, his look of panic and confusion shifted to one of obvious relief. They'd had a comfortable working relationship ever since.

Lee pointed at the mound of scrambled eggs, potatoes, and a biscuit smothered in peppered white gravy and said, "You lecture me about refined sugar, and you eat *that*?"

"Breakfast like a king," Sula said in between bites.

"Huh?"

"It's an old expression. Breakfast like a king, lunch like a prince, sup like a peasant. You know, eat a big meal in the morning, fuel your brain, but then don't overdo it the rest of the day."

"Must be one of your Norwegian expressions."

"Maybe. I'm not sure. So, what happened last night?" Sula wanted Lee to talk so she could eat.

"A Scouting group of fifteen kids and five adults was at the Wildwood Campground. Around three o'clock in the morning one of the boys woke up and heard movement and snuffling around outside his tent. He thought one of the other kids was trying to scare him, so he tried to be a tough guy and ignored the sounds. The bear grabbed his leg through the tent and dragged him, tent and all, into the woods. His screaming woke everyone up, and they started yelling and making lots of noise. The bear let go and scampered off."

"Sounds like the bear did the right thing."

"In biting the kid?" Lee looked skeptical.

"No. In taking off when they reacted to him. He showed fear of humans. The bear probably didn't know what was in the tent."

"Hm. That's a good point."

"So, what *did* he have in the tent?" Sula was certain that some bear-safety rules had been broken.

"The kid said he didn't have anything with him." The look on Lee's face indicated otherwise.

"Uh, huh. And what did you find?"

"Toothpaste."

Sula nodded knowingly. "They just love that fresh minty scent."

"The kid brushed his teeth before turning in but was too lazy to walk over to the bear locker to stow the toothpaste." Lee paused to take a sip of his coffee and then leaned back. "So, he took it back to his tent, where he also had a stash of beef jerky and trail mix."

"Geez. That's a bear trifecta." Sula shook her head at the stupidity. "What's the mayor think about it?"

"The usual. She doesn't want any bad publicity because that might mean we'll lose tourist business and then she'll have the Chamber of Commerce breathing down her neck."

"What's Parks and Wildlife doing?"

"Trying to track it. They're worried about the usual—repeat offenders and rabies."

Everything seemed under control, though she worried about the bear's well-being and hoped it had been good and scared by what had happened and didn't stop running too soon. "So why are you talking to me so early?"

"Denver news is on the way."

"I think I see where this is going." Sula put her fork down and reached into her pants pocket to retrieve her phone.

"Yeah. The mayor would like to know if you'd run some interference before they blow it out of proportion."

"Not a problem," Sula said and held up her phone. "Excuse me while I text at the table." She typed a message to her media director, who thrived in these kinds of situations. Sula knew that before the news crew's van came to a complete stop at City Hall, she'd be waiting for them, interview ready with a big smile on her pretty face and chock full of facts about bear behavior and statistics about the rarity of attacks. She'd be sure to emphasize the importance of bear safety for humans *and* bears, assure viewers that Buckhorn was a great place for recreation, and represent the conservancy with aplomb. Sula sent the message and then set her phone down on the table. "I bet you I'll have a response within two minutes."

Sula continued eating, and Lee sipped his coffee as they both stared at the phone. The phone buzzed and lit up in less than a minute, it seemed. Sula read the message.

"My media director says she's on it."

"Thanks, Sula." Lee finished his coffee and stood up. "I owe you one."

"If I had a dollar for every time you said that, we'd have a new wing at the conservancy."

"Just make sure you name it after me." Lee laughed as he walked away. "See you later, Smokey."

Sula finished her breakfast, and while taking a sip of her coffee, she wondered if she ought to go check on that bear.

CHAPTER FOUR

Hey, where are you?" The voice of Melissa's mother boomed through the speakers of her car. She had heard this question several times a day over the past three days, and her responses had been a litany of cities. "Near Nashville…just past St. Louis…coming up on Kansas City…about thirty miles from Lincoln…" Currently, Melissa was just about to exit Nebraska and enter Colorado.

"I passed Ogallala a while ago, and I'll be on I-76 soon," Melissa said loudly. She really hated using speakerphone while driving. She felt like she was yelling, but it was a safety measure.

"Great! I'm going to start dinner then. You want to talk to your father?"

"No, that's okay. I'll be there soon, and we'll have plenty of time to talk when—"

"Your mom says you're almost here!" Her father's deep voice replaced her mother's. Melissa imagined her mother handing the phone off to him and rushing into the kitchen.

"I've got about three hours left, if I don't hit any more construction. I swear, most of I-80 has been down to one lane."

"Oh, I don't doubt it," her father said and then lowered his voice. "I'll try to keep your mom from calling you every ten minutes until you arrive."

Melissa laughed. "Thanks, Dad! Hey, how's the weather your way? The sky is dark up ahead."

"A thunderstorm blew through here, and they're forecasting hail east of us, but nothing worse than that."

"Okay. I'll keep an eye on it. See you in bit."

"See you soon, honey. Drive safe."

"Will do, Dad." Melissa smiled at her parents' enthusiasm as she cruised down the interstate, buffeted by the constant wind blowing across the plains and the displaced air coming off the big eighteen-wheeler trucks and trailers. She hoped to stay outside the edge of the storm cell. She didn't have a scratch or dent on her Forester yet and wanted to keep it that way. The sky in front of her continued to darken, but she didn't see the long white streaks she associated with hail. By the time she turned on to I-76, the storm was moving northeast, so she'd avoid it. It was spectacular to watch, though. The clouds were massive, the color of a dark bruise. When lightning flashed, it illuminated the entire cloud, and for a split second, it glowed electric purple. If she were outside, instead of in the car with the windows up and the air-conditioning on, she could probably smell the ozone in the air.

One of things she missed about living in the West was the vast, wide perspective that allowed her to see weather form and dance, and sometimes stampede, across the landscape. Thunderstorms in the South were equally energetic, but in Georgia, where she lived, the landscape was densely covered in trees. She heard and felt the storms as thunder rolled over the hills and valleys, the sound shaped by the topography, but she didn't see them in their entirety as she could in a place such as this.

As she turned away from the storm, she was in the home stretch. She smiled when she passed a rustic wooden sign: Welcome to Colorful Colorado. The first of those signs had been erected in the 50s, when tourism in newly affluent postwar America started to become big business and Colorado was attracting more and more visitors year-round for camping, skiing, and mountain sightseeing.

A few years ago, her parents had complained about the governor, who thought the signs were looking shabby. He'd hatched an ill-fated plan to tear down the old ones and replace them with a new design constructed of metal. The state had almost come apart over the proposal. Needless to say, the governor didn't get reelected and the signs stayed put. The old ones that were showing their age and were riddled with bullet holes were relocated into local history museums and replaced with ones of the same design—a stone and log structure holding a wooden signboard. The letters, carved into wide brown planks and painted a bright white, always reminded Melissa of the signs in national parks and forests. They provoked in Melissa the same tingly feeling of happy anticipation.

A bit farther down the interstate stood another sign, large blocky letters propped up in a landscape dotted with silvery sage, blooming white prairie roses, and tufts of green grass. "Eat beef." The message was simple. Cattle country began somewhere in the middle of Nebraska, and Melissa had no doubt that when she arrived at her parents' house, the aroma of a pot roast would fill the air.

When she turned down the gravel drive that led to their house, the sun was setting, hovering above the mountains to the west. They lived west of the town of Welch, on a twelve-acre parcel with an unobstructed view of the foothills and both Longs Peak and Meeker Peak. It wasn't the house in which she had grown up. Her parents had sold that house in town and had purchased this property about five years ago with their eyes on retirement. The simple wood-frame farmhouse sat in the middle of the property away from the road. Melissa drove slowly past the big old barn, painted white with green trim to match the house, and the apple trees growing between the barn and the house. Tall, craggy-barked cottonwood trees ringed the structure, providing shade and a windbreak. Melissa pulled under them and parked.

As soon as she opened the car door, she heard a dog barking. It was Willy, her parents' black lab mix. When she emerged from the car, his long tail began wagging furiously, and he jumped off the porch and ran across the lawn to greet her.

Melissa braced for impact as he planted his front paws on her stomach and tried to lick her face. Laughing, she rubbed his head and ears.

"Willy! Get down!" Melissa's father scolded him as he walked around the corner of the house, though he looked nearly as happy as Willy. "Hey!" was all he said and gave her a hug while Willy danced around them, barking.

Without asking, he grabbed her suitcase out of the back of her car and carried it up to the house. Her mother came out wearing an apron and wiping her hands on a towel.

"Baby Bee!" Melissa's mom exclaimed, calling her by a childhood nickname, and hugged her tightly. When she was born, her older brother couldn't say her name, but he could say "baby." Well, sort of. According to family legend it came out sounding more like "bah-bee," and he said it over and over, *bah-bee, bah-bee*. Eventually the nickname turned into Baby Bee.

After her mother released her, they walked into the house together. Melissa, immediately noticing the mouth-watering scent of a roast, smiled knowingly to herself. In the kitchen, her mother pulled two bottles of beer from the refrigerator and handed them to her. "The roast won't be ready for another half hour. I'm making a salad, so why don't you have a beer with your father and go sit outside."

Her father smiled and held the front door open. "I think we've been dismissed."

They sat together on a wooden bench on the side of the house facing the mountains. The sky glowed orange above the blue-green foothills, and a few high, thin clouds reflected the sunlight, looking like liquid gold.

"That is so beautiful," Melissa said softly and took a swig from the bottle.

"Miss it?"

"Of course. How couldn't I?" She didn't expect an answer. "Is Robby coming for dinner?"

"He is."

Robby, her younger brother, an engineer for a company that manufactured wind turbines, lived in Boulder, about forty miles away. Her older brother, Dave, a pilot in the navy, was currently assigned to an aircraft carrier in the Pacific. Her father had recently accepted an early retirement package from the tech company where he'd worked as a software engineer, and her mother was an accountant with an auditing firm. With her love of the fine arts, literature, and history, Melissa was an anomaly in her family. They never really understood what she did, but they supported her and congratulated her on her successes.

Her father pointed his bottle toward the driveway. "Speak of the devil."

A bright-yellow Toyota FJ Cruiser turned off the road and into the drive. Robby never drove slowly, and the SUV's tires kicked up gravel as he plowed toward the house. Melissa glanced over at her father, who rolled his eyes and shrugged. "I've given up trying to get him to slow down."

"Who taught you how to drive?" Melissa yelled as her grinning, sandy-haired brother emerged from the Cruiser carrying a white bakery box.

Robby yelled back when he saw her. "My sister!"

Although the youngest, Robby was the tallest in the family. He gave her a hug, planting a kiss on the top of her head. "It's good to see you, Baby Bee!"

"Good to see you, too, little brother." Melissa's focus shifted from him to the box. "What did you bring?"

"German chocolate cake."

"Oh, my favorite!" Melissa said and then added in a stage whisper, "Don't tell Dave that you're my favorite brother."

Robby put a finger to his lips. "Lips are sealed."

Melissa's mother called them in for supper, and they sat down and ate and talked as if it were old times, minus her brother, Dave, of course. But he was present in the many photographs of him, mostly in his flight gear and posing next to, or in, his aircraft. When the meal was over, they left the table for the living room to drink coffee and eat cake in front of the television.

"So, you're going to be up in Buckhorn, huh? You know there was a bear attack there just this week." Robby shoveled another forkful of cake into his mouth.

"Really?"

"Yep," her father said. "It was on the news a couple of nights ago. A group of Scouts were camping up near—"

"Estes Park," Melissa's mother said. Estes Park was south of Buckhorn and not very close to where she was going.

"No," Robby said. "It was near Buckhorn, the Wildwood campground."

"Which is near Estes Park." Melissa's mother spoke matter-of-factly.

"Wait, isn't that near Granby?" Melissa's father asked, turning his attention away from the television.

For several minutes, Melissa ate her cake and said nothing as her parents and brother triangulated the exact location of the bear attack. Finally, she interrupted them. "So, what happened?"

"Well," her father said, "a Boy Scout troop was camping up there, and a black bear attacked one of the Scouts in his tent during the night. Dragged the poor kid, tent and all, into the woods, and the other boys and the Scout leaders yelled and made a ruckus. The bear let go and took off."

Robby nodded while their father talked. "The kid probably had food in his tent. Some smelly beef jerky or something."

Melissa's mother sat up straight and looked around as if an alarm had just gone off, then stared at Melissa. "You do have bear spray, don't you?"

"Uh." Melissa was caught off guard. "I hadn't planned on it."

"We'll get you some," her mother said. "Didn't you say you wanted to do some shopping before you headed up?"

"Yeah. I was planning to buy a new pair of hiking boots and some batteries for my flashlight."

Melissa's mother turned her attention to her father, who had been distracted by a funny advertisement on the television. "Robert!" she said sternly, pulling him back into the conversation.

"We'll get her some at Jack's Sporting Goods tomorrow. I need to get some flies anyway."

"Flies?" Melissa was confused.

"Flies. For fly-fishing," her father said.

"When Dad retired he decided he needed a hobby," Robby explained. "Turns out he actually likes it."

"Brad Pitt was so handsome in that movie," Melissa's mom said to no one in particular.

Both Robby and her father looked at Melissa's mother as if she'd lost her mind.

"*A River Runs Through It*," Melissa said. "You know, the movie. Brad Pitt is a fly fisherman. He's at the peak of his life and looking… you know…all Brad Pitt."

Melissa's father smiled weakly at her, shrugged, and turned back to the television.

Melissa slept in the guest room upstairs. It was quaint, with dormer windows and a slanted ceiling, but the two antique twin beds and dresser filled the small room. Before she crawled into one of the beds, she opened the windows in the stuffy room to let in some of the cool, dry air that was such a relief from the humidity of the South. She fell asleep to the lulling sound of crickets and woke to the sun when the early morning light broke through the windows, falling across the bed and her face.

Willy must have heard her get up, because before she made it to the stairs, he had bounded up them and then guided her back down. She was happy to find coffee brewing as her mother got ready for work.

After a quick breakfast, her mother left, and Melissa and her father went to his favorite sporting-goods store, a two-story complex that covered every kind of outdoor recreation possible. While he wandered off to the fishing section, she checked out the shoe department and found a pair of hiking boots exactly like her old ones she loved and had worn out. She knew that if she didn't go home with some bear spray, her mother wouldn't be happy. She wasn't sure of where to look for it and asked a nearby young woman wearing a blue polo shirt with the Jack's logo printed on it.

"That'll be in aisle eleven, with camping gear," she said in a perky voice and a distinctive Nebraska accent, its lilting cadence revealing its Scandinavian roots. "I'll show ya where it's located."

Stacey, her name tag said, pointed out the shelves with various brands of pepper spray intended for defense against a charging bear.

"Do you know anything about these?"

"Sure don't," Stacey said and looked apologetic.

"Okay, thanks." Melissa picked up a can labeled "Bear Defense."

"Let me know if ya need anything else," Stacey said in her friendly voice and then disappeared into another aisle.

Melissa read the label on the canister. Like the other brands on the shelf, it looked like a small fire extinguisher with a plastic nozzle and a trigger. The packaging showed a photograph of a very angry-looking bear. As she read the instructions, she realized that it sounded like it was a tactical firearm, the words *assault*, *attack*, *protection*, and *deterrent* used repeatedly. The cannister should be "fired" in short bursts, it said, and it was designed to be carried in a holster. *Don't stow it in your backpack*, the label warned.

"Put it in the basket."

Hearing her father's voice, Melissa jumped. He was standing next to her, and she had been so lost in thought, she hadn't heard him approach. He held out a plastic shopping basket, and she put the canister and a holster into it, next to an assortment of small boxes containing flies, basically small fishing hooks adorned with fancy feathers to look like insects, and a spool of neon-green fishing line that said it was guaranteed to float.

"Your mother will be happy."

"And you, too, right? What's that expression?" Melissa joked. "Happy wife, happy life?"

"Yep. That one's true."

When Melissa's mother returned home after work, she was pleased to see that Melissa had complied and bought the bear spray. Melissa assisted her in the kitchen as she reheated leftover roast and potatoes from the previous night's dinner.

"I know you don't think you need it, and really, you probably won't ever need to use it, but I'll feel better knowing you have it."

"I understand, Mom."

As Melissa carried the silverware to the dining-room table, she noticed several old photo albums on the table in the breakfast nook. "What are these?"

"Oh, I pulled those out for you. They belonged to your great-grandmother, and I found them in some of my mom's stuff recently." A look of sadness flashed across her face. Melissa's grandmother, her mother's mother, had died a little over a year ago. "I thought you might like to look through them after dinner tonight. You know, she used to go to Buckhorn. I came across some photos taken up there."

"Yes. I definitely want to look at them." Melissa didn't recognize the photo albums and resisted the urge to start inspecting them immediately.

After dinner her mother made coffee and her father retired to the living room with a cup and a piece of leftover cake to watch television. Melissa and her mother stayed in the kitchen flipping through the photo albums together, starting with the album on top. The photos were attached to heavy black paper pages with paper corners that had been glued in place. Notes written in a neat cursive script with white ink were located next to the photos that had belonged to Melissa's great-grandmother, Evelyn Llewelyn. The oldest photos were studio portraits taken in Nebraska in the 1890s, where they lived a few years before settling in Colorado.

The photos displayed somber-looking men and women dressed in their best clothing. Melissa knew that the exposure times of the cameras used then were slow and that any movement would lead to a blurred image. She always looked very carefully at people's expressions in photos from this era, trying to see beyond the serious faces they wore for the photographer, searching for clues to their actual personalities.

After a few pages, the format of the photographs changed. Instead of being mounted on thick paperboard, the photographs were printed on thin paper in a square format, an indicator that they were taken with a Brownie, the first camera produced for amateur photographers.

The pictures in the album changed, as well. Instead of posed indoor portraits, she saw landscapes, houses, and yards with people posing or doing things. The people in these photos seemed more relaxed than in those older studio portraits. They gave Melissa a better sense of who was serious, who was morose, who had a good sense of humor, and who seemed to be kind.

Her great-grandmother's written notes were helpful as they indicated where the photos were taken and when. Together, they created an illustrated story of her family: Melissa's great-great-grandparents had emigrated from Europe, traveled across America, and finally settled in a little town along the Front Range of the Rockies in Colorado.

The second album resembled the first one, but as soon as she opened it, her curiosity was piqued. On the first page, written across the top, was "Buckhorn Ranch." Melissa stared at the page in disbelief.

"Do you think that's the same place I'll be staying?"

"Probably. You said it was an old working ranch. I don't see why it wouldn't be."

The photos on the following pages included photos of mountain peaks, lakes surrounded by ponderosa pines and big boulders. She saw pictures of barns, a lodge made from large logs with a wraparound porch, and small cabins constructed from roughly sawn boards. The cars that appeared in some of the photographs looked to be from the 1920s and 1930s. There were pictures of cows, horses, and wranglers, though some of the people photographed in the saddle looked like they'd never been on horseback before and were just posing for a picture. Her great-grandmother was rarely in the photos, probably because she was taking them.

Melissa turned a page, surprised to find a photograph missing. The paper corners were there, glued in place, but the photo was absent. The note below the missing picture stood out. "Ursula." Melissa's jaw dropped.

She quickly flipped through the rest of the album, thinking that it might have fallen out and been tucked back in, but found no other pages with a missing photo.

"Could that be Ursula Bergen?"

"The artist?" Melissa's mother seemed nonplussed. "Well, I don't see why not. Your great-grandmother had those paintings by her."

"Yes, but I didn't realize they knew each other. I thought she might have purchased them from a gallery or secondhand." Melissa put her hand to her chin. "You think they could have been friends?"

"Could have…" Her mother echoed her question.

"But why is this one photo missing?" Melissa stroked and tugged at her lower lip. "It's strange."

Her mother nodded and yawned. "I'm going to join your father in the living room and watch the news."

"Can I take these with me when I leave? I'd like to compare them to where I'm staying and see if it's the same place, maybe show them to some people up there."

"Sure, Baby Bee. You can keep them." Melissa's mother stood up, putting her hand on Melissa's shoulder, and patted her. "I hope they help with your project."

CHAPTER FIVE

Melissa took her time getting to Buckhorn. Check-in at the ranch started at three in the afternoon, so she wasn't in any hurry. She decided to savor the drive on the curving mountain roads and extended it by taking a slower route, a narrow county road that followed a creek and ran between the two busier canyon highways that most people, tourists especially, took to get to the historic mountain town. She knew of a small picnic area along the way, one of her grandmother's favorite spots. Melissa remembered eating lunch with her there, listening to her complain that the road had been ruined when it was paved and widened back in the 1970s. Then, she didn't understand how an improvement could be a bad thing, but now, as an adult, she understood what her grandmother meant.

The site was small, tucked into a spot where the creek curved sharply against a rock face. It had just two old concrete picnic tables and a trash bin. If you blinked while driving, you'd miss it. As she'd hoped for, it was devoid of people and she had her choice of places to sit, so she chose a table next to an enormous boulder shaded by pine trees. While eating a sandwich she'd made earlier that morning at her parents' house, she gazed at the creek and enjoyed the gentle burbling of water flowing over the round rocks.

A gray jay hopped its way down through the branches of a nearby pine, watching her carefully from a perch on the lowest branch. When she looked up at him, he seemed to take her movement as a cue that he might get lucky. Flying down to the far edge of the table, he looked at her sideways, focusing on the sandwich in her hand.

"What a brave little beggar you are," she said quietly.

She tore off a small piece of the whole-wheat bread smeared with peanut butter and honey and tossed it toward the bird. The jay hopped forward and dipped his head, quickly snatching the tasty treat with his beak, and then, with a few swift pumps of his wings, flew back up into the safety of the pine tree to enjoy his tasty morsel.

Melissa smiled and continued eating her lunch, knowing the jay would likely come back for more. She remembered how her mother would make her two sandwiches when she was a kid, knowing that one of them would get fed to birds, squirrels, chipmunks—whatever crossed her daughter's path. If she hadn't made the extra sandwich, Melissa would have happily given up her lunch to the local wildlife. As she tore the crust off the bread, reserving it for the jay, she wished she'd remembered to make two sandwiches this morning.

After her lunchtime solitude, arriving in Buckhorn was a jarring experience. Traffic into the downtown area was backed up. The main street wasn't big, just five blocks long, but it was densely packed with restaurants and small shops selling souvenirs, clothing, candy, and ice cream to the tourists thronging the streets or driving around looking for a place to park. Flanking downtown was an equally busy shopping center with a hardware store and an outfitter, and offering groceries and pizza.

Unfortunately, Melissa had to drive through the congestion to reach Buckhorn Creek Ranch, but at least the scenery was picturesque. With a backdrop of mountain peaks, the town was festooned with baskets of blooming flowers hanging from light posts and brightly colored banners bearing iconic images associated with the town—a gold miner, a hiker, a kayaker, a fisherman, and various large animals, including elk and bears.

She lowered the car windows as she rolled through town, the traffic at a slow creep and the air cooler here. The strong scent of sugar that wafted in surprised her. She looked around and saw, on one side of the street, a candy store selling freshly made caramel popcorn and fudge, and on the other side, a taffy shop with an old taffy puller in the front window rotating slowly, stretching out a sticky blue confection.

So much for pure mountain air, she thought, while resisting the urge to look for a place to park so she could buy a sweet treat.

After she finally made it to the other side of town, she turned north on to Big Creek Road. Her directions said that the entrance to the guest ranch would be well marked five miles down the road. As the road gained in elevation, the forest became thicker and the trees bigger. A sign on the right side of the road welcomed her: "Howdy! You're almost at the Buckhorn Creek Ranch. Next Left."

In a quarter of a mile Melissa turned left on to a gravel road, driving across a cattle guard—an open trench covered with metal bars to prevent cows from crossing. She passed under a metal sign decorated with a "rocking BC" brand suspended between two tall posts. A sign along the side of the road stated that the riding stables were open to the public and directed guests to register at the ranch lodge half a mile ahead.

A second sign a little farther down the road featured an image of a serious-looking Smokey Bear holding a shovel in one hand and a sign: "Fire Danger Today." An adjustable arrow pointed to the green bar indicating a low threat level.

The road descended through the trees into a lush green meadow featuring a cluster of buildings, barns, and rows of small cabins that she recognized from the photos on the website. She pulled up to the large log building identified as the lodge. Baskets of multicolored petunias hung from the edge of the porch roof, and rocking chairs were lined up on either side of the front door. A sunburned man dressed in hiking shorts and a T-shirt sat in one of the chairs, staring at the screen of his cell phone and seeming oblivious to the world.

As Melissa walked up the steps, something buzzed past her ear, and she jerked back. She heard the chatter of hummingbirds and noticed a dozen or so of the tiny birds zipping around, feeding on the flowers and a feeder.

"Don't mind them." A stout gray-haired woman pushed open the screen door. "They're territorial little bastards, but they won't hurt you."

"Oh, I'm not afraid of them. They just took me by surprise."

"Good. You'd be amazed at the number of people who are afraid of birds, even tiny ones," the woman said and then held out her hand. "Welcome to Buckhorn Creek Ranch. I'm Betty Andersen. I'm guessing you're Melissa. You're the last person we've got scheduled to check in today."

"I am." Melissa smiled and took her hand. Betty Andersen had a firm handshake. "It's nice to meet you."

Betty invited her into the lodge and offered her something to drink, which Melissa politely declined, explaining that she had water in the car. She was trying to stay hydrated to avoid getting a headache from the low humidity and high altitude. The long room was typical of a mountain lodge: a lengthy, high-ceilinged room with exposed log posts and beams. A large river-rock fireplace dominated one end, with elk antlers mounted on the wall above the mantel. In front of the fireplace was a common area with comfortable-looking, dark-brown leather chairs and rustic pine tables and chairs. Several bookcases were jammed full of paperback books and board games. A woman and two children, a boy and a girl, were sitting at one of the tables playing a card game. The woman looked up at her and smiled, while the kids kept their noses pointed toward their cards. There was no television in sight.

"Come this way and we'll get you situated." Betty pointed to the other end of the room with her thumb toward a doorway over which hung a hand-carved and painted sign of two black bears holding up a sign that said "office." She sat down behind an old oak desk holding a computer and neatly arranged file folders and gestured for Melissa to sit in one of the chairs in front of it. Framed photographs of mountain peaks and meadows in summer and winter and a calendar, compliments of the Buckhorn Feed & Seed, with a picture of horses running across a field, adorned the walls. "Did you have a good trip? Georgia's an awfully long drive."

"I had a great trip. Thanks for asking. I didn't drive straight through. I stopped in Welch, where I grew up, to visit my parents for a few days."

"Ah." Betty nodded. She slid on a pair of tortoiseshell reading glasses and glanced at the computer monitor on her desk. After she made a few mouse clicks, the printer behind her started churning out pages. "You're a native that got transplanted elsewhere."

"It comes with my occupation. I'm a college professor. We're like highly educated migrant workers and go where the jobs are."

"Do you like it down South?" Betty asked, pulling sheets from the printer.

"I do. I like my school and my students. I'm really fortunate since there are so many qualified people and not very many full-time jobs."

"Good jobs anywhere are hard to find these days, it seems, and to have one that you love?" Betty grunted. "That's always been rare."

"I would think this would be a job to love." Melissa waved her hands in the air, gesturing at everything around them.

"Most days I'd say yes. But not every day," Betty said with a laugh. "Really, I can't complain."

Betty took a folder and pulled out a map that she unfolded and placed on the desk, flipping it around for Melissa. She pointed out the locations of various buildings, starting with the office where they were sitting, the dining hall, the horse barn and stables, and the cabins. She explained that the dotted lines were trails on the property and that a trail map was included in the folder.

With a highlighter she made a large yellow dot on one of the cabins. "You'll be staying here in Aspen Glow."

"What a lovely name."

"You'll love it. It's on the hillside tucked back in a stand of aspens. The front porch looks out over the meadow. It's a sweet little cabin for one or two people." Betty paused and looked up at her. "It's just you, right?"

"Yes, just me. I'm here to do some research about an artist who—"

The voices of the kids in the other room erupted into gleeful shouts.

"Hey, Buckaroos!" It was a woman's voice, loud and exuberant. Melissa overheard her exchanging pleasantries with the kids and their mother.

Betty took off her readers and leaned sideways to look through the door into the common area. She smiled and waved. Melissa heard the woman beg off from the kids and the sound of boots on the wide plank floors. There was also a tinkling sound that she couldn't identify. When the woman walked through the office door, Melissa realized that the tinkling was coming from the spurs attached to the woman's boots.

"Melissa, this is Kerry MacArthur, our livery manager."

"Nice to meet you." Melissa stood, stretching out her hand. Kerry took off the white straw hat she was wearing with one hand and, with the other, shook Melissa's hand.

"Welcome to Buckhorn Creek Ranch." Kerry had a dazzling smile, white teeth shining against deeply tanned skin. She was taller than Melissa and had a wiry, athletic build. Her long blond hair was braided into a thick plait that hung down between her shoulder blades. Dressed in boots, long tight jeans, and a red-checked shirt with mother-of-pearl buttons, she was the very stereotype of a wrangler.

"Sorry for interrupting," Betty said to Melissa and then looked back to Kerry. "When are you going into town next?"

"Right now. I was just coming in to see if you needed anything. We're short several boxes of horse wormer. Little Lars is getting everything set up for the chuckwagon ride."

"Would you mind picking up some blueberries if they're available at the market?"

"Not at all."

"Breakfast is served between seven and nine in the cookhouse."

Betty pointed to it on the map. "We have a chef, but I make the pancakes. With blueberries."

"Betty makes the best pancakes." Kerry, still smiling, put her hat back on. Sliding her fingers to the brim, she tipped it toward Melissa. "I'd best be off. It was nice meeting you."

"Nice to meet you, too." Melissa returned to her seat.

Betty continued talking, reminding her that the guest ranch was also a working cattle ranch with nearly two hundred head of cattle on the property and that the rules were in place for the safety of their guests. Melissa's attention wavered as she listened to the jingling sound of the wrangler's spurs.

"—and finally, we need to talk about wildlife safety."

The screen door of the lodge banged shut, and Melissa snapped back to attention. Betty handed her a booklet with black silhouettes of an elk, a bear, and a mountain lion against a bright-yellow background the color of a road sign.

"Please read this carefully, Professor." Betty peered at her over her reading glasses. When she smiled her eyes looked like quarter moons.

"My homework assignment?"

"Nope. You've got to read it right now, and then you will have a quiz."

"A quiz? Really?"

"Yep. You'll take a quiz, and if you get any answers wrong, we'll talk about it. This is a project a local wildlife conservancy started, and most of the outfitters and guest ranches are participating. We believe it's important to educate our guests for their benefit as well as our animal friends'. Between tourism and all the people moving out here, animal interactions are on the rise, especially with bears. Every year more people are moving into their territory. Our bears here are good bears, but people are the problem. When an animal asserts his rights on his ancestral land, it always loses. And by that, I mean he loses his life because he's been labeled a 'problem animal.' It's a damn shame." Betty paused and shook her head. "Would you like a cup of coffee while you read?"

"I'd love one."

"Cream or sugar?"

"Neither. Just black."

Betty left the office, coming back a few moments later with two white mugs imprinted with the ranch brand. Melissa thanked her, took a sip, and winced. The coffee was hot and strong.

Betty shuffled papers around on her desk while Melissa read through the pamphlet produced by an organization called the Colorado Bear Conservancy. She already knew most of the information it presented. It was a basic primer on properly disposing trash, how not to harass wildlife, and how not to behave like prey should you encounter a bear or a mountain lion. In other words, put all trash in the bear-proof containers provided, don't get too close to the animals, and don't run or bend over should one take a particular interest in you. The only part that surprised her had to do with staying in cabins. The pamphlet emphatically stated that ground-floor windows should be closed and locked while the cabin was unattended or at night, lest a bear be tempted by the intriguing scents inside and decide to break in. The thought of a bear climbing in through a window during the night was sobering.

Melissa put the booklet down. "I think I'm ready to take the quiz."

"All right, Professor. Let's see how you do." Betty handed her a pencil and sheet of paper with multiple-choice questions.

Melissa read through the questions, marking the correct answers as she went. The last question wasn't really a question, but it asked her to agree to help protect bears and directed her to the conservancy for more information. She slid the paper and the pencil back across the desk to Betty.

"I'm done."

Betty picked up the quiz, scanning the page, her eyes moving from top to bottom. She smiled. "Very good. You get an A plus"—she held up a Colorado Bear Conservancy decal—"and a sticker."

"Friend of bears." Melissa read aloud the words printed on the decal and then said quietly to herself, "I like that."

Melissa glanced at Betty, who stared at her with an unexpected intensity. Just as she began to feel uncomfortable, exposed almost, the look vanished, replaced with her genial smile. Betty slid the decal into the pocket of the folder with the map, information about the ranch, a map of the Buckhorn area that included information about local restaurants and businesses, and a bright-orange wildlife-safety sheet. She confirmed the terms of Melissa's reservation, asked her to sign for the cabin, and then handed her the folder and a key.

"Don't forget, breakfast is also included for the folks in the cabins that have kitchens. A lot of people like to take advantage of a hot breakfast before going out on a day trip. The common room here is open twenty-four seven. Your cabin is out of range for Wi-Fi. The signal's good in here and out on the porch, too. If you don't find a pot of coffee ready, feel free to make one. I hope you'll enjoy your stay with us."

If Melissa had any doubts about enjoying her stay, which she didn't, they would have evaporated when she saw the cabin for the first time. A classic A-frame structure surrounded by aspen trees on three sides with a deck on the front, it faced the meadow below. It was cozy inside but felt spacious because of the high and steeply pitched ceiling and front wall that was mostly glass. The main area had a living room in the front with a fireplace and a comfortable-looking couch and upholstered chairs on one side and a dining table with chairs on the other. The stairs that led up to a small loft bedroom divided the space below; underneath the loft was a small kitchen and bathroom. Melissa immediately envisioned the table as her desk, and the shelves built in under the stairs would be perfect for keeping her notes organized. Sitting on the couch or seated at the table, she'd be able to look out through the wall of glass to the meadow and the mountains beyond. That is, when she wasn't outside on the deck.

While she was unpacking and arranging her things, her great-grandmother's photo album reminded her that the arrival of the wrangler had interrupted her conversation with Betty. She had intended to tell Betty about the old pictures that might have been taken at the ranch and to offer to show them to her. She would do that soon, but since she'd be here for a month, she had plenty of time. As she placed a composition notebook on the table, she looked up and froze, stunned by the view in front of her.

The warm sunlight illuminating the trees contrasted to the cool-green grasses of the meadow and the bluish mountains in the distance. Several elk meandered through the meadow grass, grazing as they went, their big antlered heads bobbing up and down. Melissa walked quietly out onto the deck and sat down in a chair, mesmerized. Basking in the last light of day, she savored the moment, absorbing the wondrous landscape.

CHAPTER SIX

Melissa's morning began as it had for the past few days. She woke up at daybreak and made a small pot of coffee, filled a thermos, and then stowed it in her backpack along with a granola bar, an apple, a notebook, and a pen, just in case inspiration struck. The evenings and mornings were cool, almost bordering on cold. She dressed in jeans and her new boots and layered a T-shirt, a long-sleeved shirt, and a mossy-green fleece pullover.

She pulled a ball cap onto her head as she walked out the door of the cabin, into the dazzling mountain light and air. After slipping the pack on, while snapping the chest strap into place, she thought about the bear spray attached to one of the shoulder straps. It still felt odd dangling there, but she was getting used to it. She had considered not using it, but the feeling she might run into a bear nagged at her. That and the imagined look on her mother's face chastising her for being unsafe had compelled her to clip the holster to her backpack.

She walked down the hill to the road and turned left, heading away from the lodge. After a few minutes, she reached a trail that crossed the gravel road. It was wide, well-trodden, and had hoof prints as well as other, sometimes fresh and smelly, evidence that it was primarily used as a horse trail. If she stayed on the horse trail, it intersected with a hiking trail, a narrow path well marked with orange blazons nailed to trees. It traversed the hillside in a slow ascent, leading to a clearing at the crest of the hill with a marvelous view of the valley below.

Melissa stopped there and sat on a large pine log hewn into a bench. She ate her simple breakfast, drinking coffee and enjoying the morning light as the sun rose behind her. As the sun broke over the mountain peaks, it illuminated the valley below, the colors changing from cool, shadowy tones to saturated colors. She hadn't followed the trail any farther past this spot. From the trail map provided in her information packet, it looked like it went deeper into the property and eventually curved back around to the lodge, but this short out-and-back hike was perfect. It gave her an opportunity to get some fresh air and exercise to offset long hours of sitting while reading and writing. She also enjoyed ruminating on the plan for the day ahead.

Today she'd arranged to meet Betty in the afternoon to show her images of Ursula Bergen's paintings and her great-grandmother's photographs. She was eager to see if Betty recognized any of the places in them. She also planned to visit the local historical society soon. Hopefully she'd come across some scraps of helpful information, but she didn't know what, if anything, would pan out.

She finished her apple and granola bar, which she enjoyed eating in alternating bites, and poured the last of the coffee into the stainless-steel lid that served as a cup. The air was warmer now that the sun was up. Jays, chickadees, and some other birds she didn't recognize began singing loudly around her. A sharp crack, the sound of a breaking branch, pulled her out of her thoughts, and her heart skipped a beat. She put a hand on the bear-spray canister as she turned her head slowly toward the direction from where the sound had come.

Three mule deer, a young buck and two does, stood frozen nearby staring at her, their big ears alert, bodies tense and unmoving. They seemed as surprised to see her as she was them.

"Good morning," Melissa said quietly. She was relieved and felt a little embarrassed for thinking that a bear might have been sneaking up on her.

The buck's ears twitched, and he snorted in reply. He spun on his back legs and sprang back into the safety of the trees with the two does following closely behind. Melissa laughed.

"Hope you have a nice day, too."

She drank the last of the coffee, brushed the crumbs from the front of her fleece, and headed back to the cabin. It was time to take a shower and get to work.

When Melissa arrived at the lodge for her meeting with Betty, the office door was closed and had a note taped to it. The common room was empty except for a young couple seated at a table talking and looking at brochures. When they saw her go over to the door and read the note, they told her that Betty had been gone for about a half hour, but that she said she'd be back by one thirty.

Melissa was glad to know that Betty hadn't forgotten about their appointment, and she went out to the porch to wait. Sitting in one of the rocking chairs, she watched the hummingbirds dart and hover around the baskets of flowers. She checked her phone and saw she had a few messages, mostly from Beth and her mother. She replied to them quickly, saying everything was great and that she'd write more later, blaming her lack of correspondence on the spotty internet connection.

A dusty old blue Ford pickup came down the road and pulled up. Betty, her gray hair smoothly combed and pulled back in a ponytail and wearing a flannel shirt, jeans, and boots, slid out of the tall four-wheel-drive truck. She walked briskly up the stairs.

"I'm so sorry I kept you waiting. I went to check on my bees, and it took a little longer than I thought."

"You keep bees?"

"I do. It's kind of a hobby, but they're really good for the pasture, too. I put the boxes out in one of the pastures away from the buildings."

"And you get honey from them, I assume."

"Of course." Betty looked at Melissa like she'd be crazy to consider otherwise. "We rob the bees in the early summer. In a good year, we get some in the fall, too. I like the early honey the best, though. The fall honey is a little bit bitter for my taste. But some people like it better."

"I had no idea. I thought honey was honey." Melissa considered what Betty had said. "I understand that the bees pollinate flowers, but how do they help the grass in a pasture?"

"We're an all-organic operation and have clover mixed in with the grass—"

"And the clover fixes nitrogen in the soil."

"Yes, exactly. The bees love the clover and the clover feeds the grass. You must be a gardener," Betty said, squinting at her.

"I am, and I don't use pesticides. I like the bugs," Melissa said. "I take that back. I could really do without the fire ants that are all over the South."

"We don't have those here, thank goodness. I've read about them in farming and ranching magazines, though. They sound like nasty critters."

"They are." Melissa noticed a honeybee crawling across the top of Betty's shoulder, headed toward her neck. She pointed at it. "Oh! There's a bee on you!"

Betty looked at the bee calmly, raising a weatherworn finger to it. The bee kept on walking, right on to the tip of her finger. Smiling at it, she held it up to a petunia in a hanging basket. The bee flew over to it and disappeared into the throat of the flower.

"He'll find his way back to the hive when he's done here. You know, they can forage up to four miles away from the hive. Amazing little things they are." Betty smiled at the bee like it was a child.

"Wow. I can't believe it didn't sting you."

"They only sting if they feel threatened. My husband says I'm a bee charmer," Betty said with a soft laugh and then pointed to Melissa's bulging messenger bag. "Let's go in and have a look at those old photos, shall we?"

Sitting beside Betty at one of the tables in the common room, Melissa opened the photo album to the pictures that her great-grandmother had taken, pointing out the ones labeled as Buckhorn Creek Ranch. As they studied the pictures together, Betty seemed to look at her as much as at the photos.

"I bet you're a good teacher."

"What makes you say that, Betty?"

"You talk with your hands." Betty smiled at her in the same way she smiled at the bee on the porch. "And you're very, I don't know… expressive, passionate. You explain what you're talking about, but you don't make me feel dumb."

"You're not dumb." Melissa was shocked that Betty might think that about herself.

"I never went to college."

"That doesn't matter. Some of the smartest people I know didn't go to college, and some of the dumbest did. They know a lot of things about a specific topic, but they don't have a lot of life experience or common sense. There are different kinds of intelligence, you know?"

"I think I do." Betty smiled and adjusted her reading glasses on the bridge of her nose, squinting at the next photo. "I think this one was taken at the ranch. See this building here? That's the lodge we're in right now. The office was added on in the 50s, when my parents expanded the guest-ranch business."

Melissa was delighted by Betty's response, taking notes as she flipped through the photo album and talked. Betty recognized several buildings, identifying the ones still on the property and others that weren't. She knew the lake with the big trees and boulders, calling it Little Bear Lake, and said it was on the ranch.

"What was your great-grandmother's name?" Betty peered at Melissa over the rim of her glasses.

"Evelyn Llewellyn."

Betty looked thoughtful for a moment and then shook her head. "I don't think I've ever heard or come across that name."

When Melissa showed her the page with the missing photos labeled "Ursula," Betty became quiet and didn't say anything immediately.

"That *is* strange, isn't it?" Betty said after a moment.

"It is. I'm assuming it's the artist. I mean, how many Ursula Bergens could have been here at that time? I'm very curious as to why it's missing, and it makes me wonder even more about Ursula. I know I've never met her, but I figure it's okay if I call her by her first name. I'm really beginning to wonder what she looked like. I'd like to have a face to put to a name."

"Speaking of faces." Betty flipped back a few pages. "Some of the faces in these photos I recognize from my family photos. See this fellow here, on the tall black horse in the back? He's also in that photo over there by the fireplace. Don't know who he is, though."

Melissa stood and walked over to inspect the framed photo of a group of wranglers wearing chaps and big hats. They were leaning on a wooden fence, a corral, it looked like, with the blurred shapes of horses in the background. She agreed that the man on the black horse in her photo was the same man standing near the edge of the group holding a lariat in one hand.

"What a strange coincidence that I'd make reservations here not even knowing that it was connected to my great-grandmother." Melissa rubbed her index finger contemplatively across her lower lip.

When she turned around, Betty had taken off her reading glasses and was holding them in both hands gazing at her with the same intensity she had witnessed the day when she checked in to the ranch. The wrinkles in the furrow of Betty's brow deepened.

"I'm not a big believer in coincidence, Melissa. I've come to think that things happen for a reason, even if it takes you a while to figure out the reason."

Melissa nodded but didn't immediately reply. In truth, she wasn't sure how she felt about coincidence versus destiny, or if she even believed in fate.

"That's an interesting idea," Melissa said, walking back to the table. She took the prints of Ursula's paintings from her bag and laid them out on the table, explaining how she had inherited them and that she hoped she could find out where they were painted and perhaps even discover some other paintings by her while she was staying in Buckhorn.

Betty put her reading glasses back on and inhaled sharply when she looked at the painting of the woman in the clearing with the bear peering out at her from the trees.

"Yes, that one is interesting, isn't it? It's different from the others, almost like an illustration of a story."

"It is *very* interesting."

"I loved all of them as a child, but I *really* loved this one," Melissa said fondly. "I know it's silly, but I used to make up stories about it, and I pretended I was there with them. They were kind of like my childhood imaginary friends."

Betty looked at Melissa sideways, then glanced at the other two. "These are very nice paintings, aren't they?"

"Yeah. She was a good painter, and I think she deserves a place in art history. I don't want her to completely disappear. It happens to artists all the time, especially women artists."

Betty tapped a finger on the river picture. "I might know where that place is."

"Really?"

"Maybe. If it's the place I'm thinking of."

"Can I go there? Can I drive or hike? That would be amazing."

"Well, you can't drive there, but our half-day trail ride goes past it." Betty moved her glasses down the bridge of her nose and grinned.

"Oh, God, I haven't been on a horse in twenty years!"

"That's all right. Many of our customers have *never* been on a horse. And we cater to those folks. We have calm, sure-footed, and levelheaded horses just for them." Betty laughed. "Well, for you."

Melissa looked at the photo. She'd love to see the place that might have inspired the painting. Perhaps she could even take a photograph and have "then and now" images for comparison. The answer seemed obvious.

"I'll do it."

"Good. Go by the livery, or call, to make a reservation. It's a popular ride, and we offer it every day now during peak tourist season."

Melissa put her hand on Betty's arm. "Thank you so much, Betty. This feels like a good start. If you think of anything else, please let me know, even if you think it's insignificant."

"I'm glad to help, dear." Betty patted her hand. She folded her readers and tucked them into her shirt pocket. "If you'll excuse me, I've got to do some work in the office."

Melissa thanked her again for her time, packed her things, and then headed out to her car. As she stepped off the porch a hummingbird chattered, zipping past her on its way to chase off a rival at the feeder. She looked out toward the barns below, where cars parked in front of them and people seemed to be gathering. From her vantage point on the stairs she could see horses saddled but wearing halters instead of bridles. They stood in the paddock eating hay contentedly and swishing their tails against the flies, waiting for the next trail ride. Before she went back to her cabin, she'd stop by the livery and see about signing up for that ride.

As Sula pulled open the filing-cabinet drawer, the phone on her desk rang.

"Hey, what are you doing?"

Sula immediately recognized the voice as Betty's. She was an old and close friend of the family, more like an aunt than a friend, really, but it was unusual for her to call in the middle of a workday.

"I'm at the office." Sula tucked her phone between her cheek and shoulder, putting the folder in her hand into the open cabinet drawer and pushing it closed. "Is everything okay?"

"Are you by yourself?"

"Yes. What's up?" Why was Betty calling her? Sula sat down in her desk chair and grabbed a honey candy from the bowl on her desk, removing the yellow cellophane wrapper quietly before popping it into her mouth.

"I've got a guest at the ranch, an art historian, college professor from Georgia. She has some paintings by your great-grandmother and is here for the summer hoping to find out more about her. She's doing research, she said, and she's looking for more of her paintings."

"Whoa. Slow down. Someone has some of my great-grandmother's paintings?"

"Yes. Three of them."

"Really? What kind?" Sula's parents had several of her paintings, as did she and her cousins. One of them was in her office, in fact. She spun around in her chair and looked at the small watercolor painting of rocks and a waterfall hanging on the wall.

"Two landscapes and…" Betty paused. "A woman and a bear in the forest."

Sula inhaled reflexively, nearly swallowing the candy. She wasn't aware that anyone outside of her family had any of her great-grandmother's paintings, and her family preferred it that way.

"Sula, you still there?"

Sula coughed. "Yeah. I'm still here. I'm just surprised."

"I know," Betty said with a short laugh. "That's why I called."

"You said she teaches in Georgia. How did they get there?"

"She grew up here, in Colorado. Her family still lives here."

"That makes *some* sense."

"You ought to talk to her, Sula."

"Mmm, I don't know, Betty. What makes you so sure?"

"I've got a feeling about her."

"You and those damn feelings."

"You know they're usually right."

"Yeah, but—"

"But what?"

"All that's kind of personal. You know what I mean."

"I'm not telling you to kick the skeletons out of the closet, Sula. I'm just saying that she strikes me as someone with an honest question. She's not looking to make money. She's really connected to those paintings personally. Her great-grandmother used to come here back in the 20s and 30s, it looks like. I think she's got a real connection to this place and to our families."

"I'll consider it."

"Good. I'll take that to mean that I can tell her to drop by your office sometime soon to discuss it. Her name is Melissa Warren, by the way."

"That's not what I meant, Betty." Sula tried to sound firm and resolute. She really hated it when Betty told her what to do. "Betty? Betty?"

Sula looked at the phone. The call had ended. Sula wanted to tell Betty no. No, she did not want to talk to some stranger about her family. But she was also very curious, and Betty had a track record of being right. Sula rolled the yellow cellophane candy wrapper between her fingers into a ball and tossed it into the wastebasket under her desk.

If Betty thought she should do something, she probably should.

CHAPTER SEVEN

Melissa had almost forgotten what it was like to ride a horse. The elevated perspective from the back of the gray gelding, with its commanding point of view, gave Melissa a rather appealing sense of power. Looking out across the meadow, she imagined herself not as a tourist on a dude-ranch horse, but a pioneer deciding where she'd build the cabin on her homestead. In her momentary fantasy, the future lay in front of her as she guided her steady mount in the direction she wanted to go.

Melissa was well aware that the historic fantasy playing out in her head didn't match her reality. In the second-to-last position in a line of horses and riders, she wasn't doing much directing at all. Tucker, her very mellow steed, seemed fine with plodding along behind the horse directly in front of him. The only person behind her was Kerry, the livery manager she'd met when she checked in to the ranch. A confident and no doubt skilled rider, she was mounted on a muscular and lively bay mare.

Melissa twisted around to face Kerry, or "the wrangler," as she thought of her. She really dressed the part. In addition to the standard straw hat, boots, jeans, belt, and large buckle, she wore a tailored gray-and-white striped long-sleeved shirt with pearl snaps.

"Wouldn't you rather be up front instead of in the back? It's kind of dusty here."

"Once we get off the path and up into the trees, it won't be so bad," Kerry said in a reassuring tone.

"I didn't mean that as a complaint," Melissa said quickly. She didn't want to come across as some whiny tourist. "More of an observation."

"I prefer this spot. I can keep an eye on everyone from back here."

"Oh, I hadn't thought of that—you put the most experienced person in the rear."

"With these wrinkles comes wisdom." Kerry pointed to the fine crow's feet at the corners of her eyes. She lifted her hat, tucking a stray strand of her long blond hair behind one ear before resettling it on her head. "There's an old cowboy expression—if you're riding ahead of the herd, turn around now and again and make sure it's still behind you. You have to turn around *a lot* when you're leading a trail ride. You spend most of the time talking to whoever's behind you. This is a whole lot more comfortable, even with the heel dust."

Melissa looked ahead. The group consisted of two couples and two families with kids. Leading the pack was their guide, a bright-eyed young woman named Ashley, whom Melissa had guessed was a college student working a summer job. Sure enough, she was twisted in the saddle, one hand holding the reins above the saddle horn and the other propped on the rump of her brown-and-white horse, talking to the kids behind her.

"How's Tucker working out for you?" Kerry asked.

"All good. I think he's just about my speed as far as horses go."

"Tucker'll never win a race, but he'll always get you to where you want to go," Kerry said matter-of-factly.

Melissa was thankful to have been matched up with a horse for which the word *calm* could have been invented. When she'd checked in at the stables earlier that morning, the young man at the counter had handed her a clipboard with several forms to fill out. In addition to agreeing not to hold the stables liable for injury or death resulting from the "inherent risks of equine activities," it also asked her about her height, weight, and previous experience with horses. She tried to remember when she'd last been on a horse. She couldn't recall exactly—probably as an undergraduate in college. She wrote down twenty years. Being a year or two off wouldn't matter much.

The trip was described as two hours out, a half-hour break for lunch by the Blackfoot River, and then a one-and-a-half-hour ride back through meadows and forests with some gain in elevation, so Melissa hoped she wouldn't be terribly sore the next day. So far, the ride had delivered what it promised, and the weather was perfect. But the bright-yellow rain slicker tied to the back of her saddle was a reminder that thunderstorms popped up unexpectedly in the mountains, especially in the afternoon. Behind the slicker, two saddlebags held her camera, water bottles, and lunch. The stop at the river, at a spot Betty thought might be depicted in Ursula's painting, interested Melissa the most about this trip, though she certainly couldn't complain about everything else she was enjoying along the way.

Melissa asked the wrangler some questions as they meandered through the landscape. Although her responses were sometimes a bit clipped, she didn't seem to mind talking. Given the nature of her job, Melissa imagined that she probably talked to an awful lot of people over the course of a summer.

"Kerry, are you from around here?"

"Not this area, no."

"But you're from Colorado?

"Nope. Wyoming. How 'bout you?"

"Colorado originally, but I live in Georgia now."

"Is it as hot and humid down there as they say it is?" Kerry drew out the words, looking at Melissa with a cocky grin.

"It is, and then some." As soon as the words came out of Melissa's mouth, she realized that perhaps Kerry was implying something else. She felt a creeping blush and tried to be more specific. "The *climate* is very humid, and it's miserable in the late summer. And really, you know, it doesn't even begin to feel like fall until well into October."

"Huh. We have snow up here by then. You ever get snow?"

"Rarely. And when we do everyone panics, even though it usually melts when it hits the ground. As soon as the weatherman says the word 'snow,' suddenly *everyone* needs milk and bread, and they all run to the grocery store like the apocalypse has just been announced. But to be fair, the state has no snow- and ice-removal equipment, so even a little ice on the roads is really treacherous. We just stay home, wait for it to melt, and eat milk sandwiches." Melissa paused when Kerry laughed. "But I miss snow terribly, and most people there think I'm crazy for saying that."

"Well, maybe a little crazy. I get tired of it some winters." From under the wide brim of her straw hat, Kerry glanced up at the blue sky. "It sure is hard to think about snow on a day like today."

Melissa agreed. The sky was clear, and the chill of the morning had given way to a warm, but not hot, day.

"Since you're the manager, do you usually go out on trail rides? I figure livery manager would be an office job."

Kerry gestured, palm up, to the landscape around them. "Well, this is part of my office. I usually go out once or twice a week because it keeps me in touch with everything. I wasn't supposed to go today, but Little Lars called in sick this morning."

"I think I met him when I made the reservation." Melissa recalled the man she'd talked to at the stable office. He looked like he was in his

20s and was blond, very tall, and broad shouldered, not exactly what she'd consider little. "Why is he called Little Lars?"

"Because his uncle is known as Big Lars," Kerry said. Melissa wasn't sure if she planned to offer any other explanation, but after a moment, she continued. "It helps to differentiate between the two. Big Lars is Betty's husband, and he manages the cattle on the ranch."

"I thought it must be a joke. Little Lars must be six foot four, at least."

"At least. But, unlike Little Lars, Big Lars is a bit wider than he is tall." Kerry pointed her finger in Melissa's direction. "Hey, watch your head. There's a branch."

Melissa turned and ducked just in time to miss a low tree branch hanging across the trail. The near miss made her think that perhaps she should pay more attention to what was in front of her rather than the wrangler behind her. The trail wound through a dense stand of pines, but when they neared the crest of the hill, the trees thinned into a grassy meadow dotted with purple wildflowers. As they rode into the clearing, snow-covered peaks in the distance appeared.

"Speaking of snow," Kerry said and gestured with her chin. "Those are part of the Never Summer range."

"Wow…" was all Melissa could say. It was a spectacular view, and Melissa reached back to grab her camera from one of the saddlebags.

"If you'll excuse me, I'm going to take advantage of the wider path here to check in with everyone." Kerry clicked her tongue twice, and her horse shifted effortlessly into a trot.

Melissa took a few pictures, though the images wouldn't look nearly as magnificent as they did in person. She stowed the camera back in the bag for safekeeping and watched Kerry make her way along the line of riders, smiling and engaging each person in conversation as she went. Her gestures were controlled and efficient, and she was very relaxed and confident. With the reins in her right hand, she rested her left hand on her thigh and moved in unison with her horse, a slow, rocking gait. It was unexpectedly sexy.

Kerry turned her head and caught Melissa's gaze, her lips curving into a lopsided grin that made Melissa's insides quiver. Melissa had never been attracted to someone like Kerry, a wrangler, but suddenly she found herself thinking of that old expression, *When in Rome…*

Kerry turned her horse and looped around to come up alongside Melissa. "How're you doing?"

"I'm good, I think."

"You think?"

"I'm wondering if I'll be sore tomorrow."

"Probably, since you're not a regular rider. You have a good seat, though."

"I have a good what?"

"A *seat*." Kerry laughed. "The way you sit in the saddle. I've been watching you from behind. You're well balanced on the horse, and you sit on your pockets instead of pitched forward like most greenhorns. You're a natural rider." She tucked her chin and looked at Melissa coyly. "You still might need a good massage later to work out the kinks, though."

"I might." Melissa smiled back. "You know a good masseuse?"

"A what?"

"A masseuse—a woman who gives a massage. A man would be called a masseur."

"Well, Professor, around here they're just called massage therapists." Kerry's expression was mischievous. "And, yeah, I know a good one." She held up one hand and wiggled her fingers. Her fingers were long and slender, like the rest of her. Kerry looked like she had a wiry kind of strength, and Melissa imagined that under the striped fabric of her shirt she'd find well-defined muscles.

"So, you're telling me you are a woman of many talents."

"I am," Kerry said with a roguish grin and looked ahead. "We'll be at the river in about fifteen minutes, and then we'll break for lunch."

"Really? Has that much time gone by already?"

"Yep." Kerry shifted her hips, a cue, Melissa surmised, and her horse slowed his pace. She nodded and moved smoothly back into position behind Melissa.

Melissa smiled to herself. It was a little difficult to believe that she was on horseback, in the mountains, and flirting with a wrangler. As they traversed downhill to the river, Melissa thought less about Kerry and more about what she might find there. The river bottom was picturesque, the river itself narrow and shallow, but running fast. The sound of it was inviting, almost magnetic. Several picnic tables were lined up near the river's edge, and hitching rails and a mounting block were located nearby under a canopy of trees to assist those who needed help getting in or out of the saddle.

Melissa guided Tucker to an open spot at one of the hitching rails. Standing in the stirrups, she pitched her weight forward, swinging her right leg over and down to the ground, and slipped her left foot from the stirrup. She marveled at how long it had been since she had ridden a horse, yet the movement came naturally. It felt good to stretch her legs and to give her knees a break. It was easy getting down, but she eyed the mounting block, wondering if she'd need it to get back up.

Melissa handed Tucker off to Ashley, who was tying reins to the rail, grabbed her camera, lunch, and a water bottle from the saddlebag, and sat down at a table with one of the families. She ate her sandwich and engaged in polite conversation, agreeing that the weather was great, the views spectacular, and that the red-tailed hawk that had glided over them was majestic. But all the while, she glanced upriver repeatedly to where the water cascaded over several large boulders. It looked like Ursula's painting, but something wasn't quite right.

After she finished her sandwich, she excused herself from the group and meandered away, looking for a view that matched that of the painting. She didn't expect to find the fallen tree. Eighty or more years later it certainly would have rotted away or been swept farther downstream. The "storm-blasted tree" was a common motif in landscape painting, having first appeared in European painting in the sixteenth century. The fallen tree in Ursula's painting could easily have been artistic license added for dramatic effect.

As she looked at the rock formations in the distance, Melissa realized what wasn't right. The two owl-shaped rocks in the background of the painting weren't there. Surely, those formations would still exist. Only some kind of catastrophic force could have moved them. Melissa remembered when, in the early eighties, Lawn Lake Dam in Rocky Mountain National Park failed. The lake, the headwaters of Fall River, had been dammed in the 30s to make a reservoir for farmers down on the plains. When the earthen dam had failed after decades of neglect, the water had rushed out so quickly and with such devastating force, it scoured the side of the mountain bare, flooding the city of Estes Park below. Thirty-five years later, an alluvial fan of gravel, rocks, and boulders that the flood had created was still visible, a tan scar on the otherwise green mountainside.

Anything that could have moved those two rocks in Ursula's painting would have left some telltale signs. Melissa looked around, upriver and down, across the other side, and behind where she was standing. She wasn't a hydrologist, but she didn't notice anything that indicated a major flood had occurred here any time recently.

She took photos and decided to ask Kerry about a flood, or anything else that could have altered the flow of the river. If she didn't know, she'd ask Betty later. When Melissa turned back around, Kerry was waving and calling everyone back over to the horses, saying it was time to get on the trail again.

"Hey, big guy." Melissa patted Tucker on the shoulder before she got back in the saddle. He turned and bumped her chest with his big round nose and sniffed the air. She pulled a couple of carrots out of her lunch bag and slipped them to him. While he crunched his carrots, she put the remnants of her lunch, water bottle, and camera back in the saddlebag.

Pleasantly surprised and proud of herself that she was able to pull herself up without using the mounting block, she settled back into the saddle. The pure pleasure of this excursion had displaced any disappointment she felt in not finding the view.

She watched Kerry tighten the cinch strap on the horse of one of the kids. At some point during the morning her thoughts had shifted from imagining being home on the range to entertaining some romantic ideas about a certain woman wrangler. She tried, but failed, to navigate Tucker back into the last position, hoping to continue her conversation with Kerry, but got stuck in the middle of the pack between two families.

"All right, cowpokes," Kerry said after she effortlessly swung up onto her horse. "We're gonna head back a different way than we came." She gestured upriver, slicing the air with her hand. "We'll follow the river here a ways and then head up and over Widow Mountain. Then we'll be back into Buckhorn Valley and just down the road from ranch headquarters."

"Widow Mountain? That sounds dangerous," said the father in front of Melissa with a barely concealed edge of panic in his voice.

"The upper path is a little dangerous actually," Kerry said in a serious voice. "It's *real* steep and narrow, and there was a bad rock slide last year." Everyone looked at her incredulously, even Ashley, who turned around with a perplexed expression. Then, in a flash, a big smile erupted across Kerry's face. "Which is why we take the lower, safer route!"

Everyone laughed as they moved forward behind Ashley, even the worried father, who was either blushing or starting to show signs of sunburn. As they continued on the trail, Melissa became increasingly certain that it was sunburn, as the color didn't fade, and he was looking a little blotchy.

At the base of the mountain, they left the horse trail and turned on to a wider ranch-access road intended for vehicles. As promised, the road didn't go up and over the mountain but wound around it, and it seemed as if they'd reenter Buckhorn Valley by crossing a low ridge.

Melissa was admiring some boulders in a field when she heard the sound of something crashing out of the trees. The woman behind her screamed, and Melissa turned her head to see what was moving in her peripheral vision. A mule deer ran full speed directly toward her, and behind the deer, giving chase, was...*a mountain lion?*

Tucker tossed his head but didn't move quickly enough to get out of the way. Melissa stiffened, unsure what to do. The deer, an antlered buck, tried to turn away from them but made his decision too late. His momentum kept him moving forward, and as he turned, his rump hit Tucker's side and Melissa's leg. The impact forced Tucker to sidestep to keep from falling over. As the buck rolled off and then crossed in front of them, Melissa looked down to see the golden-hued mountain lion standing in front of her, tense and slightly crouched, its muscles bunched. Staring up at her with bright amber eyes and wide, inky black pupils, it was so close she could see that one of its ears was misshapen, a V-shaped piece of it missing. The big cat was as magnificent as it was fearsome. Its ears were laid flat, and its intensely unhappy expression reminded Melissa of a cornered domestic cat. But bigger. Much, much bigger.

Melissa heard voices and sounds erupting around her, but the only thing in focus was the lion in front of her and the sound of Tucker grunting as he danced around. The lion held her gaze for what was probably just a second or two, but it felt like minutes. Then, without warning, it turned and ran back up the way it had come.

Melissa didn't have the opportunity to watch the mountain lion bound back into the cover of the forest because, as soon as it moved, Tucker's flight instinct kicked in. He bolted in the opposite direction, running blindly, following the path of escape the mule deer had taken. It was all Melissa could do to hang on. She still had the reins, but gripping the front of the saddle with both hands, she couldn't rein him in.

The ride was rough. She bounced in the saddle uncontrollably and felt her right foot slip out of the stirrup, losing what little stability she had. Then, making matters worse, the saddle began to slip. Tucker kept running, Melissa kept bouncing, and with each bounce the saddle slipped sideways a little more.

Melissa grabbed a handful of Tucker's mane at the base of his neck with her right hand, instinctively thinking it was a more secure handhold than the saddle, which it was, given that it was almost sideways. At the moment she thought she would lose her grip, she felt something press tightly up against her butt, and an arm slid across her chest, below her breasts. The arm was covered in gray-and-white striped fabric.

"Kick your foot out of the stirrup!" Kerry shouted at her. "I've got you!"

Confused, Melissa then realized that Kerry and her big bay mare were running alongside them. She slipped her foot out of the stirrup as directed, and the only thing keeping her from hitting the ground was her death grip on Tucker's mane and Kerry's arm wrapped around her.

"Now, damn it! Let go!" Kerry demanded. "I won't let you fall!"

Melissa did as she was commanded, Kerry pulled her close, and they came to a sliding stop. Kerry let Melissa slip down the side of her leg, depositing her gently on the ground. "I'll be right back."

Melissa watched as Kerry took off after Tucker, who was now hopping and bucking, trying to shake off the saddle that was upside down under his belly. Kerry rode up alongside him again, leaned out, and grabbed the end of the leather cinch strap. After two sharp tugs the cinch released, and the saddle fell to the ground. He immediately stopped bucking and stood still, as though nothing had happened, though he breathed heavily, nostrils flaring and sides heaving.

Kerry trotted back to Melissa, dismounted, and walked toward her in one fluid movement. "Are you all right?"

Melissa stood there, incredulous at everything that had just transpired. "I'm fine. I'm not sure exactly how that's possible, but... I'm okay."

Kerry looked her up and down with a serious expression. "Don't move." She walked over to Tucker and grabbed his reins, flipping them over his head. Then she picked up the saddle and looked around for the saddle pad. After finding it, she walked back to Melissa.

Kerry inspected the saddle. "I can't believe he didn't bugger this up. Do you think you can ride back?"

"Yeah. I think so."

"Here. Hold the reins for me." Kerry handed them to Melissa and then placed the pad back on Tucker's back and tossed the saddle up. She pulled the cinch back under his belly and then tightened and secured it. The strap that went across his chest seemed to be broken.

"Hm. Looks like he busted the collar." Kerry untied one of the saddle strings attached to the back of the saddle, using it to devise a temporary fix. She flipped the reins back over his head and gestured to the gray horse. "You sure you're good to ride?"

"Yeah," Melissa said, though she was starting to feel a little shaky now that the adrenaline was wearing off. She put her foot into the stirrup and tried to pull herself up but found she didn't have the strength.

"It's all right," Kerry said calmly. "Let me give you a leg up. Grab the front and back of the saddle and bend your left leg at the knee."

Melissa did as she was directed, and Kerry put one hand under her knee and the other under the front of her ankle. On the count of three, she bounced and lifted Melissa up on to Tucker's back.

"If it'd make you feel better, I can put a rope on his halter so the chance of him bolting on you again is nil." Kerry's hand lingered on Melissa's leg.

"What's the chance that a deer being chased by a mountain lion will run into me again and cause my horse to flee in terror?"

"Given that I've *never* seen something like this happen before, pretty small, I'm thinking."

"Then I think I'll be okay. But I'd still feel better if you'd ride next to me."

"Not a problem," Kerry said and mounted her bay mare. "Now, let's go find out what happened to everyone else."

CHAPTER EIGHT

The tale of the mountain lion chasing a deer who ran into a horse was told several times, to the delight of the riders and livery employees who gathered to hear the unbelievable story. After the third time, they began to wander off, heading back to their vacations or returning to work. Eventually, Kerry and Melissa found themselves alone on the porch of the livery office.

"Kerry, I really can't thank you enough—"

Kerry put up her hand. "You should let me buy you a drink. What are you doing later?"

"You should buy *me* a drink? Shouldn't that be the other way around? You're the one who saved my butt out there."

"Yeah, but you didn't get hurt, so you're saving me from a lot of paperwork."

Melissa considered the logic. "You make a good case."

"I know. So…what are you doing later?"

"Having a drink with you, it would seem."

"Good." Kerry smiled smugly. "Meet me at the River Bar and Grill at six. It's on Spring Street, two blocks off Main."

Melissa narrowed her eyes at Kerry, hesitating before responding. It was unlike Melissa to be drawn in by a woman who was such a player. But she was. "All right. I'll see you there at six."

As Melissa walked away, heading toward her car, she didn't hear the creaky screen door of the livery office and had a feeling the wrangler was watching her from the porch. As she put her hand on the handle of her car door, she looked up to see Kerry, leaning on a porch post, arms folded across her chest. The light raking across the porch glinted off the spurs sticking out from under the edge of her pant legs. She smiled with a grin that suddenly struck Melissa as almost predatory, and she began to wonder what she'd gotten herself into. The events of the day had made her head swim, and although she hadn't hit it, she began to wonder if all that bouncing around in the saddle had knocked some common sense out of it.

Driving past the lodge, she remembered that she wanted to ask about the river, if there had been a big flood there. At least she wasn't that disoriented. She stopped by the lodge office to see if Betty was in.

"Well, young lady, you had quite a ride, didn't you!" Betty said when Melissa walked through the office door.

"Yes…how did you know?"

"News travels fast, even here. Ashley called me as soon as you and Kerry got back to the livery safely."

"I was so worried about the rest of the group. Everyone's horses took off for home except mine."

"Well, as you unfortunately got to experience firsthand, horses are very emotional creatures when they think something's about to eat them. It's hard to force them to behave, even for an experienced rider. I hear you did real good, though."

"That's what Kerry said. She also said that she was glad to not have to file any paperwork."

Betty laughed. "We're all thankful for that." The look on her face softened, and she put a hand on Melissa's arm. "But I'm more thankful you didn't get hurt. That's what matters most."

"I appreciate that, Betty." Melissa covered Betty's tanned and weathered hand with her own. Something about the older woman touched Melissa. She came across as tough and was a little rough around the edges, as you'd expect from a woman who ran a cattle operation and guest ranch, but a softer side appeared unexpectedly from time to time. "I dropped by to tell you that I don't think that picnic spot by the river is the place in the painting."

"No?"

Melissa shook her head. "The rock formation in the background of the painting's not there. Has there ever been a big flood through there? Something that could have altered the rock face on the other side of the river."

Betty stroked her chin. "No, not that I'm aware of. My family's owned this property for three generations. A story about something like that would have gotten passed down."

"Well, it was still a great day, even with the wild ride. I'm glad I went." Melissa tucked a loose strand of hair behind her ear. "I'll just keep looking and asking around."

"You know, I did think of something…well, someone, actually.

I have a friend, her family and mine have been close over the years. Anyway, I think she'd be good person for you to talk to." Betty handed Melissa a slip of paper on which a name and email address were written in neat cursive script.

"Sula Johansen." Melissa read the name out loud and looked up. "What do you think she knows?"

"Just talk to her," Betty said enigmatically. "I told her you'd likely get in touch with her."

"I will. In fact, I'll take advantage of the Wi-Fi here at the lodge and send her a message right now before I head back to the cabin."

"Good." Betty gave a satisfied smile.

Sula's day had started before daybreak, and she was tired, though it was a good kind of tired. Body tired rather than mind tired. She'd take time spent in the woods over sitting at a desk working on a computer any day.

She pulled her truck into the parking lot of the headquarters and visitor center for the Colorado Bear Conservancy and parked in her reserved spot under one of the solar panels that also provided shade. The lot was full, an indicator that the tourist season was in full swing. The conservancy was a private land trust of nearly ten thousand acres that her parents had established. Sula had been the executive director since her parents retired. Though now that they were living part-time in Norway working on a polar bear project, she really considered them semi-retired. Grabbing her small canvas bag and the paper sack sitting on the seat next to her, she hopped out of the truck and headed inside.

"Thank you," she said to a man who held the door for her as she walked through the entrance. Its massive wooden posts gave it the appearance of an old-fashioned lodge from the outside, but the interior, with its open and spacious floor plan, provided an entirely dissimilar experience. The building had been one of Sula's first projects as executive director, and she was very proud of it. She had worked closely with an architect to design a water- and energy-efficient structure to house the conservancy's staff and a visitors' center with exhibits and meeting rooms for seminars and workshops.

Sula walked past the information desk in the center of the atrium, nodding and smiling to the interns staffing the desk as she headed for the elevator labeled "Staff Only." After using her ID to access the elevator, she rode it to the conservancy offices on the second floor.

"Hey, Boss." Anna, her administrative assistant, greeted her when she walked into the reception area. She had started at the center as a college intern, worked for several summers, and then was hired on after she graduated.

"Hey," Sula said, holding up a paper sack. "I have something for you."

Anna took the bag and shook it. It made a dry, rattling sound, and her big brown eyes grew bigger as she smiled. "Is this what I think it is?"

"Maybe." Sula smiled back.

"Piñon nuts!" Anna exclaimed after opening it and peering into the bag. "You're the best boss ever." Anna had grown up in northern New Mexico and had a fondness for the small nuts that came from piñon pines. The nuts had a particular flavor and texture that was different from other pine nuts. They had to be harvested by hand, and because of the droughts and massive wildfires in recent years, the ones from New Mexico were sometimes scarce and always expensive. Sula had recently found them in the new health-food store in town.

"I do my best," Sula said. "Anything I need to know about before I head to my office?"

"John from the refuge called this morning. He wanted to confirm your presentation title for the meeting in Denver."

"Okay. Anything else?"

"That's it. Quiet morning today."

"I can live with that. I'm going to put in a few hours here and then call it a day." Sula walked down the hall, but halfway to her office she turned around. "Hey, is there any coffee?"

"Yeah. I made a fresh pot a little while ago."

"Now *you're* the best."

"Remember that when you write my annual review, okay?"

Sula laughed and detoured by the break room. She poured herself a cup of coffee, grabbed a carton out of the refrigerator, added cream until it was a nice blond color, and then squeezed in some honey from a bear-shaped plastic bottle sitting on the counter. The bottle was nearly empty. While stirring her coffee, she told herself to remember to ask Betty for more. She dropped the spoon into the sink and continued to her office.

This floor had offices for the staff and department heads. Although everyone had either private or shared offices, they often congregated in the central working area. The combined natural and ambient light, comfortable seating, and tables encouraged collaborative work. It made sense since each individual's responsibility usually overlapped with some other aspect of the organization. As Sula made her way to her office on the other side of building, she nodded and said hello to the staff members she passed—a biologist explaining something to the volunteer coordinator and the visitor-center director sitting on a couch next to the social-media director, both with laptops open and pointing to each other's screens as they talked.

Sula's office had two large windows, one with a view of the lake outside and the other overlooking the atrium of the visitors' center. Sipping her coffee, she watched the people down below. The center provided visitors with information and hands-on activities about the ecology of the Rockies, with a focus on how bears were an important part of a healthy environment. Outside was a popular nature trail, a short lollipop that meandered through woods, a meadow, and around the lake.

Some visitors were disappointed to find out that there weren't any bears to see. It wasn't a zoo, and Sula refused to tolerate any bear being put on display simply to entertain people. Instead, the popular BearCam monitors were installed throughout the center and streamed online. Injured bears that had been treated but couldn't be released back to the wild were housed in outdoor pens that provided them with a stimulating natural environment. High-definition video cameras were cleverly hidden in strategic locations, and at any given time, there was usually something interesting to see. Some of the video they captured had even been used in documentaries.

Sula looked toward the mountain-lion exhibit, watching as a young girl, her dark hair plaited into many short little braids with brightly colored clips on each end, reached up and repeatedly pressed the button that played a recording of the sounds that mountain lions make. She wondered if the girl preferred the growl or the purr. Most people didn't know that mountain lions purred like house cats. Sula thought about the one she'd been chasing around all morning. She called him Notch, due to an old injury to his left ear, where a chunk was missing. He might have had a run-in with a coyote as a cub, and, if so, he was lucky to have survived the encounter. Sula had recently discovered Notch near cows with calves and roaming around in areas with a lot of human activity. She was increasingly worried that he might get himself into trouble—the kind that would get him killed.

Since the spring thaw, she'd gone out once a week tracking him, no easy task, even for her. They were careful and cautious animals. Sometimes he watched her while she was looking for him. In those moments she could smell him and even feel his presence, but she didn't often see him. And when she did spot him, like today, she did her best to haze him, to get into his personal space with the intention of pushing him away from people who might do him harm and to move him deeper into the protection of the conservancy's land. She wasn't afraid of him, knowing that as long as he didn't feel cornered, he would try to get away from her. She didn't talk about her activity with anyone. It wasn't her job and was borderline illegal, but she did it nonetheless. It was normal for her to not be in the office every day, so no one had any idea what she'd been up to, and that was just the way she wanted it. If she had any say in the matter, Notch would live out his life as a mountain lion should, and no one, no human anyway, would ever notice he was even there.

She turned to look at her desk. She would rather have spent the rest of the day exploring the woods, tracking Notch. But she needed to work on a document, a letter from the executive director that would be published in the conservancy's upcoming newsletter. The deadline for the newsletter to be sent to the printer was looming. She stretched her neck and shoulders and sat down in front of her computer, deciding she'd ease into her task by checking her email first. As she scanned through the list, the subject line of one message jumped out at her: *Seeking information about Ursula Bergen.*

Sula clicked on the message, which had been sent by Melissa Warren, the professor Betty had told her about. The message, very politely and professionally written, was sent from a university email address. Melissa explained who she was, how she had gotten Sula's contact information, and asked if she could make an appointment to speak with her about Sula's great-grandmother, though it was clear Melissa had no idea of Sula's familial connection to the artist.

Sula sighed, knowing she'd talk with this woman, if only to please Betty. She responded and wrote that she'd be happy to speak with her, which wasn't exactly true, and suggested some days and times when they could meet at her office at the center. After sending the reply she turned to the task of finishing her letter for the newsletter.

Sula was startled when Anna stuck her head through the door of her office to remind her of the time.

"It's five already?"

"Yeah. I'm heading out in a few minutes. Do you need anything before I go?"

Sula leaned back in her chair and took a deep breath, blowing it out audibly. "No. I'm good. Almost done here. But thanks for checking."

"All right," Anna said in her ever-cheerful voice. "Have a good night."

"Thanks, Anna. You, too."

Sula read through the letter once more, and, satisfied, she saved it and sent it to the newsletter editor. It was time to call it quits for the day.

As she began her drive home, she realized she had two choices: grab something to eat on the way or go shopping for groceries. Shopping didn't appeal to her, so she decided to grab a bite to eat. She zigzagged through town, avoiding the worst of the traffic, and pulled into the overflow parking lot of the River Bar and Grill, looking for a space that would be easy to get in and out with the truck. The four-wheel-drive F-150 was a great workhorse, but it was tricky to park in places designed for cars. Not surprisingly, several trucks and large SUVs were in the gravel overflow lot. She spied a good spot and pulled into it.

Sula walked through the front door, heading straight to the bar, and found an open seat on the far end of the long bar, where she could survey the room. She ordered a Tin Cup whiskey on the rocks and asked for a menu.

The bartender placed a napkin down in front of her, set her drink on it, and put a menu next to the glass. The bar wasn't busy, about half full. On a weekend night, it would be packed, standing room only and no available seats. She looked over the menu.

"Ready to order?" the bartender asked after she closed the menu. A large Greek family from Denver owned the restaurant, and all its servers and the bartenders seemed to be related. The women, short and sturdily built, were warm and friendly. The men were all average height and build, with neatly trimmed, dark mustaches. They were efficient but not much for talking.

"I'll have the grilled trout with a baked potato. Thanks." Sula handed him the menu. The bartender nodded and turned to enter her order into the touchscreen register.

While Sula nursed her drink, rolling the ice around in the glass, she surveyed the room and played a mental game of spot-the-tourists, followed by guessing where they were from. Seated at the bar near her was an attractive blond woman, in her mid-30s. She sipped an amber-colored draft beer and glanced toward the door every time someone walked in. She looked at her phone regularly, too, and was smiling and texting. Sula guessed that she was waiting for someone to arrive. She was wearing tan denim jeans and a blue shirt with a pattern that looked like ripples on the surface of water. Casual, but the fabrics were high quality, expensive. Something about her made Sula curious.

Sula's phone buzzed, so she turned and fished it out of her bag hanging off the back of the chair. She had a reply from Melissa Warren.

Thank you so much for being willing to meet with me! I would be able to stop by the visitors' center tomorrow at 10, if that time is still good for you. I have not yet been there, though it is on my list of places to visit. I look forward to meeting you! Best, Melissa.

Sula's dinner arrived, and she put the phone away as the bartender set the plate down in front of her, along with a set of silverware in a red cloth napkin. Sula unrolled it, placed the napkin in her lap, and tucked in to her savory meal. They knew how to cook fish properly here, which meant not overcooking it. She was almost finished when the woman's date walked in.

Kerry MacArthur, Betty's livery manager, strutted across the room with her eyes on the woman, grinning like a coyote about to pounce. Sula swallowed and stuck her fork into the potato. It was definitely a date. Kerry was dressed in a western-style, long-sleeved turquoise shirt, jeans that had been ironed with a crease running straight down the front of each pant leg, and polished boots that looked like they'd never trod across dirt.

Kerry was great at her job. Sula understood why Betty had hired her, but Sula had never much cared for her for a number of reasons, her big ego being one. She tried to avoid situations where she'd have to make polite conversation with her. The blond woman, who was now smiling back at Kerry, was definitely a tourist. Kerry habitually hooked up with summer visitors who were amenable to…what would be the polite way of putting it? A short-term romance.

Fortunately, Kerry's attention was directed entirely at the woman in front of her. Sula found it difficult to avoid listening to their conversation.

"Hey," Kerry said as she walked up to Melissa.

"I was beginning to think you'd stood me up."

"Yeah. Sorry about that," Kerry said, without further explanation. She waved to the bartender and ordered a Jack and Coke. "I'll make up for it with the second round and dinner."

Melissa took a sip of her beer. Kerry appeared to have showered and dressed for an evening out. She looked a little flushed, and Melissa thought she detected the scent of alcohol underneath the musky perfume she wore.

The bartender slid the drink across the bar, and Kerry grabbed the old-fashioned glass and lifted it. "Here's to mountain lions and wild rides. Cheers."

"Cheers." Melissa tapped her glass against Kerry's.

Kerry tipped her glass back and took a deep swallow. As she set it back down on the bar, something behind Melissa caught her eye. An unpleasant look flashed across the wrangler's face, and then she smiled wanly. Curious as to what drew her attention, Melissa turned around to see a dark-haired woman a few seats over at the end of the bar. Holding her fork in the air, she seemed to have stopped midway through taking a bite and was looking at them. Her eyes glowed amber in the low light, reflecting the light illuminating the liquor bottles arranged on glass shelves behind the bar. The woman put her fork down, cocking her head slightly, her expression inscrutable.

"Hey, Sula," Kerry said.

"Hey, Kerry," the woman replied, picking up the napkin from her lap and dabbing the corners of her mouth. "Did you just say something about a mountain lion?"

Kerry's face lit up. "Yes, I did. Have I got a story to tell you."

Sula? How many people here have the name Sula? "Are you, by chance, Sula Johansen?" Melissa asked.

"I am." Sula looked confused.

"I'm Melissa Warren." Without hesitation Melissa smiled, stood, and walked over to Sula. When Sula got to her feet, Melissa was momentarily taken aback; she must have been over six feet tall. Sula took Melissa's outstretched hand in hers, her handshake firm but gentle. "Nice to meet you."

"Nice to meet you, too." Sula's expression shifted from a look of confusion to one of amusement. "I think you just sent me a message from five feet away."

Melissa laughed. "I did!"

"You two know each other?" Kerry asked.

"No. We just met," Sula said.

Sula was slow to release her hand, and Melissa found herself reluctant to let go. Sula was attractive, with dark, wavy hair falling just above the edge of her collar and long bangs. She wore a long-sleeved shirt the color of moss, the cuffs rolled up. The shirt was embroidered with the logo Melissa recognized from the wildlife-safety pamphlet she'd received from Betty. Her shirt was tucked into dark-brown pants, and she wore hiking boots that were a little dusty. She had broad shoulders, but she wasn't shaped like a man. Far from it. She had feminine curves. But it was her eyes, Melissa realized, that transfixed her. Up close she saw that they weren't entirely amber. Several other colors were present: deep brown with a little green mixed in and a few copper highlights.

Kerry looked back and forth at them, drained her glass, and gestured to the bartender for another drink. "Let me tell you the story."

Sula broke eye contact with her to look at Kerry and released her hand. "The one that involves the mountain lion?"

"Yes," Kerry replied with barely contained excitement. "So, Melissa here was on a trail ride I was leading today. We were going up and over the side of Widow Mountain when a mule deer, a big eight-point buck, came out of the trees, running full speed down the hillside like the devil was on his tail. A mountain lion was hot on its heels! Can you believe it? The mountain lion ran the buck down the hill, and he ran into her horse—"

"The mountain lion?"

"No, the buck. He couldn't turn fast enough and bounced off her horse and then kept on running. That mountain lion was so focused on the mulie, it wasn't paying attention to anything else." Kerry paused to sip her drink.

Sula glanced over at Melissa with raised eyebrows.

"It's true," Melissa said. "The mountain lion stopped right in front of me and just stared for a second. It was so close I could see that it was missing a piece of its ear, like a tomcat gets from fighting, you know?"

"Really?"

"Yes." Melissa smiled as she remembered the animal. "It was the most amazing and the most beautiful thing I've ever—"

"And then," Kerry said, "her horse took off running at a full gallop in the direction of the buck. Her saddle slipped, and her horse started bucking up a storm."

"Tucker didn't start bucking until after I was off him." Melissa looked at Kerry sideways.

Kerry continued, seemingly unperturbed, and stepped closer to Melissa. "I got up alongside and grabbed her around the middle like this—" Kerry tried to demonstrate by wrapping her arm around Melissa. Frowning, she squirmed out of her grasp, but Kerry seemed nonplussed. "Well, I grabbed her and set her down on the ground as gently as you please and then went back to her horse. The saddle had slid under his belly, and he looked like a bucking bronc in a rodeo, hopping and kicking. I popped the latigo strap off the saddle and he settled down." Kerry gestured to Melissa as if she were presenting a car she'd just polished. "And here she is, not a scratch on her."

Melissa felt like Kerry was showing her off, and she didn't like that she'd been touching her throughout the story. The wrangler's charm was wearing thin.

"Mountain lions rarely show themselves," Sula said to Melissa. "You're very lucky to have seen it."

"I wasn't lucky enough to have had my rifle with me," Kerry said before taking a sip of her drink. She glanced at Sula with a look that indicated that she regretted the words that had just come out of her mouth.

"What?" Melissa cocked her head at Kerry. "Why?"

Kerry looked uncomfortable, didn't say anything, and took another drink and set the glass down on the bar.

"You should answer her," Sula said. Kerry shot her a dirty look in response.

"Yes, tell me. Why?"

Kerry cleared her throat, fidgeting with the napkin under her glass, and then said unconvincingly, "To protect you."

Melissa glanced at Sula, who had one eyebrow raised, but said nothing.

"Protect me? That lion didn't seem aggressive—to me, anyway. I interrupted its chance for a meal. As soon as it realized it wasn't going to catch that deer, it ran away."

Sula nodded.

"*So*…why would you want to shoot the mountain lion?" Melissa asked pointedly.

Kerry said nothing and let out an exasperated sigh, rolling her eyes.

Sula broke the silence. "Kerry's a trophy hunter." Her voice sounded flat and cold.

"Really." It was all Melissa could think to say. She had mixed feelings about hunting. She didn't like it, but over the years she had learned that some of her students came from deep poverty and their families relied on wild game to supplement what they could afford to buy at the grocery store. But trophy hunters? She considered them as something akin to serial killers.

"Yes, I am." Kerry looked at Sula with a piercing stare and then, more gently, back to Melissa. "And there's nothing wrong with that. It's all legal. I don't break the law."

"That doesn't make it ethical," Sula said quietly.

"Fuck you, Sula. You think animals should have more rights than people. Hunting keeps things in balance so the deer and elk don't starve to death because there isn't enough forage for them all. And hunters bring a *lot* of money into this community."

"Kerry's a hunting guide in the fall." Sula spoke calmly to Melissa and then turned, looking down at Kerry. She leaned forward, speaking in a low voice that was almost like a growl. "And the deer and elk populations are so big because people like you have killed off most of the predators so you can *play* predator. Taking a life because you need to survive, because it's what you evolved to do, is a whole different thing than killing for sport, or to take home a trophy to remind you of the thrill of the kill."

Kerry said nothing in reply and took another drink, finishing it.

Sula turned to Melissa with a concerned expression. "Melissa, I'm sorry if I've ruined your date. I'm going to leave now."

"I'm done here, too." Melissa pulled cash out of her wallet and placed it on the bar.

"Oh, come on," Kerry said, reaching out and touching Melissa's arm. "We'll have fun tonight. I promise."

Melissa shook off Kerry's hand. "No. I don't think so." She grabbed her bag. "Sula, can I talk to you for a minute?"

"Of course," Sula said. "I need to pay, and then I'll meet you outside."

Melissa turned to Kerry. "Look, Kerry. I appreciate everything you did today. I really do."

Kerry opened her mouth, and when she started to speak Melissa held up her hand.

"Let's just leave it at that."

Melissa walked away, leaving Kerry standing at the bar with her mouth open like a gasping fish. Melissa had a feeling she wasn't often turned down. She made her way outside and stood in front of the restaurant waiting for Sula. The sky was turquoise and gold, and the sun, just starting to dip behind the mountains, bathed everything in a warm light. When Sula walked out the door and came toward her, Melissa noted that she moved with an easy grace. She didn't say anything and seemed to be waiting for Melissa to speak first.

Melissa looked up at her. "Should I be worried about her?"

"For her safety or yours?" A slight smile formed on Sula's lips.

"Mmm…both?"

"She'll be all right. The staff here are good people. The bartender will cut her off or find her a safe way home if she needs it."

"And me?"

"I wouldn't worry. You made yourself clear in there. She likes the chase, but she'll find someone who actually wants to play with her."

"I sort of got the feeling she's good at that." Melissa began to feel a little embarrassed and grimaced. "This isn't exactly how I thought we'd meet."

"I have an idea," Sula said with a warm smile that put Melissa at ease. "What do you say we start our introductions all over again tomorrow as originally planned?"

"That's a wonderful idea," Melissa said with a sigh of relief.

CHAPTER NINE

L ooking in the mirror attached to the back of the car's sun visor, Melissa checked her hair and makeup one more time. She wiped away a little smudge of lipstick along the edge of her lower lip with her pinkie and flipped the visor up. She got out and smoothed her dress with the palm of her hand. Walking across the parking lot of the Colorado Bear Conservancy, she tried to shake off the nervousness that had plagued her all morning. She'd gone through several wardrobe changes before leaving the cabin, from outdoorsy hiking pants to casual jeans, and then settled on a sundress and sandals. Her thoughts hovered around Sula Johansen in the bar yesterday, her curious amber eyes and the feel of her hand, warm against her own.

The entrance of the visitors' center looked like a traditional alpine lodge with large log posts and beams, but she could see that the structure behind it was a contemporary design and even had a green roof. Impressed, she walked into the brightly illuminated space beyond the front door. The information desk was directly in front of her.

"Good morning," said the young man enthusiastically at the desk. His name tag identified him: Andrew from Connecticut. "Welcome to the Colorado Bear Conservancy."

"Good morning. I'm here to meet Sula Johansen. I have an appointment with her at ten."

"I'll let her know you're here." Andrew picked up a phone. "What's your name?"

"Melissa Warren."

Andrew nodded and made the call, relaying the information, then placed the phone back on the receiver. "Ms. Johansen said she's waiting for you by the mountain-lion display. If you go straight ahead into the exhibition hall and then turn toward your right after the wildflower display, it will be directly in front of you."

Melissa smiled at Andrew, but she was really smiling at Sula's little joke. She thanked him and followed his directions. The displays were themed and organized into color-coded sections painted in natural colors, reflecting the landscape outside. There were photographs of animals and plants with explanatory information. There were also interactive displays and flat-screen monitors playing videos. Bears were featured, but it seemed that the whole local Rocky Mountain ecosystem was represented. Cleverly, the polished-concrete floor had what appeared to be tracks of various animals running in different directions. She walked past a woman taking a picture of her daughter, a young girl, as she studied some small footprints, comparing them to the ones printed on a sheet of paper she clutched in her hand.

Melissa found the wildflower section and turned to see Sula standing in front of a life-size photograph of a mountain lion perched majestically on a log. She was dressed like the day before but in different colors: dark-green pants and a tan shirt with the conservancy logo. Her dark, wavy hair was styled so that it framed her face pleasantly. She had a natural and healthy-looking complexion, like that of someone who spends a good deal of time in fresh air and light. As Melissa approached, she noticed that Sula's features were highlighted with makeup, but she wore it with subtlety.

"Dr. Warren, it's a pleasure to meet you." Sula smiled and held out her hand.

Melissa played along and extended her own hand. "Ms. Johansen, the pleasure's all mine." When she took Sula's hand, the strange electricity of her amber eyes seemed to channel through her touch. "I have the strangest sense of déjà vu."

"As if we've met before?" Sula asked with a grin and what seemed to be a mischievous expression.

"Yes, exactly that. How did you know?"

"I have the same feeling." Sula smiled. "It's uncanny."

"Yes, it is. Please call me Melissa. May I call you Sula?"

"Please do."

They laughed together at their shared joke. Melissa pointed to the picture of the mountain lion that loomed on the wall over Sula's shoulder. "Watch out for that lion there."

"Oh, she's just a big pussycat."

"Hardly."

"No. She really is. Mountain lions are the largest of the small cats and are actually closer relatives to the domestic house cat than to the big cats like jaguars and tigers. They purr like their little cousins, but they don't roar like the big cats."

Melissa studied the image on the wall behind Sula. "That's very interesting."

"Daytime kills aren't unheard of, but they're usually nocturnal or crepuscular hunters, so the sighting you had yesterday was unusual."

"Crepuscular hunter?"

"Yes. Crepuscule means twilight."

"I know." Melissa smiled slowly. "It's one of my favorite words. You don't hear it used very often."

Sula looked down at her with a thoughtful expression. "I realize you're here for a different reason, but would you like a quick tour before we sit down to talk?"

"How could I refuse a private tour with the executive director? But first I have to say that this building is impressive. I noticed the solar panels in the parking lot and the green roof."

"It was really important to me that this building be as self-sufficient as possible. Not only is the green roof attractive, but it helps insulate the building, which saves energy and money. We also generate about seventy-five percent of our own power from solar and collect rainwater for the landscaping, which consists of all native plants, by the way." Sula smiled like a proud parent.

As they walked through the hall, Melissa was impressed by the museum-level quality of the exhibition design.

"Do you have a curator?"

"No. We have a graphic designer on staff and contract an exhibition designer." Sula went on to explain how all the parts contributed to an overarching theme, the interconnectedness of biotic communities, with, of course, a heavy emphasis on bears. They paused in front of a world map showing the range of all species of bears.

"We're focusing on black bears where we are here." Sula pointed to the red heart on the map. "But we like to point out that bears live on one third of the planet's land mass—it used to be much more—and that they're an integral part of ecosystems. They're what is known as an indicator species, meaning that healthy populations of bears indicate the presence of certain other plants and animals, all signals that things are in balance. Protect bears and you help protect everything else."

Melissa listened to Sula attentively, admiring her passion. "What was it that John Muir said? When we tug at one thing, we find it connected to everything else in the universe."

"Yes, exactly." Sula smiled at Melissa like a professor pleased with her student's understanding.

"Oh, hey." Melissa pointed at a nearby BearCam monitor. "Something's going on in this one." A black bear was gnawing on the trunk of a tree.

"That's Old Bob. He's marking the tree. He'll rub on it, scratch, and bite it. The marks let everyone know they're in his territory."

"For a moment I thought maybe he had some kind of species confusion." Melissa looked up at Sula, who seemed confused, so she explained. "He was acting like a beaver."

Sula laughed. "Oh, I think he knows he's a bear." A dark look crossed her face. "He was hit by a car and lost his vision in his right eye and has some nerve damage. You know, cars kill more black bears than hunters do every year."

"No. I didn't realize that." Melissa wanted to erase the sad expression on Sula's face. "Bob's lucky to be alive and to be here."

"It would be best if he could be out in the wild." Sula gazed at the bear on the monitor with sympathy. "But this is certainly better than the alternative."

Melissa didn't ask what Sula meant, but she was pretty sure she knew that the alternative was grim.

Sula glanced at her watch. "Well, I guess we should probably talk about what brought you here. We can go up to my office. Would you like a cup of coffee?" Sula's face lit up. "We have cinnamon rolls today, too."

"I have little resistance to either of those things."

"You're in the right place, then." Sula directed her to the elevator and to the offices upstairs.

Melissa met her administrative assistant, a pleasant young woman named Anna. She called Sula "Boss," which seemed old-fashioned and endearing. It struck Melissa that Anna behaved like a puppy dog around Sula. Her face lit up when she saw her, and she seemed eager to please. Melissa wondered if young Anna might have a little crush on Sula. It was certainly understandable.

"The break room is this way." Sula gestured down the hall.

Melissa was as impressed with the office space as she was with the visitors' center downstairs. Photographs of bears hung on walls painted a pale-yellow ochre. The flooring was marvelous: bluish wood with a marbled pattern.

"What kind of wood is this? It's beautiful."

"Beetle-kill pine." Sula stopped and put her hands on her hips and regarded the floor. "The more palatable name for it is blue-stain pine. The beetle that bores into the trees carries a fungus that helps it absorb nutrients. The fungus causes the color. If trees are harvested within a few years after they die, they can be used for lumber. Unfortunately, more and more trees are 'producing' this wood every year."

"A terrible beauty," Melissa remarked and shook her head as she stared at the floor. She knew that the pine beetle was ravaging forests, and when driving to Buckhorn she had seen dead, brown splotches on the otherwise green mountainsides. When she glanced up, Sula was looking at her again with that intense gaze, causing a butterfly flutter in her chest. A creeping warmth rose to her cheeks.

"Coffee?"

"Please," Melissa said, following Sula. She smelled the cinnamon rolls in the break room before they even walked through the door.

"Cream or sugar?" Sula asked as she poured coffee.

"Black is great, thanks." Melissa took the cup that Sula offered.

Melissa watched as Sula added cream and honey to her coffee. She lifted two rolls from the box, putting each one on a small plate with a fork, and handed one to Melissa. They carried their coffee and rolls to Sula's office, which was large with two windows, one with a gorgeous view outside and the other overlooking the atrium in the visitors' center. It was neatly arranged and furnished with an interesting mix of old and new. On one side sat a gleaming, vintage, craftsman-style oak desk with a high-tech mesh office chair. On the other stretched a sitting area with modern leather and chrome chairs and couch arranged around a contemporary glass table that had cast-bronze legs resembling elk antlers. Melissa wanted to inspect several photographs of bears and two paintings more closely, but Sula gestured for her to sit down by the table.

"My God, this cinnamon roll is amazing," Melissa said after her first bite.

"They're from the bakery next door to the grocery store. Their pecan rolls are good, too." Sula settled in one of the chairs, crossing her long legs, and sat back.

"Oh, I wish I didn't know that. I'll have to do two hikes a day instead of one." Sula laughed, and Melissa enjoyed the low and smooth, sensual sound.

"So, are you enjoying your stay at the ranch?" Sula asked between bites.

"Yes. Very much. It's so beautiful there, and Betty is wonderful. I'm so glad to have met her."

"You know, she's an old friend of the family. In fact, I really consider her more family than friend."

"Betty said I should talk with you about my research project, but she didn't offer any explanation as to why. Has she told you what I'm working on?"

Sula leaned forward, putting her plate on the table, and picked up her cup. Then she leaned back, regarding Melissa with an intensity that made Melissa feel as if she was being assessed in some way. She met Sula's piercing gaze.

"Betty said you're an art historian working on a research project..." Sula took a sip of coffee slowly. "And that you are interested in my great-grandmother's paintings."

It took a moment for Melissa to process what Sula had just said— she was the artist's great-granddaughter. Her jaw dropped and she was speechless.

Melissa's silent reaction, the stunned look on her face, let Sula know for certain that the professor didn't know about her familial connection to Ursula Bergen. Sula surprised herself at being so forthright with Melissa. She'd planned to answer a few questions and keep her at a safe distance. Betty was right that there was something special about her. Sula had sensed it immediately when she met her in the bar the night before. When she'd taken Melissa's hand in hers, a sensation had rippled through her that she didn't fully understand. It almost felt like recognition, though of what she wasn't sure. She liked how Melissa had responded to her encounter with the mountain lion, with awe, not fear. Melissa's reaction was unusual. So many people seemed afraid of the world outside their homes. Melissa intuitively understood that Notch had little interest in her and recognized her experience as something rare to be treasured.

When Sula had first seen Melissa downstairs in the hall walking toward her, wearing a dress the color of blue columbine and with her golden hair pulled back, tendrils falling out along the sides of her face, her breath had caught in her throat. And when they'd walked through the hall together, she'd found Melissa's attentiveness and curiosity enchanting. Sula hadn't expected to feel so attracted to Melissa, let alone so comfortable with her—her reaction was disarming. Melissa was disarming.

Melissa sat staring at Sula and finally stammered, "Ursula Bergen was your great-grandmother?"

Sula nodded. "I was named after her, but I've been called Sula, short for Ursula, for as long as anyone can remember."

Melissa looked at her blankly and blinked. She had beautiful green eyes.

"I have so many questions, and now I don't even know where to begin."

"Take your time. I don't have any other appointments today." Sula looked at her over the rim of her cup. "Why don't you tell me about how you know about her and her paintings."

Melissa looked thoughtful for a moment, then began. "My grandmother owned three paintings by Ursula—" Melissa interrupted herself. "I've been calling her that, by her first name, I mean. Do you mind?"

"It's her given name. I don't see a problem."

"Well, I grew up seeing them when I spent time at my grandparents' house. My grandmother inherited them from her mother, my great-grandmother."

"What was her name?"

"Evelyn Llewellyn."

Sula didn't recognize the name. "Go on."

"I just always loved looking at them, and I *studied* them, you know, the way kids do. I noticed all the little details that adults gloss over, and I imagined myself in those places or invented stories that took place there. I stopped doing that as I got older, but I was always so fond of them. They might have led me to become an art historian. When my grandmother died, about a year ago, I inherited them from her. I'd wanted to do research on them even before inheriting them. I never expected that I'd find much about them or the artist. Luckily, she'd signed the back of the paintings. I was hopeful that by coming here I might find more paintings and thought perhaps I could find out just enough about Ursula to write a short essay that the local historical society might like for their archives. A local magazine might even want to publish it. But really, my interest in them is entirely personal."

Melissa's green eyes sparkled as she spoke, her enthusiasm infectious. Sula realized she was smiling as she listened. She recalled Betty's observation that Melissa didn't seem to be motivated by anything other than curiosity, and Sula agreed.

"Have you been to the historical society?"

"Yes. The people there were nice, but the museum is really cluttered, and their archives are spotty and not well organized. I didn't find anything."

"How did you know to look for her here in Buckhorn?"

"Her name was registered in the Buckhorn census records of 1920 and 1930."

Sula stood, gesturing to the wall where two paintings hung. "Would you like to see another painting by her?"

"Ah." Melissa grinned, pointing to one of them. "I knew there was a reason that caught my eye."

Melissa followed her, standing close, and peered at the painting of a tall, narrow waterfall that cascaded into a pool flanked by pines, a large boulder in the foreground. "A watercolor. Interesting. My three are oils."

Sula caught the scent of Melissa's perfume. She smelled good.

Melissa looked at the side of the wood frame. "Is this frame sealed? Could I look at the back of the painting?"

"Sure." Sula reached out and lifted the painting from the wall. She turned it around, revealing that the back was sealed with gray paper. "I had this framed when I got it from my parents…it must have been fifteen years ago. I don't remember if there was anything on the back." She pulled a small brass knife from her pocket and opened it.

"Are you sure you don't mind?" Melissa asked.

"Not at all. I'm curious now, too."

Sula placed the painting facedown on the blotter on her desk. Using the knife blade, she carefully separated the paper from the back of the frame and revealed the unmarked backing board.

Melissa gestured to the metal tabs holding the board in place, "It looks like the framer used glazer's points. They're shallow, so you should be able to slide them out easily."

Sula slid the blade in between the wood frame and the metal tabs and, one by one, pried each point out. She closed the knife, put it in her pocket again, and stood back. "Would you like to do the honors, Professor?"

"Really?"

"Please. Go right ahead."

Sula enjoyed watching Melissa. With a look of concentration, she carefully lifted both the backing board and the mat with the attached painting out of the frame. At the bottom of the back of the watercolor painting were her great-grandmother's signature and a note written in pencil.

Melissa smiled and read it aloud. "Fairy Falls, 1922. Ursula Bergen." She looked up at Sula. "Do you know this place?"

"No. The name's not familiar, and I don't know of any waterfall around here as big as that one."

Melissa turned it over and looked carefully at the picture. "This is really interesting. It's a sketch, but the composition is well considered. Notice the boulder here in the foreground versus the view of the falls. It's as if we're perched on top of the rock. That's a nice touch." Melissa paused and narrowed her eyes. Then she looked toward the other painting on the wall. It depicted a grizzly bear standing on a rocky outcrop looking down into a valley at sunset. "Tell me about that one."

"It's not by my great-grandmother."

"Yes. I know. The style is completely different. But why do you have it? And why is it hanging next to this one?"

Sula wasn't sure what she was getting at. "I bought it at an auction in Denver a few years ago. It was right before we moved into this building, and I was looking for furniture for my new office. I was at the auction because of this desk, actually." Sula tapped her index finger on the top of it. "That painting was also in the auction. It's by Bob Kuhn, who was an illustrator, and was used for a cover of *Field & Stream* magazine in the 1960s. I know all this only because it was in the auction catalog." Sula shrugged. "I bid on it because I liked it."

Melissa glanced back and forth between the two pictures. "Well, it just struck me that this picture seems to be from the point of view of standing on a rock looking out, and that picture on the wall shows a bear standing on a rocky ledge looking out. You must have made that association unconsciously."

Sula had not made that connection between the two paintings, at least not until now. Melissa's keen observation rattled her. "That's interesting. You're very astute."

"Well, I'm an art historian. It's what I do." Melissa laughed. "I spend a lot of time looking at art analytically."

"Yes, I expect you do."

"Would you like me to put this back together?"

"No. I'll take care of it later. What about those paintings you have? Do you have pictures of them?"

"Yes. I have some with me, in fact." Melissa flashed a smile. "You sidetracked me." She walked back to the couch and sat down. Then she removed the folder of photographs from her bag and laid the pictures of the three paintings out on the coffee table.

Sula sat down next to her and leaned forward to inspect them. She felt Melissa watching her, but she didn't turn to look at her. She recognized both places depicted in the two landscape paintings, and though she wasn't an expert, she could also see the similarities to the paintings by her great-grandmother that hung in her home. Betty had mentioned the painting of a woman with a bear, and as she examined the photograph of it, it seemed less a depiction of a place and more like a scene in a story.

"If you'd like to see details, I have high-resolution digital images, but I didn't bring my laptop."

"Perhaps later." Sula pointed to the image that Melissa called a river landscape. "Is this the place you hoped to find on the trail ride yesterday?"

Melissa nodded. "Yes, but that wasn't it."

"I know." Sula looked at Melissa, whose expression lay somewhere between confused and expectant. She was overcome with a desire to help her, to spend more time with her. What was it about his woman? "This place is on my property, not the ranch's. And it's a creek, not a river. Icy Creek." Contrary to her usual cautious behavior, something about Melissa prompted her to act rashly. "I can take you there if you like."

"Really?" Melissa's wide-eyed excitement shifted to a softer, more thoughtful look. "This painting hung in my grandmother's dining room, and I spent a lot of time looking at it while playing cards with my grandmother or while seated for dinner. I'd ignore what the adults were saying and get lost in exploring the space of that painting. To say I'd love to see the place that inspired it is an understatement."

"We can drive fairly close, but we'll have to hike over a mile to get to it, if you're up for that."

"I am." Melissa appeared eager. "I've been starting my days here with a short hike. I think I've adjusted to the altitude."

"That's good. How about Saturday? Would that work for you?"

"Absolutely!" Melissa said without hesitation and gathered the prints together, putting them back into the folder and sliding it into her bag. "What cabin are you staying in at the ranch?"

"Aspen Glow."

"Oh, that's a really nice one—a classic cabin with a great view. I'll pick you up at nine, and we can have lunch at the creek. Don't worry about bringing anything except your water bottle. Is there anything you don't like?"

"I'm pretty easy when it comes to food. I'm an omnivore."

"Just like bears," Sula said with a smile.

"Well, then I'll be in very good company."

"What?" Sula's heart skipped a beat. "What do you mean?"

"I assume there are some omnivorous bears out there on your property. Maybe I'll get to see one. That would be so exciting."

"Oh." Sula looked at Melissa cautiously from the corner of her eye. "Maybe."

CHAPTER TEN

Sula pulled up to the lodge and parked next to Betty's truck. She was driving her old Bronco. Since it was smaller and more agile than the pickup, it was a better vehicle for the jeep track she'd be driving on later in the morning with Melissa. Running ahead of schedule, she decided to stop by the office for a coffee with Betty.

Sula entered the lodge quietly and stuck her head through the office door. Betty was working at her desk, oblivious to her presence.

Sula let out a playful growl.

Betty jumped in her chair and spun around to see Sula standing in the doorway and grinning. "Sula!"

"If I were a bear, I'd have bitten you." Sula liked to tease her.

"If you were a bear, I would have pepper-sprayed your ass! You damn near gave me a heart attack."

"I'd rather have a cup of coffee, if you don't mind."

"Help yourself. You know where it is." Betty's mouth turned down in a frown, but her eyes were smiling.

Sula left and then returned with a cup in her hand.

"You came all the way out here for a cup of coffee?"

Sula sat down in the chair in front of Betty's desk and crossed her legs. "I'm picking up Melissa Warren in a half hour to take her out to see one of the places in her paintings."

"You mean your great-grandmother's painting."

"Yes, well, they're the same thing, right?"

"I suppose so. So, when did you talk to Melissa? I'm guessing it went well enough if you've got a date."

"It's not a date." Sula sipped her coffee. "We met last week—twice, actually. The first time was an accident."

"An accident? How so?"

"I was having dinner in the bar at the River Grill. Melissa was there. She was waiting on Kerry, only I didn't know yet who Melissa was. It was the day she went on that trail ride you suggested and saw the mountain lion. Kerry came in and, after she saw me, started showing off. You know how she is. She was a little drunk and—" Sula took another sip of coffee, pausing to figure out how to put it into words.

"You got into a fight?"

Sula winced. "Not a fight exactly, but we exchanged words."

"Uh-huh." The crease between Betty's eyebrows deepened. "You know she just quit on me."

"What?"

"Yep. She said she got a full-time government job."

"Huh. So, what are you going to do?"

"Little Lars is going to take over for now. I always thought he preferred working in the cattle operation, but he's been surprisingly good in the livery. I'll give him a chance, and if it doesn't work out, I'll advertise the position."

"I wonder what she means by a government job."

"I have no idea. I wondered the same thing. So, what'd you get in a fight over?"

"It wasn't a fight." Sula shook her head.

"Okay…so what did you exchange words over?"

"The usual—trophy hunting. She said she wished she could have shot the mountain lion."

Betty grunted her displeasure and didn't ask any more questions about Kerry. "Tell me about your date with Melissa."

Sula ignored Betty's use of the word date. "I'm taking her up above Moon Lake. There's a spot on Icy Creek that matches the view in that one painting."

"And when are you going to tell her you live in the house that's in the other painting?" Betty leaned back in her chair, clasping her hands and tapping her thumbs together while she waited for an answer.

Sula sighed. "I'm not sure. We'll see how today goes." Sula glanced at the clock on the wall and raised her cup. "Well, I better get going. Thanks for the coffee, Betty."

"You're welcome," Betty said. And as soon as Sula walked out of the office, she called out after her, "Enjoy your date."

"It's *not* a date," Sula said, not turning around, and put her cup in the bin by the coffee pot. She started to walk away but then turned and narrowed her eyes at Betty. "Why do you keep calling it a date?"

"Because I've never seen you wear makeup when going on a hike." Betty's laughter sounded like a hen cackling.

In a gesture of exasperation, Sula put the palm of her hand to her forehead and waved good-bye to Betty as she opened the screen door and left the lodge.

Melissa was standing on the deck of the cabin cradling a mug in both hands, gazing at the meadow, when Sula turned on to the driveway. She was just as attractive in a T-shirt, hiking pants, and boots as she was in a sundress and sandals. Sula parked, took a deep breath, and held it in for a second before exhaling and opening the door.

"Good morning!" Melissa smiled and waved as Sula got out. "I love your Bronco! What year is it?"

"Good morning." Sula smiled back. "It's a '76."

"I'm a little envious. My dad had a '69 when I was a kid. I loved that car and was heartbroken when he sold it before I got my driver's license."

"These old Broncos are great if you don't need to carry much, and they're better for small roads." Sula pointed a thumb over her shoulder. "I found it in North Park. It belonged to a rancher and had sat in his barn for twenty years. It didn't look like this before I had it restored."

"I haven't ridden in one in forever. That's a nice color, too. Looks like the sky this morning."

Sula glanced up at the clear azure sky and nodded. "Are you ready?"

"I am. I just need to go in and grab my pack. Be right back."

Sula unlatched the tire gate on the back and swung the spare out of the way to lift the window. While she waited for Melissa, she admired the view of the meadow below. She liked the way the cabin was den-like and secure, tucked into the trees against the mountainside. The leaves of the aspens trembled and shimmered in the breeze, their white trunks and branches standing out. Melissa, carrying a daypack and a water bottle, came around the corner of the Bronco and placed them in the back next to Sula's pack. Sula pulled the window down and swung the spare tire back in place. As she latched the gate, Melissa put a hand on her forearm.

"Thank you so much for this, Sula. It's very kind of you to take me out."

Melissa's touch, her hand pleasantly warm, startled Sula. Her eyes, seemingly greener in the morning light, were mesmerizing.

"You're welcome," Sula said. She resisted reaching out to tuck a stray strand of hair behind Melissa's ear. "Do you have a hat and some sunscreen?"

"The sunscreen is on, and the hat's in my pack."

"Excellent." Sula pulled a folded map out of her back pocket and held it up. "Would you like to see where we're going?"

"A woman with a real map? Be still, my beating heart." Melissa was joking.

Sula raised her eyebrows, a question forming on her face.

"Everyone has a cell phone and GPS. So few people actually use real maps anymore."

"I like to see the big picture…well, big," Sula said, unfolding the map.

Melissa regarded Sula with an appreciative look. "That's exactly what I like about paper maps."

"And you also don't need to rely on a signal or batteries to make it work."

"That's an even better reason to use them."

Sula gestured for Melissa to follow her to the front of the Bronco. She laid the map across the hood, holding it down with her left hand and pointing out features with her right. She showed Melissa the boundaries of the ranch, her land, and the conservancy's property.

Melissa looked at the map carefully and then pointed to a dark-green section. "So, all together they create a buffer between Buckhorn and Roosevelt National Forest here?"

"It's more like a corridor. Everything *plus* the national forest make one very large area where development is restricted. My land, the conservancy's land, and Buckhorn Creek Ranch are all in conservation easements. It's a federal program. As long as the properties are privately owned, development is restricted."

"And that's good for bears."

"Exactly, but not just bears. Protect bears—"

"And you protect everything else."

"Very good, Dr. Warren."

"I didn't earn my 'friend of bears' sticker for nothing." Melissa laughed.

"I noticed the sticker on your car." Sula smiled. Melissa was difficult not to like, and she felt unusually comfortable with her. "Okay, so now that you've got the big picture…" Sula put her finger down on the map. "We are here." She moved her finger across the surface of the map, following a solid line that turned into a dotted one near a lake. "Here, the road becomes a jeep track, and from there we'll work our way up Raven Mountain."

The dotted line made a series of zigzags.

"Oh, switchbacks." Melissa's eyes grew big. "I guess this is why you're driving the Bronco."

Sula nodded. "We'll gain some elevation and then drop down on the other side of the mountain. The road ends here, and from there it's about a mile and a half to the creek."

"Why are we standing here talking? Fold up that map. Let's go!"

Sula laughed, folding the map as she got into the driver's seat.

Melissa opened the passenger-side door and looked around.

"Do you need a hand up?"

"No. I'm fine." Melissa climbed in and slid into the well-padded bucket seat. "I'm just checking out this interior. This is not what I remember of my dad's car."

"These seats are much more comfortable than the originals, and safer, too."

"It's snug." Melissa wiggled her butt in the contoured seat and then reached over her shoulder for the seat belt. "I feel like I'm being hugged."

Sula imagined what it would be like to hug Melissa, to wrap her arms around her. No doubt she would be soft and warm. She imagined nuzzling her cheek and neck, getting closer to the source of her sweet scent. She smelled like spring flowers after a rain and a hint of sandalwood. The click of the seat belt snapped her out of her brief reverie.

"You okay?" Melissa regarded her with a curious expression. "You looked a million miles away."

"I'm good," Sula said with a reassuring smile, hoping Melissa didn't realize exactly where her mind had wandered, and started the engine.

The drive to the lake was a fairly smooth ride on a graded road that went up the valley. Along the way Melissa pointed out all the things that interested her, and there were many—a particularly large tree, an unusually shaped boulder, the colors in the landscape, and the spectacular views out the open window. While Sula tried to never take it for granted that she lived in a marvelously beautiful place, she saw it today with fresh eyes.

She downshifted, slowing the Bronco as they approached the boundary between the ranch and her land.

"Say good-bye to Buckhorn Creek Ranch," Sula said as they passed through the timber gate, the tires rumbling over the cattle guard.

"Does your property have a name? Everything around here seems to be called something-or-other ranch."

"No. I just call it my land. Sometimes just the land."

"That's interesting. Native Americans often refer to the places where they live as 'the land' and to themselves as 'the people.' Western culture likes to name everything, because it works well with the concept of private property. Naming is owning."

Sula thought about that idea for a moment. "I think of myself as more of a caretaker than an owner. This place existed long before me, and it will be here a long time after I'm gone. I have no right to destroy it."

"I wish more people thought that way. The world would be a much better place."

Sula glanced over at Melissa, who closed her eyes and turned her face to the open window. She inhaled deeply.

"Smells good, doesn't it?" Sula loved the refreshing scent of pine. It never failed to clear her mind and invigorate her senses. She took a hand from the wheel to point ahead. "The lake is just over this hill. The pines over there are dense, and the breeze is blowing their scent our way."

"How many acres is your land?" Melissa asked suddenly.

"Twenty-two thousand."

"Twenty-two *thousand*? That's huge."

"It's a lot, but many properties around here are much bigger," Sula said.

"The lot my house is on is eighty by one hundred and twenty feet. So, in comparison, twenty-two thousand acres qualifies as huge." Melissa shook her head, clearly incredulous. "How long have you lived here?"

"I grew up here. My great-great-grandparents homesteaded here and added to the original one hundred and sixty acres by acquiring all the failed homesteads around them. You had to stay on the land for five years to get the deed, and most people gave up before the five years had passed. Every generation since has added more acreage to the land. I'm currently trying to purchase a parcel to fill in a gap between my land and the ranch. But it's still modest compared to the big ranches. They're a hundred and fifty thousand acres or more."

"I had no idea," Melissa said. "Where did your great-great-grandparents come from? From your name and height and good looks, I'd say somewhere in Scandinavia."

Sula's mind momentarily faltered when Melissa described her as having "good looks." As she began to explain that her family had emigrated from Norway, they reached the crest of the hill, and the change in landscape diverted Melissa's attention.

"It's so beautiful," Melissa said in a voice that was quiet, almost a whisper.

Sula stopped the Bronco. This was where the road turned into a jeep track, and she needed to shift the vehicle into four-wheel drive. The pause also gave Melissa a chance to enjoy the fine view. The dark-blue lake reflected the sky, and its edges were dotted with large, round, gray rocks. Some boulders also poked out of the lake, forming a granite archipelago.

"This is Moon Lake. See how almost perfectly round it is? Like a full moon."

"Yes. I see that." Melissa touched her index finger to her lower lip, a habit that Sula realized meant she was thinking. "And what about the rocks in the water? They look a little like the shape of a crescent moon, don't you think?"

"Huh. You're right. From this angle it does resemble a crescent moon. I've never seen it like that before." Sula regarded Melissa, who was now looking up beyond the lake. Sula liked the fresh perspective that Melissa brought.

"Is this where we get on the road with the switchbacks?"

"It is, and it's also where I switch out of two-wheel drive." Sula shifted the car into neutral, set the parking brake, and shifted the transfer case into four-wheel drive. After unbuckling her seat belt, she opened the door. "I have to get out to lock the hubs on the wheels. It's an old car, not like the new ones where you just push buttons on the dash."

"You shouldn't insult the car by calling it old," Melissa said out the window to Sula as she watched her twist the hub locks in the center of the wheel on the passenger side. "Especially while you're driving it and are the only person in sight for miles and miles."

Sula laughed and patted the hood. "This is a good old car, and she knows it."

"She?" Melissa asked as Sula got back in the car. "Your car has a gender?"

"Yeah, like a boat. Isn't it traditional to refer to boats as 'she'?"

"Yes. But doesn't tradition also dictate that it's improper to comment on a lady's age?"

"*Shhh*…don't give her any ideas." Sula laughed.

They continued around the lake. The road was muddy where a small stream fed the lake, but it was dry again once they reached the other side and the road began to climb the side of the mountain. The jeep track was full of low spots and big rocks that had to be navigated carefully.

"Wow. You weren't kidding when you said we'd need four-wheel drive," Melissa said as they drove slowly over another big rock. As the Bronco pitched forward, she hung on to the brace mounted on the dashboard.

"Have you ever been on a road like this?" Sula asked calmly, keeping her eyes on the road in front of her and glancing at her side mirror, making sure the underside of the Bronco cleared the rock.

"No. This is a first for me."

"Are you enjoying it?" Sula glanced over at Melissa.

"Oh my God, are you kidding me?" Melissa grinned. "This is great!"

"Good." Sula smiled back. "We'll stay in the trees most of the way up, but I'll stop at the next switchback where there's a view. After that, we're almost to the top."

After they rounded the last sharp turn, Sula stopped, and they got out to admire the vista. The sun was bright, and Melissa shielded her eyes with her hand. The vantage allowed a clear view of the valley and the lake below. The raspy, insistent voice of a jay got their attention, and they turned toward the sound.

A Steller's jay, with its distinctive black head and blue body, watched them from its perch near the top of a tree. Inquisitive, it hopped down several branches, getting closer each time. Sula walked over to the Bronco, reached behind her seat, and came back with a handful of peanuts in the shell. She put one in the palm of her hand and held it out.

The jay swooped down and grabbed it, taking it back to a low branch where, holding the peanut between its feet, it pecked the nut out of the shell with ease. Sula repeated the offering several times, and a second jay swooped in for treats.

"I'm guessing they know you," Melissa said quietly.

"I always bring peanuts with me." Sula handed Melissa the rest of them. "Here. I bet they'll take them from you, too."

Sula watched Melissa feed the jays. Her ponytail had come loose, and the blond tendrils danced around her face in the breeze. A smile never left her lips as she offered the treats to the birds one by one. The second jay, a little bolder than the first, landed on Melissa's hand, perching on her thumb momentarily before snatching the peanut and taking off for the trees. The look on Melissa's face was pure happiness. Sula watched Melissa, her obvious pleasure in feeding the birds as enjoyable as feeding them herself.

"Well, I don't know about you, but I'm ready to take a little hike to our picnic spot. We're not far from where we'll park," Sula said.

"Then you'd better not give me any more nuts. I could do this all day."

Sula laughed.

"You laugh," Melissa warned her. "But I'm serious."

From what she'd just seen, Sula believed Melissa implicitly. They got back into the Bronco and continued up the road and over the mountain, then stopped where the road ended in a small clearing. Sula took a deep breath of resin-scented air when she got out of the Bronco, relaxing in a way that only happened when she was in the forest.

They grabbed their packs out of the back of the Bronco and put them on. "Are you not carrying bear spray?" Melissa asked as Sula adjusted the chest strap on her pack.

Sula looked at Melissa and noticed she had a brand-new holster with a canister of bear spray attached to the front of one of the shoulder straps.

"No." She considered telling Melissa that she forgot it, but she didn't want to lie to her. "I don't need it."

Sula always advised hikers to carry bear spray, it was a standard safety protocol, but she carried it only when she went in the field on official business with biologists or with groups associated with the conservancy.

"How can you not need it?" Melissa looked incredulous.

Sula thought for a moment about how best to respond. "I know bear habitat and behavior very well. I would never find myself in a position to have to use it."

"I'm not sure whether I should be impressed or worried."

"Worried about what?"

"That I'm about to walk into the woods with someone reckless."

"I'm *never* reckless," Sula said confidently and pointed toward the trees in front of them. "We're going this way...if you trust me."

"At this point I don't have much choice, do I? I'll just have to reassure myself with the fact that you grew up here and you're still alive." She looked Sula up and down. "I don't see any scars on you from having been mauled by bears."

"That you can see." Sula laughed mischievously and walked toward the trees in front of them.

"Touché," Melissa replied, following her.

After passing through a stand of tall ponderosa pines with the nasal calls of nuthatches and sapsuckers echoing around them, they entered a wide meadow of yellow-green grass dotted with bright colors. The wildflowers were in full bloom; the air was sweet and buzzed with insects.

"Columbines..." Melissa stepped forward to look at some of the delicate blue flowers closest to her. "I *love* these."

"I've always been fond of the owl's claws, myself," Sula said.

"Which ones are those?"

Sula pointed to a flower with a dark center and orange petals.

"Owl's claws is such a descriptive name. The petals are curved like a talon."

Sula cocked her head, cupping a hand to her ear. "Do you hear the sound of running water?"

Melissa closed her eyes as she listened carefully and shook her head. "No."

"We're close. You'll hear it soon."

They continued walking through the meadow descending gently toward the creek that Sula knew was nearby. A pattern on the ground caught her eye, so she stopped abruptly and squatted, focusing on the ground in front of her.

"What do you see?"

"Tracks," Sula said and pointed. "A black bear crossed in front of us here. See?"

"I would have missed them if you hadn't pointed them out."

Melissa bent over, peering at them. "They're so big. Are you sure those aren't from a grizzly bear?"

"I'm sure," Sula said with a laugh.

"Are you certain?"

"Very. We haven't had any grizzlies in this area since the 50s."

Melissa peered at the tracks. "You know, I read somewhere that when you step on the trail, you step into the food chain."

"That's a bit extreme. You're not really in the regular food chain." Sula looked up, brushing her bangs away from her eyes in order to see Melissa better. The sun was behind her, illuminating her hair, creating a golden aura. "But you are in the bears' house, Goldilocks."

Melissa narrowed her eyes at Sula and smiled slowly. "Well, then, I'll be sure to mind my manners and will resist eating any bowls of porridge I find along the way. I would hate to get kicked out of this beautiful house. You'll tell me if I violate any bear etiquette, won't you?"

"Absolutely, Goldie." Sula grinned.

"Oh, no…did I just get a nickname?" Melissa laughed and then became quiet and turned her head as if listening carefully. "I think I hear the creek now."

"See the blue spruce and the rocks up ahead? That's where we're headed." Sula waved her forward.

Icy Creek lived up to its name, as Melissa discovered when she crouched at the creek's edge and dipped her bandana into the clear water.

"Wow, that's *cold*. No skinny-dipping today," Melissa said as she wrung the frigid water out of the cloth and dabbed it against her face and the back of her neck. "Oh, that feels good, though."

Melissa stood, regarding the creek with a serious expression. "This really does look a lot like the river, I mean creek, in the painting, but I don't see the owl-shaped boulders."

"It's all about your perspective," Sula said. "Follow me."

Sula led Melissa up the creek a little way to a place where the water rushed around four large rocks but didn't cover them. "We'll cross here. I'll go first and help you. The first two rocks are easy, but the third one is a little tricky the first time."

Sula walked effortlessly across the first two flat-topped rocks and then scrambled up and perched on the next, taller and rounded, rock. She watched as Melissa followed her footsteps. "Okay, as you step onto this rock, give me your hand and put your weight forward."

Melissa did as Sula directed, and she pulled her up effortlessly. "Wow, that was easier than I thought it'd be," Melissa said, but realized that Sula had done most of the work.

Sula hopped down to the fourth rock and extended her hand again, helping Melissa to the last lower and flatter rock. Melissa didn't immediately let go of Sula, and they stepped onto the creek bank hand in hand. Enjoying the feel of Melissa's hand in hers, Sula led her up the creek a bit farther, to some small waterfalls. Melissa dropped Sula's hand and pointed upstream.

"This is it. I see the owls!" Using her hands, Melissa framed the view. "Add a fallen tree, a creek swollen by a passing thunderstorm, and…this is the place!"

Melissa was standing on a rock that made her the same height as Sula. Smiling her astonishment, Melissa turned around quickly, meeting Sula's gaze evenly. Sula inhaled sharply and froze, feeling like a deer in that moment when it knows she's being watched and hasn't decided on a course of action. Melissa reached out for Sula's cheeks, and before she realized what was happening, Melissa kissed her.

CHAPTER ELEVEN

Melissa hadn't planned on a kiss. Standing on a rock in the very spot where Ursula Bergen, the artist, must have stood nearly a hundred years ago, Melissa let her excitement bubble to the surface. When she turned around to explain to Sula how absolutely astonishing and wonderful this moment was for her, she was surprised to find Sula standing so close and at eye level. Sula stared at her, unblinking, with those marvelous amber eyes and long, dark eyelashes. Melissa abandoned the words she was attempting to form, reached out, and—just like that—had kissed her.

It was an innocent kiss at first, but then Melissa discovered that Sula's lips were soft, tender...and responsive. Sula leaned closer and returned the kiss, making a throaty sound like a soft growl. Melissa felt as if all her nerve endings had just woken up from a deep slumber as her awareness shifted to other parts of her body. She moved her hand from Sula's cheek to the nape of her neck, feeling the tendrils of Sula's hair brushing against her fingers. She became conscious of the weight of Sula's hand as it rested on her shoulder and then slipped slowly down, stopping against the curve of her back. As their kiss deepened, Melissa began to lose herself again in the sensations of Sula's lips and tongue, and then, with a wrenching abruptness, she felt Sula stiffen and pull away.

"I...uh...I'm...sorry." Sula's words sputtered out. "I didn't mean to—"

"What are you apologizing for?" Melissa took a deep breath and struggled to meet Sula's gaze, the wave of desire that washed over her making it difficult to focus on anything but her shapely lips.

Sula looked down at her feet. "I didn't mean to mislead you. I mean, I didn't bring you out here to...uh...seduce you. I don't want you to think I'm like—"

"Like Kerry?"

Sula nodded and hung her head like a scolded puppy. She removed her hand from Melissa's back and fidgeted with a strap on her pack. "Sula, you are *nothing* like Kerry. Trust me," Melissa said tenderly. "Anyway, I kissed you first, didn't I?"

"Yeah, you did." Sula spoke softly and smiled but kept her eyes cast down. She slipped her pack off and held it up between them. "Are you hungry? Ready for lunch?"

Melissa was hungry all right. Hungry for another kiss. But the moment between them had passed. Sula seemed uncomfortable with what had just happened, and Melissa felt as if she had inadvertently crossed some invisible boundary. Experiencing Sula's shift from confident naturalist to shy woman was unexpected, but also oddly intriguing. It intensified Melissa's curiosity. She wanted more, but for now she'd follow Sula's lead. She blew air out between her lips and hoped the whoosh didn't sound as exasperated as she felt. "Ready for lunch," she said.

Sula pulled a checkered blanket out of her pack and unfurled it in a patch of shade near the creek, and they sat down. Facing Sula, she watched as she removed cloth napkins, two apples, and a tiffin. She separated the three stainless-steel compartments, placing them side by side on the blanket in between them to reveal a smorgasbord—sliced cheese, salami, peeled hard-boiled eggs, pickles, and crackers.

"Is this all right?"

"More than all right. This is a feast."

"Help yourself." Sula gestured to the food and pulled a knife from her pocket.

Melissa sandwiched cheese and salami between two crackers and ate it while watching Sula turn the tiffin lid over to use as a plate and then pick up one of the apples and begin to slice it into pieces. Her fingers moved deftly as she carved out the seeds and tossed them aside.

Tucking a strand of hair behind her ear, Melissa observed Sula while she cut the apple and arranged the slices neatly on the lid. Melissa had never had a specific type, but she considered a woman's mind and personality to be her most attractive features. If those two aspects didn't engage her, nothing else mattered. If asked to classify Sula according to the lesbian spectrum of butch to femme, she'd have been hard-pressed to categorize her. Sula dressed practically for the mountain environment, and outdoor clothing tended to be intrinsically androgynous. She wore makeup, but only enough to highlight her natural features, especially her eyes and lips. Melissa had walked behind Sula most of the day and noticed that she moved with a confident, graceful power without even breaking a sweat, but she didn't carry herself with any kind of butch bravado.

Sula produced a small plastic bottle from her pack. Flicking the lid open with her thumb, she squeezed it, drizzling the apples with sticky honey. She wiped the rim of the lid with her finger, licked it, and looked up with a surprised expression, as if she didn't realize Melissa had been watching her all along. Melissa became aware she'd been holding her breath while watching her and mentally reminded herself to breathe.

"Dessert." Sula pointed to the apples and honey.

"You sure do like honey."

"Why do you say that?" Sula sliced an egg, placed it on a cracker with a pickle, and ate it.

"Remember, I'm observant. You put honey in your coffee, you have a bowl of honey candy on your office desk, and you brought a bottle of honey on a hike. Two's a coincidence. Three is a pattern."

"Yeah, so I like honey." Sula laughed and shrugged. "It's natural and it's good for you. Betty's a beekeeper, did you know?"

"Yes. She told me. We met one day after she'd checked on her hives." Melissa remembered the bee walking on Betty's finger. "I think she's a bee charmer."

"She might be."

Melissa waited for Sula to tell her more, but she just continued to eat. Finally, Melissa spoke. "Care to explain what you mean by that?"

"Well, one time when I was a kid, my family and Betty's family were on a picnic, and I tried to get honey from a wild hive. I'd been watching the bees go in and out of a crevice in a tree and got the brilliant idea to climb the tree and stick my hand in. Let's just say the bees were *not* happy with me."

"How old were you?"

"Ten, maybe."

Melissa gasped. "Sula, swarming bees could have killed you."

"I only got a couple of stings. Betty saw what was happening and ran over and grabbed me. The bees all flew away from her."

"That's miraculous." Melissa reached for more cheese and crackers.

"She told me that if I wanted honey that bad, she'd give me a whole jar of it whenever I wanted. I've held her to it ever since." Sula smiled, her eyes twinkling in the sunlight filtering through the pines.

Melissa narrowed her eyes. "Is this a tall tale, Ms. Johansen?"

Sula shrugged and grinned in what Melissa interpreted as a noncommittal answer and swatted her playfully, feigning a sound of irritation.

"I have an elderly neighbor who grew up in the town where I live in Georgia. She sometimes tells the most amazing stories. One day I questioned her about the veracity of her story about a dog, a deer, and a wild turkey running together down a country road. All she said was, 'Why, Miss Warren. Don't you know a story's not worth telling without embellishments?'"

Sula chuckled and picked up an apple slice, swiping it in the honey that had pooled underneath it, and popped it into her mouth.

The thought of kissing Sula's honey-sweetened lips flashed through Melissa's mind. Much as she wanted to make that a reality, Sula appeared relaxed, and Melissa didn't want to risk making her retreat again. "That reminds me of an interview with a famous artist I read years ago. She talked about her early days, before her career took off, when she had to make ends meet by teaching art history classes part-time in New York. She said she stopped teaching after she started making up stories during her lectures."

"And also when she realized that those students were going to start repeating what she was teaching to the regular professors, I'm sure."

Melissa laughed. "You're probably right about that. I've always been a little jealous of the creative freedom that artists have. They can take a fact and bend it into a new kind of truth. You know, the word 'professor' was coined to describe what we're expected to do—to profess what we know to be true. There's not much wiggle room there. I'm really just a grand storyteller explaining who did what, when, where, how, and why it's meaningful to us today."

"So, studying art is like a whodunit. That's interesting." Sula ate another slice of apple, looking thoughtful while she chewed. "Speaking of art and mysteries, I'm still mystified that you have paintings by my great-grandmother. Betty told me you have photographs from her that were taken at the ranch in the 20s and 30s."

"I'm beginning to wonder if my great-grandmother might have purchased the paintings directly from your great-grandmother. Gosh, that's such a mouthful. I'm just going to say Ursula and Evelyn."

Sula nodded. "I doubt Evelyn bought them. As far as I know, Ursula never sold her paintings. She kept them or gave them to family members. And to Evelyn, it would seem."

"It's curious, isn't it?"

"It is."

Thinking about the possibility that their great-grandmothers, Ursula and Evelyn, knew each other excited Melissa. She wasn't quite sure why it stirred her so deeply. Maybe it was the thrill of solving a mystery, not only of the artist whose paintings had been in her family, but of a possible personal relationship between Sula's ancestors and hers.

"What do you know about Ursula?" Melissa asked, then grew suddenly concerned that the question was too personal. "If I may ask."

"Well…" Sula stared up at the tree branches for a moment before answering. "She died young, so I know more about the family history than about her. Her side of the family has lived in America for a long time, since before it was America actually. Although they were Norwegian, they were part of the Dutch New Amsterdam colony that's now New York City. Like everyone else, they wanted new opportunities, so they started with land and then ventured into business and finance. Ursula's parents followed in their footsteps, I guess, by moving farther west and repeating that pattern, but keeping the land."

Sula's expression had changed. Melissa didn't know how to read it now.

"I don't want to make you uncomfortable, Sula. You don't have to tell me anything you don't want to." And Melissa meant it.

"I want to." Sula took a deep breath and let it out. "I really do, but I rarely talk about personal things. I know that must seem odd to you."

"I'm honored that you want to confide in me." Melissa took Sula's hand and held it, hoping she wasn't crossing a line. She wanted the gesture to be comforting. Sula squeezed her hand gently and smiled. Melissa's curiosity about this woman intensified. Perhaps her wealth made her cautious with people she didn't know well. Melissa increasingly realized that Sula was affluent, though she didn't flaunt it. Nonetheless she wondered why talking about her family history seemed to make her feel so vulnerable.

"As I told you earlier," Sula said, "my family started with a homestead and kept adding land to it. By the time Ursula was born in 1910, they owned one of the largest ranches in this area."

"You've never mentioned your great-grandfather," Melissa said.

"No one knows who he was. She never married."

"Really? That's unusual."

"I suppose so. But it was so remote here then, social norms didn't exist the way they did back East. Being independent was seen as—well, still is—very respectable." Sula shrugged. "I might not know who my great-grandfather was, but I do know that my grandmother, Inga, was born in 1932."

"Is your grandmother still living?" Melissa asked the question gently, noticing that Sula referred to her grandmother in the past tense.

"No. She passed away about five years ago."

"I'm so sorry. I bet you miss her."

"I do." Sula paused and took a long drink from her water bottle. "When she was eight years old her mother, Ursula, was killed in a hunting accident."

"Do you know what happened?"

"Not in detail." Sula's expression grew dark. "A hunter mistook her for a bear."

"Oh, how terrible! And she was a single mother...your poor grandmother lost her mother at such a young age."

Sula nodded. "From what I understand, her grandparents raised her, with help from Betty's family."

"So, your connection to Betty and her family goes way back." Melissa picked up an apple slice with her free hand and ate it. The sweetness of the honey was the perfect complement to the tartness of the crisp apple.

"Yes. Like I said, she's more like family than friend." Sula removed her hand and brushed something off Melissa's shoulder. "Ant," Sula said matter-of-factly and then raised her eyebrows. She raised her index finger to her lips as her gaze focused on something over Melissa's shoulder. She spoke quietly. "Look behind you...slowly."

Melissa twisted around to see three dark-brown and buff-colored adult elk cows moving toward them, walking through the lush meadow they had crossed before lunch. They grazed as they went, their heads dipping to tear off mouthfuls of grass and rising to chew and to keep a wary eye out for predators that might attack them or their calves. The calves stayed close to their mothers, nibbling the grass as they went, mimicking the movements of the much-larger adults.

They sat still, transfixed, quietly watching the majestic creatures. The meadow grass surrounding the elk shimmered in the breeze, chickadees called from the trees, and the consistent sound of water rushing across the rocks reminded Melissa that time had not stood still, though it felt like it. While watching the animals, Melissa mused on what a luxury it was to be free from the pressure of monitoring time, of having to rush off to classes or to meetings, to all the things that daily life demanded. She savored feeling fully present in the moment.

The elk approached the creek cautiously. The largest, and perhaps the oldest and wisest cow, took the lead, walking gingerly to the water's edge, where she took a long drink. One by one the other cows and calves followed the actions of their leader, though the calves seemed to be playing with the water more than drinking it.

The breeze shifted directions, and the brave leader's head jerked up. She looked directly at them, flaring her nostrils in an effort to take in their scent.

Melissa laughed involuntarily. The almost human sense of surprise the elk expressed was comical. When the elk heard her, she snorted and hopped across the creek in three bounding steps, trotting to the protective cover of the trees with the others following her.

"I'm so sorry. I broke that magical moment."

"Don't apologize. I was surprised at how close they came to us. Most people can't sit still that long without getting fidgety. I'm impressed."

"Well, thank you," Melissa said. "I'll take that as a compliment."

A low rumble prompted both of them to turn and stare at the peak in the distance. Although the sky above them was clear blue, a dark cloud was sliding over the mountain.

"We might want to head back, unless you want to get caught in an afternoon thunderstorm."

"As romantic as that sounds, I think I'd rather not." As soon as the words came out of her mouth, Melissa wondered how Sula would respond to her use of the word "romantic." But she didn't seem fazed as she put away the remains of their lunch and stowed everything back into her pack.

Melissa shook out the blanket, folding it compactly before handing it to Sula. When Sula reached for it, their fingers touched lightly, and a sharp spark of static electricity popped. Sula flinched and hunched her shoulders as if expecting to be struck by lightning. She grinned with embarrassment as she straightened her posture.

"So, the rugged mountain woman isn't so tough after all," Melissa said in a teasing tone.

"What makes you think I'm so tough, Goldie?" Sula said as she pulled her pack over her shoulders.

"Oh. I was hoping you'd forgotten you called me that."

"Nope. Sorry, but I'm afraid that name has stuck."

Melissa shook her head, resigning herself to the nickname, though in truth, she liked it. It felt like an intimate gesture, like receiving a thoughtful gift. They continued to banter as they walked back to the Bronco, and, like on most journeys, the way back seemed much shorter than the trip out. The sky overhead continued to darken, and the thunder, becoming more frequent and louder, rumbled behind them. By the time they reached the Bronco, the birds were quiet, and a few large raindrops had begun to fall.

Sula stowed their packs in the back of the vehicle and looked up at the sky, squinting. "I think we're going to get some rain."

As if on cue, the sky flashed, and thunder cracked and boomed. They hopped quickly into the Bronco while the sound echoed down the hillside. Melissa felt the resonant vibration, and after another close strike, the scattered drops of rain coalesced into a downpour.

"I'm going to let the front of this pass before we head out." Sula rested her hand on the gear shifter, her voice muffled by the sound of the rain now drumming on the uninsulated steel top.

The thunderstorm literally blew past, the wind making the big pines sway dramatically back and forth. From their position in the middle of the clearing, it was as if the trees had come alive and were dancing in a circle around them, their branches intertwined like people holding hands.

Impulsively, Melissa touched the back of Sula's hand. When she didn't flinch or pull away, Melissa lifted her hand and rested it on her thigh. She lightly ran her fingertips across the surface of Sula's hand and wrist, tracing the topography created by veins and tendons before moving upward to the tender skin on the inside of her forearm. Sula closed her eyes and smiled softly, seeming to relax to the pleasure of being touched. Melissa didn't stop until the rhythm of the rain slowed and Sula opened her eyes.

"The rain's let up."

"Mm-hmm," Melissa murmured and released her. Sula glanced at her, the sweet smile on her lips remaining in place.

They buckled themselves in, and Sula drove back down to the valley. The wind died, but the rain continued, and the road was muddy. The Bronco splashed through the low spots that had filled with rainwater. Inspired with confidence by Sula's slow, controlled driving, Melissa enjoyed the sense of being on an adventure yet feeling safe.

By the time they reached Moon Lake the sky was clear. The ground, speckled with little craters where a few heavy raindrops had fallen, was otherwise dry and dusty. The thunderstorm was moving away from them, and Melissa stared out the window at the dark clouds, looking for the occasional streaks of lighting that flashed in the distance and were followed, many seconds later, by the familiar rumble.

On the valley side of the lake, Sula stopped where she had before and got out to unlock the wheels, taking the Bronco out of four-wheel drive. When she got back in, she regarded Melissa intensely and chewed her lower lip. She appeared to be mulling something over.

"Would you like to see some more paintings by Ursula?"

"Are you kidding me? Of course!"

Sula laughed gently. "I'd be shocked if you'd answered any differently."

The road in front of them forked in two directions. Melissa knew that turning left would take them back to the ranch and to her cabin. Sula put the Bronco in gear, drove forward, and turned the wheel to the right. Melissa had no idea where this road would lead.

CHAPTER TWELVE

Sula glanced at Melissa, who was staring out the open window of the Bronco, watching the passing landscape. Golden strands of hair had escaped from her ponytail and blew wildly around her head. She'd been visibly excited when Sula invited her to the house to show her more of Ursula's paintings, but she'd become quiet once they got on to the pavement, the road noise making conversation difficult. Sula slowed the Bronco to make the turn onto the gravel road leading to her house.

"Oh." Melissa jerked and looked around. "Are we there already?"

"Almost," Sula said, turning the wheel.

Melissa scanned the area in front of them. "I don't see a house anywhere."

"It's not visible from the road. You'll see it in just a minute."

Sula chewed on her lower lip expectantly. She knew Melissa would be surprised after they passed the large boulder. From the other side of it, you couldn't miss seeing the house. It was strikingly positioned on a rise in a meadow with mountain peaks looming in the distance. Without a doubt it was the view depicted in one of the paintings Melissa had shown her. Her great-grandmother must have painted it from where the road curved around the boulder, the spot at which they were just about to arrive. Melissa would most likely be as astounded to see it in person as Sula had been to see it printed on a piece of paper in Melissa's hand.

Sula took a deep breath, hoping it would be a good surprise. She felt a little guilty that she hadn't already confessed to Melissa that she recognized the place depicted in that painting. When Melissa had shown it to her, she was uncertain about the professor's intentions, and she'd acted on instinct by not acknowledging that she knew the place. But something had shifted inside her today. It wasn't just because of that kiss, though that was extraordinary, and recalling the feel and taste of Melissa made Sula tingle. She stirred something deep inside her, a feeling powerful enough to cause her to lower her guard.

"Sula, stop the car!"

Sula hit the brakes, and Melissa grabbed the handhold on the dash. She stared at the two-story log house with a look of astonishment. Then she turned her head slowly to face Sula, cocked her head, and arched a single eyebrow. "You knew."

Sula nodded, trying to gauge the tone of Melissa's reaction before saying anything in reply.

"You knew," Melissa said again, "and you didn't tell me."

Sula met Melissa's burning gaze. She felt as if she was being examined, considered, appraised.

"You didn't trust me, did you?"

"This is my home...I'm a private person. I—" Sula stammered, stumbling in her attempt to explain herself.

"Well then, if you brought me here you must trust me," Melissa said gently, with a soft smile. "At least a little bit."

Melissa's voice, like her touch, was soothing and made her feel unbelievably good. She remembered the rainstorm, Melissa's fingertips stroking her, touching her, relaxing her, yet setting her nerves on fire...

As if picking up on her thoughts, Melissa placed a hand on Sula's arm. "I'm honored that you trust me. I truly am. I understand that you don't invite people in very often."

Sula wasn't sure if Melissa meant she didn't invite people to her house or into her life. Whether she knew it or not, she was correct on both accounts.

Melissa turned and stared at the house, pointing at it while looking at Sula out of the corner of her eye. "So, you've got some paintings in there?"

"I do."

"And you're going to show them to me?"

"I am."

"So why are we sitting here?"

"Because you told me to stop." Sula laughed and, relieved, put the Bronco back in gear.

Melissa walked up the steps slowly, admiring the magnificent two-story log house. The wood was dark with age and capped with a new green, metal roof. The roof of the house in the painting had wood shingles, but with the increasing threat of wildfires these days, a metal one made a lot more sense. To be standing in front of Ursula Bergen's house was surreal, strangely like walking around inside the painting. It seemed very real, though. The red Lyons sandstone steps under her feet certainly felt solid, and the porch posts made of mortared river rock didn't seem to be comprised of the flimsy stuff of dreams. Nonetheless, when she stepped onto the porch, she put a hand on one of the rounded rocks, in part to feel its smooth surface, but also to confirm that it was indeed real.

Sula put her backpack on the seat of a rocking chair and watched Melissa with an amused expression. She pointed behind her. "Best view in the Rockies, I think, but I'm a little biased."

Melissa turned and sucked in her breath when saw the magnificent mountain and valley vista—a pond reflecting the cerulean sky, viridian pine-covered hillsides, and craggy gray peaks still covered with snow.

"*Please* tell me you never get tired of looking at this."

"Never. I'm thankful for it every single day."

"Good." Melissa was about to ask about the house, when it was built, who designed it and so on, but was interrupted by the appearance of two svelte tabby cats—one gray with spots and the other mottled pale-orange and gray. They hopped up on to the porch railing, then immediately trotted over to Sula and rubbed against her legs. The pale one stood in between her feet and looked at Melissa inquisitively.

"What pretty cats," Melissa cooed and crouched down with her hand out. The cat walked toward her, tail straight in the air.

"That one is Tawny," Sula said and gestured to the one that stayed with her. "This one is Spotty."

Melissa petted Tawny, who immediately began purring. "I can see how they got their names."

"Not very original, I know. Their mother was one of Betty's barn cats. She disappeared when they were about a week old." Sula winced. "Probably a coyote. There were five in the litter, and we referred to them by their colors and patterns for so long, the names stuck." Sula bent over and scooped up Spotty.

"What happened to the other three?"

"Big Spot stayed to become part of Betty's barn-cat crew. Gray and Torti went to her grandkids and got renamed Ash and Butter."

Melissa laughed at the names and watched Sula cradling Spotty, petting her in long, slow strokes from nose to tail. The cat closed her eyes in seeming blissful contentment, and Melissa wondered what it would feel like to have Sula's hands on her like that, caressing her…

Sula raised her eyes, meeting Melissa's gaze. She cocked her head and arched her eyebrows as if wondering what she was thinking.

"I miss my cat," Melissa said nonchalantly and stood.

"I understand. They're good company." Sula put Spotty gently on the floor before pulling keys from her pocket. She stepped toward the front door.

"Sula, wait. Before we go in, I want to tell you something. While you were driving, I was thinking. I know you're a very private person and your paintings are unknown, and you probably want to keep them that way. But you should know that it's not unusual to write about and publish images of works of art that are listed as in a private collection, without any indication of where they're located or even who owns them. It's an option. But, more importantly, I won't share *anything* with anyone without your permission. I promise to respect your privacy."

Melissa hoped Sula could sense that she meant it. She was about to get more than she hoped for, and this was no longer an academic project. It had shifted into something more deeply personal. Sula was granting her access to her family's past, to her heritage, and considering the gravity with which Sula offered it, Melissa understood she shouldn't accept that privilege lightly. She needed to assure Sula that she would not take what she was seeing and learning and run with it. Plus, there was that little thing of having kissed Sula by the creek. Well, maybe not such a little thing. And Sula had kissed her back. The memory flooded her, quickening her pulse. *One thing at a time...*

"I appreciate you telling me that," Sula said, opening the door.

While crossing the threshold, Melissa understood Sula's reluctance to invite a stranger in. The interior of the house was spectacularly Rocky Mountain rustic. Log posts and beams supported a cathedral ceiling, and a second-floor landing overlooked the great room. The center of the wide pine plank floor was covered with a worn, but beautiful, old oriental rug, the interior walls were plastered and painted a cheerful shade of yellow, and dark-brown leather chairs and a long sofa faced a fieldstone fireplace. Bookshelves were filled with books and pottery. And there were paintings...

"Would you like something to drink? Water, iced tea, a cold beer maybe?"

Melissa barely heard Sula's question as a painting hanging across the room caught her eye. She managed to utter a polite yes to water—she needed to stay hydrated in this dry climate, and with the altitude, a beer in the afternoon would go right to her head and make her sleepy if she wasn't careful and drank it too quickly. When Sula left the room, Melissa took a closer look at the painting. It was a snowy winter landscape, the view from the porch, it seemed, and a cold contrast to what she had just experienced in person. She recognized the brushstrokes as belonging to Ursula's hand. Her ability to paint the snow, with a dozen or more individual hues of white, was impressive. What could have been a flat, dead scene was instead vibrant.

"Here you go."

Sula's sudden appearance with a tall glass of ice water in her outstretched hand startled her. For a woman with such a commanding presence, she could be uncannily quiet.

"Thank you." Melissa took a large swallow and then another, not realizing until now how thirsty she was. The glass was cool in her hand, and she pressed it to her cheek. "Ah, that feels so good."

"On hot days this painting almost gives me a chill."

"I imagine it would. I could look at this for a long time."

"Before you get lost in the snow, would you like the tour first? There's a painting in every room."

"Really?"

"Yeah." Sula grinned. "Well, almost. There aren't any in the kitchen and bathrooms."

Melissa laughed, following Sula through the house and discovering that she wasn't kidding. A winter landscape hung in the living room, a view looking down a rocky canyon in the dining room, landscapes with creeks and rivers in the guest rooms, and an autumn scene with golden aspen in the billiard room, the last stop on the tour. Melissa felt overstimulated by taking in all the paintings in addition to the house. Every room was neat and thoughtfully decorated with interesting objects, like the elk-antler chandelier in the dining room and a shiny black stone sculpture of a dancing bear on the table underneath a painting.

"Is this an Inuit sculpture?" Melissa asked, admiring the standing bear balanced on one foot with the other outstretched. Its body was twisted, one paw forward and the other tucked behind its back. With eyes made from a white inlay, it stared intensely upward. The skillfully counterbalanced pose evoked a sense of energy, grace, and strength. She had seen sculptures of this quality only in museums.

"Yes, it's a spirit bear, by Noona Parr. He lives in Canada."

"There's something about this—the tension in it. The bear seems so grounded but also intensely connected to what's above."

"In many old cultures, the bear crosses boundaries between the spirit world and our world."

"You mean the spirit bear is a shaman?" Melissa asked.

"Yeah."

"And vice versa, right?" Melissa tried to remember what she knew about indigenous cultures. "Shamans are shape-changers. They fly with the eagles and swim with the salmon."

"And dance with the bears," Sula said with a wry grin.

"And play pool with the bears, too." Melissa noticed that the billiard table behind Sula had bear heads carved into the legs.

"What?" Sula raised her eyebrows with a look of surprise and then followed Melissa's line of sight to the table legs. "Oh, the pool table. It was my grandfather's. He loved billiards."

"Do you play?"

"Yes, of course. My grandfather taught me how to shoot pool and drink whiskey when I was old enough. He never showed me any mercy. I mean billiards, not drinking."

Melissa laughed.

"Do you play?"

Melissa considered the question for a moment before answering. "I can't recall when I last shot a game of pool."

"Body memory."

"Hm?"

"You know the expression, 'it's like riding a bike'? You think you've forgotten, but your body remembers the moves. Maybe we can play sometime."

Melissa couldn't think of anything else she'd like better than to play with Sula in whatever form she wanted, but before she could respond, the trilling ring of Sula's cell phone interrupted them. She pulled the phone out of her back pocket, swiped the screen, and frowned. "I'm sorry. I need to take this. Feel free to look around."

Sula said hello to someone named Lee. Melissa wondered if a woman or a man was on the other end. She laughed at herself, recognizing a little pang of jealousy. Not wanting to eavesdrop, she walked back to the living room and perused the bookshelves. Movement caught her eye, and she looked up to see Tawny and Spotty watching her from the ledge of the second-floor landing. Having recently seen a mountain lion in person, she realized now how much they looked like their bigger feline cousin. She smiled at them and continued reading the book titles. It was always interesting to see what kind of books people read. Not surprisingly, there were many books about bears and North American ecology and conservation. A whole shelf had old books written in what she assumed was Norwegian, given Sula's heritage. One bookcase held only novels, some with well-worn and creased spines, and Melissa recognized quite a few titles as lesbian romances.

"Find anything interesting?" Sula asked as she walked into the room, tucking her phone into her back pocket.

"Yes, quite a bit."

"Sorry about taking that call. It was one of the local police officers."

"Is everything okay?"

"Yeah, sort of." A dark look crossed Sula's face. "He's been getting reports about illegal animal traps and wanted to know if I knew anything about it. Apparently, someone found their dog in one yesterday. He's alive, but he's going to lose his leg."

"That's terrible! Why would he call you? You seem like the last person to be involved in trapping."

"No, not like that. He wanted to know if I'd found any on my land. I haven't."

"That's good."

"Maybe not. I need to go take a look. I really don't like knowing that someone around here is trapping." The fierce look on Sula's face lifted. "Hey, are you hungry? I wasn't planning to have company for dinner, but I could grill some burgers, and you could tell me what you think of all these paintings."

In the kitchen, Melissa offered to help Sula prepare the meal, but Sula simply handed her a cold beer and told her to have a seat on the stool on the other side of the tall counter. The cats had followed them in and sat together on the stool next to Melissa, observing the activity. Melissa eagerly talked about how fine the paintings were while Sula pulled hamburger patties out of the refrigerator and prepared the toppings, nodding thoughtfully and occasionally asking questions.

"So, what you've seen here is more than what you expected to find?" Sula asked while slicing an onion, placing the rings on a plate with lettuce, tomatoes, cheese, and buns.

"Yes, so much more." Melissa took the last swig of beer from the bottle. It was a pleasant amber ale that she had failed to drink slowly. "I thought I'd be lucky to find two or three paintings and maybe an obituary or a couple of mentions in the local paper. I didn't expect to find Ursula's great-granddaughter with a house full of her paintings, let alone have her make me dinner and ply me with alcohol." Melissa waved the empty bottle.

Sula laughed while stacking the food, plates, and condiments on a tray. She pulled two more beers from the fridge and handed one to Melissa. "Let's go out to the patio."

The cats hopped down, following them to the back door. Melissa was impressed by their restraint. They hadn't even put a paw on the counter. The first time she turned her back, her cat, Alex, would have been on the counter and trying to steal a hamburger.

The sun had dropped to the front of the house, casting shade on the back patio. Covered with the same red flagstone as the porch, it was edged with stone planters and filled with many of the same sun-loving plants in Melissa's garden at home—yellow black-eyed Susan, purple coneflower, and red salvia. Hummingbirds chattered and darted, pausing to feed on the nectar of the blooms. Sula put the tray down on the stone table attached to the brick barbecue in the far corner and pulled out tools and briquettes from a compartment underneath. Melissa sipped her beer and walked around the patio, admiring the flowers while Sula got the coals started. The cats stalked a grasshopper, following it around the corner of the house.

"Your grandmother owned this house before you, right?" Melissa asked.

"Yeah, that's right." Sula nodded and dusted charcoal off her hands. She grabbed her beer and took a swig.

"So where did you grow up?"

"I'll show you." Sula disappeared into the house and came back with a pair of binoculars. "Come stand over here."

Melissa walked over to where Sula stood at the edge of the patio. She handed her the binoculars and then pointed across the valley. "Look along the edge of the trees over there. Find the big boulder with a vertical crack and then look up, just a little."

Melissa raised the binoculars to her eyes and adjusted the eyepiece. The trees came into sharp focus. "Damn, these are amazing." She scanned along the edge of the meadow and found the boulder Sula had described. A house tucked into the trees came into view. A modern design, it was boxy, with large windows and walls painted the color of the natural rock. She lowered the binoculars, realizing she could still see it without them, but only because she knew where to look.

"So you grew up near here. That's what you're telling me?"

"Yeah." Sula laughed. "A stone's throw away."

"With a slingshot…or maybe a catapult." Melissa lifted the binoculars again and scanned the hillside, delighted by all the detail she could see with the binoculars' high-quality optics. She continued their conversation without putting them down.

"You said your parents started the conservancy."

"Yes, that's right. After they graduated. They met in grad school when they were both students at Berkeley. My father says he struck up a conversation with my mother after she gave a passionate presentation about better, non-lethal management practices for predator species."

"You mean learning to live with them rather than shooting them."

"That's simplifying it, but yes."

"And the conservancy was a chance to show the world how it could be done. Oh! I see some deer." Melissa counted off the number of does and bucks with delight.

"My mother said it had become a time for action."

"That makes sense to me. That was in the seventies, right? So when people finally began to care about the environment, your parents were there to show them how to do things better. You know, the 'save the bears, save the planet' approach is really smart."

"How so?" Sula asked.

"People *love* bears. They're ferocious and cuddly all at the same time. They're archetypal, kind of like Beauty and the Beast."

"Beauty and the Beast?"

"Think about it. The beast is animal and human, scary and tender, powerful yet pitiful. He evokes a full range of emotions and is irresistible. Bears are a lot like that."

"That's very insightful, Professor."

"Uh-oh. Did I just go into professor mode?" Feeling self-conscious, she lowered the binoculars. Sula was looking out across the valley with a smile on her lips.

"A little." Sula glanced at her and took another sip from her bottle. "But I like it. Go on."

"Okay." Melissa raised the binoculars, refocusing them on the trees midway up the mountainside. "So, your parents took advantage of people's fascination with bears, and they put it into action. They're attracted to the conservancy because of the focus on bears, and then, hopefully, they'll take home some of the ideas you teach. It's like you're seeding hope for the future. Ooh, there's a hawk…no, maybe an owl. It's perched on a branch."

Melissa put the binoculars down when she realized Sula was watching her, staring really, with those beautiful amber eyes.

"Seeing you take delight in nature, in all the living things around us, is very enchanting." Sula said and then walked over to the barbecue and put the hamburgers on the grill.

"Really?" Melissa said, following her. "You're going to tell me I'm enchanting and then walk away?"

Sula put the spatula down and turned around, wearing an anxious expression. "I..."

"You what?"

"I think you're enchanting."

Sula stepped toward her and placed her fingers against Melissa's cheek, lightly running her thumb across her lips. Melissa's heart leapt. When Sula leaned forward and kissed her, she nearly melted. The kiss, which began tenderly, deepened into a slow, sensual exploration. Their bodies pressed together, Melissa felt enveloped by Sula's embrace, and she breathed in her alluring scent of amber and cinnamon. Being held and kissed by Sula was as comforting as it was arousing, like being drawn into a warm, gentle current. And she wanted nothing more than to take off her clothes and go all the way in. When Sula broke the kiss, she shuddered.

"You don't have to stop," Melissa said breathlessly.

"I'm afraid I do."

"Why?" Melissa was incredulous.

"Because the burgers are burning."

CHAPTER THIRTEEN

"Sula!"

When Betty raised her voice, Sula snapped to attention. "Will you help me clear the table?"

"Uh, yeah, sure." Sula glanced around, realizing she was the only one still at the table. Sunday dinner was over. Sula had been staring at the birds on the feeder outside the dining-room window when her mind wandered. *Again.* She stood, grabbed as many plates and bowls as she could carry, and followed Betty into the kitchen.

Yesterday Sula had spent most of the day and a good part of the evening with Melissa. After their meal of slightly overdone burgers they had talked...and kissed. Sula had lost track of time and didn't look at a clock until Melissa, yawning repeatedly, nearly fell asleep. Melissa apologized vigorously, but Sula took no offense, knowing that it was the consequence of the mountain air, their hike earlier in the day, and the beer. Sula drove her back to her cabin, kissed her good night tenderly, and watched with longing when she stepped through the door. She had considered asking Melissa to stay but offered to give her a ride back to her cabin instead. It seemed the proper thing to do.

Sula replayed their conversations in her head. She had learned quite a bit about art yesterday. And with her mind's eye she continued to gaze into those green eyes and delight in Melissa's easy laughter. She found it difficult to follow conversations with Betty and her family. Fortunately, she didn't need to say much when around Betty's family during Sunday dinner. Betty's husband, Lars, and her nephew, Little Lars, bantered and entertained the kids with stories. Jaymie, Little Lars's wife, was preoccupied with their new baby. John, Betty's youngest son, typically didn't contribute much to conversations, but he laughed frequently with his funny horsey snort.

It was a regular family meal. Well, everything was regular about it except Sula. She was feeling highly irregular, her mind preoccupied with all things Melissa. She didn't think anyone had noticed that she wasn't fully present, but the look on Betty's face as she scraped the leftover pot roast into a glass bowl told her otherwise.

"Sula, what is up with you? Are you feeling okay?"

"I'm fine." Sula put the plates in the sink and began rinsing them.

"You don't look fine. And you're not acting fine." Putting a lid on the bowl, Betty slid it onto a shelf in the refrigerator. She narrowed her eyes at Sula and put the palm of her hand on her forehead. "You don't have a fever."

"I'm not sick."

"Okay. So what's on your mind? Leave the plates in the sink. I'll take care of them later."

"Why do you think something's on my mind?" Sula grabbed a kitchen towel and dried her hands.

"Because I *know* you." Betty refilled her coffee cup and took a sip. "You want another slice of honey cake?"

"Sure." Sula always wanted another slice of the Norwegian dessert, a dense, dark cake sweetened with honey and flavored with cinnamon and clove.

"Coffee?"

"No, thanks. I'm good."

Betty sliced a piece and carried it over to the breakfast nook and sat down, pushing the plate across the table.

"Sit."

Sula sat and ate the cake while Betty drank coffee, stared at her, and tapped her nails lightly against the side of the cup.

"You might as well tell me now. You know you will eventually," Betty said matter-of-factly.

Sula took the last bite of cake and put the fork down with a sigh. Betty always could see through her. When Sula had figured out she liked girls instead of boys, Betty was the first person she talked to about it. They'd had the conversation at this very table tucked into the corner of the kitchen, in fact. Sula remembered that it was in the fall because Betty had handed her a slice of apple pie and commanded her to sit down and talk. Some things never changed.

"I like Melissa Warren."

"I like her, too. What's she got to do with—" Betty stopped herself and laughed. "Oh, you mean you *like* her."

"Don't laugh. It's not funny."

"I'm sorry. I know it's not funny. But you're funny, Sula. Melissa's a very nice person, very smart. Attractive, too." Betty paused and took a sip of coffee. "Is she not gay? Is that what's got you all out of sorts?"

"Oh, she's very much a lesbian."

Betty wagged her eyebrows. "Did she kiss you?"

"Betty!"

"Did you kiss *her*?"

Exasperated, Sula just grunted.

"So, did you?" Betty watched her reaction and then waved a hand at her dismissively. "You don't need to answer. I can tell by the look on your face that you did. You're blushing, too. That's a good thing, right? What's the problem? I'm really happy to see you connect with someone."

"You are?"

"Of course I am. Look, Sula. I worry about you being alone all the time. I know you value your privacy and all that, but it doesn't mean you have to be a nun, you know?"

"I know, but my life is a little complicated."

"Sure, your complications are different from most people's. But *life* is complicated, so you make it work. Your parents made it work." Betty lowered her voice. "So, what's really eating at you?"

"I asked her to go to Denver with me."

"Why Denver?"

"I'm giving a presentation on Tuesday at a symposium at the refuge, and I invited her."

"So? That sounds like a nice day trip. Visit the Mile High City and all that. You'll have a good time."

"I'm spending the night. I give the presentation on Tuesday, and then I have a meeting with someone at Fish and Wildlife on Wednesday."

Betty reached across the table and put her hand on Sula's. "If Melissa didn't feel comfortable with your invitation, she'd have declined. You have a good head on your shoulders, and you make good decisions. Do what feels right. Listen to your gut and it'll be okay. And stop worrying, Sula. You know I'm always right." Betty stood and carried her cup to the sink. "Or maybe that's what you're afraid of."

Sula fidgeted in her seat. Betty was right, though Sula was hesitant to admit it. Her attraction to Melissa felt so natural, she suspected that she had only begun to sense its depths. It felt like wading into the river to swim and putting your foot down, expecting to feel rocks against the bottom of your feet, only to feel cold water rush by as you dropped into a deep pool with the water over your head. Exciting but scary, yet her instinct wasn't telling her to run. Quite the opposite, it was goading her to get closer. Damn, she felt so conflicted.

"Stop overthinking it, Sula, or you might talk yourself out of something good." Betty tossed a hand towel over her shoulder and walked over to Sula. She put her hand on Sula's shoulder, squeezed it, and frowned. "Good grief. You're bound up tighter than spool of baling wire. You ought to go out for a run, let your hair down for a while, balance your chi, or whatever it is that happens when you're out there. You always say it makes you feel better."

Sula nodded. Envisioning a run through the forest suddenly reminded her of something she wanted to do before she left town. What Betty had just suggested would make it a lot more efficient, and she was right that it would also make her feel more in balance. Her anxiety about Melissa remained, but now she had something immediate to do to take her mind off it, even if momentarily.

"That's a good idea, Betty." Sula stood and tried her best to put on a convincing smile. She reached out, wrapping her arms around Betty in a bear hug, and kissed the top of her head. "You're the best, you know it?"

Betty patted her on the back and pulled out of her embrace, popping her with the towel. "All right, all right. Now get out of my kitchen."

Sula went home, grabbed her backpack, and headed out the front door, walking briskly toward the trees across the meadow. As was her habit in moments like this, and especially when the sun was still up, she paid close attention to her environment, to the sounds and movements of birds and animals. Or the lack thereof, as silence could tell her as much or more about what was going on around her. Even though her land was private, finding a stray hiker, lost tourist, or worse, a poacher, was always a possibility.

She unwrapped a honey candy, popped it in her mouth, and tucked the wrapper into her pocket. Everything seemed normal as she walked across the meadow. A gentle breeze cooled her skin from the warm summer sun. As she approached the pines, she heard a tremulous buzzing. Cicadas, newly emerged from the ground and singing in a chorus, were seeking their mates for the season. She wound her way through the trees and headed up the slope to a particularly old ponderosa pine.

The muscular-looking tree was tall, nearly a hundred feet. It had a flat, rounded shape, and its bark, smooth and grayish, bore the scars of old fires, some probably from a hundred years ago or more. This tree would have been a seedling when Sula's ancestors first stepped on to the docks of New Amsterdam in the seventeenth century. Putting her hand on the trunk, she touched it as if greeting an old friend. If trees could talk, this one would have some stories to tell.

She took off her backpack, unzipped it, and placed it on the ground by the tree. Then she undressed, folding her clothes neatly and stowing them in the pack. She tucked her shoelaces into her boots and placed them underneath. She had learned to do this after once coming back to find that a mouse, or some other small rodent, had been chewing on the laces while she was away.

Standing naked in the open air under the protection of the great tree invigorated her. She took a deep breath, stretched her arms out wide, and then rolled her head side to side, stretching the muscles in her neck and shoulders. Breathing slowly and deeply, she relaxed her arms, turning her palms forward and thumbs out. As her mother and grandmother had taught her so many years ago, she closed her eyes and found that indescribable place within, a spot that was a feeling, a sensation without form, yet somehow felt expansive, like a cavern deep in the earth, immense and vast yet undetectable from the outside. She folded herself into that place, and when the *hamask* came on, it took over—unfolding, bending, and stretching her.

Slow and controlled was the least painful way to shift, but that was like saying that putting your hand in a flame was less agonizing than putting it in a pot of boiling water. It was excruciating. When approached mindfully, the pain was less shocking and more manageable. Sula focused on breathing…slowly in, slowly out…but it didn't lessen the intense discomfort as much as prevent it from taking control of her thoughts. If she allowed herself to focus on the agony, it would scatter her mind.

As the forest sounds fell away, her temperature rose, and she made sure her mouth was closed and her teeth aligned. The chattering that the *hamask* often caused could break a tooth or lacerate her tongue, if she wasn't careful. The first spasm hit her, forcing her to the ground. On her hands and knees, she dropped her head as her shoulders bunched and heaved, her back arched and extended as her center of gravity shifted.

She breathed deeply, pulling air in through her nostrils and holding it, until the second spasm released its grip. She blew air out slowly through her lengthening nose. The rocks biting into the palm of her hands and soles of her feet became less noticeable as the flesh thickened into the pads of large paws and her nails extended into thick, curved claws. Her muscles shuddered, thickening and elongating in smaller rippling spasms. With an irritating tickling sensation, dense dark-brown hair sprouted all over her, lengthening into a thick coat.

The third and final spasm was the least intense; with it, her senses returned, and the pain lessened. Keeping her eyes closed, she focused on sound first—the breeze whispering through the pine needles above, a crow *caw, caw, cawing* in the distance, the nearby rustle of a ground squirrel seeking the safety of its burrow. Her sense of smell returned with acuity, her nose twitching as she inhaled the dry scent of the earth underneath her and the fragrant sweet grass in the meadow down below.

She opened her eyes, the only part of her now that didn't look much different from her human form, although her vision was now sharper and more attuned to movement. Surveying the area around the old ponderosa pine with her ursine perspective, she grunted with satisfaction. As she moved away from the old tree, the breeze shifted, bringing a subtle and unexpected scent to her nostrils.

Sula swung her shaggy head sideways, scanning the rocky hillside. Contrary to the popular myth that bears had poor vision, her eyesight was as keen as her sense of smell. In a moment she found the source of the sweet scent—red dots against a green-and-gray background, a boulder raspberry bush growing from a cleft in the rock. Clusters of bright-red, thimble-shaped berries dangled enticingly from arcing canes. The sun was hitting them, the heat causing them to release the alluring fragrance that Sula's now exceptionally sensitive nose picked up. She couldn't resist.

Sula scrambled up the rock, her strong legs propelling her with an ease that belied her massive bulk. Lowering her haunches to keep her weight centered to her rear to avoid slipping off the rock, Sula stretched forward, and extending her agile lips, she delicately grasped and plucked the dangling berries off the cane one by one. Bruins weren't the only ones with prehensile lips—horses, camels, even primates had them— but a bear's were the best. Their ability to loosen, twist, and stretch, to delicately grasp and hold tiny succulent fruits was a marvel to behold. And it was even better to be the one with the lips. Without so much as a scratch on the nose, hers could expertly navigate the thorniest of brambles to pluck a plump and ready berry.

She chewed and swallowed the last of the sweet raspberries.

With her wide, flat tongue she licked the berry juice that had dribbled down on to the fur of her chin. Would she find any more today while she explored, looking for those illegal traps Lee had described on the phone? He said they seemed to be set for mountain lion, so she wanted to check an area along the border of her land and the national forest before night fell. She skidded off the rock, landed on all four feet, and broke into a comfortable walking run.

In a few hours she arrived at a low ridge, the dividing line between her land and the adjacent national forest, although no fences marked it. The herd of elk that used it as a shortcut between the two lush valleys on either side certainly didn't care who owned the land. It was also a good place for a mountain lion to stalk its prey. Since the national forest was accessible to the public, it seemed logical it would also be a good place for a human to set a trap for a mountain lion. She stayed downwind, her nostrils quivering as she surveyed the air, trying to pick up any scrap of a human scent. She felt on edge and so remained vigilant. Finding a spot protected by trees and some large rocks, she sat, observed, and tried to think like a trapper.

Where would she set a snare for a mountain lion? The trap, or traps, more likely, would be locking cable snares or steel leg-hold traps spiked into the ground and probably secured to a sturdy tree. They'd be placed along a trail frequented by the cat; otherwise it would be a lot of work to lug the traps and set them up for a shot in the dark.

Sula scanned the area, looking for any trace of a path a mountain lion might use. They were elusive and shy, but they were also creatures of habit. While a lion might follow the route the elk were using, it was more likely to cross their path. Mountain lions liked to run along ridges and would be more successful ambushing dinner from the side.

After a few minutes of concentrated searching she noticed a thin snaking line, a delicate path crossing the elk run. She scanned the area around it for any disturbance, a pile of leaves or sticks crossing the path. A silvery glint at the base of a tree caught her eye. Aha! There it was— around the base of sturdy pine lay a cable that seemed to disappear into the ground. The poacher must have covered it with soil.

Sula tamped down her growing rage. She wanted to run right over and rip out the trap, tearing apart anything, anyone, who got in the way. But she needed to stay focused and remain extremely cautious. She had no fear of the trap itself, for she knew where it was and how it worked, but she was concerned about being so close to the edge of her land, her safe place. The poacher would be monitoring it and would also likely be armed. Her teeth, claws, and formidable strength couldn't protect her from a well-aimed bullet.

So, she sat and watched, and listened, and sniffed the air until she was certain no humans were nearby. She heard birds of different species chattering and singing in the distance. They extended the range of her senses and sounded as if nothing was bothering them, no strangers were tramping through their woods. She would have preferred to wait until nightfall to investigate the trap and remove it in the dark, but she surmised that the poacher would come back then to check the trap and, if successful, would shoot the mountain lion and drag it out without anyone seeing. She needed to do it now.

Keeping her ears pricked and her nose on high alert, she moved cautiously toward the trap. As she suspected, two snares, loops of strong steel rope cables rested delicately on a layer of aluminum foil placed on top of coffee cans set into holes dug in the ground and covered with a thin layer of dirt. A few leaves were artfully scattered and branches placed between the snares to guide the cat's feet. The mountain lion by avoiding stepping on them, an inborn habit that made it incredibly quiet as it traversed the forest, would put its paw right into the center of the cable loop. The aluminum foil would easily break under the weight of the cat, and before it could react, the snare would encircle and constrict its leg. Tethered to the tree it would panic and struggle, unable to do anything until the trapper came and shot it, if it was lucky. Some trappers would let dogs loose on live animals. The thought sickened and enraged her.

Suppressing a growl, Sula put her nose close to the covered cable, sniffing it and the area around the tree. She caught a whiff of human, masked with an acrid pine scent that was out of place, likely from some product that hunters put on their clothing to disguise themselves from their prey. She pulled the scent deep into her nostrils, the characteristic blend now imprinted in her memory. She'd hunt for this poacher, and if he was lucky, she'd find him while in human form and hand his ass over to the authorities. If he crossed on to her land and she was in fur, well, she wasn't sure what exactly she'd do, but it wouldn't be pretty.

The cables were secured with a large carabiner that was easy enough to unclip. While a bear's claws were usually associated with big, aggressive actions, they were also capable of completing quite delicate tasks. Her cousins up in Alaska regularly enjoyed clams using their claws to dig them out from the sand and then to pop them open to retrieve the tender morsels inside. Sula had once fileted a trout with hers just to see if she could do it.

After the cables were free from the tree, they were no longer a threat. She scraped them into a pile and with a single claw popped the foil-covered cans out of the holes. A couple of swats with her heavy front paws crushed the cans flat, and she folded and smashed them over the cables to make a package that she picked up with her teeth. The ground was dry, and she wasn't leaving many prints. That was good, as it would make the job of covering her tracks easier. She shuffled around, back and forth over where she'd been walking, taking care to obscure anything that looked even remotely like a paw print. No doubt the trapper would be confused when he came back.

The sun was dropping quickly and beginning to dip below the hillside in front of her. Much as she wanted to stay and wait for the poacher to return, she needed to take the evidence and report it to Lee properly. Clamping down on the remains of the trap between her teeth, she headed back home taking a different route, pausing regularly to confirm that she left no trace behind.

CHAPTER FOURTEEN

"The recycling center is down the street, Smokey." Lee Martinez took a sip of coffee from a blue mug with "Property of Buckhorn P.D." printed in large white letters, scowling at the dusty pile of steel cables, aluminum foil, and crushed coffee cans Sula had just deposited on his desk. She had stopped at his office on her way to the conservancy.

"It's a mountain-lion trap I found on the edge of my land and Roosevelt." Sula stood with her hands on her hips. Her anger hadn't dissipated since finding them yesterday, and she wasn't making any effort to mask her emotions.

Lee stroked his mustache and frowned. "Yeah, about those traps—"

"What? Do you know who's setting them?"

"Yeah. I think I do." He glanced up at her, and the creases in his tanned forehead deepened. "And you're not going to like it."

"I'm not sure I can dislike it any more than I hate this." Sula pointed emphatically to the remains of the trap on the desk.

"I got a message from the sheriff's office that Wildlife Services is working in the area."

Sula felt her blood pressure rise. "What the fuck, Lee. They've never been around here before. Why are they here now?"

"I don't know, Sula. We're just a small-town police department. The feds don't tell us anything. Hell, Wildlife Services doesn't hardly tell anybody anything. A deputy happened to see the very small warning sign they're required to post for public safety and logged it. That's all I know."

"And the next thing you're going to tell me is that you can't do anything about it."

"I'm afraid so."

Sula pitched forward across the desk, pointing her finger forcefully at Lee. "If they so much as put a toe on my land, I will—"

"Careful, Sula." Lee raised an eyebrow. "Remember, you're still talking to a law-enforcement official."

Sula leaned back, putting her hand down. "I will call you to arrest them for trespassing."

"That's better."

Sula huffed, blowing air out between her lips. "I'm not okay with this, Lee."

"I'm not either. You know my hands are tied." Lee's expression was sympathetic. She knew him well enough to see that it was genuine.

"I know." Sula didn't like his response, but she understood it. "Well, thanks for telling me." She turned to leave his office.

"Hey," Lee called out after her. "Take this stuff with you."

"That trash?" Sula paused to look at the heap of metal and then kept walking. "It doesn't belong to me."

Melissa woke up with the sun, as was her habit, and decided to put her laptop in her backpack and walk to the lodge to get internet access instead of taking her usual morning hike up the hill. The air was crisp and cool, and when she arrived, the hummingbirds were already at work, dipping in and out of the flowers in the hanging baskets. She was the first person there, it seemed. The great room was empty, and the coffeemaker was prepped but hadn't been turned on. She flipped the switch and, while waiting for it to brew, sat down at one of the long tables and took out her laptop. She scrolled through several messages on her phone while it powered up. Beth had sent her pictures of her family at a lake, the kids looking tan and happy. Her mom wanted to know if she and her dad could visit for a day or two; her father wanted to try out some fly-fishing in the area. Melissa replied that she'd check, but she was pretty sure they could stay with her at the cabin.

Melissa texted Sula to see what time they'd be leaving for Denver tomorrow. Sula had offered to drive, saying that since she'd extended the invitation, she ought to drive and let Melissa enjoy the view. Melissa explained in reply that she loved driving in the mountains, that it was a special treat. Sula acquiesced but said she'd be responsible for the hotel in exchange. That seemed fair enough.

Melissa got up and poured herself a cup of coffee, and when she returned to the table, she brought up a map of Colorado on her laptop and started planning the route she wanted to take. She felt giddy anticipating spending a couple of days—and a night—with Sula, whose manner had changed so much from when they first met. After confessing that she found Melissa enchanting and then giving her that knee-buckling kiss before dinner, Sula had lost her reserved demeanor and seemed so much more relaxed. After their meal they had sat together on the porch, side by side in a swing, and talked. Sharing kisses in between words felt somehow old-fashioned and definitely romantic. Even so, it took Melissa by surprise when she mentioned to Sula that she was planning to go to Denver to see an exhibition of regional landscape paintings, and Sula had replied that she would have to be there on Tuesday for a meeting and would she like to go with her?

Melissa had said yes without even thinking twice about it and then nearly fell asleep from the day's exertion, the beer, and the altitude. She felt bad about that, but Sula had just looked at her tenderly and offered to drive her back to the cabin. Recalling her sweet face, Melissa imagined being tucked in, among other delightful things, by this woman that she was falling for. Falling? She laughed to herself. Fallen was more like it. She shivered with anticipation and desire.

The shop bell tinkled as the lodge door opened, and she looked up to see Betty walk in.

"Well, hello!" Betty smiled at her with a big grin. "Good morning, Melissa."

"Good morning."

Betty paused and looked at her, the grin not leaving her face. "Did you have a good weekend?"

"I did. Very good, in fact."

"I'm glad to hear that." Betty went into the office, returning with a cup that said "Lady Boss" on one side and featuring a vintage image of a cowgirl with a lasso on the other. She filled it from the communal pot.

"I went on a hike with Sula," Melissa blurted, the words tumbling out. "She took me to one of the places in the paintings, and then she took me to her house. I saw *so* many paintings by Ursula!"

"I know. Sula told me." Betty took a sip from her cup and winced. "She came over for Sunday dinner."

Melissa suspected that Betty's smile and knowing expression indicated that Sula had talked with her about more than just the hike and the visit to the house. Her cheeks warmed with a blush. "I've never met anyone quite like her."

"I'm sure you haven't."

That seemed an odd thing to say, and Betty's expression changed as soon as the words came out of her mouth. She pulled a chair back from the table and sat across from her.

"Sula's her own person. She doesn't warm up to people easily."

"Yes. I've realized that."

"I'm sorry I didn't tell you about all those paintings in her house, but it wasn't my place."

"Oh, believe me, I understand. God, that house is amazing, with all the artwork in it and the decor…I'd be very careful about who I let in the door, too."

Betty looked relieved.

"But her degree of caution seems unusual. She's very guarded." Melissa hesitated for a moment. "Betty, can I ask you something?"

"Sure."

"You don't have to answer if you don't feel comfortable with the question."

Betty cocked her head and took a sip from her mug. "Okay."

"Has Sula ever dated anyone before? I mean seriously dated, like had a relationship?"

Betty looked thoughtful for a moment before replying. "Let me put it this way. Sula's not a babe in the woods. But she's never had what you'd call a meaningful relationship."

"I haven't been able to tell if she's just shy or she's had her heart broken and is being careful."

"You seem to understand her. Surprisingly well." Betty regarded her with a serious expression. "Sula is shy and she's cautious. Above all, she is *always* cautious. But, no, her heart's never been broken because she's never given it to someone."

Betty took a sip of coffee and had opened her mouth to say something when the shop bell tinkled. She glanced at the people walking in and excused herself to go talk with them.

When Betty left the table, Melissa wondered what she had been about to say.

Sula reached for her cell phone to make a call and realized it wasn't in her messenger bag. She must have left it in the truck. She'd been distracted all morning. The anger over finding the snares and then learning that Wildlife Services was responsible for them lingered, making her feel dark and melancholic. She hunkered down in her office to work but found it difficult not to brood on who was involved.

Wildlife Services was the sanitized name for a federal agency that, up until the late 1990s, was known as Animal Damage Control. The old name was better suited to its sole mission to kill any animal, no matter how large or small, that had been deemed detrimental to agricultural or ranching operations. If a rancher thought that a mountain lion or a bear was reducing his profits by picking off the cows or sheep that he should have been paying better attention to rather than sitting in the comfort of his forty-thousand-dollar pickup truck, he could call in Wildlife Services to eliminate the competition for free.

The last report Sula read calculated that, in the last twenty years alone, they had slaughtered tens of millions of animals, including endangered species. Mountain lions, bears, wolves, coyotes, foxes, bobcats, beavers, prairie dogs—the sickening list went on and on. To make matters worse, they were notorious for turning a blind eye to the sadistic methods their agents used, things like running down animals with helicopters, bombing dens with explosive cyanide capsules, strangling or clubbing pups and cubs, and leaving animals to suffer in traps for days and then turning hunting dogs on them to rip them apart instead of humanely dispatching them.

Not surprisingly, the agency operated quietly, trying not to draw unwanted attention, because when people learned about what was happening, they tended to be rightfully shocked and outraged. Much as Sula wanted public opinion to force a change of sentiment that would shut it down, that didn't seem likely to happen any time soon, and probably not in her lifetime, if ever. That was perhaps the most depressing thing about it. The people who kept the agency busy—the ranchers and large landowners who also often ran hunting operations where an elk hunt could cost a single client fifteen or twenty thousand dollars—had deep pockets and even deeper political clout.

Those bastards. Sula pounded a fist on her desk. In bear form she would have let out a roar of rage loud enough to shake the whole building and everyone in it. She jumped up, flung open the office door, and trotted downstairs and out to the parking lot to retrieve her phone. It lay in the center console of her truck, and when she picked it up, the screen flashed, alerting her to new messages.

Seeing Melissa's name in the list was like a fresh breeze pushing away the dark, angry cloud hanging over her. She smiled and opened her message first. It was written in such a cheerful tone, Sula could almost hear the excitement in Melissa's voice as she read it. She wanted to know when Sula needed to be in Denver tomorrow, so she'd know what time to pick her up.

Shit. Tomorrow. Denver. The hotel. She'd forgotten to call the hotel about changing her reservation. Hopefully it wasn't too late.

CHAPTER FIFTEEN

Melissa pulled up to Sula's house at six thirty in the morning as planned for the two-hour trip. They hoped to miss the worst of Denver's rush-hour traffic so Sula would arrive on time for her conference at the wildlife refuge. After dropping her off, Melissa would head downtown to the art museum for the day and then swing back to get Sula. Together they'd check in at the hotel and freshen up for dinner and an evening out. Sula had been intriguingly vague about where they'd be staying. Melissa teased her about maybe not really having reservations, but Sula assured her that she did and that she would like her choice.

Sula was on the porch, coffee cup in one hand and petting the tabby cats with the other. When Melissa got out of her car to open the back hatch, she wasn't sure of what was more awe inspiring—the house or the woman who owned it—though she knew deep down it was the woman. Sula was dressed a bit like a park ranger, minus the hat, in her conservancy uniform of long-sleeved tan shirt with embroidered logo and name tag, forest-green trousers, and polished dark-brown boots. Her wavy hair was styled and seemed a little shorter; she must have gotten a trim. The sight of her caused a pleasant flutter in Melissa's chest. Sula waved briskly, put the cup down on a table between two wicker chairs, and reached for her bags.

"Good morning, Goldie," Sula said cheerfully as she came down the stairs carrying a messenger bag and an overnight bag.

"Good morning, bear."

Sula stopped abruptly on the bottom step with an expression of shock. "Bear? What do you mean by 'bear'?"

"Well, if you're going to call me Goldie, the only other characters in that story are bears. So I figure that makes *you* a bear."

Sula raised an eyebrow—a well-shaped eyebrow at that, Melissa noticed. Her makeup this morning was more pronounced, accentuating her eyes, highlighting the contours of her cheeks, and drawing attention to her lips. *Oh, those lips.* Sula tossed her messenger bag into the back seat and placed her overnight bag next to Melissa's in the back. When she turned around, Melissa stood up on her toes and kissed her lightly.

"Mmm, coffee."

Sula stepped back, putting her hand up to cover her mouth. "Oh, I'm so sorry. I'll go brush my teeth again."

"No, don't." Melissa grabbed her hand, smiling mischievously. "I want more coffee."

"I only made a small pot, and I drank it all. I could brew another one if you—"

"No, silly. I want another *kiss.* A coffee-flavored kiss."

"Oh." Sula dropped her hand and put her arm around her.

Melissa gave her a lingering passionate kiss and enjoyed the feeling of being in Sula's arms. She leaned back to stare into Sula's eyes, and the morning light made the amber highlights seemed almost golden. She traced her finger down the line of her jaw and felt Sula shudder under her touch. "Much as I'd love to have a cup of coffee with you, if you want to be on time for your meeting, we better get going."

"Oh, yeah…the meeting," Sula joked, releasing Melissa from her embrace.

As they drove into Buckhorn, the main street was devoid of activity; the tourists apparently hadn't woken up yet. Melissa glanced at the gas gauge, surprised to see that the tank was less than half full. "I'd better stop for gas before we get out of town."

Sula pointed ahead. "The station on the other side of town always has a good price, and even better coffee, if you want some. I wouldn't mind another cup for the drive."

Melissa stopped at the station, which was painted such a bright shade of yellow with red trim that you couldn't possibly miss seeing it. That seemed to be the point of the paint job. It looked like a mom-and-pop operation, with hand-painted signs in large block letters advertising bait, beer, and ice. Sula went inside while Melissa attended to the gas. Standing there, listening to the whirr and click of the pump, she wondered how the evening with Sula would unfold. She was entertaining some stimulating ideas when a deep rumble jarred her thoughts back to the present. A big pickup towing a pop-up camping trailer pulled up on the other side of the pump, and a sleepy-looking woman got out, yawned, and reached for the nozzle as kids spilled out of the back seat and ran toward the convenience mart. A family heading home, it seemed; they all look tanned and like they could use a good shower.

The two-tone electronic chime of the convenience mart door dinged, and Melissa turned to see the kids go in and Sula come out, walking toward her with a large cup of coffee in each hand and gripping the top of a white pastry bag between her teeth. She wiggled her eyebrows comically when they made eye contact.

Smiling, Melissa hung the nozzle back on the pump and grabbed the receipt. "We've got gas, coffee, and whatever's in that bag. Let's hit the road."

As they descended into the canyon, Melissa heard the rustle of the paper sack and glanced over to see Sula opening the bag. "So, what did you get?" Melissa asked.

"Honey buns."

Melissa laughed. "You just couldn't resist them, could you?"

"Of course not. They're really good."

Melissa glanced at the gooey roll in Sula hand. "Well, to keep the steering wheel from getting sticky, you're going to have to feed it to me."

"Hm. You don't look like wildlife to me," Sula said with a playfully skeptical tone. "So I guess I won't be breaking any rules."

"I can imitate a squirrel pretty well," Melissa said.

"Oh, yeah?"

"Mm-hmm." And just as she was about to demonstrate her chatter, she remembered the bag of raw peanuts in Sula's vehicle. "Hey, wait a minute. You keep peanuts in your Bronco to feed the jays."

"What happens on my property stays on my property," Sula said with a chuckle. "Don't give away my secret."

"I promise not to tell anyone about your deep, dark secret."

"Well then, I suppose I can reward you with this." Sula held up a piece of sticky bun in front of her lips so she could accept it without taking her eyes off the road.

It was tender and tasted more like honey than sugar. Sula was funny, appearing so shocked when Melissa had called her a bear. Her life was devoted to bears. She studied them and protected them through the conservancy, she had bear art in her home, and she certainly seemed to like honey as much as any bear did. And based on what she had learned recently from the exhibits at the conservancy, Sula also seemed to share the bear-like qualities of being curious, watchful, cautious, and easygoing. But, as she had seen at the bar with Kerry, Sula would stand her ground if provoked. She'd be a formidable foe.

Melissa enjoyed driving down the winding canyon road, and in between bites of the honey bun that Sula offered her, she asked about her meeting. Sula explained that she'd be giving a presentation about the conservancy's mission and their collaboration with the City of Buckhorn. Melissa learned that they had been nationally recognized for not having had any bear-related human injuries in over ten years.

"So that kid who had food in his tent and got dragged off by the bear broke your record, I guess."

"Yeah."

"Hey. Whatever happened to that bear?"

"Oh, Parks and Wildlife never found him. He was a young bear, still learning the rules." Sula paused and then added quickly, "At least that's my assumption. He must have moved into another range."

"I bet that kid made you angry."

"No, not angry. Just concerned that we need to keep the pressure on education. You know, living with bears is really just about applying some basic common sense."

"Which is often lacking in far too much of the population."

"Agreed," Sula said, and balled up the empty paper sack. "Our program works because we have such strong support from the city and the community."

"You said the city sometimes calls you if there's a problem bear."

"Yeah, but that's not often. We train all the police officers, since they're first responders, on how to react to bear calls. In most cases the bears are just moving through a neighborhood, maybe pausing to take a nap in the shade of a porch. If a bear's not behaving in an aggressive or unusual manner, the officer will call one of our bear-watch volunteers. They'll help monitor the bear and, more importantly, talk to the people who gather to watch it. It's a great opportunity to educate people. If a bear's doing something that's going to get it into trouble, the police call Parks and Wildlife, who decide the best course of action."

"Like what?"

"Pepper spray, or a device called a banger that makes a loud sound near the bear. If the bear won't move on, like if it won't leave the bird feeder that shouldn't have been hung where the bear could get to it, they might have to shoot it with a bean bag. That's pretty rare, though."

Melissa nodded as she listened. "So I take it that the goal is to get the bear to associate people with unpleasant things."

"Sort of. Mostly we don't want the bears getting habituated to human food or food sources associated with humans, like bird feeders. Just moseying through the neighborhood is fine, but stopping and raiding bird feeders or climbing into an open window to get a jar of peanut butter that was left on a kitchen counter is not acceptable. A smart bear figures that out."

"Has a bear really broken into a house for peanut butter?"

"More than once."

"Wow." That put the ranch rules about keeping ground-floor cabin windows closed at night or if you weren't there into perspective. "So what happens to a bear that's not so smart?"

"It gets relocated. And I really hate when that happens, because more often than not, that bear will find its way back. And repeat offenders usually get labeled as bad bears."

"And so-called bad bears come to a bad end, I'm guessing."

"Mm-hmm. Luckily, we haven't had to do that in Buckhorn in nearly twenty years."

"That's amazing."

"It is." Sula laughed unexpectedly. "I think I just gave you my talk."

"Well, I'm impressed. I hope the people attending are equally impressed *and* inspired to take these ideas home with them to implement." The truth was, Melissa was more than impressed; she was deeply moved. "You really do make the world a better place."

"I try," Sula said softly.

As the mountains turned into foothills, which in turn gave way to the plateau below, the urban sprawl along the Front Range made the drive much less visually interesting. There were no lulls in conversation, and the time flew by as Sula entertained Melissa with stories about when she was a college intern spending the summers working in Montana. Some were funny, like a story about a black bear who had gotten drunk on peaches that a family had let collect on the ground in their backyard. After eating the fermented fruit, he'd played in the swimming pool, biting holes in all the children's inflatable toys, and then passed out cold on a picnic table. Melissa had tears in her eyes from laughter when Sula said the family didn't understand why the bear couldn't be arrested for drunk-and-disorderly behavior. Other stories, like the one about a tranquilized bear being transported in the back seat of an SUV that woke up sooner than expected, kept her on the edge of her seat.

The traffic was heavy but moving at a good pace. The Front Range had grown significantly since she'd lived there, and it was a strange experience to feel displaced in a place she knew. Aside from the immutable mountains to the west, so many things had changed, and she often didn't recognize where she was.

Following Sula's directions, she took the exit to the Rocky Mountain Arsenal National Wildlife Refuge. Fifteen thousand acres of restored grasslands, the prairie landscape was a startling contrast to the dense urban environment that surrounded it. She'd visited it years ago with her parents when it first opened to the public, and it was hard to believe that the site was once one of the most contaminated places in America from the chemical weapons manufacturing facility built there during World War II and operating until the end of the Cold War. Crossing the intersection into the refuge was like going back in time. A small herd of shaggy bison grazed nearby, the cows and calves swishing their tails to keep the flies at bay, and a hawk circled lazily, catching an updraft of air rising from the sun-warmed ground.

Melissa turned toward the visitors' center and drove past the rows of solar panels that also provided shaded parking, then pulled into the circular drive near the front door. The attractive building, constructed with local stone and stucco walls painted to match the yellow ochre-colored soil, blended into its surroundings.

"I should be done here around five," Sula said as she grabbed her messenger bag from the back seat. "I'll text you if it'll be later than that."

"Okay." Melissa leaned toward Sula. "Do I get a kiss for my superb taxi service?"

"Mmm." Sula looked at Melissa's lips from under heavy-lidded eyes and almost seemed to purr. "I think you deserve more than a kiss." Sula glanced over her shoulder as a small group of people walked past the car.

"I understand you're in professional mode here." Melissa kissed her chastely on the lips, then whispered in her ear, "You can make it up to me later."

Sula's eyes grew wide and her skin flushed pink. Instead of speaking, she smiled shyly and gently rubbed her cheek against Melissa's. Flooded with desire by the unexpectedly intimate gesture, she resisted the urge to grab Sula by the ears and kiss her fiercely.

"Have a good day, Goldie," Sula said as she got out of the car.

"You, too, Bear."

Sula smiled, shaking her head as she turned away. Melissa watched her walk toward the visitors' center and took a deep breath, blowing it out through pursed lips, then shifted her attention to navigating toward downtown. It was hard to believe it was only a ten-minute drive away from here. At least the main thoroughfares hadn't changed, so she turned off the Subaru's GPS, which wanted her to get on I-70. Instead, after leaving the refuge, she followed Quebec Street to Colorado Boulevard, passed the Museum of Science and Nature, and then turned west on to Colfax Avenue, which didn't look nearly as rough as she remembered.

The vagrants who used to loiter on the streets seemed to have been replaced with hipsters and brightly colored café umbrellas. Buildings that hadn't already been renovated for business and housing were in various states of being gutted and rebuilt. Driving through all this urban renewal, she had no idea that in metro Denver, bears would be the theme of the day, nor that she would encounter so many of them before the day was over.

CHAPTER SIXTEEN

"Turn on to Eighteenth Avenue," Sula said, guiding Melissa through downtown Denver. When Melissa had picked her up at the refuge and asked where they were going, Sula had remained steadfast in not revealing their destination. She'd have told her sooner, but once she realized that Melissa seemed to like the intrigue, she decided to draw it out. The light at the upcoming intersection, where five streets came together at odd angles, was red, and their view ahead was blocked by the Bank of Colorado building. "Veer left here on Tremont and we're there."

Melissa regarded Sula out of the corner of her eye with a sly smile, "Really? I'm so curious—"

Sula pointed forward. "Green light."

As they moved forward with the traffic into the intersection, the wedge-shaped corner of the Brown Palace Hotel came into view, its nine stories of red sandstone dwarfed by the tall steel-and-glass office buildings and high-rise apartments surrounding it. But its historic charm more than made up for the height differential. Sula watched with satisfaction as Melissa's eyes grew big.

"We're staying *there*?"

"Yeah."

"You're serious?"

"I wouldn't joke about this," Sula said with a laugh.

Melissa pulled up to the covered entrance flanked by large brass lamps. A smiling valet strode over and opened the door.

"Good afternoon. Welcome to the Brown Palace Hotel. Will you be staying with us?"

Melissa looked stunned. Sula, realizing she'd better intervene, leaned forward to speak with the young man. "Yes. We have reservations. Thank you."

They took their bags from the car, and Sula tipped the valet. As they walked toward the deep and elegantly arched stone doorway, Melissa turned to the side of the entrance.

"Look at the faces carved into the archivolts. I've never been this close to the building before," Melissa said and put her hand on the rough red sandstone.

Before Sula could ask what an archivolt was, though she assumed it was the decorative band on which Melissa's hand rested, Melissa became transfixed by the stained glass above the brass revolving doors. Two sword-wielding hybrid creatures with the head, talons, and wings of an eagle and the body and tail of a lion stood back to back.

Delight flashed across Melissa's face. "Griffins!"

"You know your magical creatures," said the smiling doorman, dressed in a black vest and crisp white shirt. He gestured to the revolving door. "You'll find more inside."

On the other side of the door, refreshing cool air greeted them. Melissa let out an audible gasp, taking Sula's arm when she saw the atrium. The ground floor was being used for afternoon tea, and nearly every table was occupied. A man seated at a baby grand in a corner played classical music—Debussy, it sounded like—and aside from the contemporary clothing of the guests nibbling on scones and elegant sandwiches, it looked like a scene from a hundred years ago. Tall arches rose to the mezzanine, and the airy space above their heads went all the way to the top of the building. Each floor was ringed with cast iron, fluted columns, and ornate grillwork painted deep forest green.

"This is so amazing…" Melissa said, looking around quickly and seeming to take it all in before she focused her green eyes back on Sula. "*You* are amazing."

Sula beamed. "Why don't you stay here for a moment and enjoy the view while I go check in."

"Okay," Melissa said distractedly, her attention now diverted by the skylight made of stained glass.

At the registration desk Sula confirmed that she had the suite she requested and signed for the room. When she returned to Melissa, she found her taking photos with her cell phone.

"Sorry." Melissa slid her phone back into her purse. "I'm not sure which has taken control of me, the tourist or the art historian."

"Maybe both." Sula laughed. "I'm sure they're used to people taking pictures. This place has a lot of history and ghosts, too, from what I've heard."

"That's intriguing." Melissa tucked a stray strand of hair behind her ear.

Sula held up the keycard in her hand. "I was thinking that we could go to our suite and freshen up—I'd like to change out of these work clothes—and then we could come back down for a drink and talk about dinner."

"Sounds perfect," Melissa said as they walked to the elevator. "On the drive over here, you said your presentation went well."

"It did. Talking about it with you on the way down helped it go smoothly. I was asked some of the questions you asked me, so my responses were polished. Thanks for making me look good."

"You're welcome. I'm glad I could help, and I learned a lot, too." Melissa peered at the brass inlays of griffins on the wooden doors. "Just like the doorman said, more griffins."

Sula pointed to the crown on which the griffin stood. "A royal griffin for the Brown Palace. I think that when the hotel was built in the 1890s, they were trying to evoke a European flair."

"Definitely. The design is a style of architecture known as Richardsonian Romanesque." Melissa paused and smiled sheepishly. "I know just enough architectural history to be dangerous."

Sula knew a few details about the hotel, but she liked learning more about it from Melissa's perspective. She liked it when she slipped into professor mode, as Melissa called it. Sula respected her scholarly knowledge, and when Melissa's voice became authoritative, she enjoyed letting her be in command of the conversation.

Melissa pointed up at the mural above the elevator. "You said the hotel was built in the 1890s, but *that* looks Art Deco, from the 1930s."

Sula had always thought the well-dressed woman in the painting stepping through the door of the propeller-driven airplane looked like Ingrid Bergman in *Casablanca*. "It is. The hotel was renovated in the 30s. You'll see more evidence of that on our floor."

"You've stayed here before?"

"Many times. This is my favorite hotel in Denver. It's such a young city and so much of the architecture is modern, I like the sense of history here." The brass floor indicator below the painting dropped from 2 to L, and the elevator dinged. When the doors slid open, they stepped in together, and Sula reached across Melissa to push the button for the ninth floor. "I can't wait to hear the details of your day."

"I can't wait to tell you all about it. But it's going to take a while, so I'll wait until dinner, when I have your undivided attention."

"Oh, I think you've had that for a while." Sula kissed her, and would have continued doing so, but after the elevator stopped and the doors opened, the sound of a man loudly clearing his throat interrupted them.

"Excuse us." Melissa suppressed a giggle and grabbed Sula by the hand, pulling her off the elevator.

"Have a nice day," Sula nodded to the glowering man as she stepped past him.

Melissa regarded the wall of glass bricks that replaced the cast-iron grillwork on this floor only. They glowed with an ethereal white light. "These glass bricks are so early twentieth-century modern, as are those Art Deco style numbers on the doors, but this hallway feels claustrophobic. And the light is so cool, institutional—like a hospital—it's a little creepy."

"Funny you should say that. This floor and the eighth floor below are where the ghostly occurrences have been reported."

"*Ghostly occurrences*? What does that mean? This is the second time you've mentioned ghosts." Melissa frowned and slowed her pace.

"Oh, nothing terrible—voices in the hall, footsteps, that sort of thing. But when you look, no one's there." Sula glanced over at Melissa, who appeared unsettled. "Are you afraid of ghosts?"

"I don't know. I've never met one, so I don't really know. And I'd kind of like to keep it that way."

"If it makes you feel any better, I've stayed on this floor several times, and I've never had anything unusual happen...well, except for that one time."

"What do you mean 'that one time'?" Melissa asked quickly. When Sula couldn't suppress her laughter, Melissa slapped her playfully on the shoulder. "You're teasing me, aren't you?"

"I am. Sorry. I couldn't resist," Sula said with a chuckle and stopped at the door at the end of the hall. "Room 922." She waved the keycard across the lock and opened the door. "Here we are."

The sitting room of the spacious suite was bright and elegantly modern, its clean white-and-gray color scheme accented with pale blue and yellow, the same hues found in the terrazzo floor on the first level. The wall in front of them curved, revealing that they were at the front of the triangular building.

"Very nice." Melissa glanced around the room, nodding with what seemed to be approval. She looked to her left at an open door leading to a bedroom and then to her right, to another open door leading to the second bedroom. She cocked her head and raised her eyebrows. "Separate rooms?"

"I…uh…" Sula hesitated, suddenly fearful that changing her reservation from a single room to a two-room suite wasn't a good idea. The way Melissa was staring at her threw her off balance. She didn't want Melissa to assume or feel any pressure that they would sleep together tonight, though the thought of kissing Melissa, slipping her out of her clothes and feeling her bare skin against her own, hadn't been far from her mind for days. Even so, as much as she wanted Melissa, she hadn't fully worked out the consequences of such intimacy. She had real feelings for Melissa, deep feelings. This wasn't some dalliance, and when she paused to think about it, that fact terrified her. She was unmoored in uncharted territory and acting on an instinct that seemed to keep poking and prodding her to get closer and closer…The jumble of thoughts went through her head in a flash, leaving her unable to form a coherent reply. Having Melissa stand there, waiting for her to say something, just made it worse. She coughed and cleared her throat.

"You're really cute when you get nervous. You know that?" Melissa smiled gently and gestured to the glasses on the counter next to a minibar. "Would you like a glass of water?"

"No. I'm fine." Sula took a deep breath and let it out. "I, um, was trying to say that I didn't want to make any assumptions…about us today…I mean, tonight."

Melissa's lips curved into a gentle smile. "Sula, I think you should assume that whatever happens, or doesn't happen, between us, it will be mutually agreed upon." Melissa kissed her on the curve of her neck, her lips warm and soft, and then unexpectedly, she felt a sharp pinch that made her flinch and take a quick breath. The jolt was like an electric shock yet pleasurable. It shot through her, coursing along her nerves to her extremities and the place in between, where it settled into an aching need. Melissa sauntered toward the bedroom nearest her. Before closing the door, she paused and locked eyes with Sula. "Give me about twenty minutes to get ready. And don't think I don't appreciate that you're a sensitive bear."

Sula put her hand on her neck, over the spot Melissa had just kissed…*and bit.* Her skin pulsed under her fingers. Hell, her whole body pulsed now. She told herself not to think too much.

❖

Melissa wasn't sure exactly what had come over her. She had acted on a wild impulse nipping Sula. It was out of character for her to do something like that. Even so, she relished the look of shock and desire on Sula's face as she closed the door. She took her phone out of her purse and tossed her overnight bag onto the bed. It had been vibrating repeatedly, and while checking it, she found five messages from Beth, responses to the photos she'd sent of the hotel atrium and one brief text about where she was and who she was with. She laughed out loud when she saw Beth's last message.

Call me when you come up for air.

While changing into her outfit for the evening and freshening her makeup, she pondered Sula's behavior. Damn, she was hard to read. The woman checks her into a historic five-star hotel, kisses her on the elevator, and then invites her into a suite with separate bedrooms. Not exactly what she'd expected. She'd have happily continued that kiss all the way down the hall and into the plush bed in front of her. Professional Sula—cool and confident—was a different creature altogether from personal Sula, the one who stammered and blushed and reined herself in. Melissa really wanted to see Sula just be herself and had an uncannily strong feeling that she'd like *that* Sula very much.

She brushed her hair and pinned it back loosely. She wanted to leave it down, but it was hot here in the city, much hotter than the mountains, and she'd be more comfortable with it off her neck. She put on lipstick, carefully accentuating the shape of her lips, and reapplied her summer fragrance, a light floral perfume with subtle notes of sandalwood that she knew Sula liked. More than once, Melissa had noticed Sula unawares catching her scent with her chin lifted slightly and nostrils flaring gently, a veiled look of pleasure on her face. Sula's almost animalistic response to her had an equally powerful reciprocal effect. Just thinking about it gave Melissa a rippling thrill.

Melissa turned away from the bathroom mirror with its terribly unflattering cool fluorescent light. Why did they always install those in hotel bathrooms? They made your skin look washed out and your hair gray. In the warmer light of the room she appraised herself in front of the full-length mirror on the closet door. She straightened the hem of the tailored sleeveless shirt, a cool hue of sage that brought out the color of her eyes. Having paired it with mossy-green pants and loafers, she'd be appropriately dressed for wherever they went. Denver prided itself on its casual attitude and dress, but it was a city nonetheless, and she was about to go out on a date. It *was* a date, wasn't it? As soon at the question crossed her mind, she clucked at herself. Sula's vacillations between confidence and reticence were starting to rub off on her. She shook her head as if that would shake off any doubts, grabbed her purse, and left the bedroom. *This* was going to be a date.

When Melissa walked through the door, she saw Sula standing by the corner window, looking down on the streets below, and she turned and smiled. Wearing light-gray denim pants with low-heeled boots and a silky black shirt with the sleeves turned up, she looked dressed for a date.

"You clean up nice," Melissa said as she crossed the room, becoming distracted by the golden beads of Sula's matching necklace and earrings. "Is that amber?"

"It is," Sula said.

Melissa examined the beaded necklace, and while comparing its color to Sula's eyes, she saw her pupils dilate. Melissa took satisfaction in witnessing the subtle response. "Mmm…it matches the highlights in your eyes."

"Why, thank you," Sula said, scanning her from bottom to top. "You look very nice yourself." She smiled and leaned forward, kissing her lightly, then brushed her lips along her cheek to her ear. "And you smell so good."

Melissa took a deep breath and let it out. "I believe it's time for that cocktail you promised me."

Sula glanced at her silver watch. "They'll be done with tea in the atrium by now, and we can have a drink there or in the Ship Tavern."

"I'm intrigued by the sound of a ship's tavern."

"Tavern it is."

Located on the first floor, past a dark-wood-paneled lounge illuminated by stained-glass windows with more griffins, the Ship Tavern was marked by a neon sign in the shape of a schooner with the wind in its sails. The bar was cozy, and the tapered room and curving wall even made the space feel a bit like being in the prow of a ship. They took a seat at one of the tables with a blue leather couch in the center of the room. Behind the couch, a thick wooden mast complete with a rigged crow's nest rose to just below the timber-and-plaster ceiling. Melissa looked around, taking in the decor—thick ropes, old maps, anchors embossed on the stools at the bar, and the numerous scale models of sailing ships mounted high on the walls all the way around the room.

"This is an unexpected theme for the Rocky Mountain West," Melissa said.

A waitress appeared and handed them menus. Apparently, she had overheard Melissa's comment. "There's a funny story. You don't know it?" Both Sula and Melissa shook their heads. "Well, C.K. Boettcher, who co-owned the hotel with his father in the 30s, bought a collection of these model ships. Don't ask me why. His wife, Edna, *hated* them and suggested they'd look a whole lot better at the hotel than in their house. Prohibition had just ended, and C.K. and his dad decided to redesign this space as a bar with a ship theme, and voilà—a new bar and a happy wife." She waved her hand. "Not much has changed in the last eighty years."

"This is considered one of Denver's classic bars," Sula said. "There would be protests if they tried to renovate it."

The waitress nodded in agreement. "What can I get for you?"

After a cursory glance at the menu, Sula ordered the blackberry bramble. Melissa looked at the ingredient list—gin, muddled blackberries, honey, and lemon on the rocks—and asked for the same thing. When the waitress returned with the drinks, Melissa admired the plump blackberry floating on top of the ice before picking up her glass.

"Cheers," Sula said.

Melissa tapped her glass against Sula's and tasted her drink. "Oh…this is so refreshing." She took another sip. It was well-balanced and fruity, but not too sweet.

"I'm glad you like it," Sula said. Using her lips, she delicately nabbed the berry from her glass and ate it.

"You chose a great drink. Do you have any suggestions for dinner?"

"I do, actually."

Melissa took another sip and gestured for Sula to continue.

"Well," Sula said, "you mentioned that you don't have good Mexican food where you live and you miss it."

"Very true. I think I might like where this conversation is going."

"I'd like to suggest a restaurant called Oso Verde. They do traditional Mexican food and have house specials that put a new spin on the standards."

"That sounds good. I haven't had a decent enchilada in over a year." Melissa laughed, picked the blackberry out of her glass with her fingers, and popped it into her mouth. Observing that Sula was watching her, she rolled it around on her tongue before slowly biting into it. The gin was starting to go to her head.

"I was hoping you'd say that, because I made a reservation there for us."

Melissa narrowed her eyes at Sula. She'd made a good call on the restaurant, but she hadn't revealed her plans until she was sure it would be well received. She was so careful that Melissa wanted to knock down those self-imposed, perhaps overprotective, walls.

Talking about the hotel while they enjoyed their drinks, Melissa explained what she knew about the style of architecture. The large atrium, made possible by the new building materials of cast iron and steel, was an engineering marvel at the time. Sula listened with interest and asked good questions.

"You'd be an excellent student," Melissa said.

"Really?" Sula signed the receipt for the drinks that the waitress had quietly left and pushed it to the edge of the table. "Why?"

"Your questions reveal that you're not just paying attention, but that you're also thinking."

"What can I say?" Sula shrugged. "I like to think."

"Which is why you'd make a good student." Melissa laughed and drained what remained in her glass. It was probably good that Sula had reservations; otherwise she'd be tempted to order a second one.

Sula glanced at her watch. "We should head to the restaurant."

While leaving the Ship Tavern, Melissa fished around in her purse for her car keys and realized that she was a little tipsy and probably shouldn't drive. When she didn't calculate the speed of the revolving door correctly and it caught her heel as she stepped into it, her suspicion was confirmed. In contrast, Sula walked through the door as though completely unaffected. And she probably wasn't. She was bigger and used to the altitude. Just as Melissa was about to ask Sula if she'd drive, Sula gestured to a woman dressed in a black suit and tie standing next to an impossibly shiny black BMW sedan.

"Our driver is ready for us," Sula said with a grin.

Melissa arched an eyebrow and dropped her keys into her purse. "Our *driver*?"

The driver nodded to Sula. "Good evening, Ms. Johansen." She turned to Melissa while opening the back door. "Dr. Warren." She smiled warmly. "Where can I take you?"

Melissa slid across the soft leather seat and watched Sula as she got in next to her while talking with the driver, who seemed familiar with the restaurant. Sula leaned back, placing her hand gently on top of Melissa's leg, her fingers resting on the inside of her thigh. Such a light touch, but it instantly sent a tingle that worked its way farther up the inside of her leg, making Melissa catch her breath when it reached its destination. *Oh...this is definitely a date.*

Getting out of the car, Melissa looked up at the neon sign for the restaurant, a green silhouette in the shape of a bear with "Oso Verde" in a fluid script next to it. She smiled to herself, realizing she had misunderstood the name of the restaurant when Sula first suggested it.

The restaurant was charming, the ambient lighting from three-dimensional perforated tin stars hanging from the ceiling almost magical. Candlelit tables were covered with striped fabric in warm, earthy colors. The hostess seated them immediately in a quiet corner, and after the waiter arrived and Melissa ordered a margarita, Sula asked for a tequila sunrise and guacamole as an appetizer.

"This menu is amazing." Melissa looked back and forth at both sides of the long card. "I think I'm going to have to order everything."

"We could order à la carte and share."

"Mmm...I like how you think."

The waiter returned with the drinks and said he'd be back in a moment with the guacamole. Melissa took a sip of hers and admired the cheerful colors of Sula's cocktail, garnished with thin slices of pineapple and a cherry.

"I'm so glad you hired a driver." Melissa laughed as she set the glass down on the table. It was the best margarita she'd ever had. The balance of sweet, tart, and salty was perfect, and she planned to savor it. Sula regarded her with a hint of a smile. The candlelight, softly illuminating her from below, flickered in her eyes and made her amber jewelry glow. Struck by Sula's beauty in that moment, Melissa didn't want to say or do anything that would make her move and break the spell that had been cast.

Instead, it was the waiter who prompted Sula to sit back, away from the light, when he arrived with a cart laden with avocado, finely chopped tomato, garlic, cilantro, spices, and a *molcajete*, a stone bowl made from gray basalt. Melissa must have had a look of surprise on her face.

"Tableside guacamole is our specialty here," the waiter explained as he expertly scooped the avocado out of its skin and, with a large wooden spoon, mashed and stirred everything together efficiently, placing it on the table alongside some freshly made tortilla chips. He said he'd give them a few minutes before taking their orders and wheeled the empty cart away.

Nibbling on chips and guacamole, they discussed their options and then settled on what they wanted. The waiter slipped in, took their order, and glided off again. The service was impeccable.

"So...*your* day. You still haven't told me how your day went." Sula took a sip of her drink and picked out the cherry with her fingers, plucking it from the stem with her lips.

"My day was very interesting." Melissa paused, watching Sula's mouth. The way her lips held the cherry was unexpectedly sensual, and the sight distracted her for a moment. "I think I've developed a thing for bears."

Sula coughed, her face turning red as she put her hand up to cover her mouth.

"Are you okay?"

"Yeah." Sula tucked her chin and cleared her voice, looking up at Melissa from under arched eyebrows. "I, uh, just inhaled the cherry... I'll be fine...go on."

"Well, bears were definitely the theme of the day. I got a little turned around downtown. I thought I could navigate my way to the museum without GPS, but I found out my memory isn't what I thought it was. It's been years since I've been in Denver, and I never came here that much when I still lived in the state. Anyway, I ended up driving around the convention center and saw the big blue bear."

"I see what you mean."

"Hm?"

"*I See What You Mean*," Sula said with a laugh. "It's the name of the sculpture. It's become an icon of the city."

"Oh." Melissa laughed with her. "That's an odd title, don't you think? I thought it was very whimsical—a forty-foot-tall indigo-blue bear peering through the plate-glass windows of the convention center."

"I guess the title is about as whimsical as the sculpture."

"That's a good response. Bonus points for you."

"Thank you, Professor." Sula grinned.

"You're welcome. And just so you know, those points aren't easy to get." Melissa paused, biting her lower lip, and then couldn't resist. "You can cash them in later, if you like."

Sula cleared her throat again and smiled shyly. "So noted."

When their meal arrived, the table was covered in bowls and plates—freshly made tortillas, enchiladas smothered in both spicy green chile and dark-red chile Colorado, and the *brazo de reina,* which was a kind of tamale made with ground pumpkin seeds that gave it a distinctive flavor and pale-green color. In between bites, Melissa described her day at the art museum. She had been surprised to find that the older North Building, Gio Ponti's fortress-like design completed in the early seventies, was under total renovation and that construction had begun on a new grand entrance designed to connect it with Daniel Libeskind's newer Hamilton Building. The two buildings were so very different—Ponti's castle covered in a revetment of gray glass tiles next to Libeskind's pointy titanium, steel-clad structure that looked like a massive crystal had popped up out of the street.

"I love your descriptions," Sula said when Melissa paused to take a bite. "You said you saw bears, more than just the big blue one. Where were the others?"

"The bears were *inside.* Since the other building is closed, the work on view from the museum's collection is much smaller, and they organized it around the theme of animals in art. To be honest, it included a lot more animals than bears, but they kept getting my attention."

"Such as?"

"Where to begin?" Melissa took the last bite of her enchilada and thought about it while she chewed. "Let's see…there was the northwest coast Native American door panel that was basically a standing bear, and the actual doorway was the bear's vagina."

Melissa thought that would make Sula laugh, but her expression remained serious, and she said, "People of the bear."

"There was a contemporary painting of a creature with the body of a bear, the head of a coyote, and wearing a cape made of vulture feathers. A sort of shaman figure, I think."

"Sounds like it." Sula nodded. "A powerful body, a cunning brain—though I think a bear is smarter than a coyote—and feathers for flying."

"An astute observation. You might have just earned an extra point. Though you do have a bias towards bears."

"True. I'll admit that," Sula said.

"Oh, the third bear was very interesting, but it wasn't in the regular collection. It was part of a small exhibition of paintings by a nineteenth-century artist I didn't know—William Henry Beard."

Melissa purposefully pronounced his last name like *bear*. "He painted landscapes and anthropomorphized animals. Apparently, he was best known for his bears."

"Anthropo…what?"

"Anthropomorphized. It means animals behaving like humans. A painting of a bear party in the forest depicted them dancing. It was amazing. Here. I'll show you." Melissa grabbed her cell phone from her purse and scrolled through her photos to show Sula the whole painting and then a detail of two bears facing each other, each balanced with one foot on the ground and the other in the air, holding the opposing front paw of their partner. Bent forward but leaning back, the bears' poses evoked the energy of dancing and were comical.

Sula had an amused expression. "That's what I look like when I dance."

"Oh, I bet you're much more graceful than that."

"You think so?"

"Yeah. I've seen the way you move in the forest and your agility climbing rocks. I bet you're a good dancer."

Sula's eyes remained on the painting on the screen of her phone, and she rubbed her thumb across her lower lip thoughtfully. "I wonder what inspired him to make paintings like that."

"That's a good question. I'll have to do a little research." Melissa put her phone away. "Oh, and there is one more bear. I encountered it just before dinner."

"Really? Where?"

"Here."

Sula raised her eyebrows in a silent question.

"This restaurant, Oso Verde—the Green Bear. When you suggested it, I thought you said 'oh, so verde.'" Melissa laughed. "I thought the name referred to fresh produce or green chile, not a green bear."

"I hadn't thought of it that way. That's funny." Sula laughed softly. "But you missed a bear."

"Did I?" Melissa looked around. Had she not seen some decoration?

"Yes, you did, *Goldie*."

"Oh," the realization hit her, "you mean you." Melissa reached out and touched Sula, running her index and middle finger slowly along the edge of her hand. "I'm Goldie, and you're the bear." She rested her fingers on Sula's wrist and spoke slowly. "My bear."

Sula made a sound, a quiet moan, or was it a low growl? Either way it made Melissa's pulse quicken. The waiter interrupted with the dessert menu and suggested the Mexican chocolate torte or the almond cake.

"Both, please," Sula said, not breaking eye contact with Melissa.

"To go," Melissa said.

Sula did not resist.

CHAPTER SEVENTEEN

I think the driver was a little surprised when you said we were coming back to the hotel after dinner." Melissa grinned as she trailed her fingers along Sula's cheek. Focused on the sensation, Sula dropped the keycard. Laughing at herself, she picked it up off the floor and waved it across the door lock.

"She was so professional, though," Sula said, opening the door. "She barely raised an eyebrow."

"Yes, but that one eyebrow spoke volumes, don't you think?" Melissa followed Sula into the sitting room of the suite and put her purse and the boxes containing their desserts on the cabinet near the minibar. She picked up a card and, after reading it, walked toward the television and removed a tablet from a charging dock below the large flat-screen. "This suite has a media system."

Sula stood behind Melissa and looked over her shoulder, her cheek very close to Melissa's but not touching. "You want to play a video game?"

"No. I want to play some music." Melissa laughed, focusing on the screen of the tablet. She turned her head and looked at Sula. "And then I want to play with you."

As if the air had suddenly evacuated from the room, Sula took a breath so quickly it caught in her throat, sounding like a hiccup. Music with a sexy downtempo beat suddenly filled the hotel suite.

Melissa put the tablet down and turned to face Sula. "Would you like to dance, Bear?"

"I'd love to dance with you, Goldie." Sula put her hands out and shrugged. "But I don't really know how."

"What?" Melissa looked at her skeptically and stepped forward. Slowly, she slid the palm of her hand, soft and warm, against Sula's and wrapped her arm sinuously around Sula's waist.

"I told you I look like that bear in the painting when I dance." Sula laughed, feeling an old anxiety creep up her. Melissa was so close to her now, her sweet, tantalizing scent filled her nostrils. "I can dance at a club where you get lost in the crowd, but like this…no, not really." Sula was telling the truth. Big boned and tall, she avoided situations that drew unwanted attention to her size, and she was always afraid of stepping on her dance partner's feet.

"Hm…so you're a shy bear who likes to hide in the forest." Melissa leaned back and regarded Sula. "Just follow how I move." Melissa swayed her hips back and forth. Sula mimicked her movements, surprised at how easy it was to match her smooth cadence. "Yes. Just like that," Melissa said softly. She stepped back, and with gentle pressure from her hand on the small of Sula's back, she guided her around the room, moving in time with the music.

As Sula picked up on the pattern, they swept in slow circles like an eddy in a gentle stream. She was surprisingly relaxed and was actually enjoying herself. "You're a good teacher."

"As I told you before, you're a good student—a fast learner, actually. You haven't even stepped on my toes."

"*Yet.*" Sula was serious, but Melissa laughed anyway. Pressed against her chest, Sula not only heard Melissa's laughter, but she also felt it, a low rumble resonating all the way into her bones.

Melissa removed her hand from Sula's back and placed it inside the collar of Sula's shirt. Brushing her nails along the nape of her neck, she slid her fingers into her hair. Sula lifted her chin, pressing her head against Melissa's hand…and bumped into the back of the sofa. She stopped abruptly, widening her stance and grabbing Melissa's hips for stability. To avoid toppling backward, she lowered herself and sat on the edge of the sofa, which had the unintended, but far from unpleasant, effect of pulling Melissa between her thighs. Melissa stared at her wide-eyed, her face directly in front of Sula's.

"Well, *that* was quite a move," Melissa said drolly and kissed her, gently at first and then fiercely. Melissa shifted, pressing her hip against the throbbing spot between Sula's legs, and a soft moan escaped from her lips. Sula felt as if she would dissolve into a puddle. Melissa broke off the kiss, leaving Sula breathless but feeling far from weak.

"Mmm…" Melissa whispered. "I like it when you growl like that."

And with those words, what little remained of Sula's reserve broke. Energy coursed through her like the torrent of a river swollen after a spring rain. She clasped Melissa tightly, stood up, and carried her to the closest bedroom.

❖

No lover had *ever* picked Melissa up and carried her off on a wave of passion. She thought that was the fanciful, overwrought stuff of Baroque paintings and romance novels. She now fully understood the expression to be swept off your feet, and it felt astonishingly good to be secure in Sula's arms. Melissa kicked off her loafers before Sula deposited her gently on the bed, trailing kisses down her neck and sweeping back the covers.

Sula undressed her with surprising efficiency; the crisp white sheets seemed to glow in the darkened room and felt cool against her feverish skin. Melissa undid the buckle of Sula's belt and unzipped her pants, pulling them and the bikini briefs she wore underneath down over the curve of her hips. Sula slipped off her boots and socks before pulling her shirt and bra over her head, not wasting time unhooking clasps or undoing buttons.

Keeping her eyes on Sula, Melissa moved backward across the smooth sheets to the center of the large bed. Sula stepped out of the clothes pooled around her feet and followed her, crawling across the bed, her hair framing her face like a dark halo. With a hungry look of desire, her amber eyes caught the light coming through the open door and glinted the color of pale gold.

Sula's mouth found hers, their kisses becoming a wet blur of lips, and teeth, and tongues. Other parts of her were wet, too, and wanting. Melissa pressed her hands against Sula's shoulders and rolled her on to her back, straddling her.

Running her fingertips lightly across Sula's breasts, Melissa followed the invisible trails with her lips. She cupped and caressed her soft, round breasts, kissing and teasing each nipple until it grew firm under her tongue and Sula began to move restlessly underneath her. She touched and kissed along the side of Sula's ribs, across the gentle swell of her belly and the shallow dip between her hips above the low rise of soft flesh between her legs. The texture and feel of her was marvelous, a play of contrasts—hard muscle underneath the soft surface of her skin.

Melissa paused to observe Sula. With her arms above her head, eyes closed, and a look of bliss on her face, she looked as languid and beautiful as Venus in a Renaissance painting. Melissa bit her lower lip in anticipation of Sula's reaction as she dipped her fingers into the soft folds between her legs, the enveloping warm wetness increasing her desire.

"Oh…" Sula raised her hips and pressed her head into the pillow. Melissa shifted, aligning her body along the long length of Sula's, and watched how Sula responded to her touch, discovering what movement and pressure seemed to bring her the most pleasure. Sula murmured incoherently, her face turned in to the pillow, her body undulating against Melissa with an increasingly urgent rhythm. Melissa felt a little drunk on the power to please.

Sula wrapped her arm around Melissa, holding her tight, and grabbed at the sheet with her other hand. They moved seamlessly together, an ancient, instinctive rhythm.

"Don't stop," Sula pleaded in a rough voice.

Melissa had no intention of doing otherwise, but before she could respond, a roaring moan erupted from deep within Sula. Her climax came in deep waves that shook the bed, perhaps even the furniture in the room; she wasn't sure because her focus remained solely on Sula. Nothing mattered more in this moment than the magnificent woman in her embrace. Sula released her grip on the bed and gulped for air. Melissa kissed her neck, damp with perspiration, and held her until she lay still in her arms, her body quiescent.

Once recovered, Sula propped herself up on one elbow and stared at Melissa with a glassy-eyed look of wonder. "I'm not sure I can put into words how that felt."

"Sometimes words aren't necessary."

"Oh, really, Professor?" Sula said in a teasing tone.

Melissa rolled onto her side to face Sula. "You know the old adage about actions speaking louder than words. I'd say your actions spoke *very* loudly." Melissa laughed softly. "Come to think of it, I'd say you *spoke* rather loudly, too."

A look of shock flashed across Sula's face, but it shifted quickly into a rakish smile. "Let's see what happens when the tables are turned."

Melissa's hair had come undone. It brushed the tops of her shoulders and fell into her eyes. Sula pushed it back with her fingers, tucking a loose strand behind her ear, a tender, intimate gesture. The base of her neck now exposed, Sula kissed and nipped it gently, working her way up to a sensitive spot below her ear. Melissa's aching need for release intensified, grew almost painful. Sula stroked her back, and with each pass, her hand went a little farther down, first over the rise and fall of each buttock, then along her hip and thigh, and finally across her stomach and lower…Melissa held her breath, anticipating Sula's touch in the place she was so desperately wanting it.

Instead, Sula put her hand on Melissa's hip and rolled her onto her back, moving with her. Hovering over her, Sula pushed her legs apart with both hands. Melissa didn't think she could be turned on any more than she already was, but experiencing the controlled power in Sula's actions launched her to a new level of arousal. She didn't just want Sula; she wanted Sula to take her in any way she wanted. Melissa moaned softly and lifted her hips, an offering.

Sula moved closer, slipping her long arms under Melissa's legs, along her sides, and sliding her fingers between Melissa's back and the mattress. With a hungry-looking smile and a low growl, Sula took her with her mouth. Melissa inhaled sharply, and cradled in Sula's arms, she was caught in a whirlwind of desire and excruciatingly pure sensation. Whatever Sula was doing with her tongue and lips, it quickly rendered her unable to form a coherent thought. She closed her eyes and clutched the sheets. Sula brought her to a point just shy of climax and held her there at the tipping point for…how long? It could have been thirty seconds or thirty minutes. Time was irrelevant. She lost all awareness of its passing until her senses, which felt like they were expanding in all directions, suddenly contracted to a single point. She cried out, and her orgasm came hard, overwhelming her in explosive pulsations.

Sula nuzzled her, planting kisses on the insides of her thighs. The heady fragrance of their individual perfumes commingled with the scent of sex hung in the air of the room that now seemed almost chilly as it cooled Melissa's damp skin.

"You are sweeter than honey," Sula said softly after she stretched out next to Melissa.

"Given your love of honey, that is high praise." Melissa laughed and put her hand in Sula's wavy hair, touseling it. It was damp at the roots from the exertions of their lovemaking. "Have you ever considered that you might have a honey addiction?"

Sula laughed and sat up abruptly. "That reminds me, we have dessert." Without waiting for a response, she jumped out of bed and padded into the sitting room. Seeing her in the light, Melissa marveled at the athleticism of her body, yet she had soft curves in all the right places. She sat up against the pillows and turned on the light next to the bed. Fortunately, it was adjustable, and she kept the light on the lowest setting, enough to see but not enough to ruin the ambience. Sula returned with the two containers, giving one to Melissa before getting back into the bed. She sat in front of Melissa and folded her legs underneath of her. "We don't have forks."

"I can use my fingers."

A devilish look crossed Sula's face. "You are very good at using your fingers."

"And you're very good with your mouth, I must say. Where on earth did you learn to do that thing with your lips?"

"Picking berries."

"What?"

Sula grinned. "Berries. I like to pick them off the vine with my lips."

"Seriously?"

"You tell me."

"Well, considering what your lips just did to me, I'd say you're serious." It was an odd thing to do, Melissa thought—pick berries with your lips instead of with your hands—but Sula's acquired skill had obvious benefits in the bedroom.

Melissa opened the box revealing the Mexican chocolate torte. She broke off a piece and held it out to Sula, who grabbed it first with her lips, then her teeth. Melissa watched her closely. Able to only feel those lips a few minutes ago, now she saw them in action. There really was something odd about how she used them to take hold of the torte. Odd, but wonderful.

Sula growled her appreciation while she chewed the cake and offered Melissa a piece of the almond torte. Together, they devoured the two pastries, and after the last morsel was gone, Melissa licked chocolate from her fingers. Sula grabbed her hand, stopping her.

"Allow me," Sula said, taking her index finger into her mouth.

"Are you still hungry?" Melissa asked. Sula ran her tongue along the tips of her fingers, causing a frisson that rippled through her body.

"I am," Sula said with a lopsided grin. "I might need more honey. But I can stop any time, if you're worried I'm behaving like an addict."

"Don't you dare," Melissa said in a low voice, pulling Sula into an embrace, kissing her hard. The taste of sweet almond mixed with her own sexual scent inflamed her, and she didn't let go of Sula until they were both entangled and exhausted. The last thing she remembered was the soft sound of Sula's slow, deep breathing, the pressure of her cheek on her shoulder, and her arm draped limply across her torso. Feeling secure and satiated, she fell into a deeply contented sleep.

CHAPTER EIGHTEEN

Melissa woke up to the smell of coffee. Opening her eyes, she discovered that Sula wasn't next to her. The bed was empty.

"Good morning, Goldie." Sula's low, velvety voice came from behind.

Melissa rolled over to find Sula standing next to the bed. "Oh, there you are...good morning, Sula Bear."

Sula, wearing a white robe embroidered with the hotel's griffin logo, smiled and offered her the cup in her hand. Her hair was wet, and when Sula leaned forward, Melissa smelled the clean scent of soap. She sat up and accepted the cup with both hands. "Ah, coffee...thank you."

"You're welcome. I hope you slept well."

"Exceptionally well." Melissa smiled. The cup was hot, and she took a cautious sip. "Do I smell bacon? And why are you up instead of in this bed with me?"

"I have a meeting this morning, remember?" Sula gave Melissa a smoldering look. "I'd *much* rather be in bed with you."

"Oh, right. The meeting," Melissa said unconvincingly. Of course, she remembered the meeting, but she couldn't resist teasing Sula. "Are you sure you can't cancel it?"

"You are such a temptress."

"Said the woman who swept me off my feet last night. And I mean that both figuratively and literally. You can't blame me for not trying to get you back into bed."

Sula laughed. "Are you hungry? I ordered room service. You were sleeping so peacefully, I didn't want to wake you up to find out what you wanted for breakfast, so I ordered several things."

"I'm famished." Melissa glanced toward the window, which was covered with a heavy drape. The room was dark, but light bled out around the edges of the curtain. She was normally up before the sun was over the horizon, but with Sula she seemed to lose sense of time so easily and in the most delectable ways. Memories of last night flashed through her mind, of Sula's body, sweaty and slick, against hers and her lips against—

"I'll get you a robe," Sula said.

Whatever Sula had ordered smelled enticing. Even though her stomach rumbled in hunger and Sula had a meeting to attend, Melissa still had a strong compulsion to untie her robe, slip her hands between the fluffy white fabric and Sula's skin, and pull her back into the bed. Sula returned from the bathroom with a matching robe, holding it out for her. Melissa flipped the covers back and eased out of the bed. Standing naked, she watched as Sula's eyes roamed over her body and she made that soft sexy sound, almost like a purr. With a fluttering feeling in her chest, Melissa turned and slipped an arm into each sleeve of the robe. Sula embraced her from behind, wrapping her long arms around her, and kissed her neck.

"Careful, Bear, or you'll never get to that meeting."

Sula sighed and released her. "All right, breakfast then."

Melissa followed Sula into the sitting room and laughed as they removed the lids from plates on a cart. They had enough food to feed several more people—scrambled eggs, bacon, roasted potatoes, pancakes, croissants, biscuits, a big bowl of fruit, little pots of jam and syrup, and a silver carafe of coffee.

Melissa surveyed the food. "Uh-oh. Something's missing."

"What?"

"Honey."

Sula's eyebrows shot up. "Oh, you're right! I'll call and order some." Sula looked around. "Once I remember where I put my phone."

"*Sula.*"

"Yes?"

"I'm kidding." Melissa gave her a teasing sidelong glance and bumped her with her hip. "Can you go a meal without honey?"

Sula looked shocked but laughed with her. "Of course, I can. But why would I want to?"

Melissa quietly marveled at the unexpected comfort of sharing coffee and the smorgasbord of a breakfast with Sula. It was as if they did this regularly, eating and talking, their conversation running a wide arc from humorous to serious. Melissa asked Sula what she hoped the morning's meeting would accomplish. She explained that it was about expanding their bear-safety program into neighboring states. Sula was aiming to use contacts in the regional US Fish & Wildlife Service office as a way of opening doors for running the program elsewhere. She envisioned hosting municipal representatives at the conservancy in Buckhorn for training and offering follow-up support after the program was implemented. She also wanted to collect data to make available to wildlife biologists and researchers.

"I could have this conversation by email or phone," Sula said in between bites of pancake that she swabbed in the maple syrup pooled on her plate. "But it's so useful to have a real conversation, you know? What they're reluctant to tell you in writing or over the phone, they'll tell you in person."

"Like what?" Melissa picked through the fruit, leaving the raspberries for Sula since she had mentioned she loved them. Additionally, Melissa was fascinated by how she ate them, the way she used her lips, though she tried not to be caught staring.

"Personalities, for one. Who's likely to be sympathetic to the cause and who isn't. Sometimes it's good to know who *not* to talk to."

"Very true. There's nothing worse than running into someone who throws up a roadblock."

"Sounds like you've had experience."

"I have. I've been trying to get another art historian on the faculty so we can develop a major in art history. Right now, we only have a minor, and I'm the sole art historian. The studio program was expanded thanks to a recently deceased and very wealthy alumnus who left us his estate. We've got the space and enough students for it. We've even lost some students who transferred to another college that offers a major. My department chair isn't against it, but he's got a lot of other things lined up that are taking precedence."

"So, who's the roadblock?"

"The dean of the College of Arts and Sciences. He's an engineer and doesn't understand the need for the study of the humanities. All he can see is science and technology as the path to the future." Melissa stabbed a piece of melon with a little more force than necessary and saw Sula wince in response.

"I thought you were happy teaching there."

"Oh, I am. I work with great people, some of whom are good friends, and I love the students. It's just that it could be better than it currently is. The program, I mean." Melissa pulled the melon off her fork with her teeth.

"You're ambitious."

Melissa thought about Sula's comment while she chewed. "Yeah,

I guess so. I see something that can be improved, and I want to make it happen." She pointed her fork at Sula. "Kind of like you."

Sula smiled. "I'll take that as a compliment."

"You should." Melissa smiled back.

Sula broke away from Melissa's gaze and glanced anxiously around the room. "I really need to find my phone. What time is it? I probably need to get dressed."

Melissa leaned forward and peered into the bedroom. The blue LED numbers on the clock on the table by the bed read 8:23. "It's almost eight thirty. When do you need to leave?"

"Eight thirty."

"Oh! I'd better get dressed." Melissa started to stand.

Sula looked surprised. "There's no hurry. I asked for a late checkout. You can stay here until I get back. I mean, if you want to. Or you could do something. I should be back before noon."

Melissa was confused. "Don't you want me to drive you to the meeting?"

"Oh, sorry. I didn't explain that part. I didn't want to trouble you, so I reserved a driver for this morning, too. I just need to dress and get downstairs."

A thought began to form in Melissa's head. "What time is our delayed checkout?"

"No later than three o'clock." Sula narrowed her eyes at Melissa. "Why do you ask?"

"You'll just have to find out when you get back," Melissa said with a mischievous grin and glanced at the clock again. "You'd better get dressed."

Sula made an exasperated sound and dashed to the bedroom, the one they hadn't occupied the previous night, where her overnight bag was located. Melissa helped Sula in an intense, but luckily short-lived, search for her phone. Standing by the door with her cell phone in hand, she looked flustered. She almost left without her messenger bag, but Melissa grabbed it, pushed it into her arms, and gave her a quick kiss good-bye. Sula just stood there like she was waiting for another kiss. With a laugh, Melissa told her to go.

Before closing the door, she hung the Do Not Disturb sign on the handle and took a shower. Afterward, she wrapped her wet hair in a towel and slipped back into the luxuriously soft hotel robe. She still had ample time before she expected Sula to return, and she certainly didn't plan to go anywhere. She didn't intend to dress either. Considering they could have a few more hours after Sula got back, she didn't see any reason not to take full advantage of the room. She laughed to herself. Taking advantage of Sula was a more accurate description of her plans. With some time to kill, she grabbed her cell phone and sat on the sofa. It was two hours later in Georgia, so it seemed a perfect time to call Beth.

"Are you okay?" Beth spoke in a serious voice, not even bothering to say hello.

"Yes, I'm fine…great, actually. Why are you worried?"

"Yesterday you texted me about being at a fancy hotel with the mountain woman of your dreams. I figure if you're calling me this morning, it's not good."

"Oh, no." Melissa laughed. "Quite the opposite."

"Then why the hell are you calling me?" As often happened when Beth was excited or agitated, her Alabama accent became more pronounced, each syllable drawn out and clearly articulated.

"Sula's at a meeting this morning, remember? It's why she was planning to spend the night here in the first place."

"Ah…so it's going good?

"Beyond-my-wildest-dreams good."

"Seriously?"

"Seriously, Beth. I've never met anyone like Sula. Aside from the fact that she has paintings by Ursula Bergen in *every* room of her *incredible* house, she's a really good person. I mean, she wants to make the world a better place—for bears and people, for all of nature, really. She knows such interesting things and has a natural curiosity, plus it's so easy to talk with her. And she has this sexy confidence, but then sometimes she gets shy and…oh my God, that might be even sexier." Melissa paused to take a breath. "Did I tell you she's beautiful?"

"Girl, you're gushing."

"You have *no* idea, Beth."

"TMI!" Beth exclaimed, and Melissa imagined her putting a hand up to stop her from going into the sticky details. But after a brief pause Beth spoke in a low, conspiratorial whisper. "So the sex is good?"

"Like I said, beyond-my-wildest-dreams good."

Beth responded with a hoot of laughter. "About damn time. Oh, hey, I'm going to have to shift to a G-rated conversation in a second. I'm picking the kids up from the pool. A storm is coming in and it's closing early."

"No problem. You said to call when I came up for air, so I did."

"I'm glad you did, honey. I'm so happy that…" Beth paused to say hello to the kids and tell them who was on the phone. Melissa heard excited voices in the background. "I'm so happy to hear that your *research* is going so well. Hey, I'm putting you on speakerphone. The kids want to say hi."

Melissa asked Emma and her brother, Jonah, about their summer. In a verbal leapfrog they took turns telling her about their boating trips on the lake, soccer camp, and archery practice. Emma explained that she was taking very good care of Alex, her cat, as promised, and when Jonah said he wished summer would never end, it suddenly struck Melissa that her time in Colorado had its limits, too. She pushed the thought away.

Beth's voice rose above the fray. "When does your research partner come back?"

"About an hour or so." Melissa heard the crack and rumble of thunder through the phone.

"Good. All right, y'all. I'm going to have to end this conversation so I can drive safely. Melissa, I'm sure you have some things to do before you dive back into your research, and we've got to get home before the sky falls out. Let me know if you come across any earth-shattering discoveries."

Melissa pressed her fingers against her lips, trying not to laugh out loud at Beth's double entendres, and played along, promising to share the results of her research as they became available. After they said their good-byes, she stretched out on the couch to ponder exactly how she'd like to greet Sula when she returned.

Seated in the back seat of a sporty black Audi sedan, Sula texted Kimbrel Smith, the assistant regional director she'd be meeting with momentarily, to tell her she was running late. She wiped a bead of sweat from her forehead. Lingering over breakfast with Melissa had her in a mad scramble putting on her clothes and looking for her missing cell phone. She knew she had turned the ringer off last night, so Melissa's offer to call her phone was no help. Fortunately, Melissa finally found it wedged between the sofa cushions. It must have fallen out of her back pocket when she was sitting on the edge of it last night. She had grabbed the phone and accepted Melissa's quick kiss before dashing out of the hotel to find her car and the driver, a middle-aged man with short hair graying at the temples, waiting for her. The day was heating up, the glass, sandstone, and concrete all intensifying the sun's effect. Heading away from downtown, toward the suburb of Lakewood, she stared out the window from the cool back seat of the car, not really looking at the passing buildings. She was glad the driver didn't seem interested in conversation, as the silence allowed her to savor memories of last night. Now that she had a moment to herself, she realized just how profoundly satisfying sex with Melissa was, and she wanted more. Just the thought of it sent a rippling tingle through her body that settled between her legs and made her breath catch in her throat. It wasn't just sex: she wanted more time with Melissa. She simply liked being with her and marveled at the way their conversations ranged across a vast array of topics. Melissa was smart and knowledgeable, but she wasn't stuffy or arrogant; she was fun and playful. Melissa stimulated her as much intellectually as physically. They were a good match. The thought reverberated in her mind. No lover had ever prompted these kinds of thoughts. This was a new experience.

Sula had dated while she was in college, but she'd never allowed herself to get too close to anyone and had developed a reputation for being cold or indifferent. The reality was far from the truth. She was just scared of revealing too much about herself. For as long as she could remember, her parents, grandparents, and older relatives had reminded her that revealing what she was to anyone who wasn't family or a close friend of the family, which was code for someone trusted who knew, like Betty, was dangerous. It was easy enough to hide in plain sight. By the time she was twelve, she was in full control of her shifts, and being a wildlife-biology major in college, she could take off for a long day hike or for the weekend to wander the woods by herself when she needed the release and stimulation that being in fur provided. And no one thought it too unusual, except her girlfriends, who didn't understand why they were never invited along. Inevitably, their feelings shifted from hurt to anger, and once that happened, as Sula had learned repeatedly, the relationship was short-lived.

After graduation, she kept her sexual encounters casual and always a safe distance from home. She had occasional opportunities when she traveled for fellowships and certifications after college, for the conservancy when she took a full-time position there, and during family gatherings in New York and Norway. It was easy enough to take advantage of a layover in a city, go to a club and get carried away by the energy of the music and dancing, to pretend for a night that she was the same as everyone else.

But Sula never felt good the morning after, and she engaged in her indulgences, as she thought of them, with increasingly less frequency than she had in her 20s. Even though she was honest about her intentions, or lack thereof, with her partners, she knew she was purposefully avoiding emotional intimacy with another woman and that she used momentary physical connections to relieve temporary aching needs. But she'd never met anyone like Melissa before now. Melissa with the sparkling green eyes and warm, golden hair, whom she had nicknamed Goldilocks and who, in turn, called her Bear. She absolutely loved hearing her say that, though she knew Melissa couldn't really comprehend the truth of the nickname.

An idea struck her. She wanted to discount it, but she couldn't. What if Melissa did know it somehow, unconsciously? And what would happen if that knowing rose to the level of consciousness? Sula could see only two possibilities: she'd either accept her for who she was or she'd run in terror. The thought of Melissa running from her broke her heart.

Her instinctual pull toward Melissa had initially terrified her, but being with her felt so natural, and now, the dreaded morning after, she felt surprisingly good. Her fears had dissipated, though anxiety born from not knowing what came next gnawed at her. Her mother had always told her that someday she'd meet someone who would be "the one," explaining that she'd feel it in her bones. Sula had never understood what she meant until now.

She suddenly wanted to talk with her mother, but she and her father were on a research vessel somewhere off the coast of Svalbard. They had access to a satellite connection, but time on the boat was valuable, so their conversations were rationed and scheduled. She wasn't due to talk with them for another week.

The driver cocked his head, the movement pulling Sula from her thoughts. She made eye contact with him by his reflection in the rearview mirror. He might have spoken, but she was so lost in thought, she wasn't sure. "I'm sorry. Did you say something?"

"Yes. We've arrived at your destination." The driver appeared emotionless, which was hard not to perceive as irritation. She looked around, realizing that the car had stopped and they were in a parking lot. He turned and handed Sula a business card. "Text me at this number when you're ready, and I'll be here within five minutes."

Sula thanked him and took the card. When she unclipped her seat belt, the driver did the same. "No need to open the door for me, thank you." The driver seemed relieved, the first emotion he had shown since picking her up.

Clutching her messenger bag, Sula stood on the curb outside a nondescript five-story concrete cube of an office building, the tallest structure in an area surrounded by strip malls. It was about the least inspiring design she could imagine for an agency devoted to conservation of the natural world. She certainly didn't know as much about architecture as Melissa, but she had learned a lot when she worked with the architects designing the conservancy visitors' center. She had needed the architects to guide her, but she knew going into the project that she wanted a building that reflected the history of the region and evoked a feeling of looking forward toward the future. This building in front of her seemed to communicate bureaucracy. And now that she thought of it, that was probably completely appropriate.

Following the directions Kimbrel had sent, Sula walked through the amber glass double doors, down a long hall of panels with images of the National Wildlife Preserves in the eight states in the region the office served. As she pressed the elevator button, she forced herself to redirect her thoughts, mentally rehearsing her pitch. Otherwise it was so very easy to think of nothing else but Melissa's tender skin and sweet lips.

Sula found Kimbrel's office on the third floor and introduced herself to the woman seated at the desk in the reception area. The room was neat, but spartan, with sturdy wood furniture that looked like it had been in use for decades and decorated with striking photographs, iconic views of the landscapes found in the states the Mountain-Prairie Region office served—wide, grassy plains, mountains, and arid desert rock formations. Kimbrel walked in, large water bottle in hand, and introduced herself. Wearing a tan polo shirt embroidered with the USFWS logo and forest-green pants, she was a lithe, middle-aged woman with blond hair, streaked with white, and styled in a fashionable, short cut. She had a firm handshake and moved like someone who had been fit her entire life. She led Sula to a small conference room and regarded her with blunt directness, as if she were the only person in the room. But she wasn't. Kimbrel had invited three others: a ruggedly handsome man in his forties, a biologist named Ben; a thirtysomething woman named Eva, a community project manager who was cute in a wholesome girl-next-door way; and Tyler, a bright-eyed grad-student intern.

Sula had thought she'd have to pitch her idea about expanding her program and knew hers wasn't the only one out there, but she was certain it was supported with good data and hoped she could make it work in other places, as well. As it turned out, they were very enthusiastic about her ambition, especially as it aligned with their national initiative to increase community engagement. Kimbrel cut to the chase, and the meeting quickly turned into a brainstorming session. By the time it concluded forty-five minutes later, Sula had a list of names of people to contact in several states and a prioritized list of places that might be good places to start.

Before she left, Sula brought up a topic on a different subject, something that had been bothering her. She asked about Wildlife Services, and before she could finish her sentence, everyone at the table looked toward Kimbrel. Sula immediately realized she had touched a nerve.

Kimbrel frowned slightly and then smiled wincingly. "You know, Sula, that they aren't within this agency. We're part of the Department of the Interior, and they come under the Department of Agriculture. How should I put it? We're by no means perfect, but we have very different missions. Ours is to conserve for now and the future, and theirs…well, they phrase their mission in carefully worded language, but let's just say they tend to see nature as a competitor that they must control in order for humanity to survive."

Kimbrel appeared to have no love for Wildlife Services, but sensing her reluctance to talk, Sula knew she had stepped into an uncomfortable, perhaps even controversial topic and felt the need to offer a reasonable explanation for her inquiry. "Well, I only ask because someone from Wildlife Services seems to be trapping for mountain lion in Buckhorn, and who knows what else in the area. I'm told that they prefer to fly under the radar, and I worry that their actions could adversely impact our bears. I'd hate to see an innocent bear get caught in one of those snare traps."

"I understand your concern," Kimbrel said flatly. "Bad things happen when there's a lack of transparency."

Sula looked at the others around the table. Ben seemed suddenly interested at his notepad, Tyler stared into her coffee cup, and Eva glared at Sula with barely masked anger but remained silent. Sula understood that one federal agent wouldn't say anything critical about another agency, at least not in this room. She wasn't exactly sure why she'd mentioned it in the first place, other than it was weighing on her mind. Maybe she thought any scrap of information she could glean might be useful.

Sula deftly shifted the conversation and graciously thanked them for their time, extending offers of hospitality should they ever find themselves in the vicinity of Buckhorn. They all commented on how beautiful the area was and that they had heard good things about the visitors' center and would love to someday visit. The pall that her question about Wildlife Services seemed to have cast lifted, and she left the meeting feeling good.

She texted the driver before she got on the elevator and, when she stepped out on the ground floor, was surprised to be greeted by Eva, breathing heavily as if she had just run down the stairs.

"Hey," Sula said. "Are you okay?"

"Yeah," Eva said, putting a hand on her rib cage and taking a deep breath. "I need to get out of the office more and get some exercise."

Sula laughed. "Were you looking for me?"

"Yeah, I just…um, I just wanted to tell you to be careful with Wildlife Services."

Sula narrowed her eyes. "Careful in what way?"

The anger on Eva's face that Sula had seen in the conference room returned. "They're using M-44s."

"Cyanide bombs?" Sula knew exactly what they were. Often called "coyote getters," they were spring-loaded cyanide capsules staked into the ground and baited so that when an animal grabbed and pulled, they sprayed sodium cyanide crystals into its mouth. Mixed with saliva, the crystals produced a toxic gas that caused a horrific death akin to strangulation. "Those are supposed to be restricted on public lands in this state."

"Yes, they are. They can be used on private lands only by request of the landowner, but I've been hearing that some of their agents are using them wherever they want to. They see it as a waste of good management tools not to use them. They don't have much oversight in the field, so they do what they want."

"Bastards."

"I'd call them something else," Eva said dryly. "Anyway, I just wanted you to know that. Off the record, of course."

"Of course."

"I hope you're not dealing with someone like that."

"Me, too." The possibility made her so angry, if she were in fur she'd have roared and torn something up just because she could. That wasn't an option, and if it were, she certainly would have scared poor Eva, so she thanked her politely instead and excused herself by saying she had a ride waiting for her.

The shiny black Audi pulled up to the curb near the entrance, and Sula got in. The driver, still professionally detached, asked her if she was heading back to the hotel. Sula said yes, and the drive back was like the ride out, quiet with no conversation required. By the time she reached the hotel room on the ninth floor, she felt better, the anger coursing through her replaced with anticipation at seeing Melissa again. The realization that she'd get to spend another day with her traveling back to Buckhorn made her feel surprisingly light.

Entering the hotel room, she called out but didn't hear a reply. Music was playing, and Sula thought perhaps Melissa didn't hear her. She closed the door, and when she turned around, she noticed a yellow wrapper, one of her honey candies, on the floor. It must have fallen out of her bag when she rushed out earlier that morning. She bent down to pick it up and noticed another candy a few feet in front of her, and another one in front of that. In fact, a trail of them led into the sitting room and then veered to the left. She followed the trail, picking up each candy as they drew her to the bedroom door. Sula laughed softly at Melissa's playful ploy to entice her into the room, which was dark and the door ajar.

"Goldie, you in there?" No response. Puzzled, Sula pushed the door open and stepped into the dark room. White flashed in her peripheral vision, and something soft hit her. Sula caught the scent of Melissa's perfume and heard her muffled laughter through the bath towel that, apparently, had been tossed over her head. She responded instinctively, pawing at the towel, but then dropped her hands to her sides. "Have I just been trapped?"

"Yep." Melissa bunched up the towel and slid it down behind her head and neck. She stretched up and kissed her on the end of her nose.

As her eyes adjusted to the low light of the room, Sula discovered that Melissa was wearing nothing but a wicked grin. "I suppose it would be futile to resist, wouldn't it?"

"Mm-hmm. I got you, Bear." Melissa tugged the towel, and Sula knew only a fool would resist following her into the bed.

CHAPTER NINETEEN

Sitting on Sula's porch, Melissa ate a slice of pizza left over from their dinner the night before and soaked up the view. It was a picture-perfect day, though some dark-gray clouds were beginning to creep over the peaks. It was sunny and warm now, during her lunch break, but another afternoon storm seemed possible in a few hours. She wasn't sure which she liked better, the energy of a thunderstorm when it blew in or the cool air, refreshed and sweetened, after it had passed.

She assumed the characteristic scent that infused the air after the rain must come from a certain mountain plant, but when she said something about it to Sula as they sat together on the porch swing after the thunderstorm the night before, Sula explained that it was a complex mix. She directed Melissa to close her eyes and take slow deep breaths through her nostrils, to focus on separating out the scents. Melissa tried, but unable to identify anything beyond pine and sage, she gave up. Opening her eyes, she watched as Sula lifted her chin, sniffed the air, and called out a litany of trees, plants, flowers…and wet dirt. Melissa laughed, but Sula had assured her that the force of the rain hitting the ground caused certain bacterial spores to erupt into the air and that they smelled very good.

Melissa was learning so many interesting things from Sula, just as she was learning so much from Sula's collection of paintings. Sula had given her free run of the house to study the paintings while she was at work, and Melissa was taking full advantage of the opportunity. With Sula's permission, and cotton gloves purchased from the local hardware store, she was methodically removing the paintings from the walls one by one and placing them on the oak table in the dining room that she covered with a cotton blanket to protect both it and the works of art. The dining room had become her study for examining and documenting them.

She took photos with her camera for reference later, when she wouldn't be able to look directly at the paintings. In her notebook, she wrote down observations about the subject matter and the physical condition of each one, knowing she'd later create a spreadsheet on her laptop and enter the notes and add photographs. At this stage, she preferred to write by hand. Translating thoughts to words slowed her down, giving her time to digest what she was seeing.

On the table now lay the painting from the billiard room, an autumn landscape that exploded with green, yellow, orange, and rusty red. She was done with it but had decided to take a lunch break before putting it back on the wall. Enjoying the porch with its magnificent view, she took a sip of the unusual and refreshing iced tea Sula had made from mint and pine needles and stretched her bare legs out into a beam of sunlight cutting across the porch. She admired the tan she'd acquired since her arrival. It was such a luxury to be outdoors without the oppressive Southern humidity, swarms of mosquitoes, and always having to be on the lookout for fire ants, whose painful, venomous stings itched for days.

She took another bite of pizza and continued watching the clouds, marveling at their mysterious beauty. They were such impossible things, seeming to exist in two states simultaneously, expanding and contracting at the same time. Suddenly something silky rubbed up against her leg. She looked down to find Tawny staring at her, the cat's green eyes focused and piercing.

"Cats don't eat pizza," Melissa admonished the cat in a gentle voice. The sweet orange-and-gray tabby looked at her as if to say, "But we do eat cheese." Spotty, her sibling, was curled up, sleeping soundly on the cushion of a chair across the porch. Melissa pinched a piece of cheese from what remained of her slice and held it out. "Shh. Don't tell your sister."

Tawny delicately took the morsel from her fingers and gave it a little shake before eating it. Even when their food wasn't alive, cats still "killed" it; some wild instincts ran deep. Melissa ate the remaining bit of pizza, brushed the crumbs off her lap, and rubbed the cat between her ears. Tawny purred and bumped her head against her hand. Missing her own cat, Melissa was glad for the company of Sula's, but she suspected that Alex might not be missing her that much in return. Every few days she received a new photo of him from Beth, usually sleeping in a cute position on the bed, the sofa, in a patch of sunlight, or Emma's lap.

Melissa stood and stretched to relieve the knot of tension that had formed in her neck and shoulders during the morning. Going back into the house, she was greeted by the subtle resinous scent that the wood of the house emanated. Like the air after a rainstorm, the scent was deeply satisfying. With a glance at the cuckoo clock as she walked through the great room, she estimated that she had just enough time to return the autumn scene to the billiard room and then take down, assess, and photograph one more before Sula returned from work.

After hanging the painting back on the wall above the dancing bear, she paused to regard the sculpture and put her hand on it with guilty pleasure. She could never touch it like this in a museum. Its black surface was cool and smooth as glass. She ran her fingers along the curve of the bear's upstretched arm, over its head, down the length of its back, and along the underside of its leg. She mused on how touching was another way of knowing. While keen observation revealed so much, touch allowed for a different kind of comprehension. Melissa cocked her head, a habit when she was deep in thought, and wondered how she might describe this type of knowing in words. Embodied observation, perhaps? She liked the sound of those words together and reminded herself to write the phrase in her journal when she returned to the dining room. Her thoughts drifted from academic to erotic as she considered how, in the past few nights, she was certainly getting to know Sula's body by touch...as well as her senses of sight, smell, and taste.

Reluctantly, Melissa pulled herself from her reverie and considered which painting she would examine next. Delicious memories of Sula unclothed and undulating with pleasure in the bed upstairs reminded her of the moonlit winter scene of aspen trees and snow hanging above the headboard. Winter came after autumn, didn't it? It seemed a logical choice.

The bedroom, located in a corner of the second floor, was cozy rather than spacious. The modest size was probably easier to keep warm. A cast-iron stove in the rock-lined corner of the room suggested that extra heat was needed on a cold winter's night. The ceiling and exterior walls in the room were exposed, and the logs, like those in the rest of the house, had darkened with age, though the room was brightened by the pale, warm yellow of the plastered and painted interior walls.

A tall dresser and low chest of drawers evidenced Sula's preference for Arts and Crafts style furniture, but the bedstead, made from aspen logs, was rustic. Beautifully crafted, it wasn't heavy looking like ones she'd seen before. The headboard and footboard of the large bed were comprised of narrow branches set into a frame at irregular angles so that they resembled a tangle of tree branches. In fact, she had joked with Sula that morning that she felt like she was sleeping in a tree house. Sula had replied sleepily, saying that, if they were actually in a tree house, she would have pulled up the ladder to keep her in bed a while longer.

Melissa crawled across the bed in order to get to the painting, which seemed to stir up their commingled scents. She smiled to herself, enjoying the intoxicating fragrance, as she reached up and lifted the painting from the wall. Once it was in her hands, she noticed that it was backed with paper. That was unusual, as all the other paintings in the house so far had exposed backs. She grasped it carefully, the way she had been taught many years ago in a museum-methods class in grad school. With a firm grip on opposite corners of the frame, she held the painting out in front of her and made her way slowly down the stairs, one cautious step at a time. She was almost to the bottom when the heel of her sandal caught on the edge of the last stair and she pitched forward, nearly falling. Catching herself, she jerked back sharply to regain her balance, and when she did, she heard a pop. Afraid she might have cracked a joint in the frame or dislodged a key—one of the small wedges of wood tapped into the corners of the stretcher frame used to tighten the canvas—she stood motionless, scrutinizing the frame and the painting's surface for any obvious sign of damage before taking it to the dining room.

She placed it gently on the padded table and took her time with it, allowing her eyes to roam over the view of a stand of aspen trees in heavy snow. The paint was thick, and the wide brushstrokes were so masterfully fluid and confident, Melissa easily visualized the movements of the artist's hand. The perspective, like many of her paintings, Melissa realized, was from a low point of view, and it gave her a sense of being in the grove rather than gazing at it from a distance. The painting of white trees in the snow was stark, but mesmerizing. The narrow tree trunks, with their characteristic dark eye-like patterns in the cool white bark, created strong vertical elements. The moon, though not visible in the sky, must have been full and either rising or setting as the trees cast bluish diagonal shadows that pulled the eye to the left. Melissa considered the way Ursula used linear perspective: the tree's shadows were orthogonals—implied lines that met up at a single vanishing point on the horizon line—which in this case was the dark area in the distance where the aspen grove seemed to end and the coniferous forest began.

Unlike the other paintings in the house, this one contained figures. Much like her painting at home, it featured a woman and a bear, but the positions were reversed. A woman in a white dress stood among the aspens in the middle ground, and looming large in the foreground was a big brown bear watching her. These figures were articulated. They looked effortlessly painted, but that wasn't an easy thing to do. Such a skill came from experience. Melissa began to wonder how many of Ursula's paintings included figures and if they would all be women and bears. Ursula, like Sula and her parents, also seemed to have had an affinity for bears; perhaps it was a familial tradition passed down the generations.

Melissa photographed the painting, and when turning it over to inspect the back, she heard what sounded like something sliding from one side to the other. Mindful to document the painting's condition as found, she resisted the impulse to immediately remove the dust cover on the back. The paper backing along the upper edge and right corner seemed to have been re-glued because the paper wasn't quite as tight there as on the other edges. A second layer of glue seemed to have caused the paper to buckle; either too much or a different kind had been used. Perhaps a repair had been made and the damaged area weakened as a result. Melissa documented the painting's condition with more photos, and then, with her Swiss Army knife, she carefully removed the backing.

What was inside came as a surprise. Instead of a loose wooden wedge, she found a thin bundle of envelopes tied with black silk ribbon. One corner of the frame was missing one of the keys, and normally two wedges were tapped in at right angles to each other. The envelopes must have been tucked into the narrow space between the remaining key and the back of the canvas and had come loose when she tripped and jerked the painting.

She lifted them out with a gloved hand and turned them over. She inhaled sharply, nearly dropping them when she saw a name and address on the front of the top envelope. Written in a beautifully elegant and fluid script was her great-grandmother's name.

Sula checked the time. It was nearing two o'clock. Her parents would be calling her soon for their video chat. Although they had internet access and email on the research vessel, they scheduled real-time conversations around their working schedules and when broadband was available. Sometimes, when the boat was moving in a direction that put the boom of the large crane in between the satellite dish and the signal, they had to wait until the ship changed its heading to get a better connection. Rather than sit in her office staring at the computer screen, Sula went to the break room for a cup of coffee and then to the front office looking for Anna.

"Hey, Anna?"

"Yeah, Boss?" Anna, grinning, spun around in her chair.

"I'm going to talk with my parents in a bit. I'll be unavailable for the next half hour or so."

"Okay." The smile on Anna's face remained unchanged.

Sula started to walk away but then stopped and turned. "Am I missing something? Why are you smiling like that?"

"I'm a happy employee?"

Sula narrowed her eyes at Anna suspiciously. "I'm glad to hear that, but you usually don't smile like a Cheshire cat."

"I'm so happy for you!"

"Why?" Sula was puzzled.

"You've been kind of funny ever since you got back from Denver, real quiet and smiling at nothing. Like, a lot." Anna paused. "I went to lunch at the diner today and ran into Betty and Lars. Betty asked how you were doing, and I told her about how you were acting. She said it probably had something to do with you and Melissa, and that explained why you hadn't called her." Anne's smile got bigger. "I put two and two together. You're seeing her, aren't you?"

Sula rolled her eyes and made an exasperated sound.

"I knew it!" Anna's smile shifted to a look of concern. "Are you mad at me, Boss? For discussing this with Betty?"

"No, not at all. Betty's sneaky. I'm sure she knew you'd talk to me about your conversation." In truth, Sula really had been in a daze while working in the office recently, and then, spending her time with Melissa in the evenings, she'd honestly forgotten to return Betty's call. She was distracted and running a little short on sleep, not that she was complaining.

"She seems really nice," Anna said softly. "She's pretty, too."

"Yeah, she is." Sula wasn't sure what else to say. She glanced at her watch. "Look, I've got to catch that call from my parents."

"Okay." Anna spun back around in her chair to face her computer, waving her hand behind her head. "Tell your folks I said hi."

"I will." Sula laughed softly to herself, thinking about Betty's sly ways, as she walked down the hall. She closed her office door, something she rarely did, and the staff knew it meant she was not to be disturbed. She took her laptop to the couch and logged into her Skype account. Sipping her coffee, she stared out the window. Clouds were building in the distance, foreshadowing another afternoon thunderstorm. The burbling ringtone alerted her to the incoming call, and when it connected, her smiling parents abruptly appeared on-screen. As usual, they were in their small wood-paneled cabin, with cool arctic light streaming through the rounded windows behind them. They looked a little weather-beaten, but happy. Her mother's gray hair was tousled, by the sea wind, no doubt. Sula had inherited her dark hair color from her mother, and she imagined that, in a few decades, hers would be similarly streaked with white. The texture of her hair came from her father, who had recently trimmed his short and grown a beard. It suited him, made him look more handsome somehow. They greeted each other with enthusiasm, Sula commenting on how it was still light there, even though it was ten o'clock at night, and asked how things were going.

"It's been great." Sula's father, Charles, spoke first. "Your mom's gotten to observe quite a few bears, and we've spent the past few days helping the marine scientists on board gather data. Interesting stuff. We're heading back to Longyearbyen now."

Longyearbyen, the northernmost town in the world, was the largest in Svalbard, with a population of about two thousand people. Situated in a treeless basin between rugged mountains and the edge of a fjord, it had begun as a mining community around the turn of the twentieth century. Now it was associated more with research scientists, nature tourism, and the global seed vault. Sula had never been there, but her parents said the views of the northern lights were spectacular and polar-bear sightings were frequent.

"We'll be back just in time for your father's wildflowers," Sula's mom, Ingrid, interjected. Charles was a botanist, and since they'd been spending so much time in Scandinavia, he'd developed a deep interest in the miniscule tundra plants and flowers that carpeted the ground in that region. With no trees or shrubs, the landscape seemed barren only at a distance.

"Yeah, and I'm talking to a curator at the Svalbard Museum. I've got him interested in a new wildflower display that addresses the impact of climate change."

"That's great, Dad."

Ingrid leaned closer to the camera, crowding out her father. "So…
we got your message about Melissa."

Charles put his hand on his wife's shoulder, pulling her back so
she wasn't blocking his view. He smiled, but the crease in the corners
of his eyes expressed concern. "Yeah. Tell us more about this Melissa."

And Sula did. In a rush of words, she related in greater detail who
Melissa was and why she was in Buckhorn for the summer. Without
going into intimate details, she also explained that they had gone to
Denver and had been spending a lot of time together.

"And you said she's at your house right now looking at paintings?"
Charles asked.

"Yes."

"And you're not there?" Charles briefly glanced sideways at
Ingrid. "You must trust her."

"Of course I do, or I wouldn't let her be there by herself."

Charles scratched his bearded chin and squinted, the lines in his
forehead deepening.

"What?"

"We've never seen you this excited about someone before," Ingrid
said.

"At least not in a long time. Since college, maybe," her father
added. "You must have strong feelings for this woman."

"Yes, I do." Sula resisted laughing. That was an understatement.

Her mother smiled at her tenderly. "Then I'm happy for you,
Sula."

Charles raised his eyebrows at Ingrid, who responded by elbowing
him gently, prompting him to agree with her. "We both are. I know we
don't need to remind you to—"

"Be cautious. Yes, Dad. I know that." Sula's happy exuberance
deflated suddenly, and she felt feel like a teenager again. "I'm always
cautious. You and everyone else in the family taught me well."

"I didn't mean to imply you were being careless," Charles said.
"I'm processing my observations here, Sula. You've never brought
anyone home before, not that I know of, anyway."

"You're right. I haven't. Melissa is…I don't know how to explain
it. She's different from anyone I've ever met."

"You know," Ingrid said slowly, drawing out the words. "Our
family, my side of the family, I mean, has a knack for knowing who the
special ones are."

Sula understood that her mother was being purposefully ambiguous, given that they were on an unencrypted video chat link. When she said "my family," she really meant her matrilineal, bear-shifting family. Her father was one of the "special ones," a regular man who happened to fall in love with a woman who could turn into a bear and who hadn't run screaming when he found out. At least she thought he hadn't. She really didn't know how he'd first responded to learning about her mother.

"How did you know Dad was a special one?"

Charles erupted in nervous laughter and leaned back in his chair. "Sorry. I was just thinking that it feels like we're having the conversation about the birds and the bees."

"You know, you and I never did have that conversation." Sula was teasing.

"We never needed to. You always liked girls."

"No." Ingrid looked sharply at her husband. "*You* didn't have the conversation with Sula, but I did. She still needed to know."

Sula nodded.

"Oh." Charles looked taken aback. "I didn't realize that."

"Yeah. I know. You were too happy feeling off the hook to give it any more thought." Ingrid laughed and shifted her focus back to Sula. "You want to know how I knew I could tell your father?"

"Yes."

"I just knew," Ingrid said flatly.

"That's it? That's all the advice you're going to give me?"

"Are you looking for advice about knowing if Melissa's the one?" Charles blinked in surprise. "Is that what you're asking?"

"Of course that's what she's asking, darling." Ingrid shook her head and patted his hand. "I think our Sula's fallen in love."

"Wait a minute. I didn't say anything about being in love," Sula said quickly, though she wasn't being entirely truthful with her parents. She was experiencing something that she could only imagine was love. When she thought of Melissa, which was all the time, she felt a little woozy and like her heart had expanded somehow and was pushing, almost painfully sometimes, against everything inside her. Still, she wasn't quite ready to confess her feelings to anyone—not to Melissa, nor her parents. "I was just asking how you knew when you could have, you know, *the conversation,* with someone."

"I think what your mom is trying to say is that you don't even consider this question unless love is involved. Love makes you want to share that confidence," Charles said.

"How did Mom tell you?"

Charles took a deep breath and squared his shoulders. "We were on a summer backpacking trip in the Cascades, and I had carried her engagement ring with me, trying to be quite the romantic. We found a place to camp near a small waterfall with a pool deep enough to swim in. It was marvelous, and I felt like we were the only two people in the world. A lot of wildlife was in the area, and all day I had been talking about what animal I wished I could turn into, although I couldn't settle on a single one. One minute it was a trout, and the next it was, oh, I don't know, a deer, or something."

"He had good reasons for each of them," Ingrid said.

"I'm glad you thought so." Charles beamed. "I kept asking your mother what animal she'd be if she could be anything other than human, and every time she'd reply, 'A bear.' I thought it was funny that she didn't want to be anything else but a bear and figured she was just being silly. That night, after dinner when we were sitting by the fire, I presented her with the ring and asked her to marry me. I believed she'd say yes immediately, but instead she told me I had to know something important about her and that what she was about to reveal could end our relationship, but she could not, and would not, deceive me any further."

"Wow…"

"Wow is right. She prepared me the best she could, but until I saw her…saw the other side of her, as it were…I thought she was just teasing, and I didn't understand why. It was very confusing."

"And how did you react when you saw this 'new side' of Mom?" Sula watched her mother turn and look at her father with an inquisitive expression.

"What do you think?" Charles laughed. "I thought I'd lost my damn mind! Or accidentally eaten a psychotropic mushroom or something."

"But you didn't freak out?"

"It was a shock, no doubt about that. But once I realized I wasn't hallucinating and that I wasn't in any danger, I was just in awe. And in love. My whole understanding of the world had changed in a flash, but once I realized that my love for your mother had not…" Charles smiled at Ingrid tenderly, and her expression mirrored his. "I knew everything would be okay. I was honored by receiving your mother's complete trust," he paused to chuckle, "in addition to her hand in marriage."

"I can't believe you've never told me this story."

"You've never asked before," Ingrid said.

"That's true. I haven't." Sula took a sip of her coffee, which had become tepid. She set the cup back down on the table next to the laptop.

"If you're going to talk to her about it, think about doing it sooner rather than later," Ingrid said as the image on the screen pixelated and the sound quality faltered. "It just gets harder the longer you wait."

"Not too soon," Sula said. "Talking about it right before her parents arrive probably isn't a good idea, especially if it doesn't go well."

"Her parents are coming?" Charles asked.

"Yeah. Her father's into fly-fishing."

"You know all the good fishing spots. He'll be impressed with you," Ingrid said.

"I don't expect to meet them."

"Sula, if Melissa is as serious about you as you are about her, she'll want to introduce you to her parents," Charles said with a knowing look.

"Oh…" Thunder rumbled in the distance.

"Don't worry, sweetheart. They'll love you," Ingrid said reassuringly.

"You're biased, Mom."

"I'm a scientist, remember? I can have personal opinions *and* be objective. Melissa sounds very nice, and smart, too. If you've invited her this far into your life, that is more significant than you seem to realize. I look forward to meeting her. And if her parents are anything like their daughter, I'm sure they'll like you."

"I guess I'll be finding that out soon."

Her father squinted and spoke loudly. "Sula, we're having a hard time hearing you. I think our call might drop."

"Okay. I love you both." Sula smiled at them, but it was hard to tell if they were smiling back. The picture had frozen, and their voices sounded tinny and fractured, but she was pretty sure they had said they loved her back. With a *blip*, the call ended.

It was good to see her parents instead of just hear their voices or read their messages. And while she felt comforted and reassured by talking with them, she felt restless. All the conversation about Melissa made her curious about what she was doing right now. She stared at her desk and confirmed that she didn't have anything pressing to complete before the end of the day. She closed the laptop and put it in her messenger bag. Then she left the office quickly, pausing just long enough at Anna's desk to tell her she'd be out the rest of the afternoon, but not long enough for her to ask any probing questions.

As she drove home, the sky darkened, and the rain came in with strong, gusty wind. Big, fat raindrops pelted the windshield, and by the time she pulled up next to Melissa's car in front of her house, it had become a heavy downpour. She ran through it, bounding up the stairs to the protection of the porch. Not wanting to startle her since she was home early, she called out Melissa's name as she pushed open the front door. The sky flashed again, and a near instantaneous crack of thunder rattled the windows.

To Sula's surprise and growing concern, Melissa was nowhere to be found. The painting that hung in her bedroom was on the dining-room table, with Melissa's notebooks and camera next to it. Her purse lay on a chair in the living room. Thinking she might be taking a nap, Sula went upstairs and quietly peeked into her bedroom. Finding it empty, she checked each of the guest rooms. Nothing. Other than an empty glass in the sink in the kitchen, she couldn't find a trace of Melissa anywhere in the house.

CHAPTER TWENTY

Sula grabbed her raincoat off the hook by the back door and put it on, pulling the hood over her head as she went out into the heavy downpour. She walked the perimeter of the house looking for Melissa or signs of her presence. Logic dictated that if her car was here, the front door unlocked, and she wasn't inside the house, she must be somewhere outside.

Sula began to worry that Melissa had gone out and been caught in the storm or, worse, had been too near a lightning strike. The front of the storm had been on top of the valley when she drove up to the house, and several strikes had been so close that, when she opened the door of her truck, she smelled the sweet, metallic scent of ozone in the air.

After completing a quick loop around the house, she stood below the porch stairs, the rain cascading off the front of the jacket's hood, and scanned the meadow, wishing she could shift into ursine form. She could make a fast shift when necessary, though it usually left her with a dull, lingering headache when she returned to her two-legged self, but with the eyes and nose of a bear, she could perceive movement and patterns with more clarity, and her sense of smell, though better than the average person's, was more finely attuned when she was in fur. Even in this downpour that obscured her vision, she'd likely be able to catch a whiff of a scent that would at least point her in the right direction.

Although the rain continued unabated, the sound of thunder rolled and rumbled from farther down the valley, and a nearby cloud-to-ground strike was still possible. Electrical storms in the high country were dangerous, and far too many people underestimated them. More fearful of large predators like bears and mountain lions, they lost sight of the fact that they were much more likely to be injured by lightning than attacked by some big animal.

Sula put her hands on her hips, scowling at the rain as she wondered where Melissa could be. She might have gone up the hill behind the house, or she could have walked down into the meadow. Sula felt compelled to move down, not up. She knew Melissa enjoyed the view from the porch, as she'd commented more than once that she'd like to take a walk across the meadow. Sula had said she'd go with her, but she hadn't yet made good on her promise—they were easily and wonderfully sidetracked; all conversations seemed to lead upstairs to her cozy bed. A rivulet of cold water rolled down her nose as she turned toward the meadow. If Melissa had decided to take a stroll across it this afternoon by herself, she had certainly chosen the wrong day.

Sula headed downhill, wincing as the rain pelted her face. The possibility that Melissa might have found shelter in the old barn at the meadow's edge struck her suddenly. She tugged the hood of her jacket forward and marched toward the old building. Framed with logs and sheathed with wide planks that were likely milled from trees felled on the property, it had been constructed to store grass hay, as well as to house horses and probably a milk cow or two. Since Sula didn't put up hay or keep large animals—the two cats were her only pets—she used it for a workshop and to store a small tractor. She walked around to the side door and grasped the handle of the side door, pulling it open. The lights inside were on.

"Melissa? You in here?"

"Sula! Over here."

Sula pushed the hood of her jacket back and looked around. "Oh, there you are…" She laughed at the unexpected sight in front of her. "Going somewhere?"

Melissa, her hair wet and plastered against her head and neck, was seated on the old tractor parked at the far end of the barn. She waved and climbed down off the weather-beaten Case, its trademark bright-orange paint having long ago faded to its current pale version of the original. Her expression was sheepish. "This rain wasn't letting up, and that was the only place to sit."

"You could have found some folding chairs in the workshop." Sula pointed to one of the converted stalls.

"I should have snooped around, then." Melissa laughed and glanced at the tractor's contoured metal seat. "Who ever thought that was a good design? That seat isn't very comfortable."

"It's functional," Sula said with a grin. She was glad to have found Melissa safe and not lightning-struck out in the field. "You weren't in the house, and I thought maybe you went for a walk and got caught in the storm. I figured I'd better come looking for you."

"That's *exactly* what happened." Melissa crossed her arms. Her T-shirt and shorts were soaked through, and her leg was smeared with black grease that must have come from the tractor. "I'm sorry I worried you."

"I'm just glad you're in here and not out there." Sula gestured with a hooked thumb toward the door. "Geez, you're soaked." Sula took her jacket off, put it over Melissa's shoulders, and gave her a tender kiss on the forehead. "Let's get you back to the house and warmed up."

"But you'll get wet." Melissa started to remove the jacket. "I'm *already* wet."

"Keep it on." Sula slid the jacket back over her shoulders. "More important, I'm warm, and you're not. Believe it or not, you can get hypothermia in this temperature." Thunder rumbled outside, punctuating Sula's words. "The worst of the storm has passed. Let's get back up to the house, and I'll make you a hot cup of tea."

Melissa didn't protest. When they stepped outside the barn, the rain was still coming down, but the sky had lightened considerably. By the time they made it up the hill and back into the house, Sula was equally drenched.

"Do you have some clothes here to change into?" Sula asked.

"Not anything clean. Just what I was wearing yesterday." Melissa clinched her arms against her torso and was now shivering visibly, the edges of her lips a little bluish. "I've got such a chill."

"Why don't you go upstairs and take a shower to warm up? I'll put the kettle on and then come up and find you something to wear."

Melissa nodded and practically ran up the stairs. Sula went into the kitchen, filled the kettle with fresh water, and set the burner to a low flame. When she got upstairs, steam was billowing into her bedroom from the partially open bathroom door. She leaned in and grabbed her towel off the hook on the back of the door, then quickly stripped off her wet work clothes and dried herself before putting on a T-shirt and a pair of jeans. She rummaged through her chest of drawers to find another pair and a soft flannel shirt for Melissa. They would be too big, but they'd suffice until she could wash and dry Melissa's clothes. Sula picked up the wet clothes off the floor, intending to take them downstairs to the laundry room, when Melissa sauntered out of the bathroom wrapped in a towel, hair dripping wet, skin pink from the heat of the water, and green eyes sparkling.

"Mmm…maybe I should warm *you* up," Melissa said when she saw Sula.

"Well, now that you mention it, I do feel a bit of a chill." Sula stepped forward, closing the distance between them.

"Poor baby," Melissa cooed, putting her hands on the edges of the towel, lifting the fabric. "I'm sure I could raise your temperature."

"I'm sure you could," Sula said in a low voice, her body instantly responding to Melissa's voice. A suggestive comment, a look, a touch... that was all it took for Sula to be consumed with desire. No woman ever had this kind of drawing power over her. Sula dropped the clothes with a wet thud by her feet, and just as she reached out to take Melissa into her arms, the teakettle downstairs began to whistle—a terrible, shrill sound, one designed not to be ignored. She grunted in frustration.

Melissa laughed and tucked the corner of the towel back in against her damp skin. "I'll take Earl Grey, if you have it."

"I do." Sula picked the clothes up off the floor again and moved toward the door, the shrieking kettle compelling her to rush downstairs. She nodded toward the bed. "I put some clothes out for you. I think they'll fit well enough."

"Thanks," Melissa said. "I'll be down in a flash. I have something you need to see."

"I can bring the tea up here." Sula paused in the doorway with a salacious grin. "You could show me here."

"I need to show you something about *a painting*," Melissa said with a laugh. "I'll show you more of me later. I promise."

"I'll hold you to it," Sula said and strode down the hall.

When Melissa came into the kitchen, Sula couldn't help but laugh out loud. Melissa had folded up the legs of the baggy jeans two turns, and the mossy-green flannel shirt could have been belted and worn as a dress. "That's a good color on you."

"At least the color fits." Melissa smiled as she finished rolling up the sleeves. "The rest of it, not so much. You won't have to worry about me ever borrowing your clothes."

"Aw, but you look so cute," Sula said.

"You think I'm cute?"

"Yes. Quite cute, in fact."

"You know, you've never told me that you find me attractive." Melissa raised her eyebrows.

"Oh...I figured it went without saying."

"Well, I've surmised that you do." Melissa's expression was

serious. "It's important to express things with words, too, you know. It feels good to hear them. Don't you like to be complimented?"

The thought made Sula uncomfortable. "I guess so."

"You don't sound very convincing."

"Well…I don't like it when too much attention is on me."

"You're funny, Sula." Melissa lifted the teabag out of her cup, squeezed it, and placed it on a shallow dish on the counter. "You're the director of a significant organization. You meet people all the time, pitch your programs, give presentations, yet you say you don't like to be in the spotlight."

"That's different. It's my job. It's the role I play."

"I get that. It's like teaching. I perform my role of professor, three shows a day."

"Yeah, something like that." Sula opened the refrigerator, pulled out a carton of milk, and set it on the counter.

"I think maybe you're an extroverted introvert."

"You're probably right." Sula opened a cabinet and heard Melissa inhale sharply behind her. She turned around. "What's wrong?"

Melissa pointed at the contents of the cabinet. "I have never seen so many jars of honey outside of a grocery store. How many do you have?"

"I don't know, exactly…a lot?"

Melissa laughed and read the labels out loud. "Orange blossom, wildflower, alfalfa, clover, buckwheat, dandelion, lavender, acacia, hawthorn, sunflower…I'm guessing the unlabeled jar is from Betty's hives?"

Sula nodded.

"That makes ten varieties."

"Eleven." Sula reached forward and picked up a jar from the back of a shelf with a label describing it as manuka honey. "I haven't tried this one yet."

"I've never heard of manuka. Is it a flower?"

"Yeah. It's in the myrtle family. Native to New Zealand. My parents sent it."

"With all this honey I'm surprised you don't have a bear breaking into this house." Melissa pantomimed a bear clawing at the cupboard.

Sula chuckled at Melissa's imitation and couldn't resist a private joke. "She doesn't need to break in…she has a key."

Melissa laughed. "On top of everything else, you're a connoisseur of honey."

"I like honey the way people like wine. You can taste the terroir, as they say. The bees make the honey, but honey is a distillation of the nectar they gather from the flowers they visit, from plants that have been soaking up the sun and nutrients in the soil where they grow." Sula reached for the lavender honey.

Melissa cocked her head and smiled. "You're a bee philosopher, too."

"A philosophy of bees." Sula pondered that possibility for a moment. "Sounds like the title of an interesting book." She poured some of the viscous amber liquid into her tea and offered the jar to Melissa. "You want some?"

"No, thanks. I prefer Earl Grey without anything in it."

Sula prepared her tea and raised her cup. "So what did you want to show me? I'm curious."

"Follow me." Melissa led her into the dining room, where a painting lay facedown on the blanket-covered table, the paper backing removed and set aside.

"This is the painting that hangs above your bed."

"I figured as much. I noticed it was missing." Sula sipped her tea and watched Melissa as she walked to the far side of the table.

Melissa pointed to a bundle of old envelopes. "I found these inside the painting."

"What?" Sula looked at them more closely. "Letters?"

"Yep."

Sula put her cup down, careful to keep it away from the painting and the envelopes in front of her. She picked up the letters, inspecting them. The envelope on top was addressed to Evelyn Llewellyn in Lyons, Colorado, postmarked 1939.

"Evelyn Llewellyn was my grandmother, Sula."

"*Really?*" Sula glanced at Melissa, her eyes wide. "And you didn't open them?"

"No. I didn't think it was right to do that without you present. I mean, technically, they're *your* letters. I was afraid I'd give in before you got home, so I decided to remove myself from the temptation and go for a walk."

"Oh, so that's why you went out. I couldn't figure out why you'd go walking in an electrical storm."

"It wasn't raining when I left, silly. It blew in so fast, I got caught in it."

"Yeah. Mountain storms do that." Sula's words trailed off as her attention shifted back to the envelopes in her hand. Absorbing the information, she stated the obvious. "These were in a painting I own, but they're addressed to *your* great-grandmother."

"Hence my temptation and decision to walk away. Even so, they don't belong to me."

"You're very ethical, Doc."

Melissa smiled, looking pleased, and bumped her shoulder against Sula's "Thanks for noticing."

"You're welcome," Sula said and untied the string. All the envelopes were written in the same hand and addressed to Evelyn. The same sender's name and city was written on the back of the envelopes, without a street address, just *Ursula Bergen, Buckhorn, Colo.*

Melissa gasped. "Your great-grandmother was writing to my great-grandmother."

"So it would seem." Sula touched the writing on the envelope lightly with her fingertips. "The handwriting is beautiful. No one writes like this anymore."

"It's very elegant but also easy to read. It makes sense when you think about it in the context of the time. Typewriters existed, but they were used more for business, and lots of things still got written out by hand, from letters to ledger books. You had to have good penmanship, or people couldn't read what you wrote."

Sula nodded and offered the letters to Melissa. "You found them, you should do the honors."

"I think we should read them together and in chronological order." Melissa sat in the nearest dining chair and selected an envelope. "This one is the oldest."

Sula moved a chair close to Melissa as she carefully removed the letter from the envelope. Sitting silently, one shoulder and thigh barely touching Sula's, Melissa read aloud the first of the letters.

August 11, 1938

My Dearest Evy,

I miss you terribly. You left the ranch two weeks ago, but it seems like you have been gone for months. I find myself turning around to tell you something, only to discover that you are not there. It makes my heart heavy, yet I feel your presence all around me. In fact, right now I have your lovely scarf that you gave to me as a reminder of you wrapped around my neck as I write. Your perfume clings to it, and if I close my eyes it is almost as if you are nearby. It is also quite useful in keeping the chill at bay. The nights are growing colder, and before long I will be skimming ice off the horses' water tank in the mornings. I put your scarf on to go outside and gaze at the full moon a little while ago. It is exquisite tonight, crystal clear and bright. I imagined that you, down there on the edge of the flatland, were looking up at it at the same time. It is a wondrous thing to believe that we could be looking at the same object at the same time and thinking of one another. It comforted me momentarily...

Melissa stopped reading abruptly, lowering the letter with an expression of shock. Sula, one hand grasping her chin pensively, met Melissa's gaze, and she suspected the look on her own face mirrored Melissa's.

"Sula, this is a love letter!"

CHAPTER TWENTY-ONE

Two cups of tea later, Melissa and Sula had taken turns reading through the letters and now stared at each other in quiet disbelief. It was a lot to take in. The letters, all from Ursula to Evelyn, made it clear that they had been secret lovers, and Ursula had commented more than once about Evelyn's parents' disapproval of their "friendship." Knowing Ursula had a young daughter but was unmarried, Melissa wondered if they were critical about that or if they suspected that their daughter's relationship to the mountain rancher woman went beyond friendly. The more she learned, the more questions she had. At the moment, she marveled at the discovery that their ancestors not only knew each other but might have loved each other.

Melissa broke the silence. "Does it seem at all incestuous to you that our great-grandmothers were lovers?"

Sula's eyebrows shot upward. "Not at all! We're not related."

"Good. I feel the same way, but I wanted to check." Melissa studied Sula's face, her expression difficult to read. "What are you thinking?"

"I'm not sure...I mean, I don't know how to put it into words exactly, but..." Sula pointed to the letters on the table. "Somehow this all seems significant where we're concerned."

"What do you mean?"

Sula stared at the ceiling as if she might find the words she was looking for floating around in the rafters. "This might sound crazy, but it's like we have a genetic predisposition for one another."

"That sounds so clinical. I'd like to think you were attracted to my intelligence and good looks."

"Oh, I was! I mean, I am. Don't get me wrong," Sula said, the sudden intensity of her gaze unexpected. Her eyes flashed like glowing embers in a fire, reminding Melissa of the first time she saw her. Sula continued. "Your intelligence and good looks are only part of what I find so very attractive about you. You teach me things, and you make me think. You make me laugh, too. *A lot.* And I love that we have shared interests. You're fascinated by so many of the things that are important to me. Nothing's been the same since we met, Melissa. And I just keep thinking about how Ursula's paintings brought you here and that our great-grandmothers knew each other—"

"Were lovers," Melissa said gently.

"Yes, *lovers...*" Sula shifted her gaze to the letters. "It feels like we were supposed to meet." Sula turned her head, and when their eyes locked, Melissa's insides quivered, an achingly sweet sensation.

"It sounds like you're talking about fate."

"I suppose I might be."

"Do you believe in it?" Melissa asked, narrowing her eyes at Sula, surprised at the unexpected shift to metaphysics in their conversation.

"I didn't use to. But I might be reconsidering. How about you?"

"I do." Melissa answered without giving it a second thought, then paused to reflect on the words that had just come out of her mouth. They surprised her...but fate, or something like it, seemed to be at play. She considered the time she'd spent in her childhood staring at the paintings in her grandmother's dining room and wondering about the places they depicted, imagining herself there. She couldn't shake the feeling that she'd been following a circuitous path leading to this summer and this place, where *there* had suddenly become *here.* "I know you shouldn't cross the Fates. My study of art, mythology, and literature has informed me very clearly on this fact. Doing that makes for compelling subject matter—very dramatic...and messy. They don't like it when you deviate from their plans."

"Well, then, we probably shouldn't do anything stupid to anger the Fates." Sula spoke in a conspiratorial tone while sliding her hand up Melissa's arm, under the rolled-up sleeve of her borrowed shirt. Her hand was wonderfully warm.

"Mmm..." Melissa hummed, closing her eyes as she relaxed into the gentle pressure of Sula's touch. Just as she began to consider how good it would feel to have Sula's hands on other parts of her body, the patter of feline feet running through the adjacent kitchen distracted her. She opened her eyes just in time to see two wide-eyed tabbies midair, about to land on the table. She leaned forward, putting her hands out, to protect the letters.

"I think they're telling me it's past their dinnertime," Sula said, shooing them away. "And speaking of dinner, are you hungry?"

"Starving, actually," Melissa said, gathering the letters. She'd been hungry for a while but didn't want to break away from the letters. "How about dinner out? Yours clothe should be dry by now. We haven't been to the Buckaroo."

Melissa wanted more of Sula's caresses and kisses, but dinner instead was probably a good idea. It would fortify her for later. "I've read about that restaurant and would love to go. But it's nice, isn't it? I'm not sure I've got the right attire here."

"It's a little upscale, but it's mountain casual—no flip-flops, no shorts, no holes in your clothes. Otherwise, a shirt with a collar and jeans or khakis are fine. Those pants and that shirt you were wearing yesterday are in the dryer, and they'll be perfect. Dress up any more than that, and people will look at you funny."

Melissa laughed, understanding exactly what Sula meant. In the South, "casual" meant something different: dress pants or a skirt for women and a button-up shirt and sport jacket if you were a man. Jeans would not qualify. While Sula fed the cats, Melissa changed into her freshly laundered olive denim pants and pale-coral blouse. Sula traded her T-shirt for a tailored light-blue button-up shirt, and within a half hour they were on the road to Buckhorn.

Melissa was content to let Sula drive, leaving her to happily observe the passing landscape. The sky had cleared hours ago, and the sun was low, the last warm light of the day falling through the trees at a raking angle, dramatically illuminating the cracked reddish bark of the pines. Approaching the outskirts of town, Sula commented that the truck was running low on gas and apologized for the delay as she turned in to a station.

While Sula pumped gas, a big pickup truck pulling up to the other row of pumps caught Melissa's attention. She glanced over at the shiny red Dodge Ram blazoned with chrome trim. With a start, she recognized the driver—it was difficult not to mistake the long, lean figure of the Buckhorn Creek Ranch's former stable manager sliding out of the tall truck. The sound of the gas cover snapping into place startled her, and she twisted around to see Sula tearing the receipt from the pump. Her gaze followed Sula as she walked alongside the truck, head down, looking at the strip of paper, oblivious to Melissa's failed attempt to quietly draw her attention to Kerry's presence on the other side of the truck.

When Sula finally lifted her head, she stopped abruptly when she saw Kerry staring at her with a sideways grin. Straightening her posture in response, Sula seemed suddenly more imposing. Without breaking eye contact, she tucked the receipt into her pocket.

Kerry sauntered closer to Sula, talking as she walked. Sula replied and they exchanged words, although from the insulated cab of the truck, Melissa couldn't hear anything. However, their body language spoke loud and clear. Thumbs hooked into the pockets of her jeans, Kerry seemed comfortably at ease. Conversely, Sula stood stiffly and glanced sideways several times toward Melissa. If Sula had hackles, they'd have been raised. Kerry turned to face Melissa and, with a wolfish grin, waggled her fingers at her. Melissa smiled half-heartedly and raised her hand in return.

Sula tilted her head and leaned forward quickly. Melissa could have sworn she saw Sula's nostrils flare. The action prompted Kerry to turn her attention back to Sula, who said something and then walked past Kerry brusquely. When Sula got into the truck she was frowning, a deep crease forming between her eyebrows. Melissa glanced through the windshield at Kerry. Still wearing that cocksure grin, she nodded to both of them, turned, and swaggered over to the gas pump nearest her truck.

Sula made a guttural sound, like a growl, but not the sexy kind that made Melissa weak in the knees. This one conveyed simmering anger.

"So, what were you two talking about?" Melissa asked as Sula started the engine and put the truck in gear.

"Not much," Sula said as she navigated back to the highway. "I asked her what she was doing now that she wasn't working for Betty, and she didn't answer. She seemed more interested in talking about you."

"Huh. Are you a jealous bear? I swear I saw your hackles rise out there."

"Oh, you saw my hackles, did you? I thought I did a better job of hiding them." Sula let out a dry laugh, and the crease between her eyes eased as a smile reappeared on her lips. "I'm not the jealous type, if you're worried about that, and I'm certainly not concerned about Kerry in that way." Sula sighed. "Something about her's bothering me, but I can't quite put my finger on it. And it's odd that she didn't want to talk about what she's doing now. She's usually one to brag."

"Maybe her new job isn't one to brag about."

"What do you mean?"

"Maybe it's not as glamorous as working at the ranch or the new job didn't work out and she doesn't want to be seen as a failure."

"You think being a stable manager is glamorous?"

"Working on a guest ranch in the Rocky Mountains? Yeah. It's kind of romantic, don't you think?"

"Only when you're not the one working on the ranch," Sula said with a short laugh.

"Point taken." Melissa was shocked to see a river of red taillights in front of them. The summer tourist traffic was backed up to the edge of town. Sula put on her turn signal. "It's like how people think being a professor is such a cushy job. I hate it when people tell me they're envious that I teach only a few hours a day and that I have summers off. They have no idea of how many *long* hours I put in outside of class preparing lectures and grading, on top of all the committee work. Summer is really just time to do the research and writing you can't do during the academic year."

Sula nodded while listening and bypassed the traffic jam, taking side streets to their destination on the other side of the town center. A sign, painted with the restaurant's name in an elaborate font embodying the flair of the Old West, hung from a cast-iron post in front of a striking two-story, polychrome Victorian.

The Buckaroo was busy, with people waiting outside on the porch, drinks in hand, but the hostess, seeing Sula as they walked through the door, greeted her by name and waved them forward. She led them through a crowd of people gathered around a massive oak bar with a long mirror on the back wall bracketed by decorative columns. The worn pine plank floors of the rooms looked original, as did the wainscoting and heavy wood trim around the doorways. Elk-antler chandeliers hung from the ceilings, and candles illuminated each rustic wood table. The hostess seated them at a table in a cozy corner of the back dining room and left them with menus.

"I see it pays to be a local," Melissa said as she opened her menu and continued taking in the details of the casually elegant space. "When we walked in, I didn't think we'd be seated for an hour, at least."

"It certainly doesn't hurt, but I hope it won't lessen your opinion of me if I tell you that I called to see if I could get a reservation while you were dressing." Sula grinned and flipped open the drink menu as the waiter, a young man with long, dark hair pulled back in a ponytail and sporting a thin mustache, arrived and greeted them.

"If you'd like to try something unusual, I recommend the Coniferous Cocktail." He smiled charmingly at both of them.

"It's good," Sula said, glancing at the waiter. "I'll have that, thank you."

Melissa read the description—rye whiskey, blue-spruce syrup, and seltzer. "Blue-spruce syrup? It's flavored with a pine tree?"

"Yeah, wild, isn't it?" the waiter said. "We make our own syrup. The spruce tips are harvested locally in the spring and early summer."

"How interesting! I want to try one."

After the waiter left the table, Melissa watched Sula peruse the menu and felt her heart swell. She couldn't think of anything that might make her feel any less impressed with the beautiful woman seated across from her. In her text messages, Beth had teased her mercilessly about being smitten with "the mountain woman," as she preferred to call Sula. But she was beyond smitten. In the last few days she'd realized that she'd crossed the boundary between smitten and love, though she hadn't confessed it to Sula. She wasn't sure if Sula's feelings matched hers equally. Sula was charming, caring, an eager and attentive lover, but she maintained a reserve that Melissa didn't fully fathom. More than once Melissa had caught Sula with a worried, almost sad, expression. When Melissa had asked what she was thinking, the look vanished, and Sula's answers were vague. She'd been at Sula's house more than her cabin in the last week, and even though they'd spent an increasing amount of time with each other and were discovering unexpected, almost preternatural, connections to one another, they hadn't talked about anything beyond the present.

The arrival of their cocktails interrupted Melissa's thoughts. "Oh!" she said after she tasted her drink. It was light and citrusy, with a subtle woodsy flavor, not overly resinous, as she had expected. "This is fascinating." She took another sip. "Who knew a pine tree could taste so good?"

"I'm glad you like it. People either love it or hate it," the waiter said. "There's rarely any in between." He pulled his order pad from a pocket in his apron, flipped it open, and held his pen in the air. "Are you ready to order?"

"I'll have the braised bison," Melissa said.

"The poached trout for me."

Melissa waited until the waiter left the table before speaking. "The trout reminds me—we haven't talked about my parents coming up this weekend."

Sula looked perplexed. "What does poached trout have to do with your parents?"

"Fly-fishing, remember? My dad intends to fish for trout on the ranch. My mom is just tagging along to enjoy the scenery and fresh air."

"Yeah, I remember," Sula said with a laugh. "But I assume they want to spend some time with you, too."

"Well, yes, that and—"

"What?"

"Sula, would you like to meet my parents?"

Sula leaned back in her chair. "Do you want me to?"

"I do." Melissa paused and took a sip of her cocktail, letting the gentle pine flavor roll across her tongue. When Sula didn't immediately reply, she said, "So…do you want to meet them?"

"If you want me to, then yes, of course." Sula gave her a sideways glance. "How will you introduce me to them?"

Melissa stroked her chin thoughtfully. "Parents are funny, you know? I could describe you as my *lover*, but that word would make them feel uncomfortable. I could say *girlfriend*, but I'm a bit too mature for that particular description. And truth be told, it doesn't accurately describe what I feel for you." Melissa paused, took a breath, and decided to just say it. "I don't know if you feel the same way about me, but I know exactly how I feel about *you*, Sula Johansen. I have quite fallen in love with you."

Sula's eyebrows arched upward, and her cheeks flushed pink. She didn't immediately speak. Melissa's hands were resting on the table, and Sula reached out, touching them and turning them over. Still quiet, she caressed her palms with her thumbs. And she looked uncomfortable. Not exactly the response Melissa was hoping for. She began to feel a quiet panic rise as she considered that Sula might be trying to figure out how to break it to her gently that she didn't share the same feelings. Sula cleared her throat before speaking in a quiet voice.

"Um…" Sula glanced around the room. "I hadn't expected I'd say something like this in such a public place, but…" She looked down at the surface of the table and then met Melissa's gaze. "I love you, too, Melissa."

Realizing she had been holding her breath, Melissa let it out in a rush. "You look terrified, Sula. Love is the most beautiful thing in the world. It's nothing to be afraid of." She squeezed Sula's hands, wishing she could transmit her surety through her touch. "And you don't need to be afraid of me."

"I'm not afraid of you." Sula took a deep breath. "I…I've never wanted something, someone, so much. But…"

"But what?

"I don't want to hurt you."

"I don't know why you think you'd hurt me."

Sula's expression became guarded. "I don't know how to do this… how to have a *relationship*."

"I don't want you to feel pressured to do or not do anything. Just follow your instincts, Sula. You seem awfully good at that." An exquisite tenderness rose inside Melissa. "We'll figure us out as we go, okay?" Melissa had already considered that they had independent lives, satisfying careers, and lived a thousand miles apart. It was a significant, but not insurmountable, obstacle to this being more than a summer affair. But it was a supremely, heart-wrenchingly inconvenient detail.

"Okay," Sula said in a more confident voice, her lips curling into a smile.

The arrival of their meal interrupted them, and after complimenting the look of each other's plates and praising the wonderful flavors of the food, they shifted the focus of their conversation to discussing the upcoming weekend. Given that Melissa's car was at Sula's house, she planned to spend another night there and then rehang the painting in the morning before returning to her cabin to prepare for her parents' arrival. She needed to do some grocery shopping and pick up supplies for grilling, which she used as a convenient excuse to invite Sula over to meet her parents.

"Would you like me to take your dad fishing?" Sula asked abruptly.

"Seriously?"

"Yeah. I know all the best places to fish on the ranch. From what you've said about him, I don't think we'll have any trouble getting along."

"Oh, I think you'll get along famously." Melissa scrutinized Sula. "You sure you haven't done this relationship thing before? It amazes me how you've gone from shy to wanting to cozy up to my dad. That's what all the serious suitors do, you know."

"Ha! No, I haven't. I'm acting on instinct here."

"Good. Keep following it. Like I said, your instincts are good." Melissa took the last bite on her plate and chewed thoughtfully. "So… sure, if you want to take my dad fly-fishing, I'm certain he'd love it. He's learning and can use all the help he can get, I think."

"I'll keep that in mind. The guides up here always complain about getting hooked by novices. The first thing I'll do is teach him how to crimp the barbs on the hooks."

"Why do that?"

"It's easier on the fish if you practice catch and release. And without barbs, they're a whole lot easier to get out of your skin." Sula made gestures like she was pulling a fishhook out of her cheek. "A barbed hook goes only one way—forward. You have to cut it or clip the line and pull it all the way through to get it out."

"Oh, God…I had no idea," Melissa said, unsure of which was more horrific—having a fishhook stuck in your face or having to remove it. The thought made her a little queasy. She reached for her drink and took a sip. "Okay, so I think we have the weekend planned. My parents arrive on Friday, and you'll come over early Saturday morning to pick up my dad. My mom and I will hang out together during the day, and I'll make sure the beer is iced and the first-aid kit handy for when you return."

Sula laughed. "The beer sounds good, but let's hope we don't need the other stuff."

"Me, too. I rather like your face the way it is." Melissa reached over, stroked Sula's cheek, and ran her finger lightly across her lower lip. "Between Ursula's paintings, the letters, and my parents' visit, I feel like I've been dominating all our conversations…how's *your* week been?"

"Good…busy…just a regular summer-season week. The visitor center is hopping. Our numbers are up, and we're adding more volunteer docents and programming. I hate to say it out loud for fear of jinxing it, but everything is running smoothly."

Melissa asked Sula to describe what her team was suggesting. While she excitedly described the possible new educational programs, the waiter cleared the table and returned with dessert menus. They both refused dessert, saying they were too full. Melissa knew that her underlying intent was to get back to Sula's house sooner rather than later, because her appetite for something that would not be satisfied by food was aroused. She asked for the check and hoped Sula was thinking the same thing. The twinkle in her eyes seemed to suggest as much.

The drive to Sula's was uneventful and comparatively quick, the downtown traffic jam having dissipated. When they pulled up to the house, the sky was darkening, and the stars were visible. Standing at the foot of the porch stairs, Melissa turned her face upward and looked for the constellation she knew so well. She smiled when she found the bright stars of Ursa Major seeming to hang in the night sky. "Ah, there you are, Sky Bear."

"What did you say?" Sula walked toward her.

"I was just talking to my old friend, the Sky Bear." Melissa pointed up at the indigo sky. "It's what my grandmother called Ursa Major, or the Big Dipper, if you prefer."

Sula stood close to Melissa, looking at her instead of the night sky above. "I prefer Sky Bear, actually," Sula said. "That's what *my* grandmother called it."

"Really?" Melissa stared at Sula in disbelief. "Huh! I have a feeling I know who they probably learned it from."

"Their mothers, I suspect."

"*Our* great-grandmothers." Melissa placed her hands on Sula's cheeks, drawing her down for a kiss. Sula responded passionately, and Melissa swiftly succumbed to her wonderfully dexterous lips. When Sula's kisses trailed down the side of her neck, she trembled and whispered suggestively into Sula's ear, "You know, earlier today I promised to show you more of me."

"Oh," Sula murmured, her lips tickling Melissa's skin. "I hadn't forgotten."

While the ancient light of the stars glimmered in the firmament above, Melissa laughed with pleasure as Sula took her by the hand and led her up the stairs.

CHAPTER TWENTY-TWO

The rising sun glinted gold off the rippling surface of Wildcat Creek. It was a picture-perfect morning: the mountain air crisp and cool, the skies overhead clear and deep blue. Standing knee-deep in the swiftly flowing water downstream from Melissa's father, Sula observed him while keeping a safe distance from the hook on the end of his line. In a misguided attempt to avoid getting his line stuck in the overhead branches of a pine tree, he had gotten impressively tangled in a thicket of willows growing along the water's edge. She resisted the urge to help him. He needed to learn how to manage himself and also to be constantly aware of his surroundings so as to avoid such predicaments in the future.

Having uttered a fanciful array of expletives, he was now disentangled and casting above the riffles as she had directed, allowing the fly to drift naturally with the current. She watched him with a critical eye; he was gently stripping the line as it moved past him. Keeping the line tight, as she advised, increased his chances of hooking a fish. He was pretty good for a novice, but like most people learning how to work a fly rod, men especially, his back cast was a mess. She reminded him to envision the face of a clock and to keep the rod within the ten-to-two positions. He had been trying to power the cast, putting the tip of rod far behind him and whipping it forward, the rod cutting the air with a *whoosh*.

But this kind of fishing wasn't about brute strength. To do it well demanded finesse and the willingness to let the long, flexible rod do the work of gathering energy and channeling it through the line. He was just starting to get the hang of it, and his casts were becoming increasingly smooth and accurate, the tiny fly dropping gently on the surface of the moving water.

Sula hoped he'd catch a fish soon as a reward for his improved technique; the stream had a healthy population of fish. She had already advised him that if they hooked any native cutthroat trout, they would release them carefully, but they'd keep any non-natives the right size and up to their bag limit in an effort to give the natives a little extra living room. When Robert asked if it would be a good idea to offer a fish or two to Betty as a token of appreciation, Sula told him it was a thoughtful gesture, and she'd love it. Her cornmeal-encrusted trout, fried in a hot cast-iron skillet, was a simple delicacy.

Sula noticed a subtle swirl in the water and a change in color indicating a trout feeding near the surface. Robert was casting in the right spot, and if he laid the fly down lightly, he might just fool the fish into taking it. On the next cast the trout rose, its nose breaking the surface of the water for a brief moment. The fly disappeared instantly, leaving behind nothing but ripples and a bubble formed by the gulp of air passing through the fish's gills when it snatched the camouflaged hook.

"Fish on!" Sula glanced at Robert's face. He was visibly excited. He lifted the tip of the rod quickly and put his fingers on the crank of the reel. "You don't need to crank, Robert. Just keep stripping the line and bring him in slow and easy. You don't want to wear him out or injure his jaw if you think you might release him."

Sula moved closer to Robert, removing her landing net from the back of her vest as she waded deeper into the cold water and took up a position alongside the grinning man. When she saw the dappled pattern and yellow spots on the fish's sides, she identified it as a brook trout, a plentiful fish that could overcrowd streams. Sula slid the transparent net under the fish, careful to avoid spooking it, and lifted it slightly, but kept it submerged. "You could keep this one if you want, or do you want to release it?"

"I'd like to learn how to release them properly. Will you talk me through doing it right?"

"Absolutely." Sula was glad he asked. He followed her directions exactly, wetting his hands before touching the fish, gently removing the hook, and then cradling the fish with one hand and holding its tail with the other, letting it rest to move water over its gills. "All right. You can let him go." The fish wriggled energetically out of his hands and dashed off.

"That was awesome!" Though graying at the temples, Robert looked like an exuberant ten-year-old boy.

Sula laughed, recognizing Melissa's expressions echoed in her father's reaction. Like Melissa, he was hard not to like. "I'm guessing you'd like to do that again?"

"Hell, yeah!"

"Okay, then. Let's work our way that direction." Sula pointed upstream and adjusted the wicker creel slung over her shoulder. She planned to end up near a pool that she knew had an abundant population of fish. She felt confident that, between the two of them, they would catch their limit and be able to stop by Betty's house to give her a couple on the way back to Melissa's cabin. Sula expected that Robert would enjoy returning to his wife and daughter in the afternoon with several fish to add to their grilled-steak dinner.

"Are you saying my grandmother was a lesbian?" Rachel, Melissa's mother, cocked her head and raised an eyebrow.

"Well…yeah," Melissa said. They sat in the Adirondack chairs on the deck enjoying the view of the meadow, each with a second cup of coffee and a cinnamon roll that Sula had brought with her when she picked up her father.

"Care to explain that?" Rachel looked skeptical.

"From what's in the letters, it's pretty explicit that Ursula loved Evelyn, and it seems like it was reciprocal. Evelyn's parents didn't like Ursula."

"But you said Ursula had a daughter."

"Yes, Inga, Sula's grandmother. Sula says Ursula never married, and no one knows who Inga's father was. She was raised by her grandparents after Ursula was killed in a hunting accident."

"That's such a tragic story." Rachel took a sip of coffee, shaking her head. "But about my grandmother, she got married. To a man. And she had a child—my mother, your grandmother."

"Are you trying to say they weren't lesbians because they had children and got married? Well, one of them got married." Melissa tore off a piece of the tender roll and popped it into her mouth.

"Maybe." Rachel shrugged. "I'm not sure what I'm saying. I'm just trying to get my head around it."

"I know. It's complicated. It was so different then. Gay people didn't have understanding and supporting parents. Some of us still don't, but at least now many of us have parents like you and Dad." Melissa paused and beamed at her mother. "That's a pretty recent change. Not that long ago it wasn't uncommon for lesbians and gay men to marry, have families, and keep their true sexual orientation a big, big secret."

"And be terribly unhappy, I suspect. I can't imagine marrying someone I didn't love."

Melissa nodded. "Do you know when Evelyn, your grandmother, got married?"

"They married when my grandfather enlisted in the navy after the attack on Pearl Harbor. If you enlisted, you were allowed a little more time to get your affairs in order before you had to report for basic training. Enough time for a wedding and a quick honeymoon."

"And to get pregnant, it seems. Wasn't she widowed? He was killed in the Pacific, right?"

"His ship hit a mine. Most of the crew survived, but he was one of the unlucky ones."

"And she never remarried…I think there's a story there." Melissa sipped her coffee and took the last bite of the roll, the soft, gooey center. Had marrying been an attempt at having a "normal" life? Or maybe Evelyn's parents had pushed her into it after Ursula died. Either way, after Evelyn's husband was killed in the war she probably felt less pressure to marry again. As a Gold Star Wife she would have had a respected status in postwar American society. Melissa let the thoughts roll around in her head. The more she learned, the less she knew, it seemed. Her desire to reveal the mystery of their lives strengthened. Suddenly, Melissa thought about her brother, Dave, a naval pilot. The mention of Pearl Harbor and the navy must have made her think of him. "Hey, speaking of the navy…how's Dave? I haven't heard from him in a while."

"The usual. He's busy and can't talk much about exactly what he's doing. Typical secret military stuff. I do know he's going to be on leave in Hawaii for a couple of weeks over the winter. Your father and I are thinking about visiting him there." She grinned and waggled her eyebrows. "He's dating a marine pilot, and we might get to meet her."

"*Dave is seeing someone?* Wow, I really need to catch up with him. I've been in such a bubble up here." She sighed and smiled. "It's been nice, though."

"I think you've had a nice distraction, too."

"Distraction?" Melissa frowned slightly. "You mean Sula?"

Her mother nodded. "I know I told you yesterday, when I first saw you, that you looked good. I was thinking it was all this fresh air and sunshine, but when Sula came by to pick up your dad this morning, you were *glowing* when you saw her. And when she looked at you, her smile went up into her eyes, as they say. You're the happiest I've seen you in a long time, Baby Bee." Her mother smiled lovingly and reached over, settling her hand on the back of Melissa's. "Are you girls serious?"

"Oh, God, Mom. Serious doesn't quite describe it." Melissa took a deep breath and let it out. "I'm in love."

"It shows. What about her? How does she feel about you?"

"She loves me back." The thought made Melissa giddy, and she smiled so wide her cheeks hurt.

"So how are you going to work it out?"

"What do you mean?"

"You live in Georgia, she lives up here—"

"I know. You don't have to remind me." Melissa didn't mean to be curt, but the words came out sharply. "I honestly don't know, Mom. We're taking it one step at a time."

"That's never a bad thing," her mother said, patting her hand. "Maybe you could get a job out here."

"Mom..." Melissa said in a warning tone. She'd had this conversation with her mother before when she suggested she get a teaching job closer to home. She didn't seem to understand how few tenure-track teaching positions existed and how very fortunate she was to have landed where she did right out of grad school. Most of her classmates hadn't been so lucky and worked in thankless and woefully underpaid part-time positions or had given up on academia entirely.

Her mother removed her hand and changed the topic. "Hey. I found some more pictures and a few other things in your grandmother's boxes I thought you might be interested in. I brought them with me."

"Really?" Melissa pulse quickened. "I can't wait to see them. I also want to show you the photos I took of Sula's paintings."

"I want to see those, but I'm not tearing myself away from this view to go inside. Not just yet anyway."

"Fair enough," Melissa said.

"Well now, look at those brookies. What fine fish!" Betty admired the dressed fish in Robert's cooler. "I know what Lars and I are having for dinner. Thank you, Robert. It's not every day you meet someone and they give you freshly caught trout!" Betty winked at Sula.

"It's the least I can do in exchange for the opportunity to fish in such a beautiful place," Robert said and nodded toward Sula. "And with such a good instructor."

"You know, Sula learned from the best. Her grandmother was an avid fisherwoman, even tied her own flies. She beat the pants off any man around here."

"Oh, I believe it." Robert laughed.

"I've got a bag in the pantry to put the fish in." She waved at Sula to follow her up the steps of her house. "Sula, come inside with me. They're on a tall shelf, you can reach them for me."

As Sula suspected, Betty didn't need her assistance. She just wanted to get her away from Robert for a moment.

"So, how do you like your future father-in-law?" Betty cackled with laughter while grabbing a plastic bag from the box on the shelf.

"Oh, so you're a fortune-teller now?" Sula huffed and then softened her tone. "I like Robert. He seems like a nice man, easy to get along with."

"Like daughter, like father, eh?"

"Something like that, yeah."

"Well, I guess you must like her a whole lot. Haven't seen nor heard much of you lately, kiddo." Betty grinned.

"Yes, I do." Sula ran her fingers through her hair, a nervous habit, as she followed Betty out of the kitchen. "I'm sorry I've been out of touch."

Betty stopped abruptly and turned around. "Do *not* apologize, Sula. I'm happy for you. I really am." She poked her playfully in the ribs with a finger. "I can't resist teasing you a little."

"Clearly."

Betty accepted two smaller trout from Robert, refusing the bigger ones that he tried to offer, explaining that he should keep those to show off to his wife. He laughed, something he did easily and genuinely, just like Melissa, and told Betty that he liked how she thought and hoped they'd meet again someday. Betty agreed and waved good-bye as they drove off.

On the way back to the cabin, Robert was quiet for the first few minutes and then spoke tentatively.

"So…um…I understand you're dating my daughter."

Sula froze on the inside. *What the hell?* She hadn't expected this conversation, and they'd certainly been doing a lot more than "dating." That sounded like something teenagers did, but it *was* what they were doing, wasn't it? She concentrated on driving and tried to speak in a calm voice. "Yes, we are."

"As Melissa may have told you, I haven't approved of all my daughter's girlfriends."

"No. She's never mentioned that."

"Really? Huh. Well, based on everything she's said about you, and the time we've spent together today, I just wanted you to know that I like you."

Sula wondered what exactly Melissa had told her parents. "I appreciate you telling me that, Robert. I've really enjoyed getting to know you today."

"It's been a beautiful day, hasn't it? Cool air, but warm in the sun. The sound of the creek was so soothing. When I close my eyes, I can still hear it. And those trout!" Robert shook his head as if he couldn't believe the day he'd had. Thankfully, he shifted the tone and topic of their conversation. "How do you get anything done up here? I'd never want to go to work. I'd just want to drive around all day in this beautiful old Bronco. Reminds me of one I used to have." He stroked the dashboard. "You really did a nice job on this restoration, by the way."

"Thank you." As they switched to the topic of cars, she relaxed. Although she really didn't know much about them other than the importance of finding a good mechanic, she knew enough to keep the conversation going, and car talk took them the rest of the way to Melissa's cabin. When they arrived, Melissa and Rachel were inside sitting next to each other on the couch, looking at something on Melissa's laptop.

"Well, hello, you two!" Rachel said, looking up.

"Look at what I've got!" Robert showed them the contents of the cooler as he stepped through the door. "There's one for each of us. Figured we could have surf and turf for dinner. Oh, wait…that doesn't really work, does it? Stream and turf?" He frowned. "Hm. That doesn't sound as good."

"How about fish and filet?" Melissa said.

"Perfect!"

Rachel rolled her eyes and gave her husband a quick kiss on the cheek as he passed by. "I take it you had a good time?"

"It was amazing. I learned so much about casting and how to read the water. And I actually caught some fish. Caught and released several more, too." Robert glanced at Sula and made eye contact with Melissa as he carried the fish to the kitchen. "*You* caught a good one, Melissa. I like her so much more than...what was her name? Terry?"

"Teresa," Rachel said flatly.

"Yeah, her. She was kind of pretentious," Robert said, putting the cooler on the counter.

"You never told me that before, Dad. I thought you liked her."

"Yeah, well..." Robert glanced at Sula as if suddenly realizing he shouldn't have this conversation with her present.

Rachel and Melissa turned simultaneously and looked at Sula with identical embarrassed smiles. Unsure of her role in this family banter and feeling uncomfortable, she remained in place, standing near the door.

"Sula, come in. You look like you're going to bolt," Rachel said, waving her in.

"Be careful or she might." Melissa crossed the room and took Sula by the arm, pulling her forward. She pinched Sula's chin and inspected each side of her face carefully. "Oh, good, no fishhooks. I can put the first-aid kit away now," she said with a laugh. "Are you thirsty? I made iced tea after lunch. And there's beer on ice."

"A cold beer sounds great."

"Sula, Melissa was just showing me pictures of your great-grandmother's paintings. They are so beautiful. You must feel fortunate to have them."

"Oh, I do. Thank you." Sula accepted the bottle of ale Melissa offered her. "Like Melissa, I grew up with them and never ever get tired of looking at them." She took a swig from the bottle. "I tend to look more at the summer scenes in the winter and the winter scenes in the summer."

"Psychological air-conditioning. That's funny," Robert said, walking into the room, beer in hand. "Let's sit outside and share stories about our day."

"Oh, God. Fishing stories. I'm going to need a beer," Rachel said, heading for the kitchen.

"Hey, Mom, grab one for me, too."

On the deck, Sula listened quietly as Robert wove a narrative describing how they had waded the creek and fought off biting insects while working their way up it slowly, how they'd paused to eat apples and peanut-butter sandwiches streamside under the shade of a big pine tree, and then concluded with fishing the pool before calling it a day. Sula didn't correct his slight embellishments, thinking it would be bad manners to do so, but also because his version of events was better and more entertaining. When Melissa asked if there was any part of the day he didn't like, he told her about getting tangled up in the willows. "I will not ever try to cast like that again," Robert said. "There was a tree branch overhead, so I was trying to do a roll cast, and I'm not exactly sure what happened. I still can't figure out how the line got wrapped around the willows and the fly stuck in the back of my vest. The more I tugged, the worse it got."

"I'm not quite sure how you did that, either, and I watched you do it," Sula said with a chuckle. She had smiled and laughed a lot today. Robert and Rachel made her feel comfortable, and her initial awkwardness meeting them had dissipated quickly. They asked her lots of questions about the conservancy and promised to stop by the visitors' center before leaving Buckhorn. When Rachel suggested it was time to start preparing dinner, she was surprised at how much time had passed. Melissa had steaks and corn for the grill and a big watermelon cut into thick, juicy slices. The trout would cook fast and make a nice first course. Sula offered to start the fire in the fire pit on the deck that also served as a grill.

"Is there a fire ban here?" Robert asked.

"No, not right now," Sula said, appreciating his concern. "And a fire pit like this one is pretty safe."

"Sula has a police-officer friend who calls her Smokey, so I think we'll be in capable hands." Melissa said.

"Thank you for sharing that, *Goldie*," Sula said with wide eyes and a smirk.

Rachel and Robert exchanged sideways glances and smiled at each other.

"I'm not even going to ask," Robert said before asking Rachel if he could help her in the kitchen and following her inside.

Sula sat on the bench by the fire pit, balled up the newspaper lying next to it, and placed it in the center of the pit. She stacked the kindling carefully around it before lighting the paper. "I like your parents," she said in between blowing gently on the fire, helping the wood catch flame.

"They like you, too. A lot. I can tell." Melissa smiled sweetly. "Thanks, again, for taking my dad out today. That really meant a lot to him."

"My pleasure." Sula leaned back as soon as the flames took hold.

"It was fun. I haven't fished that way too often since my grandmother passed."

"What do you mean? How else do you fish?"

Sula's heart skipped a beat. That was a slip. She usually fished while in fur, with claws and teeth, not a rod and reel. She couldn't honestly explain what she meant and scrambled to think of an appropriate response. "With another person, I mean. I usually fish alone."

"Oh," Melissa said, picking up her empty bottle and inspecting it. "You want another one?"

"Yeah, sure."

While Melissa was inside, Sula mentally berated herself for letting her guard down like that. With Melissa, and now with her parents, it was so easy to forget that she wasn't like them, or most people, for that matter. And it bothered her not to be able to answer Melissa truthfully. She had to be more careful. She questioned what she was doing, seemingly playing at having a normal relationship with normal people. She was many things, but normal she was not.

Melissa returned with the beer, interrupting her thoughts. She handed the amber bottle to Sula and combed her fingers through her hair, her touch energizing her nerves. It was as if she could feel the top of her head all the way down into her toes. She closed her eyes, savoring the sensation.

"You okay? You looked a million miles away when I walked through the door."

"Yeah. I'm fine," Sula said, opening her eyes to see Melissa regarding her with a tender expression. The steady gaze was intensely comforting, and her anxieties began to evaporate.

"I know meeting parents is stressful, even when it goes well. And you haven't had a lot of experience with this sort of thing." Melissa smiled and trailed a finger along the edge of Sula's ear. It caused a delightful frisson, making it difficult to think about anything other than her touch. Melissa sat down next to her and leaned into her. "I'm glad you're here."

"I'm glad I'm here, too," Sula said quietly, and even with all her unexpressed fears, she meant it wholeheartedly. She put her hand on Melissa's knee. She didn't know why or how, but Melissa grounded and centered her, and her heart felt full to overflowing. "There's nowhere else I'd rather be."

CHAPTER TWENTY-THREE

Sula stopped by the Blue Mountain Diner for breakfast before going in to the office. She'd been there only once in recent weeks, and that was the morning she took Melissa. Sula remembered it well.

They had stayed up late the night before. Sula smiled to herself recalling their lovemaking. It had left her feeling energized and not ready for sleep. When she had asked Melissa if she'd like to play a game of pool, Sula expected she'd rather stay in bed. Instead, Melissa laughed and said yes with enthusiasm. They played three rounds, Sula won the first one, Melissa the next, and the third round they called a tie. Expertly, Sula had sunk her last two balls but accidentally clipped the 8-ball on the last shot. It rolled slowly across the table and dropped into a corner pocket. They had agreed that finishing in harmonious balance with one another seemed a fitting way to conclude the evening. In the morning Melissa was groggy and wanted to sleep in. Sula thought she was adorably cute in her sleepy state and had coaxed her out with the promise of a decadent breakfast at the diner. Melissa hadn't really perked up until she finished a cup of coffee and was halfway through devouring a stack of blueberry buckwheat pancakes.

"Hey, stranger," Danni, the waitress, said with a smile, filling Sula's cup with coffee. "Haven't seen you lately."

"Yeah. It's been a little while."

"Uh-huh. Like since you've been hanging out with that cute blonde."

Sula opened her mouth to say something, but no words came out.

Danni laughed and saved her from formulating a response. "Would you like your usual?"

Sula nodded. "Yes, thank you."

"You got it, hon." With a grin, Danni took her order to the cook.

Sula sipped her coffee while reflecting on her morning. Not yet twenty-four hours had passed since she left Melissa and her parents at the cabin. Sula had awoken alone in her bed, feeling a restless pang of longing. Having been comfortable in her solitary lifestyle, it was an unusual and unpleasant feeling. She sighed, stirred cream and honey into the coffee, and scanned the headlines of the local paper she'd picked up from the stand by the front door of the diner. Beneath the fold was an article titled "Are there Grizzlies in Colorado?"

Sula knew the consensus of the scientific community was that there were no grizzlies in the state and hadn't been since the 1950s. The closest populations now lived in the Wind River Range, below Yellowstone in Wyoming. The newspaper story began by retelling the story of the so-called Wiseman Grizzly that had attacked Ed Wiseman, a hunting guide, in the rugged wilderness of the San Juan Mountains along the New Mexico border in 1979. The old female bear, killed in the fight, was an anomaly and might have been the last of the southern population of grizzlies. Regardless, it provided fuel for those who refused to believe that grizzlies had been hunted out of existence in the region.

With a soft grunt of irritation, she continued reading the story that drew upon nebulous recent grizzly sightings. They were reported with regularity but were most likely black bears that weren't black. Many had light coats and even cinnamon-colored fur, not unlike their bigger, more aggressive relatives. What irritated her most about the article was the way it was written. It made the inaccurate sightings seem plausible and undermined respected biologists. It read like a conspiracy theory, and like such inventions, it defied good sense.

Sula did sometimes wonder if an unknown shifter could have passed through, been seen, and misidentified as a grizzly. While possible—anything was possible—it seemed improbable. The only shifters she knew were members of her family, and they weren't a big group. Naturally circumspect, they took great pains not to be seen.

Sula began to mentally formulate a letter to the editor about the thoughtless article. She would write it as soon as she got to the office and send it out. She put the paper aside when Danni set breakfast in front of her, a mound of eggs and potatoes smothered in peppered gravy. While eating she considered other ways to counter the misinformation and unmerited fear of bears that the story disseminated. When she got to the conservancy, she'd talk to her media director about it and wouldn't be surprised if she wasn't already at work on it. She was admirably proactive that way.

But Sula never made it to her office. Leaving the diner, she received a call from Betty. There was a situation at the ranch, and Betty needed her help.

Sula turned on to the tree-lined drive leading up to the Ponderosa cabin. Betty had told her to meet her there but hadn't explained the problem. Betty's old blue Ford pickup was parked along the road, not in front of the cabin as Sula expected. She pulled up alongside it and lowered the passenger-side window. Betty was behind the wheel with the tip of a rifle resting against the dashboard. She cranked down the window.

"Hey, Betty. What's up?"

"Be quiet, park behind me, and get in the truck. I'll explain," Betty said and rolled the window up. Her tone and facial expression were humorless.

Sula did as directed, sliding into the passenger side of the truck and closing the door quietly. Betty's behavior perplexed her as much as the presence of the gun did.

"All right," Sula said quietly. "What's going on?"

"There's a mountain lion in the cabin," Betty said, not taking her eyes off the single-story log cabin about thirty yards in front of them.

"*What?*"

"Here. Look at my pictures." Betty pulled her cell phone out of the pocket of her denim shirt and handed it to Sula.

Sula tapped and swiped the screen, scrolling through the images. Her jaw dropped when she saw a mountain lion sprawled on a leather couch. In the next photo it was sound asleep and looked remarkably like a domestic cat, an enormous, honey-colored house cat with very large paws. Its head rested on a pillow with a pattern of pine trees, bear, and elk silhouettes.

"Bears, and elk, and lions…oh my!"

Betty took her hand off the rifle and bumped Sula's shoulder. "Not funny."

"Oh, come on. It is kind of funny. A quandary, for sure, but still funny." Sula swiped the screen of the phone one more time and audibly inhaled when she saw the shape of the mountain lion's ear, light against the dark fabric of the pillow. It was torn, an old injury in the shape of a notch. "Hey, that's my lion!"

"*Your* lion?"

Sula hadn't told anyone, including Betty, about chasing a mountain lion around, trying to keep him out of trouble. "It's the lion that bumped into Melissa on the trail ride. He's got that distinctive notch in his ear."

"So how does that make it your lion?"

Sula decided she'd better confess. "I've been chasing him around a little, trying to push him away from houses and cattle."

"Well, it doesn't look like it worked."

"Apparently not." Sula handed the phone back to Betty. She took it and tucked it into her pocket. "How'd he get in there?"

"That open window on the side of the cabin, I think," Betty said, pointing to it. A window sash was pushed up, and the screen lay on the ground below, the metal frame bent.

"How'd you find him? Did a guest report it?"

"Thank God, no. The couple staying there checked out late yesterday. They called me this morning to see if they'd left their Kindle in the cabin. It hadn't been cleaned yet, so I drove over to see if it was in there. When I walked in, I heard an odd sound and looked up to see a damn lion in the hallway walking toward me. I might have yelled a little." Betty laughed. "I'm not sure. It all happened so fast, it's kind of a blur. Anyway, he turned and ran into the kitchen, and I ran back out the front door—"

"You know, you should never turn your back and run from a mountain lion."

"Yes, I know that, Ms. Conservancy Director. He ran away from me first." Betty glared at her. "You want me to continue my story?"

Feeling chastised, Sula nodded.

"I got in the truck and sat there for a minute. Needed to catch my breath and regain my wits. That's when I noticed the window. I went back up on the porch and peeked in it, and there he was, standing on the couch. Sizing it up for a nap, I guess. Took those pictures, then drove back to where I could get a cell signal and called you. Then came back here to wait for you. Last I checked he hadn't budged from the couch."

"You think he went in through the window this morning?"

"Yeah. Guests don't follow the rules. We want them to keep the windows closed for a very good reason, and there's a damn four-footed reason in there right now." Betty pointed to the cabin, the color rising in her cheeks.

"What do you want to do?"

"Not sure." Betty glanced at Sula. "That's why I called you. Figured you could help me problem-solve this. I don't want to call any wildlife officers. When they show up, word will get out, and that'll scare the guests and create a media hoo-ha. Plus, I don't trust that they wouldn't kill him."

"All good reasons." Sula was glad Betty hadn't called it in as she should have. If they knew about a nuisance mountain lion, the Wildlife Services agent would probably know about it, too. She stroked her chin as she considered the situation. "You know, his behavior is unusual, but he doesn't look sick. In fact, he looks pretty healthy, in good weight."

"I'm recently missing a couple of barn cats."

"Oh."

"Yeah." Betty sucked her teeth. "All creatures great and small got to eat. But I'd prefer that my barn cats not get eaten."

"Oh…I'm sorry, Betty. I was thinking he was eating deer, not cats. Since there's no hunting on the ranch, the deer feel safe here and let their guard down."

"So how do you figure we get him out of the cabin without making too much fuss?"

"Well, they're most active at night, that's when they usually hunt, so unless something spooks him, he's most likely expecting to sleep here until dusk."

"And…what? We're going to let him do that?"

"Well, not all day," Sula said. "But it buys us some time to make a plan. Let me think on it."

Betty was quiet, but after few minutes she began tapping her fingers on the steering wheel. "You said it was a male mountain lion?"

"Yeah."

"If he sprays that couch, I might just shoot him."

Sula tried not to laugh. "I have an idea. You don't want him coming back, right?"

"Right."

"And you'd rather not have anyone know he was here."

"That, too."

"Let's make sure no one is too close to the cabin, especially up the hill behind it. I think he's a young male trying to establish his own territory. We can impress upon him that this is not a good place to hang out and that humans are not his friends." Sula paused. "If we chase him out the right direction, I think he'll want to head toward the ridge, which would take him away from the other cabins." Sula paused and puffed her cheeks. "I wish I could chase him on four feet instead of two."

"But you're not going to do that, right?" Betty gave her a sideways glance.

"No. I don't think engaging the *hamask* here is a good idea."

"Good. You'd risk the chance of someone seeing a big brown bear and thinking it was a grizzly. Jesus, that'd be worse than a mountain lion sleeping on a couch, for sure." Betty laughed. "How do you want to chase him?"

Sula made a mental map of the area around them. "This cabin is the farthest one back from the main road, right?"

"Yep."

"I have an idea, but I'm going to have get something from my office. You good to wait here a little while longer?"

"Sure." Betty nodded. "If you'll do me a favor."

"Another one on top of helping you deal with a mountain lion in a cabin?" Sula teased.

"*Your* mountain lion," Betty quipped back with a lopsided grin. "You said it's your mountain lion. Therefore, I'm actually helping you with *your* problem."

Sula laughed and decided not to argue the point. "Okay, what do you need?"

"Coffee. Cream, no sugar."

"You got it."

"Hey, Boss…you're a little late this morning." Anna spun around in her office chair and beamed at Sula as she walked through the door. "Have a good weekend with Melissa and *the parents*?"

"Yeah. It was great." Sula knew Anna wanted the scuttlebutt on how the family meeting had gone, but she really just wanted to get in and out of her office quickly. Still, she didn't want to be rude. "You?"

"I went down to a concert in Fort Collins, and—"

"I don't mean to cut you off, Anna, but I talked to Betty on the way in, and she's got a little situation she asked me to help her with." She pointed down the hall. "I need to grab a couple things and head out to the ranch. Can you tell me about it later?"

"And you'll tell me about your weekend in return?"

"Yes, of course," Sula said over her shoulder as she strode down the hall.

"Deal. Hey, is everything all right with Betty?"

"Yeah, she…uh…she's got some raccoons…big ones…in an attic. I'm going to help her get them out."

"Oh, raccoons can do some damage, for sure. My aunt in Albuquerque had raccoons in her attic once and—" The look on Sula's face must have reminded Anna that she was in a hurry. She stopped speaking and pointed her thumb at her computer screen. "I'm going to get back to my report and let you deal with that."

"Thanks, Anna," Sula said with relief and headed for the supply room. She opened the door and flipped on the light to reveal a space that looked like a supply closet for an outfitter. Rows of sturdy metal shelves held hand tools, outdoor equipment, and camping gear. Sula grabbed an empty duffel bag and marched to the gun safe in the back of the room.

CHAPTER TWENTY-FOUR

Melissa yawned, wrapping her fingers around her almost empty coffee cup, and watched her mother clear the breakfast dishes from the table. "When did Dad get up this morning?"

"I'm not sure exactly," her mother said, returning from the kitchen with the coffee carafe. "It was still dark out. He said he'd be back before lunch. More coffee?"

"Yes, please." Melissa held out her cup. Her mother refilled it and went back to the kitchen. The night before, her father had talked about his plans to fish the creek that ran through the meadow in front of the cabin.

Her mother returned to the table but didn't sit down. "I know you just got up, but I'm ready to take off these pajamas and put on some clothes." She ruffled Melissa's hair playfully as she passed her on the way to the stairs.

Melissa took her cup and shuffled back to the couch, where she'd been sleeping since her parents arrived. Propping herself against a few pillows, she stretched her legs out along the length of the sofa and sipped her coffee. She hadn't minded sleeping on it. It was comfortable enough, and she was more than happy to host her parents. But she missed Sula's big, cozy bed, and even more than that, she missed Sula.

Her mother came down wearing jeans and a fleece pullover. In one hand she carried a book and, in the other, a buff-colored box imprinted with the elegant logo of the long-defunct Denver Dry Goods Company. She placed the box on the coffee table.

"What's this?" Curiosity raised, Melissa sat up and swung her legs off the couch to make room for her mother.

"Things that belonged to your great-grandmother." She sat beside Melissa.

Melissa lifted the lid and peered inside. It contained postcards, photographs, and a book. "Have you looked through this?"

"Enough to see what was in there, and then I set it aside for you."

"You want to go through it with me?" Melissa felt as excited as a kid at Christmas.

"Honestly?" Melissa's mother laughed and held up a paperback book with a cover depicting a muscular dark-haired man groping a buxom woman, a large sword dangling between them. It was, undoubtedly, a romance—her mother devoured them. "I'd rather go sit on the deck and read."

"Okay." Melissa laughed, shooing her away. "Go read your book. I want to see what's in here."

Melissa removed the postcards first and laid them out on the coffee table. Photographic images printed on thick linen paper, they depicted well-known places and mountain peaks. They must have been kept as souvenirs, as none had been written on or mailed. She gathered them up and put them aside, turning her attention to the photographs. They felt flimsy and fragile in comparison. Melissa wondered if these were ones that didn't make the cut to be included in the photo album.

There were more mountain landscapes, views of mountain peaks, dark trees silhouetted against the sky, rocks and boulders, blurry elk grazing in the distance, and fat chipmunks eating peanuts that someone must have tossed on the ground for them. Some had notes written in pencil in Evelyn's distinctive handwriting on the back. Melissa recognized the names of places that tourists commonly visited, like Bear Lake and Old Fall River Road in Rocky Mountain National Park. But as she worked her way through them, the images ceased being the easily recognizable vistas in the park. They were still strangely familiar, though. Perhaps it was just because she had seen so many similar photos tipped into her great-grandmother's album.

When Melissa turned over a photo of a narrow unpaved road and read the note on the back, she gasped. It said, "On the way to Icy Creek." That was where she and Sula had picnicked…and had kissed for the first time. She reached for the next photo of a rocky creek and meadow. Her heart skipped a beat when she read, "Ursula painting." *Ursula painting!*

She hadn't seen any people in the photo. She inspected it more carefully. In the distance, in front of a line of trees, a blurry form resembling the shape of a person stood next to something, possibly an easel. A quick succession of questions ran through her mind. Would it be too far-fetched to consider that she had found a photo of Ursula painting the picture that hung in her grandmother's house and was now in her own home, in Georgia? Was this how her great-grandmother, Evelyn, came to own the painting? Were they lovers at this point? Or did that happen later? What if they kissed by the creek on the day this photo was taken? Sula's comment about having a genetic predisposition for each other reverberated in Melissa's head.

She put her hand on her chin while her mind ran wild speculating on the possibilities and parallels. She wanted nothing more than to text Sula, to tell her what she had found, but without a cell signal or Wi-Fi at the cabin, it was pointless. She glanced through the picture window to the deck. Her mother, sitting in a chair with her feet propped up on the railing, was engrossed in reading her book. She could tell her about the discovery, but she didn't expect she would be nearly as enthusiastic or as full of wonder as Sula would be. Melissa would just have to be patient and talk to Sula when she could.

She returned her attention to the photos on the coffee table and found a second photo of the artist, a woman and presumably Ursula, at work. The camera was closer to her, and it confirmed she was using an easel. The painting attached to it seemed roughly the size of the one in Melissa's living room, but she couldn't see its surface. Ursula seemed to be looking down at the palette in her hand and dipping her brush into a glob of paint. Wearing a wide-brimmed felt hat, a long-sleeved shirt with the cuffs turned up, and wool pants tucked into tall, laced boots, she looked like a quintessential artist-adventurer of the 30s. She was a mountain woman, all right, just like her great-granddaughter was today. Melissa smiled and scrutinized Sula's namesake in the photo. She and her great-grandmother really did share the same build and proportions, but her face, blocked by the brim of her hat, eluded Melissa.

She hoped to find more pictures of Ursula and maybe even one of Evelyn. Certainly, she must have been the photographer, but it would be good to confirm that she was there. Melissa looked through the remaining photos—more scenic landscapes, a few snapshots of a bright-eyed shepherd dog sitting in the back of a rugged pickup truck that they must have driven there—but no pictures of Evelyn and no more of Ursula.

All that remained in the box was the book. Melissa gently lifted it out and inspected it before opening it. Bound in green leather, the front and back covers were covered with green-and-white marbled paper. The title, *Saga av Eydís Bersa,* was printed in gold ink on the spine. Melissa knew that the word *saga* meant an epic story, usually one about a hero and his many adventures. The title was worn and faded, indicating that book had been read repeatedly and wasn't just some pretty tome that sat on a bookshelf to impress.

Melissa scanned the first few pages. It seemed to be written in a Scandinavian language, and given Evelyn's connection to Ursula, it was probably safe to assume it was Norwegian. Like most art historians, she studied French and German, and even though she couldn't read what was printed in the book, she was able to recognize some of the words and dates, enough to ascertain that it was published in Oslo in 1922.

The book was beautifully illustrated with engravings colored with rich, earthy hues, each page protected with a tissue-thin sheet of glassine paper. The linearity of the illustrations reflected the Art Deco style popular in the 20s, but they also had an organic fluidity that Melissa associated with the earlier Art Nouveau. The stylistic blend was unusual and captivating. Melissa turned the pages of the book slowly, looking for illustrations. After studying several, she realized that Eydís Bersa must be the figure depicted repeatedly in each image. Interestingly, the figure was a woman, and she seemed to be some kind of medieval warrior or knight. And if that wasn't intriguing enough, she wore a bearskin coat. The head of the bear was still attached to it and was perched on top of her head. Some images didn't have any human figures at all, only a solitary bear walking through forested landscapes.

"Huh. More bears," Melissa said quietly to herself and flipped through the pages looking for more illustrations. As she turned a page, a photo slipped out of the book. She caught it in her hand before it landed on the coffee table and saw the note written on the back:

My beautiful, camera shy she-bear.

Melissa stared at it wide-eyed. She took a breath and held it as she turned over the photo. Ursula Bergen, standing confidently with her hands on her hips, beamed at her with a broad smile. She recognized that smile. It was shocking how much Sula resembled her great-grandmother, almost as if she were seeing Sula transported back in time to the 30s. Almost. Ursula's face was more angular, her chin a little more squared, and her hair was blond and straight, not dark and wavy. But, still...Ursula and Sula were unquestionably related.

"Hello, Ursula. It's nice to finally meet you."

"Who are you talking to?" Melissa's mom asked, walking in from the deck. She looked around as if expecting to see someone in the cabin.

Melissa held up the photograph in her hand. "Mom, meet Ursula Bergen."

"Oh?" Her mother walked across the room and joined her on the couch. She slipped her reading glasses on to take a closer look at the old photo. "Wow. I see the family resemblance. This was in the box?"

Melissa pointed to the book on the table. Her mother picked it up, flipped through it, and paused to look at an illustration.

"*Whoa...*" Melissa said when the image caught her eye.

"What?"

"Doesn't that look familiar to you?" Melissa pointed at the engraving.

"Mmm...maybe?" Her mother said, frowning in concentration. "I'm not sure."

Melissa picked up the book and rested it in her lap for closer inspection. The illustration depicted a woman standing in a forest clearing. Nearby, along the edge of the woods, stood a bear on its hind legs. "This looks like Grammie's painting that I have, the small one."

Melissa's mom pursed her lips and shook her head. "I'm not seeing it."

"Well, it doesn't look exactly like it. One is a print and the other a painting, but the subject matter, setting, and composition are the same: woman in a clearing, a bear in the woods looking at her. That seems an unlikely coincidence."

"You're the art historian. I wouldn't have picked up on that, though. It looks so different from the painting."

Melissa continued to stare at the illustration and considered what was in front of her. A photo of Ursula with a note, written by Evelyn, calling her a "she-bear," was tucked into a book that had something to do with bears. Was that a private joke they had shared? Or maybe a term of endearment? The photo was placed in front of an illustration of a woman and a bear, *and* it had striking similarities to one of Ursula's paintings that had belonged to Evelyn. That couldn't possibly be a coincidence. And, if it wasn't, what the hell was its significance? And what was up with all the bears?

Melissa's questions grew exponentially. "I'm wondering if Ursula made that painting in reference to this. And why did Evelyn have both of them?"

Melissa's mother nodded thoughtfully and patted her on the knee. "You have your work cut out for you figuring that out." She stood up.

"I'm going to take a shower before your dad gets back. I forgot to tell you that he wants to have lunch in Buckhorn, and afterward I'd like to go to the visitors' center at Sula's bear conservancy."

"Bears..." Melissa shook her head slowly.

"Hm?"

"Nothing. That sounds great, Mom," she said, excited by the thought of seeing Sula and sharing these photos with her. She felt like she was playing a game of connect the dots and the image was starting to take form, but it teased her by remaining tantalizingly incomplete.

While her mother showered upstairs, Melissa took the photograph of Ursula to the dining table and grabbed Evelyn's picture album from the shelf under the stairs, then opened it to the page with the missing photo labeled "Ursula" in white ink. She carefully slid the photo into the empty corners glued to the black paper. It fit perfectly.

The visitors' center at the Colorado Bear Conservancy was busy. Melissa was happy, knowing it was good for the organization, and she felt proud of Sula as she looked at the exhibits with her parents. She had texted Sula as soon as they arrived but hadn't yet received a reply. She tried Sula's cell number, but it went straight to voicemail. Finally, she called Sula's office number. It rang twice and then was answered, but the voice on the other end didn't belong to Sula.

"Colorado Bear Conservancy. This is Anna. How may I help you?" Sula's office manager spoke in a pleasing formal voice.

"Hello, Anna. This is Melissa Warren."

"Oh, hey, Melissa!" Anna's voice immediately lost its cool "professional" tone. "How are you?"

"I'm great, thanks. I was trying to get in touch with Sula. I'm actually here at the center right now with my parents. I was hoping we could say hello."

"I'm so sorry, but she's not here. She came in but had to leave to help Betty with something. I don't know if she'll be back in today."

"I hope everything's okay. I just came from the ranch, and it didn't seem like anything unusual was going on."

"She said something about raccoons in an attic."

"Well, if anyone could charm a raccoon out of an attic, Sula would be the one," Melissa said, hearing Anna's snort of laughter on the other end. Melissa thanked her, exchanged a few pleasantries, and ended the call. Having anticipated seeing Sula all morning, and with so many things she wanted to tell her, she was disappointed not to find her at the center.

Her phone buzzed as several messages came in. She scrolled through them quickly, hopeful, but none were from Sula. Her father waved at her to get her attention.

"Everything okay?"

"Yeah…" Melissa said, looking up. "Sula's not in the office. Her office manager said she's helping Betty remove some raccoons from an attic."

"Oh," her father said. Melissa noticed he was wearing a new green ball cap embroidered with a bear paw print, which he must have gotten from the gift shop while she was on the phone. "You look so disappointed."

"I am. I was hoping to tell her about my discovery this morning. It's okay. I'll talk to her later."

"I'm sorry she's not here," her father said. "Your mom and I are really enjoying this place. You'll have to tell Sula we're learning a lot and think it's great!" He held up the visitors' guide. "There's even a nature walk around the lake. You want to go with us? Your mom's already headed that way."

Melissa nodded, pleased with his approval, and tamped down her disappointment. Her parents would be with her for only one more day, and she wanted to take full advantage of enjoying time with them. She refused to behave like some lovesick teenager and ruin a good time. Melissa smiled at her father as he put his arm around her in a tender, paternal gesture, and together they walked out into the bright mountain sunlight to join her mother.

CHAPTER TWENTY-FIVE

A h, thanks," Betty said, popping the plastic lid off the coffee that Sula handed her. Placing the lid on the dash of the truck, she blew across the top of the paper cup. "Did you remember to call Lars when you went into town?"

"Yes. He said he'd have Little Lars go over and mind the office and that he'd give him a heads-up about what we were doing." Sula grinned. "I love your husband. He's probably the only man I know who, when you tell him his wife is about to harass a mountain lion, says, 'okay, you girls have fun' and hangs up the phone." Sula wasn't being entirely truthful. Before telling them to have fun, Lars did inquire if his wife had her Winchester with her. When Sula told him the rifle was by her side, she'd heard a sigh of relief.

"Yeah, that sounds about like Lars." Betty sipped the hot coffee cautiously, watching Sula as she unzipped the duffel bag and removed a bright-yellow weather radio. "The radio in here works fine. My truck isn't *that* old."

"This radio isn't for us. It's for Notch. I mean, the lion. Some recent research has shown that they don't like the sound of human voices and will move off, even abandon a kill, if they hear humans talking. Apparently, they are most averse to talk radio."

"Huh. Never thought I'd have something in common with a mountain lion."

Sula laughed. "I figured we'd use the radio to wake him up and make him want to leave the cabin without us having to go in." Sula pulled two safety-orange plastic cases from the bag. "And then we'll use these."

"Are those what I think they are?"

"Yep. Bear bangers." Sula popped open the clasps on one case, opening it to show Betty a bright orange-and-black single-shot pistol. The pistols, part of their non-lethal nuisance bear management kits, used a gunpowder blank that made a loud bang and launched a whistling pyrotechnic seventy-five yards, like fireworks but without the colorful explosion at the end. Intended for bears that had become habituated to raiding trash cans or bird feeders, they were designed to frighten them and to reinstall a sense of fear of humans.

"That'll scare the bejesus out of him." Betty pointed to the other unopened case. "Why did you bring two?"

"Because we're going to work together and make sure he runs in the right direction."

"Away from the other cabins and the lodge."

"Exactly," Sula said.

"That's going to make a lot of noise, don't you think? I thought we were trying to keep this operation quiet." Betty held up her coffee and squinted at the logo printed on the sleeve of the cup. "By the way, this fancy coffee is really good."

"I'm glad you like it." Sula chuckled and closed the case. "I was thinking, if anyone says anything about the sounds we…well, *you* could explain that it was some illegal fireworks and the guilty parties have been dealt with."

"That's pretty smart, kiddo." Betty narrowed her eyes at Sula. "I don't think I ever realized you're so sneaky. I'll remember that. So… we're going to scare him out of the cabin with the radio. And then what?"

"Let me explain," Sula said and began to describe her plan.

Sula crept up the cabin stairs with her cell phone in one hand and the weather radio in the other. She paused, placing the radio on the edge of the porch and stepping gingerly on the floorboards. Trying not to make a sound, she made her way to the front window. Nearly three o'clock; it was time to put their plan into action. Sula figured the later in the day, the better, but she didn't want to wait too long. The goal was to startle him awake and have the upper hand.

Checking at regular intervals, Sula found him sound asleep each time, though his position varied. Not expecting anything different this time, she stood to the side of the front window and turned on the phone's camera, moving it slowly across the glass pane until she could see the mountain lion on the screen.

Head down, eyes closed, and breathing heavily, he lay on his side with his enormous paws dangling limply off the edge of the sofa. Sula leaned forward to admire the handsome cat with her own eyes. It was a rare treat to see one up close in an unguarded moment. She smiled at him, shaking her head gently, and mentally chastised him. He needed to get back to bedding down in the woods where he belonged instead of on a leather couch. But, really, how could she blame him? That sofa looked awfully comfortable. She exited the porch carefully and gave Betty a thumbs-up.

"You ready?" Sula asked when she was back at the truck.

"Yeah. Let's get going," Betty said, opening the door. "I'm tired of all this sittin' around, doin' nothing, and trying to be quiet."

Sula reached into the duffel bag, removed two packages of foam ear protectors, and handed a set to Betty. "They're as loud as a .22. You're going to want these."

"Huh?" Betty cupped a hand to her ear, amused at her own joke, the wrinkles in her cheeks and the corners of her eyes accentuating her grin.

Sula rolled her eyes. Betty pinched both foam cones between her fingers and pressed them into her ears. She took her glasses off and polished them on the tail of her denim shirt before picking up the single-shot pistol. Sula, inserting her ear protectors, watched as Betty put the blank and the cartridge in the pistol as if she'd done it before, treating it with the confident manner of someone who had been familiar with firearms her entire life. Sula prepared her pistol—a double-shot model—slipped a tin of blanks into her pants pocket, and tucked two more cartridges into her shirt pocket.

Betty took a position in front of the cabin, nearest the corner of the wall with the open window. Sula surveyed the perimeter, walking a wide arc around the cabin to confirm the area was clear and no one was nearby. It took a few minutes to complete the sweep. When she returned she nodded to Betty, who returned the gesture.

Sula went to the porch and turned the radio on, cranking the volume all the way up. The caustic voice of a man pontificating about local politics filled the air. Stepping back, she heard a loud thump and a crash from inside the cabin. She refrained from looking in to see what Notch was doing.

"He's awake!" Sula yelled, no longer worried about making noise. She scurried behind Betty, who stood at the ready with her legs slightly apart, her arm extended, and pistol pointed up into the air. Sula broke into a run, stopping next to a big pine, and turned to face the cabin.

Without warning, Notch bounded from the open window—a magnificent golden blur. BANG! Betty fired her pistol, the cartridge emitted a shrieking whistle as it traveled, throwing white sparks as it spun into the sky. Notch landed on the ground, and the cartridge exploded in the air above him. He crouched, shoulders bunched, head down, and ears flat. He seemed unsure of where to run or even if he should. After a split second of indecision, he bolted for tree cover.

"Good boy," Sula whispered as he moved toward her. She fired her pistol. The whistler flew in a corkscrew pattern, concluding with a bright explosion and a puff of white smoke. The mountain lion shifted directions and, with agility and speed, headed uphill.

Sula sprinted after him, darting between trees and around rocks. She wanted him to think he was being pursued. Though it pained her to be so unkind, she wanted him to feel as if he were in dire mortal danger. And truly, his life *was* in danger if he didn't learn to stay away from people.

As she ascended, she lost sight of him, and her speed declined as the ground became steeper, rockier, and more uneven. When she stepped on a flat rock, it shifted unexpectedly as her weight came down on it. The dislodged rock skidded downhill, and she went with it, her torso pitching forward uncontrollably, her legs going out behind her. Unable to recover her balance, she hit the ground hard and slid a few feet. She growled in frustration, knowing that, in fur and on four feet instead of two, she would not have fallen *and* would have been near the top by now.

Thankfully, the pistol was still in her hand. With adrenaline pumping through her veins, she scrambled quickly to her feet. Breathing heavily, she fired the second cartridge. The screaming pyrotechnic arced between two trees and exploded near the crest of the hill. She hoped Notch was on the other side thinking that the horrible humans and the terrible screaming things were still pursuing him.

Sula took a moment to catch her breath and considered loading another round for good measure but decided against it. It seemed like enough. At least she hoped so. She slid the discharged pistol into her back pocket and leaned forward to knock the dirt from her pant legs. Feeling a bead of sweat roll down her face, she reached up to wipe it away and witnessed a large red drop land with a splat on the toe of her boot. Shocked, she touched her fingertips gingerly against her forehead and then inspected them. Her fingers were wet and sticky with blood.

❖

"Jesus, Sula!" Betty said, seeing her coming toward the cabin through the trees.

Sula ambled toward her with blood dripping down her face, the front of her shirt stained bright red, her forehead throbbing with pain. Betty grabbed her arm and pulled her toward the cabin. "Let's use the bathroom in here, and whatever you do, don't look in the mirror."

Of course, Sula immediately stared at herself. Even though she knew facial cuts bled profusely and usually looked worse than they actually were, she was still startled by what she saw. Blood oozed from a jagged gash above her right eye, flowing in rivulets down her face. Betty grabbed her chin, turned her face away from the mirror, and dabbed the wound with a wet hand towel.

"You need stitches."

"Are you sure? Let me see." Sula tried to pull away to have a closer look, but Betty held tight.

"Trust me, Sula. I have a husband, two sons, two hundred head of cattle, forty horses, dogs, and a fluctuating number of barn cats. I know when something does and does not need stitches." She pushed her glasses up the bridge of her nose, scrutinizing her. "And you definitely need a few to close this wound. Might need to make sure you don't have a concussion, too."

Sula reluctantly agreed to let Betty take her to the health clinic. Walking through the cabin, a towel held to her face, Sula stopped to survey the living room with her one eye. One of the sofa cushions had a long tear, a ceramic table lamp lay on the floor broken into two pieces, the flat-screen TV was facedown on the floor, and an upholstered chair was tipped over backward. Betty had rushed Sula into the bathroom so fast she hadn't seen anything on the way in.

"Oh, jeez, Betty…I'm sorry."

"What are *you* sorry for? You didn't leave the window open that let the mountain lion in, and you didn't break this stuff." She paused and sniffed the air. "Could be worse. It doesn't smell bad, so I don't think he sprayed anything." Betty pushed Sula through the room, toward the door. "Come on. Let's get you to the doctor."

CHAPTER TWENTY-SIX

Standing on the deck, Melissa smiled and waved good-bye to her parents. The tires of their Toyota Highlander crunched the gravel as the vehicle rolled slowly down the hill and then picked up speed and disappeared around the curve. It had been wonderful spending time with them. Living so far away, she didn't get to do it often. She was happy they had enjoyed themselves so much and was beyond delighted that they liked Sula. Melissa had been an independent child, living on her own since she went off to college, but her parents' approval still meant a lot to her.

And it seemed that Sula enjoyed her parents' company, as well. More than once during their initial meeting, Melissa had hung back, observing their interactions. While the introductions when Sula had arrived in the early morning had been a bit stiff, she and her father had returned from their excursion as chummy as if they were longtime fishing buddies. Her mother warmed to Sula immediately, and over the course of the afternoon and evening, they had engaged in serious discussions and good-natured teasing. Laughter had been abundant, and it felt like a family gathering, though minus her brothers.

She entertained a short fantasy of taking Sula to her parents' home for Christmas dinner. Dave would be there with his new girlfriend, and by then maybe Robby might even have someone special to bring. They'd have to find some extra chairs to fit everyone around the dining-room table. She wrapped her arms around herself and sighed. Coming back to the present, she wondered if a meaningful long-distance relationship was possible. It wasn't uncommon in the academic world where full-time positions were scarce and couples often found themselves employed by universities in different states or even along different coasts. It wasn't necessarily the kind of relationship she wanted, but Sula was too good to let go.

The raspy screech of a hawk overhead jerked Melissa from her ruminations. She looked up at the blue sky and shaded her eyes with her hand, searching for a bird of prey. Then she discovered that the sound hadn't come from a hawk, but a blue jay perched in a nearby pine. The bird, clutching the branch tightly, pitched forward, and the call of a red-tailed hawk erupted from the bird's beak. "Well, aren't you clever." Melissa talked to the bird as if it could understand her. "You've learned to disguise yourself very convincingly."

She went inside and began to tidy up the cabin, putting fresh linens on the bed and cleaning the kitchen. With her parents on the way home and Sula at work, the day was hers. She pulled her notebooks, laptop, and the box containing the book and pictures from the shelves and arranged them neatly on the dining table. She opened the composition book with a design on the cover that looked like planks of wood and began making notes, recording thoughts and half-formed ideas. A few days previously, she had taken her laptop to the lodge to use the Wi-Fi and accessed research databases and museum websites to learn more about landscape painters in the American West. Specifically, those working in the early twentieth century. She wanted to see what their paintings looked like. Not surprisingly, most of them were plein air painters like Ursula, who set up their easels in the field and painted on site. From what she saw, Ursula's masterful paintings rivaled those of the artists who had achieved enough prominence to have been collected by museums, like those she saw in Denver, or to have articles written about them.

Melissa tapped her pen against her chin as she made a mental calculation. Including the ones in her house, she had documented thirteen paintings. She felt certain she had enough information to write a short article about them. Their provenance, the history of ownership of the paintings, could be established, and she could connect many of them to specific places and within a window of time. She even knew the identity of the artist and a few details about her life.

She put down her pen and opened the photo album, turning to the photo of Ursula. Photography was a strange thing when you paused to consider it. Melissa recalled the observations of an art historian she admired who poetically described a photograph as a moment snatched from the river of time. By capturing a fleeting moment and freezing it forever, it could distort your sense of time and space. Ursula smiled unceasingly at her in the photograph, the past and present compressed.

But, in truth, she wasn't really smiling at Melissa; she was smiling at her lover.

She shook her head, as if by doing so she could settle the free-form thoughts floating around in it. Sula was at work now, but she really wished she were in the room. Melissa wanted to talk with her. She felt inspired, ideas were percolating, yet she wasn't sure if she *should* write about the paintings. Writing implied publishing, and although Sula had given her full access to the paintings and encouraged her investigation, Melissa wasn't convinced that she was fully comfortable with the idea of her great-grandmother's work being known outside of the family and close friends.

Melissa flipped her phone over and stared at the "no service" icon on the screen. Feeling at an impasse, she decided to go to the lodge, where she could text Sula and make plans to see her tonight.

"Is anyone sitting here?"

"No." The man seated next to the only unoccupied rocking chair on the porch looked up at her. He appeared tired and sweaty. Melissa assumed the three children rocking their chairs furiously belonged to him.

Melissa sat and took her phone out of her bag. "It's hot today, isn't it?"

"I suppose…" He shot a warning glance at the kids, who seemed to be engaged in a game to see who could rock the fastest. "This feels cool compared to where we're from."

"Oh? Where's that?"

"Missouri." He pronounced the name of the state as if it ended with an "a."

"It's not heat. It's the humidity, right?"

"Isn't that the darned truth." The man nodded and then apologized before giving the kids a verbal warning in a stern voice. "Y'all behave while your mother gets us checked in, or you do *not* get to go horseback riding."

"No!" the children wailed in unison. They immediately stopped rocking and began to blame each other for the "stupid" game that was going to get them into trouble. Their father clutched his forehead with his hand, looking exasperated, as if he had just realized he had replaced one problem with another.

Melissa didn't try to continue their conversation, leaving him to manage his unruly brood, and unlocked her phone. She scrolled through her messages…her parents had just gotten home. Beth sent a picture of her cat sleeping in a potted plant and asked if things were still going well with the mountain woman and if she was ever coming home. Home seemed very far away right now, and she *really* didn't want to think about the fact that she was leaving soon. She and Sula needed to talk about a lot of things.

She had a message from Sula, sent late the night before, wishing Melissa a good night and asking when she'd see her again. Smiling and hopeful, she typed a reply. *Tonight?*

The screen door creaked, and Melissa glanced over to see a woman, presumably the mother of the unruly kids, holding a folder similar to the one she herself had received from Betty upon check-in.

"I hope you all enjoy your stay with us." Betty's voice and then her body followed the woman out the door, her booted foot propping the screen door open. She pointed toward the stables. "And don't forget, if you get signed up in the next half hour you can go on the chuckwagon-dinner ride tonight." The children erupted in whoops and hollers of delight as their parents herded them off the porch toward the stables.

"Hey, Betty."

"Oh, hey!" Betty turned and beamed. "Didn't see you there." She looked back and forth, her gaze sweeping across the porch. "Your parents still here, or have they taken off already?"

"They left this morning. You know, they fell in love with it here. I think you might have some new guests in the near future."

"Well, I can't complain about that. I'm very glad to hear it. Tell them I'll hook 'em up with a good rate."

"Will do. Hey…how'd your raccoon situation go?"

"My raccoon what?"

"The raccoon removal. With Sula."

"Oh, *that*." Betty chuckled. "Fine, fine…Sula's an animal whisperer, you know."

"I've figured that out."

"Have you now?" Betty gave her a sideways glance.

"Well, she has a way about her, you know?"

"I do."

"She really loves animals."

"She does."

"Bears especially," Melissa said. Betty raised an eyebrow and cocked her head while she listened. "It runs in the family, it seems. Betty, you're an old friend of Sula's family…can I ask you something?"

"Of course." Betty stepped out on to the porch, letting the screen close behind her, and leaned against a porch post, arms crossed. "What do you want to know?"

"What's up with Sula's family and bears? Why do they all love bears so much? It seems like a multigenerational thing."

Betty coughed and scratched her head before responding. "I can't answer that question for you, I'm afraid. That's one for Sula, but even she might not be able to answer it."

"You're probably right. I mean, why does one person like cats and another dogs, or prefer a chihuahua over a shepherd? Just personal preference, I suppose."

Betty made eye contact and held her gaze. "Sometimes things are the way they are because it's the way they are."

Melissa laughed at the pithy statement, even though Betty's expression was incongruously serious. "Thanks for that bit of cowboy wisdom." Her phone buzzed, so she looked at it and held it up. "Speak of the devil."

"I'll let you get on with your business." Betty put her hand on the door handle and paused. "And I meant what I said about a special rate for your parents…providing your dad catches me some more fish."

Melissa laughed. "Thanks, Betty. I'll let them know." She turned her attention to her phone and read Sula's message. It was sometimes difficult to accurately interpret the tone of text messages, but this one sounded enthusiastic.

Tonight? Yes! Chow mein, sesame chicken, or moo shu pork?
Melissa texted back, laughing softly to herself.
All of the above.

"Oh, my God, Sula! What happened to you?" Melissa put the palm of her hand against Sula's cheek and inspected her forehead. A puffy red line arced above her eyebrow, and she counted seven stitches. "Are you okay?"

"I'm fine." Sula gave her a tender kiss. "It's a little sore, but I'm okay, really. Come in and sit down. We'll eat and I'll explain."

"Please don't tell me a racoon bit you. I don't want to worry about you and rabies." Melissa took a seat at the table and surveyed the take-out boxes in front of her. Sula had gotten all three dishes, plus steamed pot stickers. She nabbed a dumpling with her chopsticks, swirling it in the dipping sauce, and popped it into her mouth.

"No raccoon, no rabies." Sula took a swig of beer. "I tripped, fell, and hit my head on a rock."

"You fell?" Melissa narrowed her eyes. "You're so agile and have great balance. I've seen you scramble up boulders like it was no big deal, so it surprises me that you'd trip on a rock. How'd it happen?"

"Well." Sula laughed nervously. "First, I need to explain that Betty and I told a little white lie."

"About what?" Melissa was intrigued and wasn't sure where Sula's explanation was going. She spooned some rice onto her plate and reached for the sesame chicken.

"The raccoon. There was no raccoon. We were hazing a mountain lion that had gotten into one of Betty's cabins."

"A mountain lion! Anna said you were getting racoons out of an attic. Why didn't you tell her the truth?"

"Because you're supposed to call your local police or wildlife officials in such situations. Betty was concerned that they'd kill Notch and the media attention, so she called me to—"

"Wait…Notch? Who's Notch?"

"Notch is the name I've given this particular lion."

"You've seen this mountain lion before?" Melissa was beginning to put separate pieces of information together, but she wasn't quite there yet. "Why do you call him Notch?"

"Because of the notch in his ear. He's—"

"The mountain lion who ran into me," Melissa said.

"Exactly."

"I think you'd better start at the beginning and explain to me how you know this mountain lion and *then* about the cabin," she pointed at the stitches in Sula's forehead with her chopsticks, "and how you got those stitches."

By the time Sula finished recounting her acquaintance with the mountain lion, why she was trying to keep him away from people, the dramatic story of how she and Betty scared him away from the cabin, and how her head had come in contact with a rock, they were sitting on the couch in the living room with after-dinner drinks. Sula had crafted two deliciously tart and sweet whiskey cocktails made with fresh lemon juice and honey. The evening was cool enough for a small fire, and Sula lit several candles around the room. In the ambient light the high-ceiling room transformed into a cozy space.

"I can't believe you were chasing a mountain lion." Melissa shook her head, letting all the details sink in. "I'm glad you weren't injured worse."

Sula rolled the ice around in her glass, staring at it. "I'm really irritated that I fell." She frowned, winced, and laughed at herself. "Ow...I guess I shouldn't do that."

"Poor Bear. I bet it bruised your pride even more than your head." Melissa put her glass on the coffee table and touched Sula's forehead lightly. "I have so many things I wanted to tell you tonight, but seeing your face I got totally distracted."

Sula smiled at her with a lopsided grin. "I'm glad I have that effect on you."

"Mm-hmm...you do. You disrupt my thoughts terribly sometimes." Melisa stroked her cheek.

In one single, smooth movement Sula set her glass on the coffee table, leaned over, and kissed her with a ferocity that cleared Melissa's mind of everything except the pressure of Sula's lips against her own. Melissa trailed the tip of her tongue along the edge of Sula's upper lip, and when Sula moaned softly, it was all the invitation Melissa needed. She pounced on Sula, though she remained mindful of her injury.

Melissa pushed Sula firmly, but gently, against the sofa pillows, straddling her. She kissed the length of her neck and unbuttoned her shirt so she could slide her hands under Sula's bra. She cupped her breasts and teased her nipples with her thumbs. Kissing the soft skin in the dip between her breasts, Melissa felt the steady beat of Sula's heart as she slid her hands around to undo her bra.

"Here, let me," Sula said in a ragged voice. She arched her back, quickly removing her shirt and bra, then tossed them aside as Melissa unzipped Sula's pants and slid them down her long legs. Sula laughed and tried to sit up when they became tangled around her ankles. "My boots."

"Nope." Melissa pushed Sula back against the pillows. "I got this. You don't do anything but sit there." Sula dropped her hands by her side and watched hungrily as Melissa untied her boots. Sula's obedient response gave Melissa an unexpected rush that inflamed and emboldened her. She stood and removed her clothing, piece by piece, teasing Sula with a deliberately unhurried pace. Sula's eyes, glinting amber in the firelight, roamed her body, and she bit her lower lip as if trying to restrain herself from action. By the time Melissa stepped out of her panties, she could hardly stand it herself.

Maintaining eye contact with Sula, she kneeled, put her hands on her knees, and slowly slid her hands up the inside of her thighs. Pushing her legs apart, she took Sula with her mouth. Sula, wet and welcoming, gasped and raised her hips, putting her arms out wide along the couch to steady herself. She might have climaxed as soon as Melissa's tongue touched her, but drunk on sexual power, Melissa denied her immediate release. Slowly, she brought Sula to the edge of orgasm twice before guiding her over the cascade the third time. Melissa grasped her hips tightly as a roaring upswell erupted from deep within Sula, her body undulating beneath her.

Melissa had intended to give Sula a moment to recover before attending to her own intense arousal. Instead, panting and raspy-voiced, Sula pulled Melissa close, flipping her over onto her back. Aligning their bodies along the length of the sofa, Sula, feverish and slick with perspiration, kissed her lips, her neck, her breasts…and slipped her hand between Melissa's legs. With abandon, Melissa opened herself to Sula's stroking caresses. Desperate for release and unable to form coherent thoughts, she was carried away by an explosive wave of pleasure.

"Mmm…I've missed you these last few days," Melissa murmured in Sula's ear after she was able to think and breathe normally again.

"I missed you, too, Goldie," Sula said quietly, in return. The soft buffalo-plaid blanket draped across the back of the couch had slid to the floor, but one corner of it was within Sula's reach. She grabbed it and covered them with it. The fire had burned down to glowing embers.

Melissa smiled, brushing her lips against Sula's cheek. "That nickname has really stuck, hasn't it?"

"I'm afraid so." Sula turned her head and raised an eyebrow. "Of course, if you hate it, I'll stop calling you that."

"Don't stop. I rather like it. No one's ever given me a nickname before. I mean, other than the obvious—Mel. Which I don't like, by the way, so don't start calling me that."

"Why not?"

"It seems so masculine, like the name of some burly truck driver or something."

"You mean a burly diesel-dyke truck driver." Sula laughed.

"Yeah. Not that there's anything wrong with that. But it doesn't really suit me."

"No, it doesn't. But it's a sweet name."

"How so?"

"Mel means 'honey' in Latin. Melissa is 'honeybee' in Greek. I read about it in one of Betty's beekeeping magazines."

"I never thought to look up my name. My mom always told me I was named for a character she liked in a book she was reading when she was pregnant. She thought the name was pretty."

"She named you well." Sula nuzzled her cheek. "Because you are sweet as honey and completely irresistible."

"Especially to a honey bear like you." Melissa laughed. Remembering one of things she wanted to talk about, she propped herself up on one arm and said, "Bears."

"Bears?" Sula glanced around as if looking for one. Seeing none, she focused on Melissa with a questioning expression. "What about bears?"

"Why do you like them so much?"

"I've always liked them."

"But *why*?" Melissa poked her gently in the ribs.

"Well…bears are easy to relate to because they're almost human-like in many ways. They're omnivores like us. Some of their gestures and expressions are like ours, especially when they stand on their back legs. They have a special place in the environment. As apex predators at the top of the food chain, they help to keep things in balance—"

Melissa placed a finger on Sula's soft lips. "You're talking like Sula the conservancy director. I want to know why Sula, the sexy, naked woman next to me under this blanket, likes bears."

Sula puffed her cheeks. "That's harder to explain."

Melissa recalled Betty telling her that Sula might not be able to explain her love for bears. "Try," she said, and when it seemed like Sula wasn't going to expound further, she tried a technique she used with students reluctant to speak in class. She prompted her with a more specific question. "Do you think it's because your family likes bears?"

"You mean my parents? Because of growing up around them and the conservancy?"

"Yes, and don't forget your great-grandmother painted bears in some of her paintings."

Sula became a little cagey. "But that's to be expected, right? Ursula was making paintings of the Rocky Mountains…where bears live."

Melissa didn't press Sula further about her love of bears. Ursula's name reminded her of the photograph she had replaced in the album, and she interrupted her own line of questioning. "I also wanted to tell you I found a photo of Ursula. It's the one missing from the album, I'm almost positive."

"Really? Did you bring it? Can I see it?" Sula was visibly excited.

"No, but I have an image of it on my laptop." Melissa rolled off the couch and out from under the blanket to retrieve her laptop from her messenger bag. The cool air gave her goose bumps. When she returned, Sula was sitting upright, so she sat next to her, and Sula wrapped the blanket around them as they looked at the picture together.

"She looks happy, don't you think?"

"She does. You know, I've only ever seen pictures of her when she was a girl. Never as an adult."

"You look a lot like her."

"You think?" Sula appeared skeptical.

"Oh, yeah…the shape of her face is bit more angular, but you really look alike." Melissa leaned closer to Sula, enjoying her warmth, but also the feel of her skin. She brought up the next image, a detail of the note on the back of the photo. "This was written on the back. I assume Evelyn took the photo. This is certainly her handwriting. And look, she calls Ursula my 'she-bear.' *Another bear*."

"Well, Ursula means 'little she-bear.'"

"Oh! Of course. That makes sense, though, given that *Ursa* Major is the Big Bear, the Sky Bear." Melissa considered the point for a moment. "And since you're named after her, that makes you a little she-bear, too." Melissa grinned, but Sula stiffened, meeting her gaze with a serious expression. "Don't you find it a peculiar coincidence that I began calling you Bear without knowing what your name means?"

"By calling you Goldie first, I kind of started it, didn't I?"

"Yeah, you did." Melissa chuckled, thinking about the first time Sula called her Goldilocks. She put the laptop on the coffee table and ran her fingers across Sula's stomach, wrapping her arm around her waist. She relaxed under her touch. "And somehow I keep finding myself in the bear's house."

"And on the bear's couch." Sula's expression softened, and she kissed the tip of Melissa's nose.

"And if I'm a good girl, perhaps I'll be invited to the bear's bed."

"Mmmmmrrrrr." Sula uttered that soft, low growl that made Melissa feel woozy.

"You're distracting me, again."

"My apologies," Sula said in a tone of mock seriousness. "What point were you trying to make?"

"I'm not really sure." Melissa was joking, but she hadn't forgotten. "At every turn I seem to find myself confronted by bears."

Sula gave her a sideways glance. "And that's a problem?"

"It doesn't seem to be, Bear."

"That's good to hear, Goldie." Sula yawned and glanced at the clock on the mantel. "Speaking of bed, would you like to come to bed with me? It is a work night for me, you know."

"I was just waiting for you to ask," Melissa said and abruptly sat up, taking the blanket with her and uncovering Sula.

"Hey! Bring that back." Sula grabbed for the blanket unsuccessfully as Melissa walked toward the stairs.

"You'll just have to come and get it," Melissa said coquettishly. She held her arms and the blanket out in a welcoming gesture and then ran up the stairs. She couldn't resist teasing Sula and hadn't even considered the extra bonus of enjoying the view from the landing of Sula's gloriously naked body as she darted around the room blowing out the candles. Sula took the stairs two steps at a time.

Melissa put on the T-shirt Sula lent her to sleep in and got into bed, the sheets smooth and cool against her legs. Sula turned out the lights, slid in next to her, and pulled the covers over them.

"Mmm…I like being under the covers of darkness with you." Melissa draped her arm across Sula.

Sula laughed. "I like it, too."

"And I could get really used to this." Melissa nestled close.

"I already have." Sula sighed softly.

"You know I'm leaving Friday," Melissa said quietly.

"What? *Really?* I thought you had another week."

"I have to go home sometime, you know." Sula faced her, and although Melissa's eyes were adjusting to the dark, she couldn't discern her expression. "We need to talk about us, Sula. How do you feel about a long-distance relationship?"

Sula was quiet for a moment. "It could work." She spoke as if she was speaking to herself more than to Melissa.

"The question is, do you want it to work?"

"I do…" Sula spoke quickly, sounding earnest, but her voice trailed off as if uncertain.

"But?" Melissa held her breath. The room felt very still, as if her heart might have paused its beating, too.

"I don't want this to end." Sula spoke haltingly. "But I don't know how to do a long-distance relationship. God, I've never even managed a *relationship.*" There was an edge of frustration to Sula's voice, or maybe it was fear.

"Well, aside from sex every night like we just had on your couch—which, by the way, I enjoyed *very* much—we'd just keep doing what we've been doing since we met. Except we'll have to commune over the phone or by Skype until I'm on break. I'd love to spend more time here in Colorado. And you'd be welcome to visit me anytime, of course. I bet there are a lot of black bears in the South, as well as people who care about them who could use your expertise. Maybe you could teach some seminars."

"The Georgia black bear population is healthy and growing, actually." Sula sounded more confident. "There's evidence that resident populations are expanding in Alabama, too."

"See, there are possibilities, already." Melissa felt brighter.

"You have a way of making the impossible seem possible."

"Just keep thinking that, okay? So, what are you doing tomorrow? I'd like to spend as much time with you as I can before I go."

"I intended to get up early, and I have a meeting, one I shouldn't cancel." Sula yawned.

"Okay, what about Thursday? Could you play hooky and we'll spend the day together?"

Sula seemed hesitant to respond. "I had planned on doing some things on the land."

"You can't postpone that until I'm gone?" Melissa didn't understand this sudden reluctance and why whatever she was planning on couldn't wait. "What are you doing?"

"I really thought you weren't leaving for another week," Sula said with a tone of exasperation. She took a deep breath and let it out audibly. "I wanted to get up early for the next few days, at least, and… um…hike through the areas where I know Notch has been before going in to the office. On Thursday, I was going to do a longer route. I don't want him feeling comfortable after all the pyrotechnics he experienced yesterday."

"Sounds like you're trying to behave like a bear, marking your territory, as it were." Melissa spoke lightly, but Sula stiffened again, the tension under her skin palpable. She sensed this was a sensitive issue for her, and she thought she understood why. "It's okay, Sula. You can trust me. I won't tell anyone about Notch and what you're doing. I won't even mention it to Betty, if you don't want me to. I could get most of my packing done tomorrow and then go with you on Thursday."

"I'm going to do it fast. I want to cover a lot of territory."

"Are you telling me I can't keep up with you?" Melissa was starting to feel irritated. "I'm not a mountain woman like you, but I'm in pretty good shape."

"It's rugged. You have to cross a boulder field to get to the lake."

"What lake?"

Sula hesitated, seeming reluctant to tell Melissa one of her points of destination. "Moose Lake," she finally said.

"You're sure I shouldn't go with you?"

"Yes. It would be better if you didn't," Sula said flatly. "I'll be back in the afternoon, though." Her tone softened. "We can spend the rest of the day…and night…together. I'll make it up to you." Sula kissed Melissa tenderly, and her irritation melted away.

"Will it involve a couch?"

Sula laughed softly. "Maybe. It might be something better. You'll just have to find out."

"Oh, you are such a tease." Melissa squeezed her, and Sula made a contented sound, a murmur of pleasure.

"Good night, Bear," Melissa said.

"Mmm…good night, Goldie. *I love you…*" Sula nuzzled her neck and spoke tenderly, in that intimate voice reserved for lovers. "And I do want to make this work. Please don't doubt that."

"We will make it work," Melissa whispered in reply. "And I love you, too."

Sula fell asleep in Melissa's arms, and by the time her body relaxed, when her breathing became slow and deep, she had concocted a plan to spend a little more time with Sula before Friday came. *And* she would demonstrate that she was indeed capable of keeping up with her bearish lover.

CHAPTER TWENTY-SEVEN

Sula stared at her reflection in the mirror, specifically at the stitches above her eyebrow. The wound was healing well and quickly, as she expected. Rarely sick with a cold or the flu, she healed rapidly, something she'd inherited with her bear-shifting genes. Although the clinic physician told her to return in two weeks to have the stitches removed, they'd need to come out in a week or less.

Sula had never needed stitches before, and they would probably tear out when she shifted into bear form, which she planned to do shortly. Informed by a quick internet search on her phone on how to remove them, she stood in the bathroom armed with tweezers in one hand and a pair of small, sharp scissors in the other. Using the tweezers, she gripped each knot, snipped the thread, and gave it a tug, yanking it out. She winced but didn't feel much pain.

She turned out the light and walked into the dark bedroom, thankful Melissa was still asleep. Trying to move about silently, she grabbed fresh clothing and went downstairs to dress. She grinned seeing their clothing in piles by the couch. Reaching for her boots, flashes of Melissa, naked between her legs, made desire rise again. Sula put her boots on and walked into the kitchen to get an ice cube from the freezer. Standing at the sink, she rubbed it back and forth across her brow to reduce the swelling and recalled delicious memories of last night. She hoped ice would reduce the fever growing inside her so she could focus on what she had planned for the day. She gazed out the window into darkness. Two sets of almond-shaped green eyes suddenly appeared in front of her as Tawny and Spotty perched on the windowsill staring at her.

"Good morning, girls. Breakfast is on the way." Sula knew they wouldn't understand waiting until later to eat and put food in their bowls. The soft tap-tap of the cat door opening and closing preceded the entrance of the two tabbies into the kitchen. They ran directly to the food, tails straight in the air. While they contentedly crunched their kibble, Sula set up the coffeemaker for Melissa. Even though she wanted a cup, she didn't want to wait on it, and the smell of it wafting up the stairs might wake her. Sula wrote a quick note, in case Melissa got up before she returned, and propped it in front of the coffee pot. She left the house at a brisk pace, heading for the old ponderosa tree across the meadow, where she quickly disrobed.

With well-honed expertise she engaged the *hamask* smoothly, and within minutes, her bones, tendons, and muscles stretched, enlarged, shifted, and reformed. Her fur came in thick and luxuriant, and her nails curved into thick, long claws. The transformation complete, she felt a stinging sensation on her brow but wasn't concerned. She lifted her head and pulled in a deep lungful of air through her nostrils, savoring it and sorting out the scents. With a grunt and a toss of her head she took off and…oh! It felt good to run on all fours.

After the initial burst of energy, she slowed her pace. She could cover a lot of ground quickly at a fast walk and not wear out. She reminded herself that she still had to go to work today and had a conference call with donors to attend. Avoiding open areas and staying under the safe cover of trees as much as possible, she traversed the land, crossing the pathways and traces where she had previously detected the scent of a mountain lion.

By the time she arrived at the spot near the boundary between her land and the national forest, where she'd discovered the mountain-lion snares a few weeks earlier, the sky was beginning to lighten. She walked slowly and methodically. As she neared the crest of the hill, she caught a scent. Instinct told her to stop…be quiet, look, and listen. And smell.

A slight breeze ruffled her fur; it was good to be downwind. She sniffed and again caught the faint, confusing scent. It was purposefully perplexing, she realized, a fragrance engineered to mask the scent of being human. But it wasn't perfect. An underlying olfactory tone, distinctly human, gave it away. She recognized this particular mix of synthetic and human pheromones as the stench that had been all over the place the day she tore out the traps.

Sula felt secure and in command on the higher ground. The human, undoubtedly that damn trapper, was below her unawares. She lay down, reducing her profile, and continued to quietly observe with her ears and nose. Concentrating, she heard movement, unhurried footfalls, moving away from her, which meant the person was heading deeper into public land. She waited patiently after the sound and the scent disappeared, letting some additional time pass before cautiously making her way down to where the deer path intersected with the mountain lion's trace. In the early morning twilight Sula carefully inspected the area and found no evidence that the snares had been reset. Having expected to find traps or, worse, evidence that a mountain lion had been caught and killed, she was perplexed at finding nothing of the sort. She continued nosing around until the shape of something that didn't belong in the woods caught her eye. She realized she was staring at a boxy, camouflaged object attached to a tree with a nylon strap—a trail camera!

She sauntered over to the camera and sniffed around the base and bark of the tree. The trapper had definitely been there. The camera was within easy reach. Removing it wouldn't have been a problem even if it wasn't. Contrary to popular belief, brown bears and grizzlies were adept at tree climbing when they felt compelled to do it. She stood on her hind legs and reached up. Hooking her long claws under the strap, she gave it a quick tug, tearing it loose from the tree in one swipe.

Curious about what she'd find on camera's storage card, she grunted softly to herself, the closest thing to laughter she could manage while in fur. She picked up the camera gently with her teeth and headed for home.

Melissa woke to the sound of purring. Very loud purring. She opened her eyes to see Spotty…no, it was Tawny, the orange-and-gray tabby, seated on Sula's pillow next to her head, who greeted her with a slow feline blink of the eye. Unless Sula had magically transformed into a cat, she wasn't in the room. Melissa stretched and yawned, remembering that Sula was planning to go for an early morning hike to chase away a mountain lion. A few weeks ago, such a thought would have sounded crazy to her, but today, it seemed quite normal. Funny how much could change in a short amount of time. She caught the scent of coffee as it wafted into the room and heard the clatter of dishes coming from the kitchen downstairs.

"Good morning," Melissa said, walking into the kitchen and wrapping her arms around Sula. Sula gave her a quick kiss. Her hair was damp, and she smelled good, like sandalwood and pine. "Did you take a shower already?"

"I did." Sula smiled.

"You must have been quiet as a mouse."

"You were *sound* asleep." Sula smiled and pointed to the coffee pot with the wooden spoon in her hand. "Coffee's ready and the oatmeal is almost done."

Melissa poured a cup of coffee, holding it with both hands, and leaned against the counter, watching Sula at the stove. "Did you go on that hike already?"

"I did." Sula portioned the thick oatmeal into two bowls.

"Any sign of Notch?"

"Nope," Sula said, smiling as she carried the bowls to the kitchen table. "No signs at all."

"That's good, yes?" Melissa sat and poured honey and milk on her oatmeal. Sula's preference for honey over brown sugar had grown on her.

"Yes, very good."

Melissa lifted a spoonful of oatmeal, and looking across the table at Sula, she noticed the thin black threads missing from her forehead. "Hey, what happened to your stitches? We didn't pull them out last night, did we? I was trying to be careful not to hurt you."

"No, you didn't hurt me." Sula chuckled. "Quite the opposite. You made me feel *very* good." She put her fingers to her brow. "They...um...felt like they needed to come out. I removed them before I left earlier."

Melissa stared at the wound, though it would now be better described as a scar. A healthy shade of pink, it appeared mostly healed. "You must have an amazing immune system, Sula. I wouldn't have thought it would look so good after just a couple of days."

"I've always healed fast," Sula said quickly.

"Clearly."

When Sula left for work shortly after breakfast, she gave Melissa a kiss that made her want to drag her back to bed...or the couch. She refrained, knowing that Sula had an important meeting. Perhaps she'd also removed the stitches because she wanted to look good for it.

Melissa took a quick shower and used Sula's pine-scented soap. While getting dressed she noticed the small bottle of Sula's fragrance and took the liberty of dabbing a little on the sides of her neck. She liked the idea of having Sula's scent on her, a subtle sensual reminder she could carry with her during the day.

Before falling asleep last night, Melissa had hatched a plan to surprise Sula with a picnic at Moose Lake, which she deduced was one of the points on the long hike Melissa hadn't been invited on. In those hazy moments before sleep, it had seemed like a brilliant idea, but in the clarity of the morning she realized that, first, she would have to find the lake and, second, figure out if she could even get to it. She grabbed her laptop and took it to the porch to enjoy the morning light and air while doing some research.

Using satellite images from Google Earth, she found Moose Lake, one of several small lakes in a cluster. The map didn't show private-property lines, but it did identify public lands. The lake was close to the edge of the national forest, and she assumed it must be on Sula's property, or maybe it was a part of the conservancy's land. There was a road nearby, but it didn't seem particularly close to the lake. Wondering if a topographic map might give her more detailed information, she opened a new window and found a website where she could view topographic maps for free. She wasn't adept at reading them, but she knew enough to get a sense of the steepness of the terrain and identify the road types.

After finding the right quadrant she scrolled and zoomed in on the lake. She was delighted to see a road on this map that wasn't denoted on the Google Earth map. It skirted around the lakes and was marked by dashed lines, indicating it was unimproved, one step up from a four-wheel-drive track.

Melissa recalled watching a video playing at the Subaru dealership when she was buying her Forester not long ago. The video demonstrated the off-road capabilities of cars like hers. Driving on muddy roads, she had used the mode that put the transmission into low four-wheel drive, increasing its traction and control. What was the point of having such a feature if you didn't use it? Trekking up to Moose Lake was as good a time as any to test it out on an unpaved mountain road.

Buoyed and resolved, Melissa noted the name of the map section and flipped the lid of her laptop closed. She headed into Buckhorn to do some shopping, and her first stop was Buckhorn Outfitters, the local outdoor-recreation store. The shop bell attached to the door tinkled cheerfully as she walked in. The front of the store was full of brightly colored clothing and footwear. Equally colorful kayaks and nylon kites hung suspended from the ceiling. It was all rather visually overwhelming.

"Can I help you?" A fit-looking and tanned young woman with long dark hair peered at her from behind a rack of light jackets. She wore an orange T-shirt with the store's name printed on it and a cute graphic of a smiling bear holding a cup of coffee.

"Yes. Do you have local maps?"

"We do." The woman, whose name tag identified her as Marley, waved her toward the back of the store and showed her the shelves lined with books and maps. "Are you looking for something in particular?"

"Yes, I am. Do you have the Sylvan Glade topographic map?"

"If it's around here, we should." Marley scanned the maps. "We have paper and laminated. Do you have a preference?"

"Laminated seems practical."

Marley selected a map and handed it to her. "You doing some hiking?"

"I am." Melissa didn't really want to go into any more detail.

"Well, if you need anything else, we probably have it."

Melissa hadn't fully considered what she might need to complete her little adventure. "This will probably do it, but I'm going to browse a bit."

"Okay," Marley said with a friendly smile. "If you need help just let me know."

"I will, thank you."

Melissa left the store with the map, a collapsible five-gallon water container, and a pack of Mylar emergency blankets. Walking through the first-aid section she had realized she should be prepared. Should she get stuck on the road, fail to get to the lake, and need to be rescued, she'd at least demonstrate that she wasn't stupid enough to go out unequipped. Also in the bag were two tees with the store's coffee-drinking bear logo: a green one for herself and a blue one for Sula. Melissa just couldn't resist.

She went to a casual riverside café for lunch. It was busy, and although her beer arrived quickly, the service was otherwise slow. She enjoyed the soothing sound of the water and the energetic chatter of hummingbirds as they darted between feeders hanging along the edge of the deck. It gave her time to study the map she had just purchased and to devise a plan. Sipping a draft of the local amber ale, she unfolded the map on the heavy rustic wooden table and studied it. Corresponding the laminated paper map with a digital map on her phone, she figured out how to get on the county road that intersected with the road leading to Moose Lake. She made a rough estimation that it would take her at least an hour to drive there, longer if the going was slow on the unimproved road. Since she wasn't exactly sure when Sula would arrive, she'd want to arrive early. She'd take an art history book or two with her and a notebook. She couldn't read without taking notes, an academic habit. She checked the forecast and saw little chance for rain. Her plan was coming together perfectly.

"Excuse me. Can I put this down?" A server, balancing a large, round tray laden with food in one hand, held a plate with a massive burger and mound of fries in his other hand, hovering it over the table.

"Oh, I'm so sorry," Melissa said and folded the map quickly, setting it aside to make space for her lunch.

"Enjoy!" the waiter said, seemingly unperturbed. He set the plate in front of her and dashed off to deliver more orders.

Melissa took a bite of the burger, which tasted so good, perfectly cooked and thickly stacked with cheese, lettuce, onion, and a ripe tomato. Why did everything seem to taste better in the mountains? Watching the swift water flow past and listening to the hummingbirds' chatter, she ate slowly, enjoying each bite, and imagining the look of surprise on Sula's face when she found her at the lake tomorrow.

Sula returned to her office after her two-hour video-conference meeting. The group of major donors was an enthusiastic bunch, mostly successful businessmen and women with a passion for the outdoors or environmental issues, and they were eager to help with an upcoming fund-raising gala. Her staff ran most of the meeting; she only had to give an introduction and comment when necessary. She was thankful for that, as the storage card from the trail camera she had nabbed early in the morning was in her pocket and seemed to be burning a hole.

She inserted the card into her desktop computer and was pleased to see files, hundreds of them, sorted into dated folders. When she opened the first image file, she was delighted to see a GPS coordinate included with the time-date stamp. She grabbed a notepad and a pencil and wrote down the coordinates as she scrolled through the photos. The images were a mix of black-and-white infrared images taken at night that revealed animals in ghostly shades. Less frequent were color images when the camera shifted to daylight mode. Most of the images were on par with what you would expect to find—numerous deer and elk browsing past the camera's field of view, a black bear with a cub, a few raccoons, an owl swooping past, and an industrious mouse that triggered the camera repeatedly as it darted back and forth across the trail the camera was monitoring.

The photos in the last two folders were the most interesting ones. The folder dated two days ago held three images of a mountain lion. In one, the shape of the lion's head was distinctly outlined against the dark background. Sula zoomed in and saw the misshapen ear. Notch! She picked up her pencil and wrote down the GPS coordinates.

An unexpected number of images was on the card from this morning. The first image was tantalizingly incomplete. The person who set the camera was recorded, but only partly. It could have been anyone wearing a hooded sweatshirt. She wrote down the coordinates even though she knew exactly where the shots had been taken. When Sula opened the next photo, she jumped in her seat and then laughed as she clicked through the next few images. A large brown bear, looking directly at the camera, walked up to it and then obscured the lens. Sula knew that occurred when she ripped the camera from the tree. A dozen or more pictures had been recorded after that, blurry views of the ground taken while she carried the camera back home. She had been careful to put the camera facedown on the ground before she shifted, and when back in human form, she had opened the case and turned off the camera. She viewed the images with fascination. She'd never seen pictures of herself in bear form before and was intrigued by how much she recognized herself. It was her eyes. Bears' expressive eyes, set close together and in line with the bridge of the nose, were not so different from human ones. Not surprisingly, she looked a lot like her mother in fur. She was a good-looking bear, if she did say so herself. Much as she wanted to save these photos, she deleted the files with regret. It was just too dangerous to keep them. She was obviously not a black bear, and her shape and size were remarkably close to that of a native grizzly. While grizzly sightings in Colorado continued to be reported, physical evidence or photographs had never corroborated them, and she wanted to keep it that way.

Now that she had viewed all the photos, she was curious to know where they had been taken. She opened a mapping program and typed in the GPS coordinates to produce a topographic map marked with five bright-red dots. She added a layer showing property lines and another delineating roads to help visualize the locations. She leaned back in her chair and crossed her arms, glowering at the map on the screen. Each dot was located along the boundaries between the national forest,

Buckhorn Creek Ranch, the conservancy's land, and her private land. Her skin prickled, and she felt as if a predator was stalking her. Indeed, there was a predator out there, albeit a human one. And she also knew she wasn't the prey it was searching for. She was fairly certain the target was Notch, the mountain lion she was trying to educate and protect, or perhaps any mountain lion who happened to be unlucky enough to step into the trapper's snare.

She stared hard at one particular red dot and, leaning forward, zoomed in on the map, enlarging the terrain and an irregular blue shape representing a body of water. The red dot was very close to Moose Lake, the area she was planning to patrol tomorrow. She muttered an inelegant expletive to herself when she realized that the camera had been placed on conservancy land. The trapper had trespassed, and these photos with their embedded GPS tags were proof.

Not exactly sure how she'd do it, Sula silently vowed to stop the trapper.

Melissa returned to her cabin after a last stop at the grocery store, where she picked up a loaf of French bread, an assortment of deli meats, cheeses, fresh ripe fruit, and some locally made chocolates, hoping to rival the smorgasbord Sula had prepared for their first hike to Icy Creek. She carried the bags into the kitchen and put the perishables in the refrigerator. When she turned and faced the great room, the reality that this wasn't home suddenly hit her. In two days, she had to pack her things, load her car, and drive back to Georgia. And rather than being ready to go home, as she would have normally expected after more than a month away, she felt strangely displaced and a deep melancholy brewing.

She walked into the living room and stood in front of the wall of glass. As she stared at the verdant meadow and the blue mountain hillsides in the distance, her vision blurred. Tears were streaming down her cheeks in salty, warm rivulets.

CHAPTER TWENTY-EIGHT

Sula left the house before daybreak after a breakfast of toast and coffee that Melissa made. When Sula nuzzled her cheek in the dark and told her she could stay in bed, Melissa explained that she wanted to spend as much time as she could with her and would get up. And that was true, even if she wasn't completely forthcoming about her plan to intercept her at Moose Lake.

After Sula left, Melissa dressed quickly and drove to her cabin to get the picnic supplies. Walking into the cabin she was confronted by what she had packed the day before in preparation for the drive back to Georgia. Her grandmother's photo album, notebooks, and art books were stowed back into the box she had brought them in. Next to it were several bags full of souvenirs and gifts for friends. She grabbed a pen and a sticky note from a box and went into the kitchen. *Going to Moose Lake,* she wrote on the bright-yellow paper and stuck it to the counter. If her plans went awry, she wanted someone to know where she was headed. After loading a cooler with food and ice, she hoisted it and carried it out to her car, away from all the reminders that her time in Buckhorn was ending very soon.

Using her car's GPS, she followed the route she had planned, taking a two-lane state highway to the unpaved county road that led to Moose Lake. It was a beautiful drive on the smooth highway, the sky clear and the rising sun bathing everything in a crisp, clear light. The road curved gently, following the terrain of the lower edge of the mountainside for a few miles and providing views of lush meadows. Gaining in elevation, the road twisted and turned as it traversed coniferous forest. Occasional breaks in the trees provided stunning vistas of the peaks in the distance. In many areas the trees created a patchwork mix of green and rusty brown, evidence of the devastating forest fires that had ravaged this area a few years ago. In a few places, healthy stands of trees had been thinned first by fire and then by chainsaws. Dry dead trees had been removed to prevent them becoming fuel for a future fire. It was a heartbreaking sight.

As she approached the crest of the mountain, a yellow sign indicated the road she was looking for lay ahead. It appeared quickly on the left, just before a sharp turn to the right. Watching carefully for oncoming traffic, Melissa turned off the paved road. She paused to read the routered and painted wooden signs identifying a church camp and a ranch ahead. Another sign stated that the public road became private in four miles. From her maps, Melissa knew Moose Lake should be a few miles more past that point.

Excited, she drove forward and ran through a mental checklist of the things she had packed—the cooler that contained more food that she needed for a picnic lunch for two, a blanket, emergency Mylar blankets, and a full five-gallon container of water. Stowed in the back of her car, in a pocket above the spare tire, was the first-aid kit she always kept on hand. Her backpack was loaded with a couple of books, a notebook, pens, and a waterproof jacket for an unexpected rainstorm.

The gravel road was well-graded and snaked down into a valley, where turnoffs for the church camp and the ranch were clearly indicated with more wooden signs. She lowered the window as the road continued along the meadow's edge, the air fresh and sweetly scented. She saw a small lake and paused to glance at the open map on the passenger seat, confirming its presence on the printed page. Ahead of her the road turned, and before entering a stand of trees, she spotted another sign, this one metal and professionally fabricated. In stern language it indicated that beyond the sign was a nature preserve owned by the Colorado Bear Conservancy and that access without a permit was not allowed. A second sign, in all capital letters, explicitly stated that no hunting was allowed.

Melissa read the signs. Technically, she was trespassing, but considering that she was planning a surprise romantic picnic for the conservancy's director, it seemed like the rules didn't really apply to her. The road narrowed and was less well maintained, but she didn't find any ruts or large rocks like the jeep track Sula had driven on in her Bronco. Taking it slow, she continued on the road, winding up and down the hillsides.

Coming down the last hill she had glimpses of the lake, its surface shimmering in the morning light. At the bottom, the road widened into a pullout with a sign displaying the conservancy logo and reading "Moose Lake Access."

Elated, almost giddy, at her success in finding the lake, Melissa pulled over and stopped. It had been so much easier getting here than she expected. But she hadn't anticipated seeing a big red Dodge pickup, trimmed in chrome, parked in the pullout. She had seen this truck before, and it took her a moment to connect it with the details of her memory. It was Kerry's. She'd noticed her getting out of it when Sula stopped for gas before they went to dinner at the Buckaroo.

What was Kerry doing here? Sula didn't know what her job was, though she said Kerry claimed to be working for the government. If that was the case, it didn't make sense that she would be on the conservancy's preserve, which was private land. She knew Kerry was a hunting guide in addition to being an avid hunter herself, something that riled Sula. And given that Sula intensely disliked and distrusted Kerry, it didn't seem likely that Sula would allow her access to land she managed. Could Kerry be poaching?

Impulsively, Melissa got out of the car and walked slowly up to the truck. She glanced around and saw no sign of Kerry. Standing on the running boards, she looked into the cab, seeing nothing out of the ordinary, but a foul scent filled her nostrils with the stench of death and putrefaction. Afraid of what she might see, she turned and peered into the bed of the truck anyway. It was empty, but a line of blood, thick and coagulated in the sun, pooled between the ridges of the black plastic bed liner and had begun to attract flies. Melissa walked around to the back and saw red drops smeared on the ground, forming a trail leading toward the lake that she could glimpse beyond the trees.

Melissa ran back to her car and got in, breathing heavily less from exertion than from fear and a rush of adrenaline. She locked the doors. Crazy thoughts went through her head, including the possibility that Kerry had murdered someone and was hiding the body. She forcibly calmed herself and attempted to rationalize her skittering thoughts. Kerry was a player, a womanizer, but she didn't seem like a killer. But, really, how could you know? Serial killers got away with murder for years, sometimes decades, and their neighbors often never had a clue.

Melissa stopped her mind from going down the path of what might be and instead focused on what she knew was true. Kerry was a hunter, not for food, but for the sport of it. She worked as a guide and was hired by other trophy hunters. She enjoyed hunting, and hunting meant killing. She must have killed an animal. That seemed the most plausible reason for the blood. But it was still unclear as to why she was here by the lake. Not only was it private property, but the Colorado

Bear Conservancy owned it. It just didn't make sense. The more she thought about it, the more she felt a growing unease. Whatever was going on, it didn't seem good.

Something was dead, and whatever Kerry was doing with the dead thing on conservancy land, she probably didn't have permission to do it. Melissa started the engine, intending to abandon her plans for a picnic and telling Sula about what she had witnessed as soon as she could, but before she could get back on to the road, Kerry emerged from the trees, walking along a narrow path.

Wearing matching brown and olive-green forest camouflage shirt and pants emulating branches and leaves, she appeared emotionless and inscrutable. As she approached, her countenance changed noticeably the moment she seemed to recognize Melissa. Her body relaxed as her purposeful gait shifted into a slow swagger. She lifted her chin, a nod of greeting, and flashed a wolfish grin, her teeth white against her tanned skin. Melissa had witnessed this expression before, but now Kerry seemed only a facsimile of friendliness as the coldness in her eyes persisted.

Sula paused to survey her surroundings. She knew from the terrain that she was nearing Moose Lake, and sniffing the air, she could smell the water. If no one was nearby, she planned to circle it, searching for evidence of the trapper or the trapped. The trail camera had been placed there a few days ago, and it seemed possible that the site might give her some answers to her questions. After a thorough inspection, she planned to cut across Buckhorn Creek Ranch, steering clear of its horse and hiking trails, and make her way back to her land to be home by noon.

She'd maintained a fast pace all morning, slowing only to inspect the places where the trail camera had been located. Twice, she found evidence of traps that had been placed and removed, but she didn't see blood or the telltale signs of struggle: disturbed ground and broken branches where an ensnared animal flailed in desperation to free itself. She'd caught the marking scent of a lion a few times along the way, but it was faint, not fresh.

She neared the lake following a shallow draw where the ground was soft and moist, dampening the sound of her movement. Catching the scent of raspberries, she slowed her steps, swinging her head from side to side, looking for the tantalizing treat. She rationalized that a few ripe berries would be a good energy boost. Finding the shrub, Sula stripped the ripest berries from the canes, enjoying the sweet fruit, but then dropped the berry between her lips, interrupted by the sound of human voices. She pitched her ears forward, seeking the location of the sounds, which seemed to be coming from the direction of the lake.

She moved slowly and methodically toward the water, taking up a position next to a boulder, where she peered carefully around the rock, continuing to rely on her sensitive hearing as she scanned the lake's edge. The breeze was blowing laterally across the lake, and she didn't detect anything out of the ordinary with her keen nose. A gleam of light caught her eye, and when she focused on it, she realized she was looking at the reflection of sunlight on metal, the trim on a truck, it seemed. The breeze shifted direction suddenly, coming toward her and allowing her to discern two voices and bringing valuable information to her keen nose. She tilted her head, putting her long snout to the breeze. With nostrils flared she inhaled deeply and caught several scents. The strongest held the pungent odor of death and a musky tone she associated with deer. Her lower lip quivered on the next deep intake as she recognized the smell of something particular and peculiarly unnatural…the trapper's cover scent. The trapper was here! Sula fought the urge to huff and snort in anger. She had more smells to sort out. A third deep intake revealed a distinctive fragrance that triggered an entirely different emotion. This was a very, very good scent that tickled her insides. This one she knew intimately.

Sula's mind roiled as she questioned why Melissa would be here at Moose Lake, and, more important, why she was here with the damn trapper. Confused, Sula stood on her hind legs, letting her front legs hang loosely along her sides as she stretched her neck upward and held her head high. Staring hard across the lake she finally saw the upper bodies of two people. She recognized Melissa by her silhouette. Her hair was pulled back in a ponytail, and she wore her bright-yellow jacket. In front of her was a…woman in camo? This was the trapper? She was taller than Melissa, and thin…*Kerry!*

Suddenly, disconnected bits of information knitted together. Sula knew a Wildlife Services agent had been working the area around the time Kerry quit her job at the ranch. She had bragged about leaving for a government job but strangely didn't want to reveal what it was. Of course, she wouldn't tell Sula that she was a contract wildlife killer.

Sula dropped to all fours with a grunt and pawed the ground in agitation. When she had seen Kerry at the gas station recently, something had bothered her deeply, but she couldn't figure out what it was. Now she realized it was her unique identifying scent that she tried to cover up with hunter's trickery. Sula had perceived it, but given that human sense of smell was vastly inferior to a bear's, she couldn't clearly recognize it for what it was.

A rage engulfed Sula like a wind-blown wildfire. Taking long strides and staying under cover of the trees, she made her way to the other side of the lake to figure out what the hell was going on.

"Wow, so you're out here doing government work?" Melissa tried to sound innocently enthused. Sitting in the car she thought about driving off to tell Sula that Kerry was doing something suspicious by the lake. But Sula was on her way to the lake completely unaware of what was going on. Melissa decided to engage with Kerry until Sula arrived… whenever that would be.

"I am," Kerry said with a cocky grin.

Melissa didn't buy it. If she was doing anything official on conservancy land, Sula would have mentioned it. Melissa knew that Sula didn't know where Kerry was working, and it bothered her. Kerry was lying. But why?

"Is this some kind of special ops, top-secret kind of thing?" She kept smiling and wagged a finger at Kerry's camo outfit.

Kerry narrowed her eyes. "Sort of."

"So, you can't let me in on it?" Melissa forced a laugh. "I hate to tell you this, but your camo's not working. I can see you. You can't be *that* undercover."

Kerry laughed at her stupid joke and seemed relaxed, but she didn't answer the question. "So why are *you* out here? This is off the beaten path. Tourists don't usually come out this way."

"I'm not your average tourist."

"No, you're not," Kerry said salaciously, raising a single eyebrow. Her expression made Melissa feel uncomfortable, and she hoped her reaction didn't show on her face.

"I grew up in Colorado, remember? I like to go to the places where the tourists don't go."

"Yeah, I get that."

"Anyway, I was planning to go for a little hike around the lake and enjoy a beautiful day far away from the madding crowd."

"Away from what?"

"The madding crowd," Melissa said while opening the passenger-side door and grabbing her backpack. "It's an expression, the title of an old book, actually. It means to get away from hustle and bustle of city life."

"Always the professor, huh?"

Melissa didn't respond to the dig. She wanted to come across as friendly, not adversarial. She shrugged, put the pack on, and pointed in the direction Kerry had come from. No doubt, whatever she'd dragged out of the bed of the truck was out there in the woods. "Well, I'm going to take my hike and let you get back to work."

As soon as she stepped forward, Kerry put a hand up, stopping her. "You shouldn't go that way."

"Really? Why not?"

"There's something you won't want to see."

"Such as?"

Kerry crossed her arms and frowned. "A dead deer."

"Oh! How *terrible*." She focused on a dark stain on Kerry's shirt. "Is that deer blood on your clothes? Did you shoot it?"

"No. I didn't shoot it." Kerry frowned, giving her a sideways glance, and unfolded her arms. "It was hit by a car." Melissa twisted around to get a better view of the front of Kerry's truck. "I didn't hit it, if that's what you're wondering."

"I was." Melissa smiled. "Why did you bring it out here? Are you hiding the body?"

"Yes," Kerry said quickly, too eagerly. Melissa sensed that she was lying again. "That's exactly what I'm doing. I thought I'd let scavengers take care of it. Circle of life. What better place than here? I'm not the bad person you seem to think I am."

"Well, I'm not the delicate flower you seem to think *I* am. I can handle seeing a dead deer." Melissa wasn't convinced that was really true. Driving past a deer that had been struck by a car was one thing, but getting close to one was not something she was sure she had the stomach for. She started walking in the direction Kerry had come from, hoping she would take the bait. The longer she stayed with her, the greater the chance Sula would show up and catch her at whatever she was doing.

"We'll see," Kerry said with a harsh laugh. "Okay. If you're determined to go that way, I'll walk with you, at least until the deer. I'll point you away from it. I'm sure you don't really want to see it."

"Oh, are you going to be my knight in shining armor?" *Or should I say bloody camo?*

"I'll be whatever you want," Kerry said huskily. "I still regret we never finished our date."

Melissa inwardly cringed. Where was Sula? She felt a rising panic when she considered that Sula might have changed her plans and wasn't actually coming to Moose Lake. In that case, she'd do her best to keep her shit together, politely walk past the deer, and say good-bye to Kerry. And then what? She didn't know, but she'd figure it out. She hooked her thumbs in the straps of her pack and gently rested her fingers against the canister of bear spray, mentally rehearsing how it worked. She was beginning to wish she hadn't reconsidered her initial plan to drive away.

Sula knew the deer was close. In human form, she could have detected the smell as unpleasant. In fur, as she was now, it was overwhelming. Looking ahead, she saw the mangled remains a few yards away. A young buck, its flesh torn and body mangled, appeared to have been hit by a car. Sula assumed the trapper put it out as bait for a mountain lion and looked around, expecting to see leg-hold traps or snares, but saw none. Melissa must have interrupted Kerry before she had a chance to set them, on conservancy land, no less. Sula's smoldering anger was about to ignite.

Sula heard their voices, the sounds coming closer. She backed away, moving up the hillside. A large downed tree caught her eye, and she scrambled over it, intending to lay low, listen, and observe. On the other side she was surprised to find a tree stand and climbing equipment leaning against the log. She sniffed it and picked up Kerry's altered scent. It seemed she wasn't planning to set traps around the deer. She was going to climb the tree and wait for Notch to check out the carcass, then shoot him from above, no doubt.

She had figured out what Kerry was planning to do later, but she still had no clue what was going on right now, nor why Melissa was here. When she heard Melissa's raised voice, she sensed anger and an undertone of fear. Sula stopped thinking and went into action.

"Touch me again, Kerry, and I will pepper-spray you." Melissa pulled the canister out of the holster attached to the shoulder strap of her pack and pointed it at Kerry

"Oh, come on..." Kerry put her hands up and laughed. "I was just going to give you a kiss. Sula's not here, so she'll never know. This is your big summer adventure, isn't it? Live a little, Professor. I'll give you a story to tell all your friends back home." Kerry grinned and stepped forward.

Melissa popped the safety latch off with her thumb, the orange plastic tab falling to the ground. "I'm not kidding. *Back off.*"

"Fuck!" Kerry's eyes widened, and she took several steps backward, then froze in place. "What the...*fuck!*"

Melissa, stunned at her ability to impress Kerry with how serious she was, realized that Kerry wasn't looking at her. She was staring behind her. Suspicious that it was a trick to get her to put her guard down, Melissa resisted the urge to turn and look. But when she heard rustling and an agitated hoarse, huffing sound, she knew something really was behind her. And it was big.

Melissa turned, pepper spray in hand, and witnessed the dark form of a bear. It stood still, perched on a downed tree, and stared at them with an intensity that was almost palpable. It was unlike any of the black bears she had seen in pictures or videos. Her heart pounded, and she felt like she'd just received an electric shock. This bear was massive, with dark-brown fur and a lighter face and muzzle. Broad, long-legged, and high-shouldered, it lowered its head and fixed its gaze on Melissa. The bear's warm golden eyes, glinting in the sunlight, bore into her. She froze, aware she was in extreme danger. The bear became agitated and began swaying its head from side to side, blowing air through its nostrils and making throaty, guttural sounds. Melissa couldn't look away. It was the most magnificent and beautiful thing she had ever seen. Fear competed with awe.

"It's a goddamn grizzly," Kerry said in a low voice.

"There are no grizzlies here." Melissa repeated what Sula had told her.

The bear huffed loudly and pounced forward, landing on its front feet. Kerry shuddered. "That's no black bear. Trust me. *Shit.* The deer... the deer...it thinks we're competitors for the carcass."

"Hey, bear," Melissa said in a calm, but firm voice, employing the bear-safety strategy she had recently learned, and stepped sideways.

The bear responded with another guttural huff. Fixing its gaze on Kerry, it moved quickly forward and stopped abruptly, a bluff charge.

Kerry jerked in response, almost falling over backward. "Use the spray!"

The bear snorted and clacked its teeth.

"Stay calm," Melissa said, keeping her eye on the big bear. Movement in her peripheral vision prompted her to glance over at Kerry. She had raised her shirt and was pulling a black handgun from a holster tucked inside her pants.

"What are you—"

The bear charged, closing the gap between them. Melissa flinched, and, as a cloud of pepper spray jettisoned forward, two shots rang out in rapid succession. Kerry yelled and coughed. The bear let out a terrible sound of anguish and stumbled, falling to the ground.

"Oh, my God, you sprayed me!" She wiped at her face and raised her gun again, pointing it blindly at the bear, who was writhing on the ground in front of them.

"No!" Melissa said without thinking and sprayed Kerry again, this time intentionally.

Kerry coughed and sputtered. She went down on her hands and knees, retching. But it was nothing in comparison to the sounds the bear was making. Melissa shifted her gaze to the bear. Maybe it was the adrenaline, or perhaps she was going into shock, but she couldn't focus on the animal. It was the strangest thing. Everything else was clear—the sun shining through the needles on the branches of the trees, the dappled light on the rocks, the dusty ground. But the bear was strangely indistinct. She watched with horror as the animal heaved and rippled. It uttered sounds that chilled her to the bone, and she wondered if she was hearing what peopled called the death rattle. Was she watching this animal die? Kerry groaned and coughed, yet Melissa's only concern was for the bear.

She walked toward it, shaking her head and rubbing her eyes. Head tucked, it lay facing the ground with one front leg folded under its chest and the other extended with the massive dark paw turned up, revealing thick black pads and the tips of curved claws. Not only was it out of focus, but its shape was changing. It seemed to be growing smaller and was losing its fur, which wasn't falling out; it was just disappearing, like a drawing being erased. The shape of its face was shifting, too, its snout shortening. The anguished sounds intensified, causing her ears to ring. Melissa kneeled, reaching out to the pitiful creature, as if touching it would confirm that what she was seeing was real and not some kind of hallucination. When her fingertips made contact, the pads of its toes felt hot and prickly, almost as if an electric current were passing between them.

"Don't touch me," the bear said thickly. Its voice was unmistakably Sula's.

CHAPTER TWENTY-NINE

Melissa snatched her hand back. "Sula?"

The dark form of the creature on the ground in front of her coalesced into something more human than bear and recognizably like Sula. What she beheld made absolutely no sense. She had no rational explanation for what she was witnessing, but right now none of that mattered. There was no more bear, only Sula sprawled facedown on the ground, naked and bleeding. She responded instinctively. She rolled Sula on to her side and put her hand on her cheek.

Sula opened her eyes, but unable to focus on Melissa, she mumbled incoherently. The flesh along the side of her ribs was jagged and torn, as if one of the bullets had grazed her. Two nearly perfect round holes penetrated either side of her upper arm, entrance and exit wounds from the second bullet, Melissa guessed. They bled profusely, bright-red blood pooling and rolling across her skin. Melissa took off her backpack and searched it for a bandana. Finding it, she wrapped it tightly around Sula's arm, tying the corners in a knot to hold it in place and hoping the pressure would help slow the bleeding.

"Is that Sula?" Kerry sat on the ground, still coughing, her face blotchy red and her eyes puffy. Saliva dripped from her chin, and vomit mixed with the blood stain on her shirt. "How can that be *Sula*? I shot a bear."

"Melissa," Sula said slowly, meeting her gaze. Her eyes were the same amber color as the bear's just a few minutes ago. Melissa's mind faltered.

"I shot a bear," Kerry said again, raising her voice like a petulant child. "A grizzly bear!"

"Kerry, *shut up*." Melissa maintained eye contact with Sula. "I need to get you to a hospital, Sula. Do you think you can stand? I don't think I can carry you."

Seeming to come out of a stupor, she nodded and grunted.

Melissa stood, and avoiding touching the raw flesh along her ribs or her wounded arm, she helped her into a standing position.

"Melissa—"

"Hospital, Sula." Melissa had only one goal in mind, and she could focus just on that single thing. If she let her mind think about other *things*, she'd lose it. "Let's get you to the hospital. Here, lean on me. Put your arm over my shoulder." Melissa wrapped her arm around Sula's waist, steadying her and taking some of the weight off her feet. Sula stumbled but took a halting step forward and then another. "The car's not far. Just keep walking with me."

They shuffled past Kerry, who seemed disinclined to get up. Melissa didn't care if she stayed there. In fact, she preferred it. As they continued down the path, Kerry said repeatedly that she had shot a bear.

The drive to the local hospital in Buckhorn seemed to take forever. Sula, wrapped in the picnic blanket with a silver emergency Mylar sheet over the top, was obviously in pain. Every sharp curve and bump in the road caused her to gasp, and she looked pallid. Melissa focused on driving as carefully and smoothly as she could manage. Keeping her mind on that task and monitoring Sula with quick glances helped keep her from replaying what she had just witnessed by the lake.

She pulled under the covered emergency room entrance at the hospital and told Sula not to move while she went inside. Stepping through the sliding doors into the harsh fluorescent light of the hospital disoriented her. She must have looked it, too, as a nurse, a young, dark-haired woman, immediately asked if she needed help. As soon as she used the word *gunshot* in explaining Sula's condition, a young man in scrubs ran out to her car, followed quickly by two orderlies pushing a gurney. The nurse put her hand gently but firmly on Melissa's elbow and guided her to an examination area, explaining that she needed to make sure she was okay. A second nurse, an older woman with wavy red hair and wielding a clipboard, joined them, requesting her identification and insurance cards, and asked her a lot of questions. The brunette nurse directed her to sit on the bed and attached an automated blood-pressure cuff to her arm. Her ID card dangled in front of her: Courtney Stone, RN. As the machine hummed and the cuff tightened, Nurse Stone examined her, looking for bullet holes, no doubt, while Melissa tried her best to answer the questions being asked by the redheaded nurse.

"Your blood pressure and respiration rate are a little high," Nurse Stone said.

"I just saw someone shoot my girlfriend." Melissa didn't add the part about her girlfriend also being a bear. A bear who transformed into a woman. All this attention on her made her feel like she was being sidetracked from the reason she was here. "Is Sula okay?"

"I can't answer that for you right now," said the redheaded nurse standing at the foot of the bed. "But I'll see if I can find something out." She peered over the shoulder of Nurse Stone at the computer monitor. "You can rest here until things get back to normal." She patted Melissa's leg and left the room.

Things were never going to get back to normal, not after today. While Nurse Stone quietly worked on the computer, Melissa leaned back against the pillow and stared at the holes in the ceiling tile above the bed, as if focusing on them could somehow anchor her and prevent her mind from swirling. After several minutes, it was clear her strategy wasn't working. She lifted her head when the curtain was drawn back, expecting the redheaded nurse with news of Sula. Instead it was a handsome, dark-haired, mustachioed police officer. He nodded at her when they made eye contact.

"Hello, Miss Warren...Dr. Warren. I'm Officer Martinez, and I'd like to ask you a few questions." He stood at the foot of the bed, holding a small notebook in one hand and a pen in the other, seemingly ready to take notes. He looked her directly in the eye.

Melissa glanced at his name tag—L. Martinez—pinned above the pocket of his shirt, opposite his shiny silver badge. Sula had mentioned an officer named Lee Martinez, the one who called her Smokey, and talked about him more like a friend than a business acquaintance.

"Yes, of course." Knowing that Sula respected him made her feel more comfortable, but still...how was she going to describe what had just happened without explaining the giant bear that had appeared and turned into Sula? She'd end up in a psychiatric ward, for sure. "I'm sorry, but could I have some water first?"

"I'll get you some," Nurse Stone said and left.

Officer Martinez stared at the floor and chewed on the edge of his mustache. Melissa closed her eyes and put her head back on the pillow. While the nurse was gone, Melissa realized that she could tell the story exactly how it happened, but just not mention anything about a bear. The nurse returned with a large cup full of ice water and a warm blanket that she draped across her. It felt surprisingly good. She took a deep drink, sucking the cold water through the straw, draining half the cup.

"Do you know who shot Sula Johansen?" Officer Martinez asked.

"Yes, I do. It was Kerry MacArthur. She used to work for the Buckhorn Creek Ranch. I'm staying there, so that's how I know her." Officer Martinez raised an eyebrow almost imperceptibly as he wrote in his notebook. "And can you tell me how it happened?"

"I can." Melissa took another sip of water, a deep breath, and described how her plans for a romantic picnic had gone terribly awry. Like a good student, Officer Martinez took notes while she talked. "So, as I said, Kerry was making me feel uncomfortable."

"Describe what you mean by 'uncomfortable.'"

"She kept touching me and tried to kiss me. I told her to stop and she wouldn't."

"That's when you pulled out the bear spray."

"Yes…I really just wanted her to back off, to leave me alone, I didn't intend to actually spray her. But then Sula showed up unexpectedly— she jumped over a big log—and I guess it startled Kerry. She drew a gun—"

"What kind of gun?"

"A handgun."

"You didn't know she had a firearm?"

"No. It was under her shirt. She pulled the gun, and I guess I flinched. I sprayed her accidentally." Melissa paused and considered the fact she was talking to a police officer. "The first time."

"You sprayed her more than once?" Officer Martinez's mustache twitched almost imperceptibly.

"The second time was on purpose because I thought she was going to shoot Sula again." Melissa took another drink of water, sucking it through the straw, watching as he wrote everything down.

"How many shots were fired?"

"Two, one right after the other."

"Did Ms. MacArthur fire the gun before or after you sprayed her?"

Melissa chewed on her lower lip and shook her head slowly. "I'm not sure, it might have happened at the same time. It's all a blur."

A call came in on the officer's radio, and he put a finger up, cueing her to pause while he cocked his head, listening to the message. He put his hand on the radio mic draped over his shoulder, turned his head, and replied quickly in coded police jargon. "I'm sorry. Please continue, Dr. Warren."

"Well, that's about it, really. Kerry fired twice, Sula went down, I pepper-sprayed Kerry again, and then I got Sula to the car and drove her here to the hospital."

"And you said you left Ms. MacArthur at the lake."

"Yes, she was sitting on the ground. She seemed okay, but—"

"But what?" Officer Martinez looked at her with raised eyebrows. "She kept saying she shot a bear and that she couldn't believe it was Sula." Melissa shrugged, raising her eyebrows. "Honestly, I was more concerned about getting Sula to the car."

"Is there anything else you think I should know?"

"No. Not that I can think of right now."

"All right," he said, making a few more notes. "That'll be all for now." He flipped his notebook closed and clicked his pen, slipping both into his shirt pocket, then pulled out a business card and handed it to her. "Can you come by the department anytime tomorrow and give us a written statement? If you think of anything between now and then, you can add it."

"Sure." Melissa stared at the card in her hand, feeling the gravity of being a witness.

"You take care," Officer Martinez nodded and left Melissa alone in the room. She watched the clock and listened to the activity and conversations happening on the other side of the curtain. Not sure who else to contact, she pulled out her cell phone and sent a message to Betty, telling her that Sula had been shot and was at the hospital. She was relieved when the nurse finally returned with an ER physician, who asked her the questions she'd already answered and looked over the notes the nurse had made.

"Your vitals are improved. Unless you have any complaints," the doctor said with a smile, "I think you're good to go."

"I'm good," Melissa said, though she wasn't entirely sure about that.

The doctor signed her release forms, and the nurse handed her the discharge papers.

"What about Sula?" Melissa asked. The red-haired nurse had never come back with information about her.

"Oh…" the nurse said. "Why don't you have a seat in the waiting area, and I'll see what I can find out."

That was the second time she'd heard that promise, but not knowing what else to do, Melissa went to the almost-empty waiting area. It seemed to be a slow day in Buckhorn. The room was cold, and she wished she still had the warm blanket. When the automatic doors swooshed open, Melissa looked up to see Betty walk in and waved to her. She strode over with a look of deep concern.

"What happened to Sula?"

Melissa opened her mouth to speak but wasn't sure where to begin. "Kerry shot Sula."

"Kerry MacArthur? Is Sula okay?"

"I think so?" Melissa felt tears well, and her throat constricted, the emotion she had kept under tight control spilling over. "I don't know. I don't really understand anything."

Betty stood in front of her, hands on hips, frowning, as the doors opened and a voice they both recognized filled the waiting room. They turned to see Kerry, wide-eyed and yelling. She was handcuffed and flanked by two police officers.

"I shot a bear! A bear! She was a bear! Sula was a bear!" Kerry saw them across the room and lunged toward Melissa. "Melissa! Tell them!" The officers hooked her elbows and dragged her back to the admitting desk. "I shot a *bear*!"

Lee Martinez trailed behind Kerry and the other officers. After watching Kerry's outburst, he walked over to Melissa and Betty. He glanced over at Kerry with a sad expression. She looked a mess, her hair coming out of her usually neat braid and still dressed in her soiled camouflage outfit. "She's angling for a psychiatric evaluation."

Melissa leaned forward, putting her head in her hands and groaned. "Can you make that two?"

"Excuse me?" Martinez said.

"Nothing," Betty said, putting her hand on Melissa's shoulder. "I'll take care of this, Lee."

"She's had a rough day," Officer Martinez said, gesturing to Melissa, his tone sympathetic. "If you need anything, Betty, you let me know."

"I will, Lee," Betty said in a confident voice. "Thank you."

After he left, Betty sat next to her, putting her hand on her knee. "Melissa, honey. I need you to tell me what happened. And you've got to keep it together, okay?"

"Okay," Melissa said, sniffling.

Betty glanced around, seeming to survey the room. The only other people in the waiting area were on the other side, near a television they were watching. "So, what happened?"

After just having given a full—well, *almost* complete report to the officer, Melissa didn't feel up for describing the details again. She tried to explain as concisely as she could. "Sula went for a hike early this morning. She's been looking for signs of that mountain lion, and I knew she was going to Moose Lake, but she didn't want me to go with her. I planned a picnic and drove up there, intending to wait there and surprise her. But when I arrived, Kerry was there. I don't know what she was doing, but I think she might have been poaching. There was a dead deer."

"A dead deer?" Betty repeated her words, looking confused.

"Yeah, like I said, I don't know what she was doing, but she was behaving weirdly and...inappropriately. And then Sula showed up, scaring us. Kerry shot her in the arm. And I sprayed Kerry with bear spray."

"Sula scared *you*?"

"Yes, at first," Melissa said hesitantly. "I didn't recognize her at first."

"Mm-hmm." Betty looked her in the eye. "And Kerry says she shot a bear?"

Melissa nodded.

"*Did* Kerry shoot a bear?" Betty's expression was strangely calm, given what she was asking.

Melissa bit her lower lip, hesitant to answer the question truthfully. She hadn't lied to the officer; she just hadn't been so specific. But he wasn't asking questions with Betty's precision. It was if she already knew the answer. Melissa took a deep breath and exhaled. "Yes."

Betty seemed unfazed. "Did you tell Lee Martinez that?"

"No."

"Why not?" Betty narrowed her eyes.

"Because I thought he'd think I was crazy, just like he thinks Kerry's crazy."

"Because the big bear you saw turned into Sula?" Betty's voice was nearly a whisper.

Melissa jerked upright, staring at Betty. "What? How do you—" Melissa sputtered, unable to form a question.

"What you saw was real, Melissa."

"I'm not crazy?"

"No, you're not crazy," Betty said reassuringly, a subtle smile forming on her lips. "But you did experience something very special and rare."

"You've seen it before?"

"I have. And we'll talk more about it later, but right now I need to know that you're not going to talk about this with anyone else but me so I can go find a nurse and see what's going on with Sula."

"Yes, the nurse…" Melissa felt like her brain was in a fog. "The nurse was supposed to come back to talk to me, but she didn't." A wave of anxiety hit her. "Do you think that's a bad sign?"

"Not necessarily." Betty patted her back and squeezed her shoulder. "I'll go see what I can find out, and I'll be back." Betty stood and was intercepted by Nurse Stone.

"Is this Sula's mother?"

"No," Melissa answered.

"I'm her aunt," Betty said quickly. "How is she?"

"She's stable," the nurse said to Betty, but glanced at Melissa with a reassuring smile. "She's being prepped for surgery right now. The bullet nicked the bone, and the surgeon want to remove a few fragments and clean up the wound so it'll heal properly. If you'd like to see her before we move her, now would be the time."

"I would, thank you." Betty looked at Melissa. "Are you good here?"

Melissa nodded.

"I'll be back."

"Hey, Sula."

Hearing a familiar voice, Sula opened her eyes, blinking against the harsh light. Betty stood in the doorway smiling at her. "Hey…"

"How're you feeling?"

"I'm okay…well, I mean I guess I'm not okay if I'm here…" She started to point to her bandaged shoulder, but the movement caused a spasm of pain. Wincing, she held her breath until it ebbed. "I'm going to have surgery. Did they tell you?"

"The nurse told me. And I talked to Melissa. She's in the waiting room. You had an *exciting* morning, didn't you?"

"Is she okay? I tried to explain, but she kept telling me to be quiet."

"You scared her. In more ways than one. She's got a good head on her shoulders, though, that's for sure. She's understandably confused right now. I'll talk with her, so don't you worry about that."

"Thanks, Betty." Sula closed her eyes. She felt a little woozy and was having a hard time keeping Betty in focus. She opened them again. "Hey, Betty?"

"Yes?"

"Kerry was setting traps." Sula frowned. "On conservancy land and other places. She set out bait and was going to shoot Notch."

"That explains the dead deer. And why you got angry enough to show your true colors."

"And Melissa...she was scared of Kerry. I heard the fear in her voice, and I felt very protective." Sula panicked. "I might've messed up, Betty. I was...Kerry saw—"

"I don't think you need to worry about her." Betty chuckled, although Sula didn't think it was a laughing matter. "The police picked her up. She seems to have the *crazy* idea that she shot a bear. She's getting a psych evaluation."

"But Melissa saw—"

"Melissa says Kerry shot *you*, not a bear."

Understanding, Sula closed her eyes and laughed softly. She felt better with her eyes closed. "Hey, Betty?"

"Right here."

"Could I see Melissa?"

"If that's what you want, sure. I'll go get her."

Melissa put her head in her hands and closed her eyes. Snippets of the day flashed through her mind. A big, big angry bear. Kerry in a cloud of pepper spray. Sula on the ground bleeding after several excruciating minutes of a mind-boggling metamorphosis. And Betty sitting next to her, patting her and all but telling her that everything was okay. *Okay? What the hell?* Truth be told, she was glad Betty was here. It seemed like she was taking command of the situation.

Her head felt like it was spinning. Was she experiencing shock? Perhaps the doctor had released her too soon. She opened her eyes and stared out the window overlooking the parking lot while she tried to process her thoughts. Sula was...what? A shape-shifter? A were-bear? This was the stuff of horror movies, fairy tales, and ancient art—the products of imaginative, creative minds. This did not exist in the real world. At least that's what she'd thought until this morning. What she knew to be fact and fiction had shifted beneath her. A shift of seismic proportion. It was an awful lot to take in. She felt destabilized, adrift in an ocean of uncertainty. Just hours ago, she had been certain about a lot of things, of feeling wonderfully, deeply in love with Sula, for one. And now...God, she didn't know what to think.

"Melissa?"

Startled, Melissa flinched and sat up to see Betty in front of her.

She was so lost in thought she hadn't seen or heard her walk up. "How's Sula?"

"She's all right, considering. She'll be going into surgery soon."

"That's good."

"It is." Betty scrutinized her. "She'd like to see you before she goes."

Melissa bit her lower lip, feeling unsure.

"Listen," Betty sat next to her and looked her directly in the eye. "That is Sula in there. The same Sula you've always known. Today you learned something new about her. But it doesn't change *who* she is."

"How long have you known?"

"I've never not known," Betty said, a gentle smile forming on her lips. "Our families have been good friends for a long time, going back to the old country. It runs in her family, you know. She's not an anomaly."

There were *more* people who could turn into bears? Melissa's head started to spin again. She hadn't gotten past the shock of knowing there was one. "Are you…?"

"Ha! No. I'm just a plain ol' regular Norwegian-American. Nothing fancy in my genes," Betty said with a half-smile. She tucked her chin and raised her eyebrows. "So? Do you want to see her?"

"I do," Melissa said, but still felt uneasy about facing Sula.

Before she could change her mind, Betty led her down the hall to the pre-op area, where the beds were arranged in bays with a privacy curtain at each end. Betty gestured to a closed curtain on the far side of the room. "She's in the bed at the end."

Melissa heard voices, people talking, and one of them was Sula's. She took a step forward and a nurse stopped them. "She's on her way to surgery now."

"Sula asked to see Melissa before she went," Betty said.

"Okay, but…" The nurse glanced over her shoulder as the curtain was drawn back. "It'll have to be quick."

Melissa moved forward slowly and peered around the curtain. Sula lay in the bed, eyes closed, dressed in a hospital gown with a blanket neatly draped across her. Her shoulder and upper arm were wrapped in thick layers of gauze, and an IV was attached to the hand of her other arm. An orderly stood behind the bed, ready to wheel her out.

Sula opened her eyes and raised her head. Her lips curved upward gently, an expression as disarming as it was charming. Melissa returned the smile without thinking, but the dizzying happiness she felt seeing her was edged with a gnawing anxiety that churned inside her, a strange emotional cocktail. Sula lifted her arm, extending her hand, the gesture striking her like a jolt of electricity. Melissa froze. All she could see was the shape of a bear paw. Suppressing the memory, Melissa stared at the long fingers…not claws, she reminded herself…it was the strong hand that hoisted her up boulders and brought her pleasure during their lovemaking. She moved to the side of the bed, cautiously taking her hand.

Sula squeezed her hand gently. She sighed and put her head back on the pillow, closing her eyes. When she spoke, her words were slow and thick. "Glad you're here."

The orderly cleared his throat. "I'm sorry, ma'am, but I need to take her to surgery."

Melissa nodded to the young man. Sula released her hand, and as she watched her roll past, she held on to the feel of her skin, soft and warm…and human.

Betty walked her back to the waiting area. "The nurse said the surgery should take about an hour and a half."

"Okay." Licking her lips, Melissa realized her mouth felt sticky and dry. She remembered that her car was packed for a picnic, including bottles of strawberry lemonade in ice. "I'm going to get something to drink from my car. Can I bring you something?"

"No. I'm fine. Thanks." Betty touched her arm. "Hey, you don't have to stay here, you know. It would do you some good to go back to the cabin, get a shower, maybe take a nap. I'll keep you posted, and you've got my number."

Melissa walked through the doors, out into the heat of the day. She retrieved the bottle from the cooler in the back of her car, but her hands were shaking so badly she could barely twist off the cap. Sitting in the car, she held the bottle with both hands to steady herself, took a deep drink, and noticed the hospital band still on her wrist. She thought to cut it off with the Swiss Army knife in her backpack, but with her hands trembling the way they were, she feared she'd only cut herself. Maybe when the sugar kicked in, her nerves would settle. She stared at the hospital through the windshield, the white walls reflecting the sun so brightly it hurt her eyes. Looking down, away from the glare, she realized she had blood on her hands, in the creases of her palms, under her fingernails. Startled, she wondered how she had been unaware of it. The world was apparently starting to come back into focus bit by bit.

She took another swallow of lemonade and looked at herself in the rearview mirror. She looked awful…although her hair looked kind of nice. She hadn't realized how spending so much time outdoors had turned it really…golden…just like Goldilocks. Sula had been calling her Goldie all summer. It had seemed a cute, sort of flirty term of endearment. But now she realized the joke was on her. She really *was* Goldilocks sleeping in the bear's bed. A bear's bed, for crying out loud. A fucking bear! And she'd been fucking the bear, too. Melissa stared at herself in the mirror, curled a golden lock of hair around her finger, and began to cry.

Betty was right. She needed to wash up, go back to the cabin for a shower and a clean change of clothes, then try to calm herself and hopefully get some sleep before beginning her three-day drive home to Georgia. The mundane reality she'd been dreading returning to was now a lifesaver, something tangible to hang on to. Her thoughts raced away from the present, forward to Georgia, to her university, to her teaching position. She had meetings to attend and classes to prepare for. She couldn't miss a day of work, couldn't miss a thing this semester. It was her tenure-application year, and not showing up for her first day back would jeopardize her good standing and reputation. The new provost paid attention to who attended and, more importantly, who did *not* attend the formal faculty convocation before the start of the term. Barring a death in the family or any other extreme emergency, Melissa *had* to be there. If she didn't get tenure, she wouldn't have a job.

It was time to leave. Time to go home.

CHAPTER THIRTY

"Hey, Boss, here's your coffee..." Anna put a cup of fresh coffee on her desk and pulled a plate out from behind her back, "and a cinnamon roll."

"Ah...you're the best administrative assistant ever, Anna." Sula lifted her nose to inhale the sweet, aromatic scent wafting toward her.

Anna beamed. "Did you hear the news? The weather forecast changed. We're supposed to get several inches of snow this afternoon."

"Really? Then I guess we'll be closing the office early today." It was an office tradition to close early the day of the first snowfall and let the administrative staff go play in the snow. The visitor-center employees would get two extra hours of personal time.

"Awesome." Anna grinned. "Snow day! Shall I share the good news?"

"By all means, let everyone know. I'll send an official email."

Anna practically skipped out of her office. Sula sipped her coffee and looked to her calendar. The twentieth of September. Snowfall this early wasn't unheard of, but it was unusual. Looking at the calendar reminded her that over a month had passed since Kerry had ruined everything between her and Melissa, and she was still causing her trouble.

After the shooting, Sula's immediate concern for the conservancy was news coverage. Kerry's initial assertion of having seen a bear-woman had been reported by the Denver stations and spread quickly through the internet, with spinoff speculative stories about fabled grizzlies and even the possibility that freaking Bigfoot was tramping around Buckhorn. Worried that it would cause a public-relations problem, she discovered that the opposite was true. Her media director explained that it was being perceived as just another all-too-frequent example of a troubled individual acting out violently. If managed correctly it would benefit the conservancy by providing more opportunities to share the organization's noble work and to preach the good word about living with bears.

Sula didn't want the conservancy to press trespassing charges. The district attorney's office was already pursuing reckless-endangerment charges. The local newspaper quoted Kerry as saying that, blinded by pepper spray, she thought she was shooting at a large bear in self-defense. Trying to portray herself as the victim, she also said she had lost her job. Strangely, her story contained elements of truth. Sula in fur had huffed and popped her jaw in anger and begun to charge when Kerry fired the pistol. Sula couldn't help it. A deep protective instinct had kicked in, and her mind had emptied of everything except getting Kerry away from Melissa. At least Kerry seemed to have stopped talking about the bear turning into a woman with reporters. But Sula knew not to trust her. The woman was wily, and who knew what she was saying privately?

Sula's hands trembled with mounting anger, and she put the pencil down before she snapped it in half and threw the pieces across the room. Kerry had given up a respectable job to work as nothing more than an unconscionable contract serial killer. If she had any moral compass whatsoever, she had abandoned it when she took that job with Wildlife Services. As far as Sula was concerned, when she started trapping for them, she became complicit in the agency's slaughter of millions of animals—bears, mountain lions, wolves, bobcats, coyotes, foxes, the list went on and on—butchery that was unjustified, horrific, and tragic.

She wanted Kerry to pay for her crimes against nature, an intentional misuse of the term, she knew, but it described her heinous actions well. Sula also needed to protect the conservancy and, the more she considered it, herself, too. The last thing she needed was some Bigfoot hunter, inspired by Kerry's fantastic story, nosing around, hiding in the woods with recording devices. Finding Kerry's trail camera had warned her that even forests weren't as safe as they used to be.

She was the source of every damn thing wrong in her life right now. If it weren't for Kerry, she and Melissa would still be speaking. Sula would have had the time she needed to find a way to explain to Melissa carefully and gently what she was. It would have been difficult, but Melissa would have understood, and they would still be together. Instead, the love of her life, the only woman she had *ever* loved, had driven away as quickly as she could without even saying good-bye.

Sula had still been groggy the day after surgery when Betty let it slip that Melissa was on her way back to Georgia. She only vaguely remembered having seen her as she was being wheeled to the operating room. Recalling her last clear memories of Melissa broke her heart—seeing a look of terror on her face as she witnessed Sula in fur and the metamorphosis of the *hamask*, the rampant fear as she drove her to the hospital. Sula had texted Melissa from her hospital bed, asking her to let her know when she arrived safely. Her heart was heavy when she received a terse text several days later that just said, "Home." Sula replied immediately, saying she wanted to talk, to explain things, to make things right between them, but received no reply. *Nothing*...not another word from Melissa.

Sula's chest constricted; pain and heartbreak twisted and spun into white-hot anger. She wanted to lash out, but at what? The feeling of helplessness made her even more frustrated and angry.

She went to the window and gazed out at the trees and the lake beyond, hoping the peaceful view of the landscape would soothe her agitated nerves. She pressed her forehead against the cool glass and closed her eyes.

She fantasized about taking Kerry down. If she hadn't been shot, she very well might have sunk her teeth into an arm or a leg and given her a swift bone-breaking, tendon-snapping shake, before dragging her into the woods where nobody would have ever found her. Sula ran her hands through her hair and sighed deeply. As much as they gave her guilty pleasure, she recoiled from her thoughts. She had never hurt anyone while in fur, not even with her cousins when they were kids playing rough-and-tumble with fangs and claws. But she'd never been pushed to the edge like this either. Clearly Kerry was a predator. She shuddered to think about what might have happened to Melissa had she not arrived.

She considered the irony of working to protect apex predators when she had one nearby that she wanted to cull. But Kerry wasn't the kind of natural predator that maintained balance in the ecosystem. Quite the contrary. She was nothing but a malicious canker—

Mercifully, her office phone rang and interrupted her dark thoughts. Not surprisingly, it was her father. Her parents had offered to fly home when Betty alerted them about the shooting and surgery, but Sula had assured them it was unnecessary. They promised to call every day, and they did for a few weeks. Now they phoned every few days.

"Hey, Dad. What's up? Checking on me again?"

"I'd like to think of it as checking in." He laughed. "How're things?"

"Fine." Nothing had really changed in the last few days. "Oh, we're going to close the office this afternoon. We're forecast to get snow."

"So soon? Usually the first snowfall isn't for, what? A few more weeks."

"Yep. Blame it on climate change."

"No doubt." Her father sucked his teeth. "I saw a news story about some bad storms with tornadoes in the South, and I thought about Melissa. Have you heard from her yet?"

Sula sighed deeply. "No."

"Have you tried contacting her again?"

"No."

"Why not?"

"I told her I wanted to talk, and now I'm waiting. I guess she needs some space, or…" Sula hesitated to say she thought it was over.

"Or what?"

Sula didn't speak for fear of making it real. "I don't want her to think I'm pressuring her. I scared her, Dad, and I feel terrible about it. I hate thinking she's afraid of me."

"I'm not so sure that keeping your distance is a good idea, Sula. This is a shocking thing for someone to deal with. Trust me. I know. You can't talk about it with *anyone*, not even your closest friend, without fearing they'll think you've gone off the deep end or you're perpetrating a hoax. It's very isolating. And it makes you question a lot of things. Like *everything*." He laughed gently. "If she's struggling— and she probably is—she needs someone to talk to, and the only person she can be truly honest with is *you*."

"I hadn't considered it from that perspective."

"If you really love her, and I think you do, she needs to know it. If you don't act like you love her, she'll never be sure."

Sula had always thought her father was a kind and thoughtful man, but her admiration just hit a new high. "How'd you get so smart, Dad?"

"He's been married to a very smart woman for many years," Sula's mother interjected unexpectedly. "I think it's rubbed off on him."

"Mom! I didn't know you were on the call. You need to tell me when you're both on the phone."

Her mother laughed. "I didn't want to interrupt, sweetheart. Your father understands what Melissa is probably experiencing more than I do. I agree with him. If she hasn't reached out for you, you need to reach for her. Don't leave her twisting in the wind."

"And don't make it too heavy," her father said. "Don't ask her how she feels about your relationship and stuff like that. Just let her know you're thinking of her. I'll bet she'll return in kind."

"And that's the beginning of a conversation," her mother said.

"So exactly how much have you two been talking about this?"

"Oh...not much," her father said unconvincingly.

"Mm-hmm."

"All right, Charles. We've probably taken enough of Sula's time. I'm sure she's got things to do."

"Yes, I do." They said their good-byes and Sula returned to work, considering renewed possibilities.

The morning passed surprisingly quickly. As promised, she closed the administrative offices two hours early, to everyone's delight, and went home. The cats greeted her on the porch, rubbing against her legs with tails straight in the air. Their coats had become thick recently; even they knew winter was coming soon. Sula had been seeing the signs— migratory birds had begun an early journey south, and she'd observed chickarees, the little pine squirrels, furiously tearing through pinecones to get at the seeds at the base of the scales. "Squirrels gathering nuts in a hurry will cause snow to gather in a hurry," her grandmother used to say. She petted the cats while taking in the view that filled her with a sense of beauty and awe. Even on an overcast day, such as this one, it never failed to provide a balm for her soul.

Since talking with her parents, she'd thought even more about Melissa, if that was possible. Going into the house, she focused on forming the words she'd send in a message. She wanted to say so many things, but she couldn't put them all down in a single message. It would be overwhelming. She would take her parents' advice and let Melissa know she was thinking of her. They were right. Melissa wouldn't know her feelings if she didn't express herself.

Sitting on the couch, Sula took her phone out of her pocket. Opening the messaging app, she tapped Melissa's name and stared at the blank white message box. She started a message and erased it. She began another and erased that one, too. She didn't know how or where to begin.

Feeling overwhelmed, she took the phone to the kitchen, putting it in a charging dock on the counter while she went upstairs to change into a pair of jeans and a T-shirt. In the mud room, she put on her hiking boots and a coat and headed up the hill behind the house, intending to take a short hike and hoping the fresh air and physical activity would provide her some clarity.

The cats followed her halfway up the hill. She was thankful for their company, especially recently. They seemed to sense her sadness, sleeping with her every night and entertaining her with their antics. It was hard not to smile and laugh at them as they zoomed around her, playfully pouncing on invisible prey and each other. They didn't follow her past the edge of their territory, so they eventually parted ways. Sula continued on, weaving around boulders and pines, unhurriedly making her way to the crest of the hill. It was quiet. The birds and animals knew the weather was changing and had already taken shelter.

The golden-hued grass in the meadow below rippled like water as the wind picked up.

The temperature was dropping, and the steely gray clouds obscuring her view of the peaks were a color she associated with snow. Tucking her hands into the pocket of her coat, she descended into the meadow. As she meandered through the dry grass, the first snowflakes began to fall. Pausing to watch them, she put her hand out to catch a few, and landing in the palm of her hand, they almost instantly dissolved into droplets of water. By the time she arrived back home, the snow was beginning to stick, and she was thirsty.

Entering through the back door, she didn't see the cats anywhere. She removed her boots, leaving them on a mat in the mud room, before going into the kitchen to fill a tall glass with water. After several big gulps of it, she leaned against the counter, taking small sips and staring at her cellphone with ambivalence. The phone nested at an angle in the dock, and its slick black surface reflected her frowning face. She tapped the phone. No new messages.

While walking into the living room, she wrestled with ideas on how to begin a conversation with Melissa. She was not very good with words, at explaining her feelings, so maybe she shouldn't rely on them so much. Perhaps she could send something other than a message. She stared out the front window, watching the falling snow, and thought about flowers, yet that didn't seem quite right. Flowers were for dates, birthdays, or funerals. Flowers made her think of greeting cards, and she had never seen a card for this situation. Cards, like flowers, seemed impersonal, too generic. Above all, whatever she sent had to be meaningful.

A thump, a sound like something falling on the floor, came from the back of the house. Curious, Sula walked through the kitchen and down the hall but didn't see anything out of place. When she walked into the den, she spied a cat sitting on the billiard table.

"Uh-uh, no." She waved her hand at Spotty, who gazed at her with a feline expression of indifferent innocence. "Bad cat."

Sula inspected the felt on the table, which didn't appear damaged, and then she saw the cue ball on the floor by a cabinet. The cat must have knocked it off. This was an old house and the floors weren't exactly level, so that fact wasn't noticeable until you dropped something that could roll. She walked over and bent down to pick up the ball, and when she straightened up, something in the room caught her eye. That was it. She knew exactly what she would send Melissa. It was perfect. She glanced at Spotty, who blinked slowly at her as if to say, "See. I'm not such a bad cat, after all."

CHAPTER THIRTY-ONE

With one more class to go for the day, Melissa was on her third cup of coffee and warding off a nervous breakdown. She felt ragged, exhausted, but at least she wasn't still wearing her pajamas. She didn't want to see anyone or leave the house all weekend, so hadn't found any reason to change clothes. However, Monday demanded she dress for work. Freshly showered, with hair and makeup done, she knew she looked better on the outside than she felt inside. When she'd first returned to Georgia, colleagues and students kept remarking on how tanned and fit she looked from her trip to Colorado. At one point she thought she might scream if one more person commented on how golden her hair had become.

She was only keeping it together on the surface. Underneath she felt raw and vulnerable, wavering between confusion, bouts of heartrending longing, but also anger from having been played the fool. Her emotions were dangerously close to the surface, easily bubbling over, and she didn't trust that she wouldn't burst into tears at an inappropriate moment. Time was supposed to heal all wounds, but with every passing week she felt worse, not better.

Each time she passed the water fountain down the hall from her office, she stared at a poster hanging above it. In bold letters, it asked, "Do you have signs of depression?" She did. For one, she was isolating herself, which wasn't a good thing to do, but she didn't have anyone to talk to, not even a therapist, because her issue hinged on something any right-minded person would identify as the product of delusional thinking. She wasn't delusional—she knew what she had seen, and Betty had confirmed its reality.

Even so, she had distanced herself from the only two people with whom she could talk. After a brief stop at the Buckhorn Police Department to write a statement about witnessing the shooting, she'd just taken off from Colorado. Although it had been time to leave, she could have handled her departure much better. She didn't even say good-bye to Betty. She quietly left the keys to the cabin in the lodge mailbox. Since returning she'd felt stupidly paralyzed.

In the evenings she prepared for her classes until she was mentally exhausted, and then she cleaned her house or found little odd jobs that needed doing until she was so fatigued, she fell asleep immediately. She dreaded the nights, because keeping herself busy during the day made whatever she tried to avoid then find her in the middle of the night. Without fail, she'd wake up either revisiting the horrific moments of seeing Sula transform from a bear or reminiscing about Sula the woman—missing the rich timbre of her voice, her infectious laughter, and the feel of her soft, warm skin.

This morning Melissa awoke with her arm outstretched. She'd been dreaming about Sula taking her by the hand, helping her climb a boulder. She felt light-hearted, awash in a feeling of contentment, but as the warmth and pressure of Sula's dream touch ebbed, Melissa broke into tears that quickly turned into uncontrollable sobs. Her cat, Alex, nestled close to her and purred loudly. Although it was a sweet gesture, it couldn't ease her pain.

Even now, sitting at her desk cradling the cup in her hands, staring at the inky black coffee inside it, she was having a hard time shaking off the lingering bittersweet feeling from the dream. She glanced at the clock. It was nearing three o'clock, almost time for class. She gathered her things and left her office for the classroom.

A seasoned instructor, she shifted easily into her role as professor when she entered the room, like an actor taking the stage. She called roll, bantered with the students, and picked up where they had left off the last class discussing the work of Pablo Picasso. She framed the mercurial painter as a problematic individual, a charismatic, misogynistic narcissist whose art practice nonetheless expanded the boundaries of art and deeply affected the course of Modern art in the twentieth century. The final image in her lecture was the *Minotauromachy*, the "minotaur battle," an etching made in 1935 when his marriage was falling apart.

"The figure of the minotaur you see here," Melissa pointed, the digital projector casting a shadow of her hand across the screen, "represents Picasso. He might also be the bearded man on the ladder observing the scene. Also watching are the women in the window with the doves—a symbol of peace, and don't forget his father specialized in painting pigeons, or European rock doves as they're also known.

But our focus is here in the center where we see that the minotaur has gravely injured a bullfighter—"

"Is that a woman?" Steven, a student sitting in the front row, asked.

"It is. She's holding the sword used to give the killing blow to the bull in the ring. She's draped over the horse, eyes closed, her jacket open, exposing her breasts—"

"And the horse is wounded." His eyes big, Steven looked disturbed by the graphic violence, as did many of his classmates.

"Yes. Its intestines are spilling out," Melissa said, and the class groaned collectively. "Yet this ferocious creature is stopped in his tracks by a mere girl holding a burning candle…a light in the darkness."

"Is the minotaur afraid of the girl or mesmerized by her?" The question came from Kiley, a shy but thoughtful student, who always sat in a dark corner of the back row.

Melissa moved to the side of the room to a position where she could see the overall image more clearly. "It's a good question, isn't it? What do you all think?"

The room was silent. She knew to be patient and to wait, for someone would eventually break the silence. Several students spoke at the same time, expressing different points of view. Some thought the minotaur looked terrified, while others saw him as menacing. One student thought he was fascinated by the flame of the candle, but another interpreted the creature as reaching to snuff out the flame. "What if I told you that the girl in this etching looks a lot like Picasso's young mistress who had recently informed him that she was pregnant?"

"*Ohhhh…*" several students said.

"So, let's consider the possibility that it's all of those things simultaneously. What he wants and what he's afraid of are the same thing." Melissa paused, shocked by how her words seemed to illuminate her own current inner conflicts. She walked to the back of the room. "Let's take a moment to unpack his use of the minotaur as a personal symbol. He chose this creature from Greek mythology to represent the root of his conflict. Remember, the Greeks saw beauty in order, rationality, and logic—all products of human intellect. Think about what the minotaur is: the body of a man with the head of a bull. A human body without logic, ruled by bestial passions was an ancient Greek's worst nightmare."

"Are you saying the minotaur is the boogeyman?" Steven asked, making the class laugh.

"Sort of, but the way Picasso illustrated him here, he's the epitome of conflict. While he is fearsome, he's also a pitiful creature who doesn't fully belong in either the human or the animal world." Melissa saw heads nodding. She glanced at her watch. "And with that, we are out of time for today."

Melissa stayed in the back of the room, leaning against the back wall, while the students gathered their notebooks and laptops, stuffing them into backpacks and bags. As they cleared the room one by one, some wishing her a good afternoon before they left, she ruminated on the expressive, almost human, countenance of the minotaur's face. It wasn't the shape of the nose or the set of the mouth but the eyes that held a spark of humanity. She'd seen something similar in person when she made eye contact with a bear by Moose Lake. A bear whose eyes glinted amber like her lover's because, as it turned out, they *were* her lover's. She took a deep breath and blew it out through pursed lips. Talk about simultaneity and conflicting emotions.

She retrieved her folder from the lectern and walked back to her office while continuing to reflect on the ideas that had surfaced during her lecture. She hadn't planned to explain things exactly the way she did; it was as if she had been speaking for her own benefit. Perhaps her subconscious was working things out like a computer program running in the background.

She put the folder on her desk and picked up her messenger bag, ready to go home even though she still needed to finish tomorrow's lecture on ancient Roman art. She'd do it at home…in pajamas. She slid her laptop into her bag and picked up her phone to find a message from Beth asking if she'd like to meet for a quick drink. Melissa had been dodging having a real conversation with her, knowing she couldn't postpone it forever. She responded, agreeing to meet her at the Depot restaurant.

When Melissa arrived, Beth was already in the bar with a glass of red wine in hand. She waved Melissa over.

"Thanks for meeting me." Beth gave her a quick hug. "I thought I'd take advantage of Ben being on soccer-practice duty tonight with the kids." She held up a menu. "I ordered dinner to go. I know. I'm a terrible mom, I should be in the kitchen right now preparing a well-balanced meal for my beautiful family."

Melissa laughed. "Let me see that menu. I'm going to copy you." Scanning it quickly she saw that it hadn't changed over the summer.

She waved the bartender over and ordered a draft beer and a burger with fries to go.

"You got it," the bartender said and turned away to place her order.

"So…" Beth stared at her over the rim of her glass as she took a sip. "What's up with you and the mountain woman?" She narrowed her eyes. "You've been vague, to say the least."

The bartender slid the beer toward Melissa, and she lifted the bottle and took a swig before answering. It was cold and tasted good. "We're not talking."

"What? Did you leave on bad terms?"

"I didn't leave on any terms."

"What do you mean?"

Apparently, either news of the shooting hadn't reached the Southeast or Beth hadn't seen the story. Either way, she was thankful for that.

"Sula was preoccupied with some…" She considered how to describe the situation ambiguously. "Work stuff. And then it was time for me to go. The semester was about to start."

"And you didn't talk about the status of your relationship before you left?" Beth looked at her incredulously.

"Pretty much." Melissa took a deep swallow of beer.

"It's been what? Two months now?"

"Six weeks. I know. It doesn't make sense."

"Oh, I think I get it." Beth narrowed her eyes. "Will you indulge me in analyzing you for a moment?"

"Sure?" Melissa said. She didn't think Beth would have accepted a different answer.

"Everything was perfect between you two. You really liked the mountain woman—"

"Sula. She has a name, you know."

"Okay, so you really like *Sula.*" Beth said her name slowly, drawing it out. "And she really likes you. But you have a job *here*, and she has a job *there*. By leaving things unresolved, you didn't risk ending the relationship over the inconvenient matter of mileage."

It was true. The distance had been an issue for Melissa, but they could have worked it out. Once she'd discovered Sula was a werebear, that such creatures actually existed, it became the least of her concerns. Explaining that to Beth would require a conversation she didn't want to have, so she simply said, "That's very insightful, Beth."

"And that means I'm right, yes?"

"Maybe."

Beth swatted her arm playfully. "Mm-hmm, I'm right. I bet she hurt your feelings and you hurt hers. You didn't talk about it, so now you're both miserable."

Melissa opened her mouth to speak but couldn't.

"You don't have to reply to that, honey." Beth smiled smugly and set her glass down on the bar. "I can see I hit the nail right on the head."

"Did you know my name means honey?"

"Hm? What?"

"Melissa…my name is from the ancient Greek. It's derived from the words for 'bee' and also for 'honey.' Sula told me that. I didn't know, it surprised me."

"Yeah. Bears like honey—Winnie-the-Pooh and all that." Beth downed the last of her wine. "I imagine the director of a bear-protection agency would know such things."

Melissa laughed at Beth's description of the Colorado Bear Conservancy. Maybe the beer had already gone to her head because she visualized bears in witness-protection programs, bears with secret identities. Hm…kind of like Sula. But she wasn't really a bear, was she? At least not all the time. Just some of the time. Did that make her a human who turned into a bear or a bear who turned into a human? And how exactly was she able to do that? Betty said it ran in her family…

"Earth to Melissa," Beth said, waving her hand in front of her face.

"Oh! Sorry, Beth…yes?"

Beth gestured to the two large paper sacks on the bar. "My dinner has arrived. I need to go. The bartender said your order would be out soon."

"Oh, okay. I guess I zoned out there for a moment."

"Yeah, I noticed." Beth smiled at her. She grabbed the bags and pursed her lips, giving her an air kiss. "I need to get going. Listen. You have to talk to her. If any more time passes, whatever you have will be irrecoverable. Go home and figure out a way to talk to Sula before it's too late."

Melissa opened the door of her car, the heat and humidity hitting her like a warm, wet blanket. Getting out of the car, she slung her messenger bag over her shoulder and grabbed the paper sack with her dinner, remembering her last conversation with her parents last week. Her mother, as usual, asked about Sula. She knew things had fallen apart between them, but she didn't understand why because Melissa hadn't explained it in a way that made sense. How could she? Her father kept conversations to safe, tangible things like the weather. Lately, he'd been commenting on how winter seemed to be coming early to Colorado, the evening temperatures were dropping, and the prevailing winds had shifted. First snowfall was usually mid-October, but her father speculated it would be sooner this year.

Perspiration had beaded on her forehead by the time she walked from the car to the front steps of her house. On days like this, when it was so damn humid, she thought it was condensation more than sweat. Here, in the Deep South, it wouldn't even begin to feel like autumn until close to Halloween, but even then, it was often still T-shirt weather.

She was surprised to find a large box by the side of the front door; she hadn't ordered anything recently. She carried her things inside and returned for the box. It was heavy. She rotated it to see the label. It had been sent from Colorado…from Buckhorn…*from Sula.*

While she carried it into the kitchen, Alex followed her, meowing loudly, demanding his dinner. "Just a minute, sweet boy."

Melissa put the box on the kitchen table, grabbed a sharp knife out of a drawer to slice the tape, and opened the box. Inside was a smaller box, surrounded by packing peanuts. She removed it, and opened it to find something swaddled in bubble wrap. Unrolling it, she gasped when she realized what it was.

In her hands was the dancing-bear sculpture she'd last seen on a cabinet in the room with the pool table at Sula's house. She placed the sculpture on the table and put her hand back into the box, fishing around in the packing peanuts for a note. Instead she found another, smaller, bubble-wrapped object, an unmarked jar of honey. Taped to it was a note, written neatly in black ink.

The honey's from Betty.

Melissa stared at the sculpture in disbelief. The bear's gleaming white eyes, contrasting the glossy finish of the black serpentine stone, seemed to stare back with an intense, focused expression. She couldn't believe there wasn't a letter, some kind of explanation. She grabbed the box and turned it upside down, shaking it, spilling the packing peanuts on the floor. Alex pounced, batting them across the tiled kitchen floor as she checked under the bottom flaps of the box, but she found nothing. Alex began meowing insistently, his hunger overriding his delight with new toys. Melissa fed him, then sat down at the table to eat her lukewarm food in the company of the dancing bear. She hardly tasted her meal, leaving it unfinished as she considered the sculpture. It was puzzling, and like any puzzle, it required a solution. She liked the sculpture, had admired it when she first saw it and said so. Slowly she recalled her conversation with Sula about it. She had described the dancing bear as an Inuit spirit bear. The dance wasn't entertainment; it was a ritual, one in which the shaman took on the form of a bear. The shaman was a shape-shifter…just like Sula.

Still, Melissa didn't understand why Sula had sent it to her. She knew this already about Sula, so why just reiterate it? There had to be something else, some other meaning. She was an art historian, for goodness' sake. She was adept at decoding works of art, so surely she could figure this out. Yet no more illuminating ideas came to mind. She was stumped.

Approaching the sculpture's message like an unknown work of art reminded Melissa that she had work to do before her class tomorrow morning. She cleared the table of everything except the bear and swept the floor, leaving a few packing peanuts for Alex to play with. Sitting down at the table with her laptop, she began searching for images to complement a lecture on ancient Roman commemorative sculptures. Tomorrow included Trajan's Column, a massive, nearly one-hundred-foot-tall stone column covered from bottom to top with a spiraling band of images carved in low relief. Depicting the Romans' victory over the Dacians, it was highly detailed, demonstrating all aspects of a military campaign, including leaders giving speeches, the building of boats and fortifications, and the battles. Created as a form of propaganda, it showed the Romans in the best light, as organized and well-equipped. Their enemies, on the contrary, often looked rather unkempt and shaggy. Needing more images to illustrate her lecture, she turned to an academic website with high-quality photographic details of the entire sculpture. As she scrolled through the image gallery, some figures in one section of the column caught her eye.

Four bearded men, clearly different from the clean-shaven Roman warriors, stood out in the crowd. Instead of helmets, two of the men had what looked like wolf heads on top of their heads, and the other two had those of bears. Melissa zoomed in on the image. The men seemed to be wearing animal-skin cloaks with the heads still attached. She had seen this costume before in the illustrated book, *Saga av Eydis Bersa*, that belonged to her great-grandmother. Intrigued, she clicked on the information button, and after reading a brief description, she went down a rabbit hole of research.

Two hours and another cup of coffee later, she learned that the soldiers were Germanic Scandinavian warriors of Odin, kind of like a military special-forces unit. In Old Norse they were called *Ulfhednar*, "wolf-warriors," and *Berserkers*, or "bear-shirts." The contemporary expression, "to go berserk," came from the bearskin-wearing warriors. Described as ordinary before battle, they became overheated, their teeth chattered, and they bit their shields as they were overcome with an all-encompassing rage that propelled them to fight with a ferocity that defied logic. Berserkers terrified the Romans, who fancied themselves civilized and above such barbarian behavior. Melissa imagined legionnaires shaking in their sandals facing such formidable foes. Perhaps it helped explain why the Roman Empire never expanded very far into northern Europe.

Her discovery of berserkers led her in other directions. Though unclear, there seemed to be a connection between them and shape-shifting bear shamans found in ancient cultures all across northern Europe, Siberia, and North America. The relationship between humans and bears seemed to run deep and wide. Although a fearsome animal, the bear represented good, even noble, qualities associated with teaching, leadership, healing, balance, and courage. She was reminded of her conversation with Sula when she said that bears had human-like qualities. She found an article about an ethnologist who had lived with and studied the Inuit in Canada around the turn of the century. A quote from a woman he interviewed riveted her.

In the old time, people and animals lived together in harmony. An animal could be human, and a human could be animal. Sometimes they were the one and the same. There was no explanation and no need for it; it was just the way the world was.

Melissa read the quote several times slowly, letting the words sink in. The last sentence echoed Betty's enigmatic response to Melissa's question about why Sula liked bears so much. *Sometimes things are the way they are, because it's the way they are.* Melissa closed the lid of her laptop, staring at the dancing bear in the middle of the table. Frozen in a position with one foot on the ground, the other reaching for the sky, it linked the earthly and spiritual realms as she and Sula had discussed. Now she fully comprehended why the sculpture appealed to Sula, for it also represented someone who shifted between the states of human and animal. And it was beautiful.

Having just talked about Picasso and the minotaur earlier in the day, she recalled how archeologists believed that myths could be rooted in the histories of real places. The legendary labyrinth where the minotaur roamed might have been the elaborate palace complex that now lay in ruins on the island of Knossos in the Mediterranean Sea. Melissa entertained the possibility that berserkers were based in reality, too. She had seen a bear transform into a woman, and Betty had explained it as a trait that ran in Sula's family. Perhaps in the long-ago past, berserkers weren't just wearing bearskins, pretending to be bears, but they *were* bears.

Her sense of reality was expanding at a dizzying pace, and the more she learned, the more questions she had, but the pieces of the puzzle were falling into place. Although she didn't yet have a complete image, she had enough to make some sense of what she was seeing. It had been in front of her all along, but shock and fear had occluded her ability to see it.

The ideas coursing through her mind left her breathless, and her heart was pounding, but not with fear, as it had in the woods when confronted with a Sula as a bear. This was something else, the thrill of observing with fresh eyes, of making discoveries and considering previously unthinkable connections.

Feeling antsy, she stood and got a glass of water, drinking it in several deep swallows. Leaving the empty glass on the counter, she went out the back door, walking slowly into the middle of her tired, overgrown garden. Most of the plants were spent, barely hanging on after the late summer heat that continued well into fall. She reflected on how it had been so easy to start calling Sula "Bear" as a term of endearment. She had so many bear-like qualities, including her love of honey and those agile berry-picking lips... Melissa shivered although the evening air was warm. With sudden unexpected clarity, she understood that she hadn't been played a fool. She *was* a fool for stupidly trying to walk away from what, deep down, her heart and soul knew.

While the songs of night insects filled the air around her, she stared into the evening sky, hoping to glimpse the sky bear, Ursa Major, the big bear. But she didn't see it. A smile crept across her face as she realized she knew exactly where a big she-bear, *her* she-bear, was located. She wasn't in the sky circling the North Star. She was to the west and terrestrially bound.

Melissa marched into the house to the kitchen and grabbed her phone to call Sula. Finger hovering over the screen she paused, thinking about all they needed to discuss. No, a phone call wasn't the right way to do it. This required a face-to-face conversation. Her university was on a four-day teaching schedule, with no classes on Friday, but that day was usually jam-packed with committee meetings. She checked her calendar, and to her amazement, she didn't have any meetings scheduled this week. She couldn't help but interpret that as a sign that she was doing the right thing. She put the phone down and went back to her laptop. If she could find a seat on a Friday-morning flight out of Atlanta to Denver, she could be in Buckhorn by dinner.

CHAPTER THIRTY-TWO

Leaning the snow shovel against the wall by the back door, Sula knocked the snow off her jacket before entering the house. With the second snowstorm of the season, it seemed that winter wasn't just coming early. It had arrived. She hung her coat and hat on the hook in the mud room and kicked off her boots, shivering as snowflakes slid down the back of her head, under her collar, and melted against her bare skin.

She padded into the living room and lit a fire. The cats followed, jumping up on the chair closest to the hearth, which would soon be the warmest spot in the room. Watching as the logs caught flame, she wished their light and warmth could do more to cheer her. A metallic rattle reminded her to check the pot of chili on the stove in the kitchen. She went in and gave it a stir, then turned down the flame to let it simmer. As she looked out the kitchen window, she could barely see the barn down the hill because of the big, fluffy snowflakes drifting down slowly like little parachutes. She'd need to sweep the front stairs soon, but she wasn't ready to go back out into the cold.

She picked up her phone from the counter, checking for messages or a missed call. None. On Wednesday she'd checked the tracking number of the package containing the spirit-bear sculpture she'd sent Melissa. It had been delivered Monday, but now, Friday, she still hadn't heard a word.

After putting the phone down, she picked up the Sierra Club magazine from the stack of mail by the phone and took it to the living room to read by the fire while waiting for supper. Featured on the cover was a story about the intelligence of black bears that presented interesting new research demonstrating them to be as smart and social as primates. The cover illustration of a thoughtful-looking bear, paw under chin, reminded her of the last email she'd responded to before leaving the office. She'd received and accepted an invitation to be a speaker at an upcoming black bear conference in the Smoky Mountains of Tennessee.

Abandoning the magazine for an atlas pulled from a bookshelf, she stood flipping through it until she found a two-page map of the southeastern states. The location of the conference near the national park wasn't far from the Georgia border. She turned to the state map of Georgia, scanning it for the town where Melissa lived. It was just a few hours' drive.

A loud pop from the fire drew her attention from the maps in her hands, and she gazed at the dancing flames, her thoughts wandering. She pictured herself driving to Melissa's house and knocking on her door. She wasn't sure if she was bold enough to do something like that, though. She was the biggest, baddest beast in the forest, but when it came to matters of the heart, she was as timid as a mouse. Sending Melissa the sculpture was her attempt at a grand romantic gesture, one that seemed to have failed. She wasn't sure what made her think she would have the audacity to arrive unannounced knocking at her door. If Melissa opened the door, she might just slam it shut in her face, or maybe she wouldn't even open it.

She put the atlas on the shelf, sliding it back into place. Moving to another section, she looked for something else to read, wanting a novel that would distract her from her own thoughts. Hopefully she could find a story to get lost in for the evening…someone else's story, one with a happy ending.

Comfortably settled on the couch with a book, Sula responded to a loud sound after the cats, eyes wide, jumped off the chair and ran away toward the back of the house. It was a thud, like something heavy had fallen on the porch. A tree branch, she thought, but then she heard a muffled voice.

"Ow! *Shit!*"

Snapping the book shut, Sula jumped off the couch and, unlike the cats, moved in the direction of the sound.

"Hello?" Sula said loudly, standing by the door.

"Sula?"

Sula thought she recognized the voice on the other side, but it wasn't possible…was it? Opening the door, she was hit by a blast of cold, but more shocking than the frigid air was finding Melissa sitting on the stairs near the edge of the porch.

"Melissa! What are you doing here?"

"Slipping on the steps, apparently." Melissa looked up at her with a grin. She was wearing jeans with cowboy boots, a dark-gray puffy jacket, and a knit hat the color of moss.

"I see that, but—"

"I had prepared an eloquent speech to convince you to open the door. Clearly I hadn't considered falling on the stairs." She looked down at her feet and then back up at Sula, extending her hand. "But it worked quite well. Will you help me up…please?"

Sula nodded mutely. Reaching for Melissa, Sula saw that her footsteps had compacted the snow on the steps into ice. She took Melissa's hand, startled by the sudden contact, and pulled her to her feet.

"Why wouldn't I open the door for you?"

"After all this time, and silence, I was afraid you'd be done with me. And I wouldn't blame you. I behaved stupidly, just running away. You were going to have surgery and I…I just took off like an idiot. And then I never responded to your message. That was cruel and unkind. I haven't been myself since I left, but I don't think that's a good enough excuse. I should have talked to you. You deserve better than that. And Betty, too."

"I thought I'd never see you again," Sula blurted out, beginning to feel the cold seeping through her clothes. "It's freezing out here. Come in." Sula gestured to the open door and followed Melissa, still in disbelief. "How are you here?"

"How did I get here? I flew."

"To Buckhorn?"

"No. To Denver. I rented a car at DIA and drove up." She removed her hat and ran her fingers, nervously, it seemed, through her honey-colored hair. She looked as anxious as she was beautiful, although in the light of the living room, Sula saw dark circles under her eyes.

"How are you?" Melissa said softly. "You look good…really good."

"I'm healed. No permanent damage."

"I'm so relieved. God, how could I not have asked you before? I just assumed you'd be okay, but what if you weren't? I was so foolish, so selfish." Melissa shook her head, pressing her fingers against her lips, looking on the verge of tears. "I'm so sorry. Can you ever accept my apology?"

"I owe you an apology, too. I kept a big secret from you."

"Yeah, you did." Melissa cocked her head. "Does that make us even?"

"Well, I don't know about even."

Melissa's face fell. "What do you mean?"

"You owe Betty an apology, too. She's kind of mad at you for running off. And let me tell you, that woman can hold a grudge."

"Tell me about it. I had a long talk with her this morning from the airport."

"She knew you were coming?"

Melissa hung her head and nodded, looking so pitiful Sula wanted to soften her words. Melissa's stomach rumbled, and she put a hand on her stomach, her look of shame shifting to embarrassment.

"Are you hungry?" Sula asked. "I made a pot of chili and was just about to eat."

"I'm famished. I rushed from the plane to the car-rental counter, and when I saw the snow, I was afraid to stop. It's been a long time since I've driven in a snowstorm."

"It's probably good you got here before the canyon road iced over." Sula gestured to the dining room. "Take your coat off and have a seat. I'll bring it out."

Sula put down bowls of chili, cheese, and crackers and then took a seat across the table.

"Oh, this is so good," Melissa said after the first spoonful. "Thank you."

"You're welcome." Sula ate two bites of chili and set her spoon down, realizing that, for the first time in weeks, the nagging ache in her chest had disappeared.

"Is something wrong?" Melissa held her spoon mid-air.

"I'm just still shocked that you're here...in front of me. What happened? Why are you here now?"

"On Monday, when I received the spirit-bear sculpture you sent, I was probably as surprised to get it as you were to see me on your porch."

Sula looked at her sideways, raising her eyebrows.

"Okay, maybe not *as* surprised," Melissa said with a smile that Sula couldn't help but return. "Trying to figure out why you sent it to me made me think through our situation. Not including a note was a good strategy. That was like something a professor would do—make the student figure it out so they really learn the lesson."

"I'll take that as a compliment." Sula added more cheese to her chili and stirred it in.

"Why didn't you tell me you were coming?"

"I started to call you and…you know, the plane ticket was an impulsive decision. Maybe the most impulsive thing I've ever done. When I realized I was letting fear rule me instead of being guided by love, I recognized how badly I'd behaved. I should have responded when you said you wanted to talk. After so much time I was afraid you'd say no if I told you I was coming. I didn't want to take that chance."

"I would have said yes in a heartbeat." Sula smiled ruefully.

"Really?"

"Really. Would you believe that earlier today I was thinking about knocking on *your* door?"

"Are you kidding me?"

"No. I'm going to a conference in Tennessee and was looking at a map. It's at a place not far from where you live."

"That would be *really* nice." Melissa smiled gently at her. "It's funny we were thinking along the same lines."

"Mm-hmm. Parallel lines of thought, it would seem. You said the bear sculpture made you realize some things. What things?"

"It was a puzzle. At first, I didn't understand why you sent it other than I had said I liked it. But when I thought about how it represents a shaman, a person who moves not just between worlds, but between human and bear bodies, I realized that it represented you, a beautiful woman *and* bear."

Sula blushed and nodded, listening attentively as Melissa continued to explain how earlier that day, she had given a lecture about a minotaur, a hybrid creature, and then, when she was preparing a lecture on Roman sculpture, she came across images of Germanic warriors.

"Germanic warriors?"

"Yes. Wearing the skins of wolves and bears. They were hiding in a crowd, just like you. Then I did some research and learned some very interesting things…"

"Such as?"

Melissa put her spoon down and looked Sula directly in the eye. "You're a berserker, aren't you?"

Sula inhaled sharply, not expecting the point-blank question, though she anticipated where Melissa's line of thinking was taking her. No one had ever asked her that question before. "Yes, I am."

"How is that possible?" Melissa said, her tone somewhere between wonder and incredulity.

"It just is." Sula shrugged. "I mean, I can't explain how I exist any better than you could explain yourself. You and I are both the product of millions of years of evolution. Can you explain how *you* came to be? But I'm not a berserker like you're thinking." Sula noticed both of their bowls were empty. "It'll take some time to explain...would you like to sit by the fire? I can make some coffee or tea. Or a hot toddy?"

"Anything with alcohol would be appreciated. It's been that kind of a day."

"It'll just take a few minutes. Go enjoy the fire." Sula carried the bowls to the kitchen and put the kettle on to boil, while she sliced a lemon and got out a bottle of whiskey. When she returned to the living room carrying two steaming mugs, Melissa was sitting on the couch. She put a mug on the table in front of Melissa and sat in the chair by the fire.

Melissa lifted the cup and took a sip. "Mmm, lemon, *honey*, of course...and is that whiskey? You'd make a good bartender." Melissa took a second sip and smiled, her expression mischievous. "Or should that be *bear*tender?"

Sula, the edge of the cup pressed against her lips, laughed and almost inhaled the hot liquid. Making a joke about being a bear shifter was the last thing she expected from Melissa.

Melissa lifted her mug. "I'd better drink this slowly. Otherwise I'll end up passed out on this couch. I had to get up really early to make it to the Atlanta airport, and with the time difference, it feels like two hours later than it is here on Mountain Time." She put the cup back on the table. "Betty said it runs in your family. Your parents are beserkers?"

"No. Just my mother." Sula held the warm mug between her hands. "It seems to be a matrilineal-gene expression. That's what I meant about not being a berserker like you think. Those berserker warriors were men wanting to be like us. I guess they sort of stole our identities, in a way. They wore the animal skins and worked themselves into a bestial frenzy before going into battle, but they weren't true shape-shifters. More like wannabes." Sula eyed Melissa, monitoring her responses to this information. She leaned forward while Sula spoke and seemed intrigued, not frightened.

"But what about the story of Eydís Bersa that I came across in that book with my grandmother's photographs? She was a berserker warrior, wasn't she?"

"In that story, yes. As I'm sure you know, sagas like that were based on oral tradition. The original stories probably had bits and pieces of truth and fiction, and the first person who wrote them down probably altered the stories, too. I think Eydís Bersa weaves together the stories of women who could become bears, the true berserkers, and the male-wannabe berserker warriors."

Melissa looked lost in thought for a moment. "If berserkers are real, are the *ulfhednar*, the wolf-warriors in that sculpture, real, too?"

Sula shrugged. "I don't know. I've never met one. If they exist, I imagine they live in secrecy like we do. There aren't that many of us, you know, and we try to live quietly and go about our lives. If our truths had ever been revealed, we would probably have been hunted to extinction."

"And your father? He knows about your mother?"

"Of course. My mother told him when he proposed." Sula paused, taking a deep breath. "They kept asking when I planned to tell you, but I just couldn't get up the nerve."

Melissa's eyes opened wide. "You told them about me?"

"Yeah. I was trying to figure out how to explain it all to you in a way that wouldn't make you think I was crazy or scare you. And then you saw the *hamask*—that's what we call the shift—in the worst form. Having been injured, I had no control over it."

"Does it hurt?" Melissa grimaced. "It seemed awful."

"It's not so bad when I initiate it. When I don't have control of it, it is…unpleasant."

"And by 'unpleasant,' I assume you mean it's horribly painful."

"Yeah." Sula laughed, a lightness coming over her from being able to be so open, so unguarded. Melissa's expression shifted to apparent bewilderment. "Oh, I'm not laughing about the pain. Trust me, that's no laughing matter. It feels good to talk about this with you."

"Yes, it does. I think I was still in shock when I left. It was like my brain couldn't process everything I'd seen. I just shut down everything except school and teaching…and I've been so miserable. And I've missed you terribly." Melissa searched her eyes. "Sula, can we start over?"

Sula's heart skipped a beat. "Even knowing all this, you still want to be with me?"

Melissa nodded. "I'd like to try."

"I would, too." Sula grinned. "You know, they say the third time's a charm."

"The third time?"

"Yes. Remember when we first met? In the bar with Kerry?"

"Oh! I didn't even ask about Kerry!"

"Yeah. I'd like to forget about Kerry, too," Sula said bitterly, taking a sip of her toddy.

"So, what happened to her?"

"She lost her job, and charges were brought against her, but she'll probably just get probation. I wish she'd go back to Wyoming, where she came from."

"I hadn't thought about it before, but you tried to protect me from her in the bar just like you did in the woods." Melissa's face lit up. "And after the incident at the bar, we agreed to reintroduce ourselves at the visitors' center the next day. That would have been our second time."

"Yes, making now the third time." Sula stood and stepped over to Melissa, extending her hand. "Hello, Dr. Warren. It's nice to meet you, *again*."

Melissa stood and took her hand. "Why, hello, Ms. Johansen. It's nice to meet you again, too."

"I hear you'd like to talk with me about some paintings," Sula said, joking.

"Yes, and I still want to."

"Yeah? What'd you want to talk about?"

"For starters, you know the one I was calling *Aspen in Moonlight*?"

"The one upstairs in the bedroom?"

"Yes. Can we go look at it?"

"Sure. But bring your drink. Otherwise one of the cats will stick a paw in it." Sula led Melissa to her bedroom, as she had done before many times, only this time her intentions remained chaste. She turned on the light. It wasn't seduction she wanted right now.

Melissa stood next to the bed, near the headboard, sipping her drink and staring at the painting hanging over it. "I've been thinking a lot about this painting."

Sula sat on the edge of the bed, holding her mug in both hands, looking up at it. "About what?"

"About how works of art don't change, but we do. As our perspective changes, it impacts how we interpret the things we see. I didn't understand this painting before, and it seemed like some dreamlike fantasy. My experience in the woods changed my outlook beyond anything I could have ever imagined." Melissa glanced at Sula with a soft smile. "And then I unexpectedly received your bear sculpture. I considered it from new angles, and that caused me to think differently about this painting." The tone of Melissa's voice was gentle, but she spoke with professorial authority. Sula liked it. "I think your grandmother, Ursula, is the bear and my grandmother, Evelyn, is the woman. If I'm right, then this painting acknowledges that Evelyn knew Ursula's secret."

"How so?" Sula felt like she was a student again.

"For starters, how can she *not* see that big bear in the foreground? It's as if they went out for a walk together to enjoy watching the moonrise. Remember that comment in one letter about how they were looking at the moon at the same time but from different places?"

"Of course. It was very romantic but sad and full of longing."

"What if this painting was made in reference to that love letter? That letter, among others that makes their relationship explicit, was hidden in this painting. It seems possible that Ursula hid the letters in the painting to protect Evelyn. We know her parents disapproved of her."

"Or Evelyn herself might have hidden the letters there. You told me that the paper backing had been cut and re-glued clumsily."

"Oh, I hadn't even thought of that." Melissa's eyes grew wide. "That's an equal possibility, isn't it?"

Sula nodded. "Back to the painting, you're saying that it demonstrates that Evelyn knew Ursula was a bear. That's an interesting idea. These are the only two paintings that I know of with bears and women in them, and one belonged to your grandmother, the other to mine. So maybe they do contain hidden messages about their relationship and what Evelyn knew."

"Exactly. Bonus points for you. You should have studied art history." Melissa flashed a smile. "Now, with my new knowledge and perspective, when I look at these paintings, they tell me that Evelyn knew and loved Ursula for what she was. I can't help but think that they might have had a life together if it wasn't—"

"For the bullet that ended Ursula's life," Sula said gravely, touching her arm where a different bullet had passed through. "It's weird, isn't it? The parallel?"

"Don't you mean parallels? Our great-grandmothers were lovers, *and* you were shot by a hunter, just like Ursula, your namesake, was shot by one."

"Fortunately, I *survived* being shot." Sula finished her drink and put the cup on the bedside table.

"Life is strange. If Ursula had survived, then they might have found a way to stay together. Evelyn would have never gotten married and had a child..." Melissa put her fingers to her lips as an idea seemed to jolt her, "and I wouldn't have been born."

Sula frowned at the thought that she might never have met the love of her life. "That just reinforces this feeling I've had that it's like we're completing something left unfinished."

"What do you mean?"

"I'm not sure exactly, just a feeling of setting something right," Sula said.

"Maybe you're feeling us setting ourselves right. You know, Sula, there is something that seems unfinished...for me, anyway."

"What's that?"

Melissa drained the contents of her cup and placed it next to Sula's. "I need to see you as a bear again."

"Really?" Sula bit her lower lip, anxious. No one had ever asked her this. Of course, because she'd never allowed herself to fall in love, she'd never let someone get close enough to know, let alone ask.

"I need to see it, in part to replace the bad memory I can't get out of my head. But also, because I need to see you fully as you are. I know this Sula," Melissa put her fingertips against Sula's chest, then pointed to the bear in the painting, "but I need to see the *other* one, too."

"You want to see me in fur? Right now?"

"No. Not right now." Melissa stifled a yawn. "But if my great-grandmother could handle it, I can, too."

"I'll do whatever you want, whatever it takes to make things right between us." Sula scanned Melissa's face. "You look tired. You can sleep here if you like, or there's the guest room."

Melissa sat down next to Sula, putting a hand on her thigh. "I want to sleep here with you."

"Like I said, whatever you want." Sula smiled. "Did you bring a bag? I can get—"

Melissa interrupted her with a kiss, tender and sweet, and pulled her down to lie with her on the bed. They held each other and talked, taking turns saying sorry and kissing away bittersweet tears until they agreed to stop apologizing to one another for what was done and instead to focus on the future together. After Melissa fell asleep in her arms, Sula pulled a blanket over them and watched the snow outside the windowpane falling slowly and silently until she drifted peacefully into a deep sleep.

CHAPTER THIRTY-THREE

Melissa awoke in the bed by herself, still wearing yesterday's clothes. Her suitcase remained in the car outside. The last thing she remembered before she fell asleep was making plans for Sula to visit after her conference in Tennessee. Sula had asked her if she'd be visiting her parents for Christmas, hoping they could also spend time together over the holidays. Already it seemed like they were working out the details of a long-distance relationship.

After getting out of bed, she looked out the bedroom window. The weather had passed, and it was a crystal-clear morning, the kind you see only after a snowstorm. She ran her fingers through her tangled hair. It would be good to retrieve her bag from the rental car, take a shower, and put on clean clothes. Where was Sula? The house seemed quiet as she walked along the landing. The irresistible scent of coffee met her halfway down the stairs, and she followed it to the kitchen, where she found the pot freshly brewed and two cups waiting. It looked like Sula was about to make breakfast, for an empty bowl, a box of pancake mix, and a package of strawberries sat on the counter.

"Sula?" Melissa called out, looking around. No reply came.

She poured a cup of coffee and couldn't resist sneaking a strawberry out of the plastic container. They were out of season, but the big, red berries looked good. Turning the tap on to rinse off the strawberry, she was startled by movement that caught her eye through the window.

Walking slowly up the hill, halfway between the house and the barn, was a bear. An enormous brown bear, whose dark coat shimmered in the morning light. It had to be Sula. Melissa was no expert, but that was most definitely not a native black bear. Transfixed, Melissa watched her amble closer, her broad feet with their long, arcing claws making deep depressions in the snow with each step. Sula must have seen her as her direction shifted, and she walked directly to the window, stopping inches away from the glass. Her big black nose was so close to the windowpane, it was fogging up from her exhaled breath. Sula tossed her shaggy head, nose pointing toward the back patio, and then moved away, disappearing from view.

Melissa went to the back door. She'd left her shoes upstairs, but several pairs of boots stood lined up next to each other in the mud room. She slipped her feet into a pair nearest the door. They were several sizes too big, but Melissa didn't care. Opening the door, she shuffled through the snow, into the cold air and crisp, bright light.

Sula was waiting for her. Melissa held her breath as Sula took a few steps forward and stopped, lowering her massive head so that they were eye to eye. Melissa held her gaze, the eye contact grounding her, reminding her that she was indeed facing Sula, the woman she loved.

Sula blinked slowly and lowered her head, looking toward her left hand. Melissa followed her gaze, realizing she still held the strawberry between her fingers. She stared at it, surprised it was still in her hand. She held it up, and Sula responded by smacking her lips softly.

"Oh…you want this?"

Sula uttered a soft huffing sound that Melissa interpreted as an affirmative. She held out the berry, watching with fascination as Sula took the berry with her lips, which were surprisingly delicate. She chewed once before swallowing it. Melissa wished she had brought the whole carton with her.

"May I touch you?"

Sula huffed a reply, the moisture in her breath condensing into a thin cloud between them. She cocked her ears forward inquisitively, it seemed. Melissa reached out to touch Sula's fur. Coarse on the surface, it felt soft and fuzzy underneath. Sula pressed her cheek against Melissa's hand, closing her eyes. With both hands, she rubbed her cheeks, marveling at the size of her head, which was the width of Melissa's shoulders. She touched the edges of her ears, smoothed the fur that arced across her eyes, and ran her fingers lightly along the velvety fur of her long snout before tracing the edges of her thin, black lips. Sula opened her eyes wide.

Melissa suddenly became aware that her cheeks hurt. She'd been so focused on Sula she hadn't realized how hard she was grinning. Sula was a truly magnificent creature in both human and bear form, and Melissa's heart swelled with love.

"In case you wondered, Sula," Melissa said, gently tugging the fur on her cheeks, "I think I can handle this. But if you want more of those strawberries, you're going to have to change back and make those pancakes for breakfast."

Sula grunted softly, swatting her gently with an enormous paw, a playful, teasing gesture. Then she turned quickly, pivoting on her back feet, and began to walk down the hill.

Melissa followed her a few steps, then stopped. "I'm not going to follow you, Sula, if that's what you want. It's freezing out here."

Sula paused, lifted her head to the side, seeming to listen, and then picked up her pace. Squinting against the sunlight reflecting off the snow, Melissa noticed two sets of tracks—one set made by two feet going downhill, the other made by four bigger ones coming up. Sula, now running and kicking up snow, was following the same path down toward the barn. The double doors of the old barn were wide open, and Melissa wondered if Sula had changed, engaged the *hamask* as she described it last night, down there. Curious, she continued watching, turning the collar of her shirt up against her neck, crossing her arms and tucking her hands under her arms, trying to conserve her body heat.

Within seconds Sula was inside the barn but staying within view. With a whole-body shake, she cast off the snow clinging to her fur after her quick romp. Melissa was finding it difficult to focus on Sula. At first, she wondered if it was the bright mountain light. Surely snow blindness couldn't happen that quickly. Then she realized that her eyes weren't the problem. It was Sula. Her body became less distinct, the contour edges softening, and Melissa realized she was witnessing the beginning of the *hamask*. Sula appeared to shiver at first, and then her body heaved and roiled. Little clouds appeared in the air around her head. She must have been breathing heavily, exhaling hard, the moisture from her lungs condensing in the cold air.

Fascinated, Melissa watched as every part of Sula's ursine body reduced in size, its angles and proportions shifting as muscles contracted and reformed. Her fur shortened, then disappeared entirely, as pale skin replaced it. When Sula came back into focus, she was crouching naked, balanced on her hands and feet. She stood up quickly, stretching her neck and rolling her shoulders, and dashed out of view.

There. She'd seen it. It wasn't the grotesque metamorphosis that had been haunting her dreams and waking thoughts. It didn't merit fear. If anything, it was a miracle in the truest sense of the word—a thing of wonder. Melissa forced herself not to smile only because it was so damn cold that she was clenching her jaw, trying to keep her teeth from chattering.

When Sula reappeared, she was wearing a barn jacket and jeans tucked into pac boots. She closed the doors and walked up the hill, following the path in the snow she'd already walked twice. Melissa's heart felt as happy as Sula looked, a big grin plastered on her face.

"Good morning, Goldie," Sula said as she approached.

"Good morning, Bear." Melissa reached for Sula, kissing her, tasting the strawberry that lingered on her lips.

"Pancakes for breakfast?" Sula raised an eyebrow.

"Yes. Pancakes with strawberries." Melissa laughed. "*Lots* of strawberries."

"Good," Sula said. Wrapping her arms around her, she kissed her again. "Let's get you inside and warmed up."

As much as Melissa wanted to go back into the house where it was cozy and warm, she didn't want to abandon this moment or its wonderful magic. As the sun continued to rise above the trees behind the house, the world seemed refreshed and renewed with a smooth blanket of snow that sparkled and glittered in the crisp, dry air. Suddenly, it struck her that today was a new beginning in so many ways. She couldn't wait to find out what the rest of the weekend—the rest of her life—held in store.

About the Author

Kelly Wacker (www.kellywacker.com) is a Western native currently residing in the Deep South where, as a professor of art, she teaches art history and environmental studies. Deeply connected to the natural world, she spends as much time as she can observing, thinking, and daydreaming while walking with her canine companion in the fields and along the creeks near her home. She is also prone to staring at the night sky, looking for the moon, and searching for Ursa Major. She has yet to see a bear in the wild but hopes that will change soon.